QUEEN ESTHER

QUEEN ESTHER

JOHN IRVING

SCRIBNER

London · New York · Amsterdam/Antwerp · Sydney/Melbourne · Toronto · New Delhi

SCRIBNER

First published in the United States by Simon & Schuster, LLC, 2025
First published in Great Britain by Scribner, an imprint
of Simon & Schuster UK Ltd, 2025

1 3 5 7 9 10 8 6 4 2

Simon & Schuster UK Ltd, 1st Floor, 222 Gray's Inn Road
London WC1X 8HB

Simon & Schuster Australia, Sydney

Simon & Schuster India, New Delhi

www.simonandschuster.co.uk
www.simonandschuster.com.au
www.simonandschuster.co.in

The authorised representative in the EEA is Simon & Schuster Netherlands BV,
Herculesplein 96, 3584 AA Utrecht, Netherlands. info@simonandschuster.nl

A CIP catalogue record for this book is available from the British Library

Hardback ISBN: 9781-4711-7912-9
Trade paperback ISBN: 978-1-4711-7913-6
eBook ISBN: 978-1-4711-7914-3
Audio ISBN: 978-1-3985-5157-2

Printed and Bound in the UK using 100% Renewable
Electricity at CPI Group (UK) Ltd

For Marty Schwartz

For we are sold, I and my people, to be destroyed, to be slain, and to perish.

—ESTHER 7:4

CHAPTERS

QUEEN
ESTHER

1.

The Townspeople of Pennacook

Josiah Winslow was born in Plymouth, Massachusetts, in 1629—his father, Edward Winslow, was a Separatist Puritan who'd traveled on the *Mayflower* in 1620. Edward's younger brother John sailed on the *Fortune,* arriving in Plymouth in 1621. Beginning in Puritan times, more Winslows kept coming.

The present-day James Winslow, who was called Jimmy as a child, was unimpressed by his Winslow ancestry—he'd learned not to care who his ancestors were. "When it comes to your forebears, you deserve no credit, you should take no blame—you don't get to pick your parents, do you?" Jimmy's grandfather, an English teacher, had told him.

James Winslow would be a student abroad for only one year, yet what happened to him in a foreign country confirmed his belief in his intrinsic foreignness. It seemed a contradiction that Jimmy Winslow would always say he was just a New Hampshire boy. He wasn't New Hampshire enough for the townspeople of Pennacook; the townsfolk had made it their business to know where the Winslows came from.

If you grew up in Pennacook, in southeastern New Hampshire, in the 1940s and 1950s, where you *came from* mattered. You knew there was a class system in America; you were aware of a ruling class, and you sensed your place in society. The town is situated around the falls where the freshwater Pennacook River meets the tidal, saltwater Squamscott—once the land of the Squamscott Native Americans, a subtribe of the Pennacook Nation. The name *Pennacook* comes from the Abenaki word *penakuk,* meaning "at the bottom of the hill." The town's founder had left England to escape religious persecution; he'd also been exiled from the Massachusetts Bay Colony for sharing his sister-in-law's dissident religious views. The English Puritans bought the land from a Squamscott sagamore. There were similar small towns throughout New England—factory towns or mill towns, where your social standing was clear. Class consciousness wasn't unique to Penna-cook, where there was a textile mill (as long ago as 1830) and a shoe factory (since 1884). What set Pennacook apart, and gave the town an acute class consciousness, was a private school for boys.

Established in 1781, Pennacook Academy was an independent school for boarding and day students, ninth grade to twelfth. The academy was one of the oldest secondary schools in the United States. In the 1950s and 1960s, when James Winslow was a student there, he was aware that his social standing at the academy wasn't evaluated by his fellow students in the same way it was by the town.

In the 1950s and 1960s, unlike the town, Pennacook Academy was a meritocracy; the school cared if you were good in the classroom. To the academy, your grades mattered—to the boys, not so much. Your wit was what mattered to the boys; they cared if you could entertain them. You were forgiven for not being entertaining only if you were a jock. To Jimmy Winslow, the way he was evaluated at school made more sense than the scrutiny he withstood in town.

What did the *Mayflower* matter to those Pennacook Academy boys? Their class consciousness wasn't aroused by America's first settlers—least of all, by the ship they sailed on. The day boys distrusted the boarders and vice versa. In an international school, nothing is universally true, but the boarding students were generally more worldly; in comparison, the townies seemed unsophisticated.

James Winslow was distrusted by both the day boys and the board-ers, because he was in a subclass of townies. Faculty children were in a difficult position, but Jimmy Winslow was an unusual faculty brat. He was the grandson of the most revered member of Pennacook's English Department. Thomas Winslow was the most popular teacher at the academy; his students adored him. You might suppose, then, that James Winslow would have been trusted by his fellow students and welcomed by the faculty, above all the other boys—but he wasn't a real Winslow. Jimmy was a nobody's boy. This much was understood: his mother had adopted him; his father was an unknown. As for the boy's birth mother, she put no one at ease. For starters, she was an orphan.

To the townspeople of Pennacook, James Winslow was (and would always be) the orphan's kid. The academy was kinder. To the students and faculty alike, maybe Jimmy wasn't a real Winslow, but there were a whole lot of Winslows and they all loved and looked after that boy. (Well, no wonder, the townspeople of Pennacook pointed out—Jimmy was the only Winslow boy.)

Years later, whenever James Winslow was being modest, or he was otherwise at a loss for words—and he always spoke excruciatingly slowly—he would repeat he was just a New Hampshire boy. Naturally, the townspeople of Pennacook thought they knew better; the Winslows weren't like the rest of the locals, the orphan's kid included. For all their meddlesomeness, what the townspeople of Pennacook actually knew amounted to only this. The circumstances of James Winslow's birth were fraught with irregularities. When babies are born and transferred in such a way that you don't even know whose babies they are—not exactly—aren't things bound to go off the rails in a family? The townspeople of Pennacook were poised for things to go awry with the Winslows—with that adopted boy, especially. Maybe then those Winslows wouldn't seem so proud. The townspeople of Pennacook were sick and tired of the respect shown those Winslows as a model family, even when it came to their adopting an orphan's child.

2.

A Fourth Daughter

Constance was the steadfast matriarch of the Pennacook Winslows. Her maiden name had been Bradford. William Bradford had been onboard the *Mayflower*. The townspeople of Pennacook imagined Constance was no less steadfast when she'd been a Bradford; becoming a Winslow merely served to steel her moral certainty. The woman was unwavering. Constance was the one responsible for the virtue names bestowed on her first three daughters—Faith, Hope, and Prudence (in that order).

Virtue names appeared to matter less to Thomas Winslow, the little man of the household. Mr. Winslow was the epitome of an English teacher; to the townspeople of Pennacook, the diminutive man was the essence of teacherly. His forebears didn't matter to him. "You can't improve your ancestors—you can only improve yourselves and inspire your children," Thomas Winslow told his Pennacook Academy students on the first day of every English class he taught. He meant he could teach them to read well, beginning with what they would read. "And if you learn to write well, you will speak well, too," he told those boys. As for what they would read—the poems, the plays, the stories, the novels—"the more make-believe, the better!" the English teacher told his students. What Mr. Winslow further said was the gist of his belief in fiction. "If you can imagine yourself in someone else's shoes, this might make you a better person," Thomas Winslow would tell those boys.

What grated on the townspeople of Pennacook was the way Thomas Winslow tried to teach them. The adults of the town didn't want an English teacher telling them how to improve themselves. It wasn't Thomas Winslow's business to tell the townsfolk how to inspire their children.

The well-to-do adults of the town were most annoyed at the tiny English teacher. Why would they want to imagine themselves in someone else's shoes? How did Thomas Winslow dare to make them better people? And Constance, in her own way, could be a busybody; she got under the skin of the townspeople of Pennacook, too. Those two were always pushing what they'd read on you. What they'd read wasn't all those Winslows were pushing, but the town's awareness of being pushed began with the books.

Thomas Winslow wasn't self-conscious about his smallness. It irked the town's menfolk that Thomas was not a bit bothered by his tiny size.

The women felt differently. Thomas Winslow was handsomeness in miniature to them. "Isn't he *a little doll*?" the ladies of the town teased one another. Don't think Constance didn't know how the women felt.

Yet the prevailing impression of Thomas Winslow was teacherly. To the townspeople of Pennacook, the pretty little man did not bring spontaneity to mind. If Constance was the one who named Faith, Hope, and Prudence, the exactness of the two-year span of time between each of the daughters' births seemed in keeping with the specificity of detail in those plotted nineteenth-century novels the tiny English teacher loved. On the surface, the deliberate difference in the ages of those virtue girls was characteristic of Thomas Winslow, wasn't it?

After Prudence (the third virtue daughter) was born, the townspeople of Pennacook counted the years. Given their esteem for Thomas as *a little doll,* the ladies of the town kept the closest count. Two years after Prudence was born, it looked like the Winslows were done having children. Prudence was five when the Winslows let the last of their nannies go. When those virtue daughters were little girls, they had a succession of nannies—three in a row. Constance insisted on calling them "au pair girls." The *au pair* designation caused a hullabaloo in town. For one thing, it was inaccurate—they weren't foreign girls, they spoke English, and (above all) those girls were *orphans.* To the townspeople of Pennacook, where the Winslows' nannies *came from* mattered.

Constance, of course, could not be criticized for her use of language. "I call our girls *au pair,* from the French—literally, 'on equal terms.' Our girls help with housework or childcare in exchange for room and board—they're part of our family," Constance said; she would not use the word *adopted,* nor did she ever say the Winslows were a *foster* family for those girls. "We don't give our girls a salary—we give them an allowance, the same as you would give your older children," Constance told anyone who would listen. "These girls are like our children," Constance said of those orphans—to the consternation of the townspeople of Pennacook. "We buy their clothes, we help them with their homework—all our children know school is important," Constance couldn't stop herself from saying. The Winslows would see to it that their au pair girls got into college; those nannies knew they were expected to do well in college, too.

There had to be something wrong with one of the Winslows' orphans, or so the townspeople of Pennacook hoped. Not enough was known about where those orphans *came from.* With orphans, too much is missing; there's always something you don't know. The townspeople of Pennacook understood (albeit vaguely) what happened to unadopted orphans; when they were only fourteen or fifteen, they became what was called "wards of the state." That didn't sound good. There were ladies in the town who said childcare was too important a job for minors. And you would be asked, or you might think to yourself: Would you let wards of the state look after your children?

Not a speck of dirt could be found on the Winslows' first three nannies. Those three were model students in the Pennacook public schools; the way they sailed through college (they got into good graduate schools, too), you would have thought they were Winslows. The way those three unadopted orphans came "home" (as they called it) for Christmas or their vacations sorely vexed the townspeople of Pennacook, too. The way those three virtue daughters adored seeing their old au pair girls, you would have thought the Winslow kids were like sisters to those wards of the state.

And those nannies spoke no ill of their treatment in the Winslow household. "I felt accepted from the beginning, like I'd always been part of the family—and now I always will be," the oldest of those orphans had said. She'd been the nanny for Faith, the firstborn.

"You can't just give someone a home, not someone like me, who's never had a home, but that's what they gave me—they made me feel I was home," Hope's nanny, Lucie, told the mothers of her friends at school, the ladies of the town, who (for once) were speechless.

Then there was Denise, the au pair girl for Prudence, the youngest of the virtue daughters. Denise was the taciturn one. Her reticence to speak made the townspeople of Pennacook imagine she might have something to hide. Yet the quietest of those orphans was just a shy girl, reserved in her speech; if she seemed reluctant to join a conversation, she was wise to be wary of the ladies of the town (and their penchant for gossip). "I was treated like one of the kids—we were all treated equally," the youngest of the Winslows' three nannies said. "I was just supposed to be one of the more responsible kids, because I was a little older"

Grasping at straws, the way the ladies of a small town will do, one of the older women inevitably asked: "But what do you call Mr. and Mrs. Winslow—how are you supposed to address those two?"

"Oh, those two are just bigger kids—I call them Tommy and Connie, like they call each other!" the suddenly excited nanny said; she was not so taciturn anymore.

The ladies of the town wouldn't dream of calling Constance Winslow *Connie*, no more than the menfolk could imagine Thomas Winslow—the little boss man of the English language—as a *Tommy*. And the Winslows' wards of the state even embraced Constance's maiden name—her Bradford business, her *Mayflower* lineage. To hear those orphans talk, you would have thought their ancestors—from those families that had given them up or abandoned them—had sailed on the *Mayflower.* "Poor Dorothy!" those au pair girls exclaimed, bemoaning the fate of William Bradford's first wife. She was only sixteen when she married Mr. Bradford. They'd left a three-year-old back in Holland with Dorothy's parents. Dorothy drowned; she fell (or she jumped) overboard when the *Mayflower* was anchored offshore in Provincetown Harbor. There was no doubt in the minds of the townspeople of Pennacook—Dorothy definitely jumped overboard! She could see from the ship what a wilderness awaited her; she knew she would never see her darling three-year-old again. *We would have jumped,* the ladies of the town were thinking and nodding their heads to one another.

Not those nannies. They would have gone ashore and faced the wilderness. "William Bradford remarried!" Faith's au pair girl declared, as if a man's remarriage were an act of heroism.

"William Bradford became the governor of Plymouth, and he wrote a history of the Plymouth Colony—*Of Plymouth Plantation,*" Lucie had told the entire town.

"Bradford's history is still taught in collegiate American-history courses!" Denise would add—still a shy girl, but less reticent over the years.

Even Constance's first name had some ancestry attached to it. "*Constance* comes from the French, via Latin," Faith's nanny was the first to say, dutifully repeating what she'd been told.

"It's a medieval form of *Constantia*—that's the Latin," Hope's au pair girl, Lucie, had reported.

"It was the name of the daughter of William the Conqueror," Prudence's ward of the state, Denise, said, not so shyly.

And then, when Prudence was ten, it became apparent that Constance was, once again, pregnant. At four months along, she was starting to show. When she gave birth to a fourth daughter, Prudence was eleven;

Faith and Hope were teenagers. The virtue daughters were old enough to rebel against the very idea that they might be called upon to be the new kid's babysitter, but (true to their names) they were virtuously eager to do it. As for those three nannies who'd moved on, one of them had children of her own, yet they all volunteered to come "home" (as they continued to call it). The old au pair girls were competing with one another; they had a fight over who would be the one to look after the newborn.

"Oh, my dear girls—don't be silly," Constance said.

"You have your own lives to lead, dear girls," Thomas told them.

To the townspeople of Pennacook, the fourth daughter didn't appear to be planned. The ladies of the town questioned the possibly premature impression of Thomas Winslow as teacherly; maybe there was something spontaneous about the little doll. Then along came the cleaning woman; she was the one who told tales about the Winslows' sleeping arrangements, but not even a small town in New Hampshire could presume to know all there was to know about that. (Not even a cleaning woman knows everything.)

The ladies of the town had long wondered about the Winslows' sleeping arrangements. When the first three daughters were little girls, Thomas Winslow had dorm duty; the whole family lived in a faculty apartment in a Pennacook Academy dormitory. Imagine one of those underage orphans living in a boys' dormitory; yet there'd been no fooling around between the academy boys and the au pair girls. Thomas and Constance must have read the riot act to the boys in the dorm. The academy boys—the older boys, especially—knew the nannies were off-limits. Yet the quarters were cramped for a family of five (plus one); faculty housing hadn't been designed for three small kids (plus an au pair girl). And the townspeople of Pennacook were left to ponder: Did the academy dock Thomas Winslow's salary because the nanny ate with the family at their faculty table in the school's dining hall? (It irritated the townspeople of Pennacook that the academy's business was no business of the town's.)

The Winslow's long-suffering cleaning woman would let you know she was sorry she'd left Boston; she'd followed her husband north to New Hampshire, but he hadn't amounted to a pot to piss in, which she would let you know, too. If you gave her more time, she would tell you why her whole family should have stayed in Kildare. Gertie Eustis was an Irish woman whose first name had been shortened from Gertrude; she may have been angry about that, too. She'd been the Winslows' cleaning woman from the start—in their first days in faculty housing and after they moved off campus into a house of their own in town.

"Those kids have no sleepin' rules—those Winslows are a liberal family when it comes to sleepin' arrangements," Gertie told the town. "Those kids' pillows keep movin' around," was the way Gertie put it. To the townspeople of Pennacook, the word *liberal* was sufficient condemnation, before Gertie got to the part about the pillows movin' around. Changing the bed linens was the cleaning woman's job; Gertie found all the kids' pillows in one kid's bed, or in the nanny's bed. In the Winslows' dormitory days, there were never enough bedrooms—there were barely enough beds. The nanny never had her own room there—just her own bed. "The so-called au pair girl always has a kid, or all of 'em, climbin' into her bed—an *orphanage* sleepin' situation," Gertie Eustis called it.

On the centermost streets of Pennacook, there were white colonial houses—like the one with five bedrooms the Winslows would move into when Thomas had paid his dues as a young teacher, when he was done with dorm duty. Each of the virtue daughters had her own bedroom, although those three shared the same bathroom. The nanny had not only her own bedroom but her own bathroom, too. The au pair girl's "quarters" (as Constance called the nanny's bedroom and bathroom) were at one end of the second floor, above the kitchen. The master bedroom and bathroom were at the opposite end of the upstairs. Like the Puritans themselves (befitting Thomas and Constance Winslow), the seventeenth-century colonial displayed scant external ornamentation. There was a steep roof with two chimneys, and a front entry with a portico supported by columns. There were narrow clapboards, painted white, with black shutters on the windows.

Yet the Winslows' cleaning woman would tell the townspeople of Pennacook that no detail of old New England decorum, or the right number of bedrooms, could persuade those virtue daughters and the teenage ward of the state to stay in their own beds. "Those kids and the orphan are sleepin' all over the place," Gertie told the town. The cleaning woman saw herself as the Winslows' personal housekeeper; Gertie had a managerial mindset. The sheets and pillowcases were in her care; they were her business. It mattered to Gertie where the kids' pillows ended up—not to mention the nanny's pillow. Most mornings, all the pillows were in one bed—more often than not, the nanny's bed. Even after what looked like the last of those orphans went away to college, the virtue daughters piled into the same bed together. "Migrants sharin' a bunkhouse have better sleepin' boundaries—I'm just guessin'," Gertie Eustis would say, to anyone who listened.

As for the Winslows' young daughters piling into the same bed, the townspeople of Pennacook didn't give a hoot. What got the town's attention were the new *sleepin' boundaries* of Thomas and Constance. Thomas had moved into the orphan's vacant quarters. In Pennacook, there surely were other married couples who slept in separate bedrooms; yet the town talked obsessively about the distance between the two bedrooms where Thomas and Constance slept. To get to the master bedroom from the former au pair girl's quarters, Thomas had to tiptoe past the children's bedrooms, or he had to traipse downstairs and traipse back upstairs, after he'd trekked through the whole house.

Why this journey between bedrooms mattered so much to the townspeople of Pennacook had something to do with how different the fourth daughter turned out to be. To begin with, the perhaps unplanned (or more spontaneous) daughter didn't have a virtue name— not exactly. It may have sounded virtuous to the ladies of the town, but Constance made two things clear: Tommy had named her, and *Honor* was an "expectation" name. "*Honor* is a name like *Chastity*—an expectation isn't necessarily a virtue," was the way Constance put it. To the townspeople of Pennacook, especially the ladies of the town, *Honor* nonetheless sounded like a hard name to live up to.

So much for poor Dorothy—the Bradford who went overboard, the young wife who drowned when the *Mayflower* was anchored in Provincetown Harbor. The Winslows' fourth daughter wouldn't be a Dorothy; she would be an Honor, not the easiest cross to bear. Surely the townspeople of Pennacook were wondering: What will Tommy and Connie do? With those two sleeping at opposite ends of their house, who would the Winslows find to look after Honor?

We wouldn't get another orphan, the ladies of the town were thinking and nodding their heads to one another. In the town's judgment, those Winslows would be pushing their luck with a fourth ward of the state. In truth, the townspeople of Pennacook didn't know much about orphanages. But like many folks in small New England towns, the citizens of Pennacook knew only what they had heard, and what they'd heard was good enough for them.

3.

Where the Orphans Came From

M any New Englanders had heard of the New England Home for Little Wanderers. In Pennacook, the most prevalent opinion was that it was created by Boston businessmen in 1865 to help children orphaned by the Civil War. It was actually founded in 1799. As few people in Pennacook knew, it was Boston's first orphanage for young girls—then called the Boston Female Asylum. The smaller orphanages in northern New England weren't as well known as Little Wanderers.

The first orphan train had left Boston in 1850, carrying homeless children north to New Hampshire and Vermont. Thomas and Constance had seen photographs of the children on the orphan trains. They didn't look old enough to become wards of the state. Maybe some of those kids had found homes with good parents, but the Winslows had heard stories about the children who were indentured as servants; they were treated as slaves, or they were otherwise abused.

In the beginning, when the Winslows went looking for unadopted orphans who would soon become wards of the state, Thomas Winslow wouldn't look outside of New Hampshire. They found their first three au pair girls in New Hampshire orphanages. Constance realized sooner than Thomas that they would need to expand their search for a fourth au pair girl. She reminded Tommy that there were orphanages in Maine. The one in St. Cloud's had been a logging camp for the first half of the nineteenth century—when the woodcutters were doing their damage, before the forest was gone. St. Cloud's was one of those river towns that remained after the loggers had moved on. The sawmill had stayed (only for a little while), along with the lumberyard (for a little longer); a dying mill town was what the loggers left behind. Their bunkhouses were where the orphans slept; their cookhouse was a kitchen and a dining hall, where the kids ate. From the orphanages they knew in New Hampshire, the Winslows heard mixed messages about the physician who ran the orphanage in St. Cloud's, Maine.

First of all, the Winslows were impressed that a doctor was in charge, and they'd been told the doctor was a reader. He read aloud to the children; he encouraged the kids to be readers. But the Winslows were also told that the orphanage physician was "prone to tirades."

"What about?" Thomas Winslow had asked. To an English teacher, a tirade wasn't necessarily a bad thing—not if it was justified.

The doctor raved about "the rape of the forest"; he said the logging industry and the paper companies had failed to replace the trees that they had cut down. "When the river valley surrounding St. Cloud's was cleared, and the second growth sprang up everywhere, like swamp weed, what was left behind?" the doctor in charge of the orphanage would ask you. Then he told you: "The sawdust; the scarred bank of the river, where the log drives had gouged out a new shore; the mill with its broken windows with no screens; the whore hotel; the church, which was Catholic, for the French Canadians, and which looked too clean and unused to belong in St. Cloud's, where it was never half as popular as the whores, who had the good sense to move on with the loggers." And here the orphanage physician paused, to catch his breath or to contain himself.

"Why did the Catholic Church leave town after the whores and the loggers had left?" the doctor asked, almost innocently. The physician who was prone to tirades answered the question himself. "Because there was no one who had anything to confess—an orphan's conscience is clear."

"The doctor does sound a little crazy, Tommy," Constance said.

The Catholic Church had expressed an interest in participating in the running of the orphanage in St. Cloud's; the orphanage physician had vetoed the idea. "We're not an orphanage with a religious affiliation," was all the doctor said. The Winslows were not churchgoers; they had no religious affiliation. They weren't knowledgeable about the alleged evils of the logging industry or the paper companies. Maybe the orphanage physician was a little crazy about the rape of the forest, or whose fault it was for failing to plant new trees; the Winslows knew next to nothing about forests or trees.

"I like the sound of the reading—encouraging the kids to be readers doesn't sound crazy, Connie," Thomas told his wife. Constance was the librarian at the Pennacook Public Library—a yellow-brick, late-nineteenth-century building bordering the academy campus on Front Street. To the townspeople of Pennacook, Constance Winslow was as much of an annoyance as her husband—those two were always telling you what you should read.

"I like the sound of the reading, too, Tommy—I'll bet you like the sound of an orphanage with no religious affiliation even better," Constance said. In addition to hearing her husband say (more times than she could count) that religion was the bane of civilization, she knew he had a grudge against the state of Maine.

"St. Cloud's is a very hard place to get to—Maine is just too far to go, Connie," was all Thomas Winslow would say. (St. Cloud's is nowhere near anywhere, as they say everywhere in New England.) Inland Maine was snowed in during the winter months—nor was there any spring in that part of Maine, a period of time distinguished by thawing mud. The old logging roads were impassable, immobilized by the mud. If you went there in the winter or the spring, you were advised to take the train.

Furthermore, the Winslows were told, your fellow passengers would look down on you if you got on or off the train in St. Cloud's. The orphanage was all that was there. You were stigmatized for your association with the orphans. This forewarning of the passengers' contempt only served to confirm Thomas Winslow's grudge against Maine.

Maine's Public Laws of 1840 and 1841 included the country's earliest anti-abortion legislation; it made attempting the abortion procedure on any woman "pregnant with child" an offense, "whether such child be quick or not," regardless of what methods were used. Performing an abortion was punishable by a year in jail or a one-thousand-dollar fine, or both. If you were a doctor, you could lose your license to practice. Other states followed. By 1910, abortion was illegal throughout the United States; it remained so until 1973, when the *Roe v. Wade* Supreme Court decision held that a woman had a constitutional right to an abortion.

The Winslows were abortion-rights advocates before the townspeople of Pennacook were thinking much about abortion. If you listened to the town, you would have thought abortion had always been illegal. The history of abortion in America was not well known to most Americans—the townspeople of Pennacook included.

But abortion didn't inspire the Town Talks—Constance's contribution to adult education in the town of Pennacook. The Winslows were irritating advocates of trying to improve town-gown relations. The relations between the town of Pennacook and Pennacook Academy were forever strained and in need of improving.

The Town Talks were the librarian's idea, but the Pennacook Public Library, where silence was the rule, was not an ideal venue for a speakers' series. Finding a forum for the Town Talks was easy; the academy's lecture halls were not in use on weekday nights, during the students' study hours. As for choosing subjects for the Town Talks—topics that were mutually agreeable to the townspeople of Pennacook and the academy faculty—this was harder. "Tommy is the teacher—the subjects are his business," was all Constance told the town.

The ladies of the town were interested in fiction. For Thomas

Winslow's Town Talks about novels or novelists, the ladies of the town turned out in droves. "Women are the fiction readers—we live in our imaginations more than men do," Constance Winslow said. (She would have you believe she was speaking strictly as a librarian, oblivious to the fact that the ladies of the town thought her husband was *a little doll.*)

Thomas gave two Town Talks on Charles Dickens; he had the ladies of the town read *Little Dorrit* and *Great Expectations* (in that order), making the case that *Great Expectations* was the better novel. Thomas Winslow would discover that the ladies of the town (even the ones who were smitten with him) were not as easily persuaded by their teacher as the academy boys were. The ladies loved the prison-to-riches story and the kind-hearted Little Dorrit. There were only three or four men at the Dickens Town Talks. "You're talking to a bunch of women, Tommy—women are going to like a marriage melodrama more than a boy's bildungsroman," Constance said.

"Right you are, Connie," Thomas told her. He gave two Town Talks on George Eliot's *Middlemarch.* There were a surprising number of men in attendance at the first of the Town Talks on the Eliot novel. "I saw seven or eight men, Connie," Thomas said. But no men attended the second *Middlemarch* talk. Thomas Winslow was crestfallen.

"Maybe the men who came the first time didn't know George Eliot was a woman, Tommy," Constance told him.

"Right you are, Connie," Thomas said. He gave four Town Talks on the Brontë sisters' best-known novels—the first two talks were on Emily's *Wuthering Heights,* the last two on Charlotte's *Jane Eyre.* Constance asked him why he began with Emily. Didn't Thomas know that Charlotte was the older of the two—not to mention that *Jane Eyre* was published a little before *Wuthering Heights,* if only by a month or two? "Right you are, Connie," was all her husband would say.

Constance knew him so well; she knew he had a reason to begin with Emily, but not why he wouldn't tell her what the reason was. Thomas was good-humored about the total absence of men at his Town

Talks on the Brontë sisters—not one man showed up. "At last we know exactly how smart the townspeople of Pennacook are, Connie—smart enough to know the Brontë sisters were women," Thomas told her.

Constance was smiling when she whispered to him, wagging her index finger. "Not something you should say publicly," she chided gently.

It surprised her how her Tommy began the first of his Town Talks on the Brontë sisters. The lecture hall was packed to the topmost (hindmost) tier. Constance admired how her husband stood, with no notes, in front of the lectern; if he'd stood behind it, he was so small that the ladies in the first row of seats could not have seen him. "I wonder if you can tell me whether Emily or Charlotte wrote this," he began. When he started reciting, from memory, his eyes never strayed from the faces of those women in his audience. Thomas Winslow was quoting what Emily or Charlotte Brontë had written, but Constance could see what her husband was doing; he was reading the expressions on those women's faces. From where she sat—in a lone chair on the speaker's platform, to one side of the lectern—Constance could see the women's faces, too. The ladies of the town were caught off guard by what they were hearing; for once, the artful faces of those women could not conceal what they were feeling. By no means were all the thoughts of the ladies of the town revealed—only the ones who were affronted by what they heard, only those women who felt resistance or hostility to what the English teacher told them.

"'Conventionality is not morality,'" he recited, noticing the ladies who looked like they'd been slapped. "'Self-righteousness is not religion,'" Thomas continued. "'To attack the first is not to assail the last,'" Thomas concluded his recitation in a reprimanding tone of voice.

That was when Constance recognized the churchwomen in the audience, the ladies who'd pursed their lips and narrowed their eyes; the churchwomen were the ones her husband's recitation had exposed. Constance Winslow had studied the ladies of the town more closely than her husband had. He'd wanted to draw them out, Constance understood—to identify who the churchwomen were. But why did this matter to him? Constance wondered. They were only reading the Brontë sisters. And the passage he'd recited puzzled Constance—only at first, and not for long.

The ladies of the town had been instructed to start reading Emily Brontë. In the first talk, some of the women wouldn't have finished reading *Wuthering Heights*—almost no one had dived into *Jane Eyre,* except those women who might have read the novel when they were in high school or college. And what would they remember from *Jane Eyre?* Constance was imagining. Maybe that novel's wonderful first sentence, Constance thought—her lips moving slightly, as she silently repeated it to herself. ("There was no possibility of taking a walk that day.")

Why would her Tommy quote from Charlotte Brontë's preface to the second edition of *Jane Eyre* to a group of ladies who were only starting to read *Wuthering Heights?* That was when Constance saw why he began with Emily. Thomas Winslow wanted Charlotte's didactic themes of conventionality and morality, of self-righteousness and religion, to catch *all* the women in his audience by surprise. Constance knew her husband's thoughts about the religious ending of *Jane Eyre.* Constance understood that Thomas was setting the table for what he would say about Jane's conflicted feelings about Christianity. Jane chooses to be happily married to Rochester, on her own terms, and not to marry St. John, whom she very much admires (in her Christian way). Jane doesn't choose to join him in India, where St. John is dying—awaiting his dear Lord Jesus. Constance loved what a good teacher her husband was, but she knew her Tommy too well. He wasn't only setting up his talk on the ending of *Jane Eyre*—when he hadn't yet said a word about the beginning of *Wuthering Heights.* Constance knew Thomas was a planner. He was looking farther ahead than his talk on the ending of *Jane Eyre*; Constance saw that he was setting up his talk about the history of abortion in America. She knew he was worried about that one; she was worried about it, too.

Constance also saw that not one of the ladies in the lecture hall would venture to guess which Brontë sister wrote what Thomas had recited to them. Those women were dreaming of Heathcliff and Catherine, or they'd read far enough in *Wuthering Heights* to be having nightmares about that monster of a man. Those women weren't thinking about *Jane Eyre,* much less Charlotte Brontë's preface to the second edition.

"I suppose Connie knows which Brontë it is," Thomas said, not turning to look at her. (Her Tommy was committing to memory the indignant faces of those churchwomen, Constance could see.)

"It sounds like Charlotte to me, Tommy," Constance told him.

"Right you are, Connie," he said, sighing. There were titters from the assembled women, the ones who thought he was *a little doll,* but Thomas Winslow moved on. "Charlotte will wait her turn," Thomas told the ladies of the town. "Emily is our Brontë girl today—what a Gothic story she has written!" he suddenly cried, raising his arms above his head. "But don't dwell on what a monster Heathcliff is," he exhorted them. "It's Catherine you should care about—poor Catherine," he said softly.

Constance saw the ladies' lips move. Inwardly and involuntarily, without a sound, those women were repeating what he'd told them— *poor Catherine.* In her heart, Constance could hear Catherine's own words—when Catherine is ill and remembering the past, when she could freely be with Heathcliff. ("I wish I were a girl again, half savage and hardy, and free," Catherine says.)

Her empathy for Catherine notwithstanding, Constance willed herself to go against her husband's teacherly instructions. While she sat unmoving on the speaker's platform, while Thomas talked on and on, Constance allowed herself to dwell on Heathcliff. Constance knew the most troubling aspect of Heathcliff to dwell on. Heathcliff is an orphan—not a good one, as it turns out.

The more immediate matter of concern in the Winslows' life was Honor, their fourth daughter; with former au pair girls overrunning the house, offering unasked-for assistance, the back bedroom often had two grown women sleeping in a queen-size bed. Worse, the Winslows were hearing it from Faith and Hope (even from Prudence) that they, their own children, were perfectly capable of looking after a newborn sister. Thomas was once more sleeping in the master bedroom. At night, if Honor cried, you could get trampled rushing to the dear child's assistance.

If the townspeople of Pennacook imagined the Winslows were pushing their luck with a fourth ward of the state, luck wasn't what Constance worried about. Constance knew her whole family had benefited from three terrific au pair girls, now three wonderful young women. Yet Constance understood why those orphans hadn't been adopted. People who were brave enough to adopt an orphan usually wanted one of the newborns. They wanted a kid with a clean slate—not one who'd been abandoned at the orphanage, not a kid who was old enough to remember a previous life (and the people in it).

Weren't the orphans who remembered being abandoned the ones who might be full of rage? You couldn't blame one of those orphans if they were angry, Constance couldn't help thinking; she just didn't want to bring a bad one into her family, knowing this was the last orphan she and Thomas would endeavor to save.

Oh, Tommy, Constance thought, because she didn't believe in prayer—*please give up the grudge you have against Maine!* Her lips weren't moving; facing the ladies of the town, she sat as still as a stone. Constance wanted to give the orphanage physician in St. Cloud's a try—the reader, as she thought of the doctor who ran the place. Constance didn't care how hard it was to get there, or that you had to take the train. She shared her husband's grudge against religious institutions. The Winslows weren't believers; they were wary of those people who thought nothing of imposing their religion on you. As for the orphanage physician in charge of St. Cloud's, the nonreligious part surely appealed to the Winslows; only the Maine part stood in their way.

4.

A Letter from Dr. Larch

There were other orphanages in Maine. The one in Augusta, the Maine Children's Home, was farther north than St. Cloud's, but it was easier to get to—you could drive there. Constance heard they had a good record of placing children in reliable homes for foster care. "It's still in Maine, Connie," was all Thomas said about going to Augusta.

There was the one in Lewiston, which Constance knew not to mention—not only because it was an orphanage for boys. It was run by nuns from the Sisters of Charity; the nuns had come to Maine from Saint-Hyacinthe, Quebec, in the late 1800s. Constance could only imagine how her husband might imitate the accent of an unfortunate child who'd been taught to speak English by French-speaking nuns.

Constance knew that nun-run orphanages were not on her Tommy's list—not even in New Hampshire. The one in Manchester—St. Peter's Orphanage—was also run by the Sisters of Charity. ("Those nuns from Quebec are everywhere!" Thomas exclaimed.) The Sisters of Mercy had been running St. Mary's Orphanage in Dover since 1887. "No nuns, Connie," was all her Tommy would say. He wasn't worried that Honor would be inadvertently strangled by an au pair girl's rosary beads, although there were rumors that the Sisters of Charity had beaten bed-wetters. What Thomas Winslow was worried about were the potential proselytizers—those unadopted orphans (soon to become wards of the state) who'd been indoctrinated by the nuns.

There was a second orphanage in Dover, one the Winslows were also worried about. The Dover Children's Home had been founded by the Woman's Christian Temperance Union.

"They don't say they only take children of alcoholics, Tommy," Constance cautioned him.

"They don't say we'll be subjected to random sobriety tests, Connie," Thomas told her. They were just fooling around; they weren't really worried about the temperance part. It was the Christian part that worried the Winslows.

The Winslows had worn out their welcome at Coit House in Concord, one of the many orphanages founded for children orphaned by the Civil War. The Winslows had found Faith's nanny there, but they had asked too many questions about the orphanage's affiliation to St. Paul's School and the Episcopal Church. With the passage of time, the Winslows would not countenance so much as a hint of religious affiliation. They'd never made an appointment at the Daniel Webster Home in Franklin after learning it had been founded by Chaplain August Mack—the *chaplain* word turned away the Winslows.

"Aren't we burning our bridges, Tommy?" Constance had asked him. In truth, Faith's nanny was a great girl, despite coming from Coit House; she'd not tried to brainwash Faith into becoming an Episcopalian. The Winslows had originally thought of getting Faith's au pair girl from a nonreligious orphanage in Berlin, in northern New Hampshire—less than sixty miles from Quebec.

The waterpower in Berlin was provided by the Androscoggin River—it ran the pulp and paper mills. "Paper City" as Berlin was known, was so far north, so close to Quebec, there were many townspeople of French-Canadian descent; yet the orphanage in town had always been run by a doctor and nurses, not nuns.

A physician-run, nonreligious orphanage was right up the Winslows' alley, but the name of the place put off Thomas; the Androscoggin Children's Mission sounded Catholic to him. The English teacher's interpretation of the word *mission* might have been too literal. "I take *mission* to mean 'the sending of the Holy Spirit into the world,' Connie," Thomas told her.

"Perhaps the doctor didn't mean *mission* in the Latin way, Tommy," Constance cautioned him, but the Latin meaning of *mission* was why the Winslows had gotten Faith's au pair girl (their first unadopted orphan) from Coit House. Meanwhile, the name of the nonreligious orphanage in Berlin kept changing. The word *mission* was the first to go. The new name was misleading in a different way.

The "Androscoggin Wayward Children's Home" made Thomas Winslow think of the orphanage physician as a failed novelist—one who couldn't do titles. The word *wayward* made it sound like the children were responsible for being orphaned. The Winslows were told that a third name was found, thanks to one of the nurses. "That doctor should not be allowed to name anything, Connie—not even a new medicine!" Thomas told her.

"More to the point, Tommy—certainly not a new *orphan*," Constance corrected him.

"Right you are, Connie," Thomas said; he was gracious when he was bested. And because one of the nurses (not the orphanage physician) got the name right, the Winslows would take their second and third wards of the state from the Androscoggin Children's Shelter in Berlin. For no better reason, Constance wondered, than it wasn't in Maine?

The Winslows would like Dr. Roland Remillard and his nurses a lot. "They were certainly French Canadians, Connie, but there was not a crucifix in sight," Thomas had observed, to his satisfaction. Nurse Bergeron was their favorite, but Nurse Pinette was very nice. The two au pair girls the Winslows took from the Androscoggin Children's Shelter, Lucie and Denise, were unadopted French Canadians. Those two wards of the state were wonderful young women. As the Winslows observed, Lucie occasionally went to Mass; Denise did not.

In southeastern New Hampshire, the townspeople of Pennaccok were not as accustomed to French Canadians as their neighbors up north; yet even the ladies of the town loved Lucie and Denise. There was nothing not to like about those orphans from the Androscoggin. The good results were presented to Constance as a fait accompli. She knew her Tommy was dead set against going anywhere but Berlin for Honor's nanny.

A shortage of fourteen- or fifteen-year-old girls at the Androscoggin Children's Shelter was what worried Constance. She needn't have worried that Berlin would run out of unadopted orphans. As Lucie would one day tell the Winslows about being abandoned at the Androscoggin, "We were transitoire the whole time we were there, just waiting for someone to take us."

"If nobody wants you till you're fourteen or fifteen, you'll always be transitoire—that's just what it's like to be an unadopted orphan," Denise told the Winslows. Those two au pair girls spoke excellent English. Constance always said that Lucie and Denise must have found it less painful to say "transitory" in French.

"Right you are, Connie," her husband said. Their Hope and their Prudence would excel in the French they took in school, because of the help they had from those wonderful French Canadians.

As for the French-Canadian kids they met in the Pennacook public school, Lucie and Denise had befriended them. Lucie and Denise were surprised that most of the French Canadians in Pennacook didn't speak French. (It wasn't that way in Berlin.) The Pennacook French-Canadian kids didn't even take French in school. Lucie and Denise had met some of their classmates' parents, too, and they didn't speak French at home. Occasionally, there were grandparents who spoke French— not willingly, Lucie and Denise told the Winslows. Speaking French had isolated them, the grandparents said to Lucie and Denise. "I don't want my grandkids to speak French—if they start speaking French, my grandkids will be as isolated as me!" one of the grandparents told Lucie.

It turned out that half the French-Canadian kids Lucie and Denise had met in school came from one Pennacook family. The Winslows weren't surprised. The Beaudette clan was renowned for procreation. In a different way, the townspeople of Pennacook were as unkind about the Beaudettes as they were about the Winslows. No one in town would accuse the Winslows of overbreeding, but even the ladies of the town said the Beaudettes were "breeding like rabbits."

The Winslows' French-Canadian nannies took pity on the Beaudettes, as did Thomas and Constance Winslow. The Beaudettes were nice to everyone, their nonstop childbearing notwithstanding. The mother and father, Josephine and Antoine, had only girls—one after another, until Josephine was too old. The Beaudette girls were good-natured about having too many sisters to count.

The townspeople of Pennacook were of the opinion that old Antoine must have wanted a boy; this was why he couldn't stop. The ladies of the town were more of the opinion that Josephine couldn't say no. Just look what became of those Beaudette girls. Some of those girls got pregnant when they were still in high school. Almost all the Beaudette girls had babies instead of going to college; the one who went to college, Chantal, was the only one who spoke French. And those Beaudette girls mostly had more girls; there were only four Beaudette boys in the whole family. Those boys behaved themselves. They stayed in school; all four finished college. Except for Arnaud, they married late and had small families.

Arnaud Beaudette would be Jimmy Winslow's friend—he was the only Beaudette to attend Pennacook Academy.

Chantal was the smallest and youngest of Antoine's and Josephine's daughters. It was weird that Chantal was only a few years older than Arnaud, who was her nephew—one of her sisters' children. *Poor Chantal,* the ladies of the town silently commiserated with one another;

they meant her clothes, the hand-me-downs. Chantal wore the outsize blouses and sweaters of her older, bigger sisters. "And a good thing, too, Tommy—those Beaudette girls are too well-endowed for their own good," Constance Winslow said.

"Right you are, Connie—Chantal deserves a chance to finish school and not attract undue attention," Thomas told her. "You're well-enough endowed for me, Connie," he couldn't resist telling her.

"Stop it, Tommy," she always said. Constance and her daughters were modestly endowed.

And Chantal Beaudette was nowhere near as broad in the beam as her older, bigger sisters; she could never wear their skirts or dresses. No one in Pennacook had seen Chantal in a skirt or a dress. Chantal wore jeans or slacks; they must not have been hand-me-downs, because they fit her. Jimmy Winslow loved her.

Even the townspeople of Pennacook were smart enough to imagine that Chantal must have inherited the Beaudette breasts. Even in those baggy blouses and sloppy sweaters, the ladies of the town were observant enough to see something big under those loose-fitting tops. Chantal Beaudette had to have big boobs, didn't she? A long time later—long after the Winslows would find their fourth unadopted orphan—the cruelest speculation would gain traction in the town, concerning the lack of definition to Chantal's breasts under her floppy clothes. What if she'd been born with only one boob, a big one? What if Chantal had a *onesie*?

Before the townspeople of Pennacook would become transfixed by the bosomy Beaudettes—long before Jimmy Winslow was born—the undistracted Winslows didn't lose their focus on finding a fourth unadopted orphan. Those wonderful French Canadians, their last two unadopted orphans, had served them well. Understandably, the Winslows wanted another girl from the Berlin orphanage.

What exactly happened at the Androscoggin Children's Shelter would never be adequately explained in what passed for the news in

New Hampshire—not in those days. Between the end of World War I and the beginning of World War II, orphans weren't the only ones who felt a lack of permanence, but the Winslows understood that orphans should be allowed to take transience personally. An orphan is simply more of a child than other children—in the way all children want the things they love to happen daily, on schedule. For everything good that promises to last, to stay the same, an orphan is permanently longing.

When the Winslows tried to make an appointment, they were informed that the Androscoggin Children's Shelter had closed. The orphans were being relocated to other facilities providing care for unwanted children. It would not console the Winslows to hear that "church groups" were offering their assistance in relocating the kids.

When the Winslows tried to contact Dr. Remillard directly, they were informed that he was no longer allowed to practice medicine in New Hampshire. When the Winslows inquired after Nurse Bergeron and Nurse Pinette, someone rather rudely said: "Those nurses might have gone back to Canada—maybe Dr. Remillard went with them, not that anyone in Quebec would want them."

In what passed for the news in New Hampshire, the only information the Winslows would read concerned a local Berlin physician, a Dr. Patrice Grenier, who was "on call" to the former orphanage—in case one of the kids was sick, or otherwise needed to see a doctor. The church groups were reported to be watching over the orphaned children who had yet to be relocated.

The Winslows guessed their two orphans from the Androscoggin would know what was going on in Berlin. Lucie and Denise had always been smart girls, including when they were only fourteen or fifteen. Their two French Canadians just confirmed what the Winslows had guessed.

"Dear Dr. Remillard—they must have caught him, or one of the women he helped might have told someone!" Lucie exclaimed.

"Nurse Bergeron or Nurse Pinette would never have told anyone—

it was one of those women who got knocked up, and she needed to blame someone," Denise said.

"Dr. Remillard gave those women what they wanted—either a baby they would leave behind, or an abortion," Lucie explained, but the Winslows had figured it out. In that period of time, when abortion was illegal in the United States, a woman with an unwanted pregnancy might find a physician who was willing to give her an abortion in an orphanage. A doctor in an orphanage would know what happened, or what *didn't* happen, to those children who were left behind—the ones who weren't babies, the ones who weren't taken (like Lucie and Denise).

As for Dr. Remillard, who gave those women what they wanted, the Winslows wished him all the best—as they did Nurse Bergeron and Nurse Pinette (wherever they went, however they might manage to start a new life).

Even the townspeople of Pennacook knew a little about what was going on in some orphanages. When a girl in high school (or in junior high school) missed six months or more of school, the ladies of the town would whisper among themselves. You might hear one of them say the schoolgirl had gone to the orphanage. The townspeople of Pennacook were capable of occasional common sense. If a girl got pregnant, she would stop going to school before she started to show; she kept out of sight till she went to the orphanage and had her baby, leaving it behind. The ladies of the town watched closely. If a girl stopped going to school for only two or three months, she still might have gone to the orphanage—not to have her baby, but to have an abortion.

Ever since illegal abortion became the status quo, the Winslows had noticed an entrenched cruelty in the townspeople of Pennacook—most of all, in the ladies of the town. The churchwomen were the cruelest. Of an unmarried woman or girl who got pregnant, those women said: "She's paying the piper." Meaning she deserved to give birth to an unwanted child—she deserved to *pay for* getting pregnant. The Winslows were of the opinion that the anti-abortion crusaders (both the men and the women) didn't care what happened to the unwanted child—not after the child was born. What those crusaders cared about was punishing the mother.

As for the long drive north to Berlin, the Winslows weren't going. "Maybe it's for the best, Tommy—there are more than enough of us to look after Honor," Constance told her husband. But Thomas Winslow wasn't worried about the new baby. With three daughters dying to look after their little sister, and their former au pair girls refusing to move on, Honor would not go uncared for. An army of caregivers was poised to look after the Winslows' fourth daughter.

"I already bought our tickets for the train, Connie—I thought we'd give that reader in St. Cloud's a try," Thomas told her. For once, he didn't mention Maine.

"You should buy a third ticket for the train back to Pennacook, Tommy—in case there's a girl who wants to try us," Constance said.

"Right you are, Connie," Thomas said. He showed her the third ticket for the train from St. Cloud's. Constance understood how he felt compelled to help the unadopted orphans, the ones no one had taken—the wards of the state who would soon be cast out.

When Thomas Winslow first wrote to the orphanage in St. Cloud's, Maine—describing his family's circumstances, and their happiness with those three au pair girls who'd once been wards of the state—the orphanage physician in St. Cloud's had not delayed in writing back. (Thomas Winslow would say the delay had everything to do with the postal service to and from Maine.) From the date on the doctor's letter (which Thomas showed her), Constance could see that her Tommy must have written to St. Cloud's before the Winslows were informed that the orphanage in Berlin had closed. Of course it pleased Constance to know her husband had a backup plan all along.

The doctor didn't beat around the bush. His name was Wilbur Larch. "Here in St. Cloud's, we need to know more about your financial resources," Dr. Larch's letter began. "You're a schoolteacher, Mr.

Winslow—your wife is a librarian. With four children of your own, it would seem you're a family of modest means. It is commendable that you and your family have provided a college education for three former wards of the state, but how can you afford this? Tell us how this is within your means, Mr. Winslow." And that wasn't all the doctor would ask of the Winslows.

"Goodness gracious, Dr. Larch is certainly direct—isn't he, Tommy?" Constance asked her husband.

"It's a fair question, Connie," Thomas answered.

As the Winslows were aware, it was a question that had long plagued the townspeople of Pennacook—not least the ladies of the town, who were dying to know where the Winslows' money came from. Naturally, there was no one in the town who would ask the Winslows about their family money—not as directly as Dr. Larch did. In the class warfare that permeates small New England towns, your family money was everybody's business—not to mention an advantage, one you didn't deserve. To the townspeople of Pennacook, the Winslows' family money mattered more than their *Mayflower* ancestry.

5.

The History of Abortion in America

A s Thomas Winslow would write to Dr. Wilbur Larch, there were wealthy Winslow and Bradford families living in the greater Boston area—where he and Constance came from, where they'd grown up. They were sent to private secondary schools; they were boarding students at Pennacook Academy and at Abbot Academy. (Abbot was a school for young women in Andover, Massachusetts.)

Thomas and Constance were prep-school students when they met one summer in Marblehead, Massachusetts, where both the Bradford and Winslow families had summer homes. If you've seen the Emanuel Leutze painting of *Washington Crossing the Delaware,* those were Marbleheaders who rowed the general across. The Marblehead militia became a regiment of George Washington's army. At the end of the Revolutionary War, the town of Marblehead was left with 459 widows and 865 orphaned children.

First a fishing village, later a Boston bedroom community—in the summer months, Marblehead was mostly a sailing and tourism town. Both Constance Bradford and Thomas Winslow would remember the sailboats in Marblehead Harbor, though they were not sailors. Those two were always reading. When the summer kids in Marblehead were sailing, those two readers remained on shore. That's how Constance and Thomas met. In Marblehead, and all around Marblehead Harbor, it's possible those two were the only ones their age who were reading.

During the Salem witch trials, the town of Marblehead had only one witch. She was found guilty of witchcraft and hanged in 1692. Her name was Wilmot Redd; her husband was a fisherman. For some reason, young Constance Bradford took to heart that Wilmot was known for her irritability. "Poor Wilmot must have been a *reader*, Tommy—her fisherman probably hated her because he never read anything," Constance told the young man she would one day marry.

"Right you are, Connie—poor Wilmot was found guilty of *reading*, and they hanged her for it!" Thomas told his teenage sweetheart.

"In other parts of the world," Dr. Wilbur Larch would one day write to Thomas Winslow, "what you and your wife were thinking and feeling when you were teenagers might be entirely your own business. But here in St. Cloud's, we need to know what you two were like at that age— before we commit one of our young teenagers to your safekeeping."

This was why the Winslows wrote Dr. Wilbur Larch and told him everything; they began by telling him they weren't real Marbleheaders. As the Winslows would further explain, they were just a couple of kids who started a summer romance; it happened only because they were reading instead of sailing. Those two would spare the doctor no detail; their story of the one witch hanged in Marblehead made Dr. Larch imagine that Wilmot Redd must have been a relative of the Bradfords or the Winslows, and that poor Wilmot had been *hanged* for reading.

Constance waxed lyrical about Abbot Academy and her schoolgirl days. Constance said she was inspired by Abbot's Latin motto: Facem Praetendit Ardentem—She Holds Aloft a Burning Torch. "No, I was not inspired to be an arsonist," Constance wrote to the orphanage physician, "but I aspired to a higher education—and to more reading!" Constance couldn't restrain herself from branching out beyond her teenage years. "I have a master's in library and information sciences," she wrote Dr. Larch, "and Tommy has a master's in English literature."

Not to be outdone, Thomas Winslow regaled Dr. Larch with his thoughts concerning Pennacook Academy's Latin motto: Finis Origine

Pendet—The End Depends Upon the Beginning. "My schoolmates, all boys, weren't inclined to divulge their innermost feelings to me, and none of us had any actual experiences worth sharing," Thomas Winslow wrote the orphanage physician in St. Cloud's. "It was the brave young characters in the novels I loved who shared their innermost feelings (and harrowing experiences) with me—those characters in literature taught me who I was." The English teacher named certain characters, beginning with Pip in *Great Expectations* and including Catherine Earnshaw in *Wuthering Heights*. Thomas was just getting started. Dr. Larch had to hear all about Ishmael in *Moby-Dick*—then it was James Steerforth in *David Copperfield*, and Thomas got carried away with the incomitable Jane Eyre.

It's a wonder Thomas remembered to tell the doctor about the philanthropy of the Bradford and Winslow families—the wealthier members of their respective families, the ones who made much more money than a schoolteacher and a librarian.

Thus was Wilbur Larch informed about those Winslows who were coming to St. Cloud's. When he wrote back to the Winslows, confirming their appointment at the orphanage, Dr. Larch was brief and to the point.

"Here in St. Cloud's, I believe we have a young woman who might meet your needs—most certainly, she will benefit from your family's educational guidance and support," the doctor wrote. "Pay no attention to our stationmaster if you meet him when you disembark or board your train. He's a religious fool—he believes in Judgment Day," Dr. Larch added.

"Goodness gracious, Tommy," was all Constance could say. Despite the Judgment Day stationmaster in St. Cloud's, she was looking forward to getting out of Pennacook—chiefly to get away from the Town Talks. Thomas wasn't the only member of the academy's English Department to contribute a talk or two. The one on Wordsworth, Coleridge, and the later Romantics was well attended. Almost no one came to the one on literature in translation; Dante, Cervantes, Balzac, and Zola were virtually alone. The two talks by faculty members in the History Department were a similarly mixed bag. The one on the colonial era of the United States was more popular than the one on the American Civil War, although Thomas Winslow would complain to his two colleagues on the Pennacook faculty; he found fault with both historians. They should (at least) have mentioned, he told them, that abortion was widespread and not illegal between the 1620s and the mid-nineteenth century.

"Well, Thomas, I wouldn't say abortion is *germane to* the colonial era of the United States," one of the historians replied.

"Well, George, if you were a pregnant woman who didn't want a baby, abortion might be *germane to* you—in any era," Constance said, jumping into the conversation.

"Right you are, Connie," Thomas told her.

"Well, Constance—and you, too, Thomas—I can assure you that the availability of abortion was of no relevance to the American Civil War," the Civil War historian said.

"Well, Frank, if you were a pregnant widow whose husband had been killed in the First Battle of Bull Run, the availability of abortion might matter to you," Thomas told him. (You could not marginalize the abortion subject around the Winslows.)

The problem with the Town Talks, as the Winslows would figure out, was that no young people came to them. Thomas should have been talking to teenage girls and women in their early twenties—the ones with the most to lose because of an unwanted pregnancy.

No Town Talk was as sparsely attended as the one Thomas Winslow gave on the history of abortion in America; that one was the most unpopular of all the Town Talks, ever. Not one faculty member from the History Department showed up; there were only a few from the English Department. Among the ladies of the town, only the churchwomen were represented, and they had come to cause trouble.

"In the time of the Puritans, America's deeply religious founding fathers, abortion was permissible beyond the first trimester—up to four or five months," Thomas began. The churchwomen's lips were pursed, their eyes already narrowing. "For more than two centuries—beginning when the Pilgrims landed in Plymouth, Massachusetts—abortion was largely allowed," Thomas Winslow went on. "With the help of mid-wives, the choice to have an abortion or a child belonged to the woman who was pregnant," Thomas told his meager audience, mostly women. The only men (not counting the few from the English Department) were doctors—just three doctors. Constance sat there, same as usual, still as a stone; she knew the part about the doctors was coming.

Then one of the churchwomen stood shakily, like a reluctant school-girl called on in class. Constance whispered the woman's name—so quietly only Thomas could hear her. "Aren't you overlooking the child in the womb, Mr. Winslow?" the churchwoman asked. "The child in the womb is a human being, too." She suddenly shouted: "The child in the womb has a soul, you know!" The word *soul* should do it, Constance thought to herself.

"Respectfully, Mrs. Sweeney, if you believe an unborn fetus has a soul, you shouldn't have an abortion—no one's making you have one," Thomas told her. Surely Mrs. Sweeney was beyond childbearing years; no one could imagine her having a baby or an abortion.

"Even *you* have a soul, Mr. Winslow—everyone has a soul from the moment of conception!" Mrs. Sweeney cried.

"But, Mrs. Sweeney, if I don't believe I have a soul, I don't believe an unborn fetus has one," Thomas told her.

Constance pushed back her chair and stood; she went straight to her Tommy, in front of the podium, taking the microphone from him. For such a small audience, those two Winslows didn't need a microphone. "Women have always been undermined by men in power—back then, in the case of abortion, the men who did the undermining were doc-tors," Constance said; she made a point of not looking at the three doctors, only at Mrs. Sweeney, who was at a loss for words. Mrs. Sweeney just stood there.

"Right you are, Connie. I think the microphone is unnecessary," Thomas added. Constance put the microphone on the podium and returned to her chair. Mrs. Sweeney just went on standing.

"Beginning in the 1840s, doctors sought to gain control of the reproduction business," Thomas Winslow began again—this time speaking to the three doctors, ignoring Mrs. Sweeney. "Doctors were establishing their new profession; midwives were their competition. The doctors wanted the money the midwives were making," Thomas said.

Constance tried to stop wishing Mrs. Sweeney would faint and fall down, thus distracting the three doctors. "Maybe the doctors underestimated how great the need for abortion was. We know what the doctors wanted, and they achieved it—doctors drove midwives out of the abortion business. But we don't know the doctors' reasons for making abortion illegal," Thomas Winslow went on. That was when the first of the three doctors stood up and started to leave.

Constance knew the other two would follow the first one. "Maybe the doctors changed their minds about wanting the job when they realized how many abortions the midwives had been performing. Childbirth is a lot more dangerous than a first-trimester abortion, but the doctors lied about the dangers of performing abortions in order to take midwives off the job. Midwives are still delivering babies!" Thomas called to the departing doctors. Now the churchwomen were following the offended doctors—all but Mrs. Sweeney, who appeared to have taken root in the floor of the lecture hall.

Constance once more pushed back her chair and stood, calling after all of them. "The history of how midwives lost the abortion business makes doctors and men look awful!" Constance called. At that moment, the only remaining members of the audience were a small number of men—a few of Thomas's colleagues in the English Department.

"Connie doesn't mean you men—thank you for coming," Thomas

told them. What the Winslows would remember was how thrilled the men from the English Department were to be there; they'd not seen Thomas fail to hold an audience's attention before. "The history of abortion in America is not one of those nineteenth-century novels I love," Thomas was telling his colleagues, while Mrs. Sweeney just went on standing. "It has no discernible plot, there are no delineated characters, there is no foreshadowing of an ending—as storytelling, it's a mess," Thomas told his colleagues, who were loving every word. His fellow English teachers found Thomas entertaining, even when he'd failed to hold an audience.

Not Mrs. Sweeney, who stood ramrod straight. Constance knew Mrs. Sweeney was waiting for her turn, a parting shot. "Thank you for coming, Mrs. Sweeney," Thomas said sincerely.

"Maybe you *don't* have a soul, Mr. Winslow—maybe you're just a *blasphemer,*" Mrs. Sweeney said.

"Good night, Mrs. Sweeney—no one has a soul," Constance told her. So much for improving town-gown relations. No one walked out of other Town Talks, including the clunkers. More people showed up at (and stayed for) the geologist's talk on the rocks of New England. The biologist's talk on genetics got bogged down in anecdotes about his students' botched experiments with fruit flies. Notwithstanding the fruit flies, no one walked out.

Pennacook Academy was not a school with a religious affiliation. There was Morning Meeting, not Morning Chapel. On the weekend, students were required to attend a religious service of some kind—of their own choice. Many of the boys who weren't religious chose the Catholic Church because the first Mass of the morning was the quickest. The Jewish students were driven by bus to Temple Israel, a synagogue in Portsmouth. The school minister was Presbyterian; he taught the academy's history-of-religion courses. In his nondenominational way, the school minister gave a Town Talk on comparative religion. The turnout was of moderate size, both men and women.

The Winslows were impressed that the school minister asked a member of the English Department to stand beside him on the speaker's platform. Daniel Rosenthal and his wife, Naomi, were one of the Winslows' favorite young couples at the academy. The Winslows saw a lot of the Rosenthals socially. "Daniel is Jewish—he's with me to answer any questions you may have about Judaism," the school minister told the townspeople of Pennacook.

No one asked Daniel Rosenthal a question; the Winslows felt badly for their young friend. They'd already noticed that Naomi hadn't come to the Town Talk; she must have known it would be awkward. The silence of the townspeople aroused the Winslows' suspicions that many New Englanders were silently anti-Semitic.

Constance sensed that her husband was about to ask Daniel a question; she knew he was having a hard time with what to ask. Given all the books they'd read, and how well educated the Winslows were, they knew nothing about Judaism. "Don't ask, Tommy—poor Daniel will know you're just feeling sorry for him," Constance whispered. If there ever was a *Right you are, Connie,* situation, Thomas Winslow knew this was one, but he didn't whisper a word to his wife. He knew the Jewish people originated from the Israelites and the Hebrews; he scarcely remembered that they came from historical Israel and Judah, and only because Daniel Rosenthal had recently reminded him. Thomas Winslow knew there'd been a Kingdom of Israel and a Kingdom of Judah, but he couldn't keep them straight. Daniel and Naomi were always reminding him that both were destroyed.

From the Jews they knew at Pennacook Academy—both the faculty and the students, all of whom the Winslows liked—the Winslows thought Judaism was a refreshingly secular religion. Daniel and Naomi laughed when Thomas told them this. "The Jews at Pennacook are as secular as we can be!" Naomi said.

"There are very religious Orthodox Jews—Naomi and I don't have much in common with them," Daniel Rosenthal had told the

Winslows. There'd been some conversation about the apparent lack of proselytizing that Jews do. The Winslows approved of no proselytizing.

"No Jew has ever tried to convert me!" Thomas told the Rosenthals, who laughed. The Rosenthals weren't interested in converting someone who wasn't Jewish to Judaism. As for the Jewish kids at the academy— all of them were boarding students—the Rosenthals wanted those boys to feel they were part of a family. The Winslows got the feeling that the Jewish people were most of all a community with a history; they just happened to come from a part of the Levant known as the Land of Israel.

"Even in exile—or just a boy at school, away from home—a Jew feels some solidarity with the Jewish people," Daniel Rosenthal told the Winslows. As unreligious as they were, the Winslows felt an unaccustomed solidarity with the Jewish people—at least with the Rosenthals.

All these thoughts distracted the Winslows from the school minister's Town Talk on comparative religion. The Winslows wouldn't remember a word. Their thoughts were with what little they knew of Judaism and the Jewish people. What little the Winslows knew, they liked. Besides, the talk on comparative religion was the last Town Talk the Winslows would attend before they boarded the train to St. Cloud's. The Winslows were already thinking about the orphanage and the orphan they would meet there. Naturally, they hoped that their last orphan would be the best one.

6.

The Jewish One

The train to St. Cloud's left as early as a milk train, and it made as many stops. The train stopped at stations where no one got off or on the train, but the Winslows scarcely noticed their fellow passengers. More people disembarked and boarded the train in Portland, and again in Lewiston, where the Winslows were vaguely aware of the Androscoggin River. As the crow flies, you could follow the Androscoggin north-northwest to Berlin, New Hampshire, but the train to St. Cloud's went its own way—due north. It wouldn't keep company with the Androscoggin for long. North of Lewiston, where the Winslows parted company with the big river, looked foreign to them, though there were other rivers around. Maybe the Winslows were wondering about their closeness to Quebec, or Thomas had his own reasons to say, "Another French Canadian would be okay with me, Connie."

"I just want a good one, Tommy," Constance said.

A new conductor passed through their car, where the Winslows were almost the only passengers. A younger couple sat across the aisle, and two elderly, quarrelsome men were seated on the same side of the train as the Winslows, a little ahead of them. There were no words with the old codgers when the conductor checked their tickets. The young couple and the conductor also refrained from conversation. In Maine, Thomas Winslow was thinking, there must be a strict observance of silence in the presence of men in uniform. Constance had the tickets in her purse; she handed them to the conductor, a squat man with a gray mustache, his eyes concealed under the visor of his conductor's cap.

"We're going to St. Cloud's!" Thomas Winslow announced to the entire passenger car, causing the two codgers to cry out in consternation. There was a sharp intake of breath from the young woman across the aisle, and the conductor's cap was knocked askew when he suddenly stiffened. That was when the Winslows saw the conductor's one glass eye, and his one good one.

"You have the right tickets—St. Cloud's is where you're going," the conductor with the glass eye told Thomas, handing the tickets back to Constance.

The two codgers had been whispering to each other, like a couple of hissing snakes, when one of them turned around and shouted over the back of his seat. "You don't have to raise a ruckus about where you're goin'!" he cried.

Constance held her Tommy's hand. She knew he would have been disappointed if he couldn't incite their fellow passengers on the subject of St. Cloud's. For the same reason, the Winslows were disappointed not to encounter the Judgment Day stationmaster on the platform when they got off the train. There was no one in or around the forlorn-looking railroad station; no other passengers had disembarked or boarded the train in St. Cloud's, where the dirt road to the orphanage was not as muddy as the Winslows were expecting. They'd worn their mud boots, but they needed only to avoid the wheel ruts. Spring had come to Pennacook—not yet to this part of Maine. There were mounds of unmelted snow in the woods as the Winslows trudged on. Dusk was falling; in the darker stage of twilight, the orphanage buildings were unclear. The Winslows faintly discerned what looked like three structures—two separate bunkhouses with a building between them, probably a dining hall with a kitchen.

Where was the hospital? There had to be somewhere for the babies to be born, and for the infants, Thomas Winslow was thinking. There were no children's voices. It was the time of the evening for kids to have supper, Constance thought. At the first building they came to, they saw steps leading to a porch and (perhaps) an entrance.

Nurse Edna heard the Winslows knocking and let them in; she said she'd been expecting them. As she led them along a corridor, through the glass panels on a pair of double doors, they got a glimpse of cribs for infants and a nurse holding a baby. "Nurse Angela will be joining us, as will Dr. Larch when he finishes his supper—he's in the dining hall with the children," Nurse Edna told them. She explained the layout of the orphanage as patiently as she might have spoken to a newly abandoned orphan. The building they were in was the boys' division; the boys bunked upstairs, where their washrooms were. The ground floor, where the infants were, had two delivery rooms equipped for surgical operations. Dr. Larch slept in the boys' division, where he also had an office. The building on the far side of the dining hall was the girls' division. The boys and girls did everything together, but they slept and washed and dressed in separate buildings.

Nurse Edna left the Winslows in Dr. Larch's office while she went to get the doctor. Constance quickly looked away when she saw the stirrups on the gynecological examination table. The Winslows whispered about the smell in the doctor's office. It was an antiseptic smell, or something medicinal. Constance thought she recognized the smell, but she couldn't name it. It made her queasy.

The office was a maze of books and instruments, but the doctor's desk drew the schoolteacher's attention. The typewriter was the centerpiece; the surrounding stacks of pages had a writerly symmetry, an orderliness that reminded Thomas Winslow of Dr. Larch's letters. Just then, the nurse they'd seen with the infants breezed into the office—automatically opening a window. "Some fresh air might be nice—you must be the Winslows," Nurse Angela said. Thomas introduced himself and Constance, who inquired about the smell. "Oh, that's just ether," Angela answered, as breezily as she'd walked in.

47

Nurse Angela saw no reason to tell the Winslows that Dr. Larch was addicted to ether. Besides, the Winslows were looking with approval at the doctor's framed diplomas—the ones from Bowdoin College and Harvard Medical School. Angela didn't know the sordid story of what had happened to Dr. Larch between those two degrees. Not even his nurses knew why Larch was disenchanted with the Portland of his youth—only that he was definitely disenchanted with it.

In his first year of medical school, Wilbur Larch had had a bacterial infection that pained and ashamed him. It was gonorrhea—a gift, indirectly, from his alcoholic father. His old man had been so proud of Wilbur, he sent him to medical school with a present. He bought the boy a Portland whore, setting up his son with a sexual experience in one of the wharf-side boardinghouses. It was a present the boy had been too embarrassed to refuse. Young Larch was touched that his father had given him anything. The whore's name was Mrs. Eames. "She rhymes with screams!" Wilbur's father had told him.

It was no small feat that his father managed to be a drunk in the Portland of Mayor Neal Dow's time. Dow was responsible for the Maine law that introduced Prohibition to the state. In those days, all Larch's father could find to drink was a Scotch ale or a bitter beer—he had to drink these weak brews by the bucketful to get buzzed enough to think it was a good idea to buy his son a whore.

These were pre-penicillin days. The gonorrhea lived on for months in young Larch, giving him a passionate interest in bacteriology before burning itself out. It left his urethra scarred. It left him fond of ether, too—because the ether sleeps Larch administered to himself relieved him of the burning. This singular encounter with sexual pleasure—in combination with Wilbur's memory of his parents' loveless marriage—convinced the med student that a life of sexual abstinence was medically and philosophically sound. The road that led young Larch to obstetrics was strewn with bacteria—his own. Every morning, he would milk a drop of pus from his penis onto a stained slide. Magnified more than a thousand times, the gonococci he saw under the microscope were still smaller than common red ants. By the time the gonococci were gone, Larch was an ether addict.

While they waited for Dr. Larch in his office, the Winslows were now looking at a framed photograph on a corner of the doctor's desk. Among the soldiers on cots and the doctors attending to the wounded, the Winslows would not have recognized Dr. Larch—they hadn't met him yet. Besides, Dr. Larch wasn't pictured with the doctors—as Nurse Angela knew, Larch had taken the photograph.

"Is this a field hospital—was Dr. Larch in the war?" Thomas Winslow asked Angela.

In the grainy black-and-white photo, the soldiers' bandages were a brighter white. Angela knew what Dr. Larch was dealing with there—the shell and grenade fragments, the shrapnel, the dirty bits of a soldier's uniform that were carried with a missile into a wound. There was a recurring bacillus infection, but why did the Winslows need to know?

"It was an Advanced Dressing Station in France—we missed Dr. Larch here when he was over there," was all Nurse Angela said.

That was when Dr. Larch and Nurse Edna got to the doctor's office. There was no folderol about the seating arrangements. From the two chairs in front of the doctor's desk, the Winslows' view of Dr. Larch was partially blocked by the big typewriter. The two nurses sat together on the examination table; the stirrups didn't bother them.

"Here in St. Cloud's, nothing is ideal, but we do the best we can," Dr. Larch began. "The one we're thinking of, the one who might work out for you, is a special girl—she is loved and looked up to by all the girls."

"The boys look up to her, too," Nurse Edna added.

"She's fourteen, almost fifteen, but she seems much older—she's very mature for her age," Dr. Larch continued.

"She's very tall, too—and she keeps growing," Nurse Angela said.

"She must be fully grown—she can't keep growing!" Nurse Edna cried.

"Knowing her, she'll keep growing—she likes being tall, and she's very determined," Dr. Larch told the Winslows.

"She sounds wonderful!" was all Constance could say.

"Well, we only know what we can see for ourselves—we were told so little about her," Dr. Larch said; now his voice sounded doubtful.

"She *is* wonderful, Wilbur," Nurse Angela interjected, as if she knew what the doctor was going to say and she wished he wouldn't say it.

"The circumstances of her coming here were, at first, familiar to us—she was left here when she was a child, after dark, with no explanation and very little information," Dr. Larch began, but he paused; he was looking at his nurses on the examination table. "Your turn," the doctor told them.

It was a cold, snowy night in 1908 when the little girl was left on the front porch. Nurse Edna was with the infants when she heard the loud knocks on the door. Edna had to settle down a baby before she went to see who it was. Dr. Larch had gone to bed, but he was still awake; the knocking was loud enough for him to hear it.

"When a child is left on the porch after dark, a child that young is usually crying—not this girl," Edna told the Winslows. The abandoned girl was angry; she was kicking the newel post at the top of the porch stairs, but she didn't try to go after the woman who'd left her. In the dim glow cast by the porch light, Nurse Edna could see the woman who was leaving—already on her way back to the train station. "Please don't go—please tell me something about her!" Edna called to the woman. That was when Nurse Edna realized there were two women. One of the women was beyond the reach of the porch light, in the darkness. The unseen woman's voice resonated in the dark.

"She's Jewish!" the invisible woman shouted.

"She knows," said the woman Edna could see. "She also knows her name and how old she is—that's all she knows," the woman added; she was receding from the porch light, into the darkness.

"Is one of you her mother?" Nurse Edna asked the woman she could still see.

"She has no mother!" the invisible woman cried; by now, the two women had disappeared in the darkness.

"What is your name, dear child?" Edna asked the angry little girl, who was still kicking the newel post.

"Esther, like the queen—Queen Esther," the girl answered. She enunciated with unusual clarity; she didn't speak like a child.

"Queen Esther! I'm just Edna," Nurse Edna told the little girl.

"I'm just Esther," Esther said, giving the newel post a gentler kick.

"How old are you, Esther?" Edna asked; she guessed the girl was five, a tall five-year-old with strangely adult enunciation.

"I'm almost four," Esther answered.

A very tall three-year-old, Edna was thinking, when she heard one of the infants crying—maybe the baby she had tried to settle down before she went out on the porch. Esther heard the infant crying, too.

"Is that a baby? I've never seen a baby," Esther said. She was indignant when Edna asked her if she had a cough or a cold. "I'm not sick—I'm just tired!" the girl told Edna. "Are there other kids here? I don't know any kids," Esther added. (The Winslows were getting the picture.)

Nurse Angela had heard the invisible woman shouting (and what she shouted) all the way from the girls' division; some of the girls who weren't asleep had heard what the unseen woman shouted, too. It was hard not to hear the *She's Jewish!* and the *She has no mother!* if you were awake.

Angela told Edna that Dr. Larch was not in bed; he was waiting to meet the new orphan in his office, in his pajamas. He'd heard the *She's Jewish!* and the *She has no mother!*—as some of the boys had. Children repeat what they've heard. What the angry-sounding woman had shouted would get around.

In an orphanage, many children have no mother. The significant part of Esther's story was her Jewishness—being a Jew mattered to

Esther. In Dr. Larch's office, it had been strange when Esther started speaking of herself in the third person.

"Esther has no mother and no father," the girl began—her first words to the doctor.

"I'm sorry about that, Esther," Dr. Larch told the girl.

"The king loves Esther more than the other women," Esther said.

"Good for the king!" Dr. Larch cried. He'd stood up from his desk and was searching his bookshelves for his Bible, seldom used.

"Haman is the bad guy—he wants to kill all the Jews," Esther went on with the story.

"Haman sounds like a very bad guy," Larch said; he'd found his Bible and was opening it to the table of contents.

"Esther and Mordecai save the Jews—they're Jews," Esther explained to Dr. Larch.

"Mordecai sounds like a good guy," Larch said. Esther just nodded; she would let no one interrupt her story. "Shouldn't Esther tell the king what Haman is plotting against the Jews?" Dr. Larch asked Esther. He knew the story was biblical; definitely the Old Testament, Larch was thinking.

Esther sighed, nodding again; if she didn't like to be interrupted, she would let no one rush her story, either. "The king hangs Haman," Esther said; she approved of the hanging.

"Good for the king!" Larch cried again.

"Haman's kids get hanged, too—ten of them," Esther added.

"They had it coming!" Dr. Larch cried. It was evident that Esther thought so, too, from the vigorous way she nodded. Who would read or tell a kill-or-be-killed, Old Testament story to a child? Larch was wondering. He'd found The Book of Esther in the Old Testament. "You were named for the Esther in the Bible?" Dr. Larch asked her. This time, when she nodded, Esther smiled—only a small smile. "Who told you that you're Jewish?" Dr. Larch asked Esther.

"My mother wanted me to know," the girl answered firmly.

"But who told you, dear—was it one of those two women who brought you here?" Edna asked the child.

"Not them. He said he was a rabbi," Esther answered. "Another man was with us—he wrote everything down."

"The rabbi in your synagogue—you were brought up Jewish?" the doctor asked Esther, who fiercely shook her head.

"I don't know any Jews—I really want to!" Esther cried. "I don't know any other rabbis," she added.

"Is your mother dead, dear—do you know if she's alive?" Nurse Edna asked Esther.

"The rabbi told me she was dead—I just know I'm a Jew," Esther said. "My mother wanted me to know," she repeated softly.

"There are other kids here, Esther—you're going to make some friends," Nurse Angela told the abandoned child. "We'll find a Jewish family for you. Won't we, Wilbur?" Angela had asked the doctor.

7.

Fear Is Love

From their time on the train, the Winslows knew St. Cloud's was closer to Lewiston than it was to Portland. Dr. Larch told the Winslows that the first Jewish families had settled in Lewiston in the 1890s. At that time, most of them lived in the area of Lincoln and Chestnut Streets, where the first synagogue was established. By the turn of the century, some Jewish families had moved across the river to Auburn—near the Barker Mill and Second Street.

After Esther's arrival, Dr. Larch had met with a rabbi and two men from the Auburn Jewish community. The men were sympathetic to Esther's plight, but they were candid with the doctor. The rabbi would explain the abandoned child's circumstances to Jewish families in his congregation, but the two other men feared some families would question the lack of documentation concerning Esther's Jewishness. The rabbi who told Esther about her mother had no name. Was Esther's mother Jewish? the rabbi in Auburn had asked.

The word *documentation* was sufficient to set Larch off. "Here in St. Cloud's, many of our children lack documentation—yet we were expected to know the story of Esther's mother!" Dr. Larch cried.

"No tirades, Wilbur," Nurse Angela cautioned him. No Jewish families came forward following Dr. Larch's visit to the Lewiston-Auburn area. The Winslows were wondering why Larch hadn't begun by looking for Jewish families in Portland. The second-largest seaport in New

England, Portland was older and bigger than the twin cities of Lewiston and Auburn. Wouldn't Portland have an older, bigger Jewish population? the Winslows were thinking.

By the summer of 1917, when Dr. Larch was in France, the Jewish community of Auburn had moved into a new synagogue on Second Street. Nurse Angela met with the new rabbi there. Angela liked him and he empathized with Esther's situation, but the unadopted orphan was now almost a teenager, making her more unadoptable. There was no verifying the Jewishness of Esther's mother, notwithstanding that Esther's Jewishness was her foundation—being a Jew was the mainstay of her identity.

As she got older, the history of the Jews was of such interest to Esther—it was truly equal to her passion for novels. In reading to her about Judaism, Larch and his nurses had learned more about the Jewish people than they could imagine. Yet the new rabbi in the new synagogue in Auburn feared that some Jewish families in his congregation would think that Esther was old enough that she should have received some proper religious background and training.

This set Larch off on another tirade. "Here in St. Cloud's, what has proper religious background and training done for us?" the doctor cried.

"Wilbur, you weren't here—you were off in France," Nurse Angela said. (She made it sound as if the doctor had been on vacation.)

Six months later, in early 1918, as Nurse Edna explained to the Winslows, a fire destroyed the new synagogue on Second Street. Angela and the rabbi would stay in touch, but no families in the Lewiston-Auburn area were interested in adopting Esther.

As little as the Winslows knew about Jews, they were right about Portland. From the 1860s till the early 1900s, the Jews who immigrated to Portland came mostly from Eastern Europe. They spoke Yiddish. However, since the early twentieth century, Portland's Jewish population had changed. There were Conservative and Reform synagogues in Portland, not only Orthodox synagogues.

When Larch came back from France, Esther was old enough to behave herself in a synagogue. The girl was also old enough to be critical of an Orthodox synagogue, where men and women sat apart. By the time Larch had corresponded and met with a rabbi in Portland—in a Reform synagogue, where men and women sat together—Esther had read the Torah, through Deuteronomy. She'd already decided she didn't believe in God.

"Right you are, Esther!" Thomas Winslow cried.

"Tommy," Constance said. Then she asked Dr. Larch why Esther didn't believe in God.

"What has God done for Esther?" Larch asked. Esther counted all the references to God's strong hand or outstretched arm in the Exodus; yet she doubted that God did *enough* to help the Israelites. "God didn't do *enough* to help Esther, or her mother," Dr. Larch told the Winslows.

"Esther listens to *you*, Wilbur—she thinks what *you* think about God," Nurse Angela said.

"The apple doesn't fall far from the tree," was how Nurse Edna put it.

"Here in St. Cloud's, what has God ever done for us?" Dr. Larch asked his nurses.

"That's what we mean, Wilbur," Angela said.

"The Book of Esther came from the Hebrew Bible—it's one of what's called the Five Scrolls," Larch told the Winslows. "The Book of Esther and Song of Songs are the only books in the Hebrew Bible that do not mention God," Larch added. "King *Ahasuerus*, a Hebrew name, comes from the Old Persian name for Xerxes I. Esther must be fictional," Dr. Larch went on. "Persian kings didn't marry outside Persian noble families—there probably wasn't a Jewish queen. And Esther is a Jewish *orphan*—she doesn't reveal her Jewish heritage when she's crowned as queen. Esther tells King Ahasuerus she's Jewish only when she reveals that Haman is plotting to kill her people—including herself!" Dr. Larch exclaimed.

"What a good story!" Thomas Winslow cried.

"Yes, but it's just a story—Esther is the pick of Ahasuerus's harem, so she gets her way," Larch said.

"Wilbur," was all Nurse Angela could say. All Constance could think was that Dr. Larch was like her Tommy, the way Larch went on and on.

Dr. Larch described a Rembrandt painting, *Ahasuerus and Haman at the Feast of Esther.* The way the nurses rolled their eyes, it was clear they'd heard about the Rembrandt before. The Winslows were mystified when Larch started talking about Purim, the Jewish holiday celebrating the saving of the Jewish people from Haman—a day of feasting and rejoicing, a day of deliverance for the Jews. "There are cookies that look like Haman's ears," Larch told the Winslows.

"They're called hamantaschen, which means 'Haman's pockets' in Yiddish. In Hebrew, it translates as 'Haman's ears,' because of the cookies' shape," Nurse Edna explained. She could see the Winslows were lost, overwhelmed by their unfamiliarity with Jewishness.

"People wear Halloween-like masks and costumes—lots of drinking, there are also parades," Larch went on.

"There are donations to the poor, Wilbur—it's not just partying," Nurse Angela said.

"I found passages about Purim in *The Jewish Encyclopedia.* I read the passages aloud to the kids one night, when Esther was twelve or thirteen," Dr. Larch told the Winslows. "Your turn," the doctor said to his nurses.

As Nurse Edna and Nurse Angela explained, the descriptions of Purim made all the children happy for Esther—the parades, the costumes and masks, the young people having fun. But the Purim stories made Esther sob. "I'll never learn how to be a Jew—I have too much catching up to do!" Esther had cried. No one had seen her in tears before.

"We'll help Esther catch up—we'll put her in touch with other Jews. She'll find her people," Thomas said to Dr. Larch.

"You should know that Esther will want to go there one day," Larch told the Winslows.

"Go where?" Constance asked the doctor.

"The historical kingdoms of the Israelites and the Hebrews, the historical Israel and Judah—as if she could travel there!" Dr. Larch cried.

"Wilbur," was all Angela said.

"The Promised Land, the Holy Land," Edna explained to the Winslows.

"Wilbur, Esther just wants to go to Jerusalem," Angela said.

"Oh, what a relief—just Jerusalem!" Larch cried.

"Esther means she would like to go to Jerusalem when she's older—when she's an adult and she can make adult decisions," Edna explained to the Winslows.

"Adult decisions!" Dr. Larch exclaimed, holding his head in his hands.

"You should tell the Winslows about Esther's tattoo, Wilbur—speaking of adult decisions," Angela said.

"Esther has a tattoo?" Constance asked the doctor.

"That's putting the cart before the horse," Nurse Edna said.

Edna meant that Portland was the horse that came before the tattoo. Portland was the linchpin of where Esther came from. Because Dr. Larch didn't want to return to the city he'd left as a young man, he had put off making inquiries of the Jewish community in Portland. What came of Larch's first meeting with the Reform rabbi in Portland would change everything. Larch had emphasized that Esther was only three (almost four) when she was left at St. Cloud's; yet her pronunciation and enunciation were very grown-up. She didn't speak like a child. Esther had informed the doctor and his nurses that she didn't know any children.

"Whoever her mother was, she did much more than read to Esther—the child had virtually memorized Esther's story in the Bible," Larch told the rabbi. "It must have been her mother who taught Esther how to speak."

"It sometimes happens here, in Portland, that we see Jewish immigrants who've learned English as a second language before they get here," the rabbi told Dr. Larch. "When those new immigrants teach their children English, the children speak like adults," the rabbi said. His name was Leopold Herzfeld; he reasoned that Esther might have been born in Europe. Her mother would have confided in a rabbi—if she'd landed in Portland when she was pregnant or Esther was only an infant. Rabbi Herzfeld further reasoned that Esther's mother would likely have turned to Congregation Shaarey Tphiloh, if she'd confided to a rabbi around 1905 or a little later.

In 1904, Shaarey Tphiloh built a synagogue on Newbury Street, in the Old Port district. Most of its members were from Eastern and Central Europe—some newly arrived, some children of earlier immigrants. Two groups of Orthodox Jews had come together to create the synagogue. *Shaarey Tphiloh* means "Gates of Prayer," Larch told the Winslows.

"You pronounce it *Sha-a-RAY T'-FEE-la,* Wilbur," Nurse Angela corrected him.

"I don't care how you say it—the synagogue had the goddamn documentation!" Dr. Larch exclaimed.

"The synagogue knew the story of Esther's mother," Nurse Edna told the Winslows. "You've still got miles to go before you get to the tattoo," Edna added.

Rabbi Herzfeld was right to inquire about Esther at Shaarey Tphiloh. One of the synagogue's leaders found Esther's history in the congregation's records. Esther Nacht was born in Vienna in 1905. Her mother's maiden name was Meyer—from the Hebrew word *meir,* which means "enlightened." Hanna Meyer, who'd also been born in Vienna (in 1880), married Simon Nacht. He was born in Bremen, Germany. Simon died during the voyage to Portland—as did other passengers onboard the German ship from Bremerhaven. It was a bacterial pneumonia, like streptococcal pneumonia, but Hanna Nacht didn't know what it was—she just prayed her infant daughter wouldn't die of it. Her husband's name, *Simon,* meant "to hear" (or "to be heard") in Hebrew. All Hanna had heard, on the ocean passage to Portland, was her husband's cough.

The former Hanna Meyer lived up to the expectations of her maiden name. In explaining her circumstances and describing her fears for her daughter—with every word she spoke to the rabbi at Congregation Shaarey Tphiloh—Hanna was enlightening. As it sometimes happened with Jewish immigrants who were new to Portland, her story was so complicated that the rabbi asked one of the synagogue's leaders to transcribe the conversation between the rabbi and the new immigrant. The rabbi at Shaarey Tphiloh shared those records with Larch. The extensive recordkeeping in the case of Hanna Nacht's conversation with the rabbi at Shaarey Tphiloh was unusual in one way—due to the direness of Hanna's circumstances. She was afraid for herself and for her two-year-old daughter. Neither the rabbi nor the synagogue leader had ever seen Hanna Nacht before. Her prayers on the long voyage from Bremerhaven notwithstanding, Hanna was not an observant Jew; she'd made no friends among the members of Congregation Shaarey Tphiloh. Dr. Larch had just assumed that Esther was too young to attend Hebrew school.

"You don't know anything about Hebrew school, Wilbur," Nurse Angela interrupted the saga.

"At this rate, we'll all die before we get to the tattoo," Edna interjected.

In Vienna, both Simon and Hanna Nacht had been trained to teach English as a second language. Hanna told Simon she wanted to immigrate to the United States or Canada when their child was born. As always, she was enlightened—ahead of her time. She knew anti-Semitism was proceeding in a gradual, subtle way—even more so in Austria than in Germany, in Hanna's opinion. In Portland, two German-speaking Jews who were trained to teach English as a second language might have eked out a living for themselves and their new daughter. There was

61

a growing population of new immigrants; Hanna and Simon would have taken turns with the teaching and looking after Esther. But now Hanna was a widow and a single mother; what little money she made as a teacher was spent on childcare, and Hanna found only two teenagers to babysit Esther. Wilbur Larch was aware of the undesirables in the Old Port, on those streets that paralleled the waterfront. They lived in boardinghouses like the one Hanna moved into.

An older prostitute who had a room there told Hanna she could make more money as a prostitute than she did teaching English to immigrants. "Restless young men are everywhere," Hanna told the rabbi. Of course this was written down by the synagogue leader transcribing the conversation. Hanna must have been thinking of the young sailors who roamed around the Old Port. There were some young sailors in the pretty teacher's class, learning English as a second language. One of the young sailors told Hanna he'd jumped ship in Portland. He intended to see the world this way, he said—signing on as crew in one port, jumping ship in another. This wayward sailor was not a suitable young man for a pretty widow and a single mother to be talking to. Thus did Hanna express her fears to the rabbi and the synagogue leader at Shaarey Tphiloh. Yet Hanna said she was more afraid of "those Christian women" than she was of the young sailors. Hanna didn't mean only the women from the Woman's Christian Temperance Union; she said there were "other women like them." Hanna was more afraid of these women than she was of possibly becoming a prostitute. "If anything happens to me, please don't let those women steal Esther," Hanna said.

Hanna had sensed that anti-Semitism was insidious in Vienna. And in Portland, the temperance types were opposed to more than alcohol; they were opposed to immigrants, too. Those Christian women were watching Hanna because she was a pretty Jew. The women could see how the men looked at Hanna; they could see how much Hanna worried about Esther, too. "Your daughter would be safer if she wasn't

Jewish," a woman who purported to be from the Woman's Christian Temperance Union told Hanna.

"Is your daughter old enough to know she's Jewish?" one of those women asked Hanna. "Esther would be better off if she never knew she was a Jew."

"It seems anti-Semitism is insidious in Portland, too," Dr. Larch told the Winslows, but the Winslows already suspected this. That day at St. Cloud's, when Larch and his nurses and the Winslows were together, they all felt ashamed. Of course it crossed their minds that Esther might be better off if she never knew she was a Jew.

At Shaarey Tphiloh, Hanna told them she wanted Esther to know she was Jewish. Then Hanna gave the rabbi their travel documents— her passport and Esther's, which included their birth records. "If anything happens to me," Hanna began again, "Esther should have our passports—she should know who she is and where she came from."

What happened to Hanna would remain murky. Her body was found in the laundry room of the boardinghouse, where she'd been bludgeoned to death. No one said she'd succumbed to prostitution; if a client had killed her, it likely would have happened in one of the bedrooms. Hanna's students were interrogated by the police, including the wayward sailor who'd jumped ship in Portland. Her students were obviously innocent; the young sailor in question struck everyone as the most innocent of all. It was probable that two people had done it. Whoever did it had held Hanna over a sink, where her head was repeatedly pounded with a wrench—a tool that anyone could have taken from the laundry room's utility closet. There were no indications that Hanna had been abused sexually.

Hanna had the foresight to tell Esther's babysitters where to go, should she come to harm. As Rabbi Herzfeld later said to Dr. Larch, they'd done the best they could do—truly, all they could do—at Shaarey Tphiloh. Esther's memory of her meeting with the rabbi was remarkably intact; she'd been three (almost four) when the rabbi told her that her mother was dead. What Esther had forgotten was what she'd said when the rabbi told her that her mother wanted her to know she was Jewish. "I know!" Esther said. The synagogue leader wrote this down, too.

The babysitter who'd brought Esther to the synagogue had informed the rabbi of Hanna's murder. Naturally, the rabbi did not tell Esther how her mother died. Not in Esther's hearing, one of the synagogue's leaders tried to prepare the babysitter for everything that would happen next. A "delegation" (in the sense of a "deputation") of women from Congregation Shaarey Tphiloh would come get Esther at the boardinghouse. In no way did the rabbi or the synagogue leaders at Shaarey Tphiloh distrust this babysitter—she was just an anxious teenager who was understandably distraught at Esther's predicament.

The young babysitter wasn't Jewish, but she was very protective of Esther. The problem was how long it took to find and inform the women in the Jewish community. Though Esther was a Viennese Jew who spoke and understood English, and her mother had been Jewish, no women in the congregation knew her. Furthermore, whoever adopted Esther would eventually have to tell the child that her mother was murdered.

It took until the morning of the following day, when three women from the Jewish community agreed to take responsibility for Esther. The three women would share between them the essential care of Esther, until a Jewish family could be found to adopt the child. When the Jewish women went to the boardinghouse, they found Hanna's room in disarray; Esther's babysitters, two teenage girls, were sorting through the strewn clothes, Hanna's and Esther's. The babysitters were sobbing. Two women had taken Esther a day ago. The babysitters hadn't realized that the women who took Esther weren't from the synagogue—the women weren't Jewish.

"We thought they were you," one of the teenagers told the women from Shaarey Tphiloh.

"Esther doesn't cry—she just gets angry," the other girl said.

It was everyone's opinion that those two women who took Esther may not have been from the Woman's Christian Temperance Union. They might not have been temperance types at all; it's possible they weren't even Christians. But whoever those two women were, they were anti-Semites. Whoever they were, they did their best to prevent a Jewish child from being raised as a Jew in a Jewish family. Yet those two women must have talked to Esther; those two must have realized it was too late to dissuade Esther of her Jewishness. So they took her to St. Cloud's, where they left her. Those two just guessed that a Jewish family wouldn't venture there.

Rabbi Herzfeld arranged the doctor's meeting with the rabbi and synagogue leader at Shaarey Tphiloh—Larch's second trip back to Portland. Larch was grateful to the synagogue for showing him the written account of Hanna's transcribed story. What stood out for him was what Hanna told the rabbi about her daughter when Esther was only two—almost three. "She's going to be tall—she already has her father's long legs, and his long fingers. Esther already has his strong hands."

In his office at St. Cloud's, Larch told the Winslows what he'd said at the synagogue the year before. At thirteen (almost fourteen), Esther was taller than all the kids (and all the adults) at the orphanage; she also had the strongest hands. The cook at St. Cloud's was fond of canning fruits and vegetables. He was devoted to Mason jars with screw-on lids. When the cook couldn't unscrew one of them, he would send for Esther. "That girl's hands are so strong, she can unscrew anything!" Dr. Larch had declared to the rabbi and synagogue leader.

"I want to meet her—I want to give her the passports that belong to her," the rabbi at Shaarey Tphiloh told Larch.

The synagogue leader, an older man, was in tears. "We've been hoping someone like you would find her, Dr. Larch—we've been praying she would end up in safe hands," he said.

While the Winslows and Dr. Larch weren't among the faithful, they had respect for these men of faith, who'd not abandoned hope for Esther. Of course Larch agreed to bring Esther to the synagogue, notwithstanding that she didn't believe in God (and Larch knew Shaarey Tphiloh was an Orthodox synagogue). Larch had confided to Rabbi Herzfeld that Esther wasn't a believer, but he'd not told them at Shaarey Tphiloh. Maybe Esther's lack of belief was more acceptable to a rabbi in a Reform synagogue than it would be to a rabbi in an Orthodox synagogue or a Conservative one—or so Larch ventured to ask Rabbi Herzfeld.

"Given Esther's experience, it's not for me to judge what she believes," Rabbi Herzfeld told Dr. Larch. "Esther deserves to know who she is and where she came from, and how much her mother was afraid for her. Fear is love," the rabbi said.

8.

A Bra for Esther

The window Angela had opened in Dr. Larch's office was still ajar. The Winslows could hear the hullabaloo all the way from the girls' division, where the girls were weeping and wailing. "Esther has been packed and ready to go for hours—she wouldn't wait till she met you," Edna explained to the Winslows.

"Esther read your letters—she decided she liked you," Larch told them. "If you decide you don't want her, she'll try to go with you anyway," the doctor forewarned the Winslows.

"She is taking forever to say goodbye to the girls—it's her long goodbye that makes them cry!" Edna exclaimed.

"Esther will keep it short with the boys, but they'll cry harder," Nurse Angela predicted.

"All of them should be happy for Esther—Esther has found a family!" Larch shouted.

"They're happy for Esther, Wilbur—they're just sad for themselves; they're going to miss her," Angela said.

"We're all going to miss her," Dr. Larch told the Winslows.

"You should tell them about the tattoo before Esther gets here," Edna reminded the doctor.

The Winslows watched Nurse Angela close the window. Either the girls stopped crying or their lamentations no longer penetrated Dr. Larch's office. The tattoo story turned out to be interwoven with

Larch's third trip back to Portland—the one he took with Esther. He'd had time to prepare her for the meeting with the rabbi at Shaarey Tphiloh. Esther understood that one of the synagogue's leaders would be there; she knew why they wanted to meet her, not only to give her the passports.

Before they boarded the train to Portland, Dr. Larch told the fourteen-year-old that she'd been born in Vienna, and what had happened to her mother. Esther's reaction to her mother's murder was very composed, Larch said to the Winslows. "Those two women should be found and killed, but that won't happen," was all Esther said about it.

More surprising to Larch was Esther's reaction to Portland; she remembered more of the Old Port than he expected. They'd arrived the night before their appointment at the synagogue, and they stayed in a hotel near the waterfront. They had dinner in a fish place, where they overheard a conversation. A tattoo shop was going under, or it was sunk from the start. It had never worked. "Sailors get tattooed, don't they? Why would a tattoo shop sink to the bottom in Portland?" Esther asked Dr. Larch.

"I haven't the slightest idea—a tattoo is indelible, you know," Larch told her. "The pigment is inserted into punctures in the skin—it's permanent, Esther."

"I know. I want one. I want to talk to a tattooer about it," Esther said. This was when the story of the sinking tattoo shop was interrupted by the boys—their piteous cries were coming from the floor above Larch's office, where they were supposed to be in their beds. No boy could have slept through the sounds of such unrelenting sorrow. The boys' plaintive howls reflected their unending misery.

"Good grief!" Larch exclaimed, getting up from his desk. He stomped off to the staircase in the hall, shouting upstairs to the boys. They were beside themselves with anguish over Esther's departure. "She has found a *family*—be *happy* for Esther, you whiners!" he shouted to them. "And don't take all their clothes, Esther!" Larch called to her

A BRA FOR ESTHER

When Dr. Larch came back to his office, Nurse Angela was perturbed. "The boys aren't *whiners*, Wilbur—they just love her, like the rest of us," Angela told him.

"Esther has already taken some of the boys' clothes. She's taller than they are—most of their clothes are too small for her," Edna explained to the Winslows.

"Esther doesn't need another flannel shirt—the boys must be out of flannel shirts, and they don't have anything else that fits her," Nurse Angela told the Winslows.

"Esther doesn't like to wear women's clothes?" Constance asked the nurses.

"She likes men's clothes better," Edna answered.

"Esther won't wear a bra at all—she just plain refuses," Angela said to the Winslows.

"Esther is small-breasted, and she's only fourteen—I think she can get away with not wearing a bra," Dr. Larch told them all. As for the three women in the doctor's office, Constance included, their united expressions stood in contradiction to Larch's opinion.

All Constance said was: "We'll do our best to find a bra for Esther—one she likes."

"I wish you luck with that," Larch told Thomas, who just smiled. Given all the women in the Winslows' extended family, Thomas had learned to mind his own business when it came to bras.

The sounds of distress from the boys upstairs were somewhat subdued when Edna urged Dr. Larch to hurry up and finish the tattoo story.

It was after dark, but not late at night, when Larch took Esther to Anchor Al's on Commercial Street. Al was a maritime tattooer—from New York, another seaport. When they arrived, he was packing up his tattoo flash: anchors and mermaids, tall ships at sea, true-love tattoos—bleeding hearts pierced with daggers. For Esther's sake, Larch was hoping against a mermaid; he still didn't know exactly what Esther wanted.

69

Al knew Esther was the one who wanted a tattoo, notwithstanding that she most likely wasn't old enough to get one.

"If I had to guess, young lady," the tattooist began, "you're not lookin' for a bleedin' heart, or a tattoo of a seafarin' kind."

"She's not old enough to get a tattoo, but she has imagined one in her future," Larch told the tattooer.

"It's just words, no pictures—no sharks or sea serpents," Esther began. She sounded apologetic.

"Words mean as much as pictures, young lady," the old maritime man assured her. "I'm goin' back to the Bowery, but tell me what words you're thinkin' of, and where you imagine puttin' 'em."

Dr. Larch knew Esther well enough to know that he should have been watching her, but he wasn't. The bare breasts of the mermaids might have distracted him; as Larch later told the Winslows, the mermaids' breasts were "harbingers" of Esther's tattoo. When Larch belatedly turned his attention to Esther, she'd already unzipped her parka and unbuttoned her flannel shirt; she was untucking her T-shirt. Before Larch could stop her, Esther had hiked her T-shirt up to her chin—exposing her long torso, from her collarbones to below her navel. Anchor Al maintained a respectful dignity.

"No bra, Connie," Thomas reminded her.

"I know, Tommy," Constance said crossly.

"I want the words here—if they'll fit, if the letters won't be too small to read," Esther explained to the old New Yorker.

"Not that you'll be showing this tattoo to everyone, I hope," Dr. Larch cautioned her.

"You know the words I want—you know everything I've read and what I like," she said to Larch. "I don't care if no one but me ever sees it, and I'll have to read it backward in a mirror—where the letters will be reversed." Larch knew then what the tall girl's tattoo would be, provided Esther's torso could accommodate the lengthy passage. Larch had heard her read *Jane Eyre* to the girls—later, to the boys. When she was reading aloud, Esther always read a certain passage twice. Larch knew Esther believed the passage merited repeating, especially to the boys.

"'I care for myself,'" Esther started reciting. If not her words, her pretty breasts held the Bowery man's attention. Esther's breasts were noticeably smaller than those on the surrounding mermaids.

"'I care for myself,'" Thomas Winslow repeated in reverence; as if on command, he stood at attention in Dr. Larch's office. Constance knew how many times he'd taught *Jane Eyre* to the uncaring boys at Penna-cook Academy. He'd hammered some sensitivity into those insensitive boys. Thomas had made them memorize the passage near the end of Chapter Twenty-seven. Even the dullest of those boys would remember this about Charlotte Brontë; the passage was the epitome of Jane's indomitable spirit.

"'The more solitary, the more friendless, the more unsustained I am,'" Esther went on reciting to the old tattooer, "'the more I will respect myself.'"

Larch was looking at the tattoo flash. Sharks and sea serpents beat staring at Esther, who went on showing herself to the maritime man. "What are you lookin' for?" Anchor Al asked Dr. Larch.

"If you have a scrap of paper around, I could write out the passage—so you can see it as a whole," Larch told him.

"Sure thing, I got paper—I'm always drawin' when I'm not tat-tooin'," the old New Yorker said. When Larch began writing, Esther finally lowered her T-shirt. She watched what he wrote to make sure he got every word right.

"I know this passage almost as well as you do," Larch told her.

"There are twenty-one words and five punctuation marks—three commas and two periods," Esther informed the old tattooer. She'd not yet buttoned up her flannel shirt. Larch thought she wanted to be ready to show herself again.

"With tattooin', you count the spaces, too—when you're letterin', you count the spaces and the letters, young lady," Anchor Al told her.

As Larch wrote out the passage, Esther counted the spaces and the letters; she would learn there were about the same number of spaces as there were words.

The old maritime man was sorting through his tattoo flash; he found some lettering fonts to show Esther. She didn't like the Luminari, a boldface font—a composite of medieval styles. "Maybe it's too dark and serious for you," Al told her.

"It's too religious-looking for me—it looks like sacred scripture, or something," Esther said. She also didn't like the Harrington font—from London, late nineteenth century. "It's too feminine for me," was all Esther said about the Harrington. (Larch thought the Harrington was too flowery for her, but he kept this to himself.)

Esther liked the Goudy Old Style. "Just plain Goudy," the maritime man called it. It was an American font, a new one. "You don't think it's too plain, do you?" Anchor Al asked her.

"I think too plain works for me—I'm too plain, and I always will be," Esther answered. She liked the Didot font, too—a French typeface, from the eighteenth century. "It's too thin, but so am I—too thin works for me," Esther told the old tattooer. He showed her where the line breaks should be. Her tattoo had a vertical shape; it ran the length of her torso. The line breaks had their own weird symmetries. "Would you tattoo my breasts, or would you work around them?" Esther asked the Bowery man. (*Don't tattoo her breasts—work around them!* Larch was thinking, but he didn't say it.)

"When the time comes, that's up to you, young lady. I'd prefer to work around your breasts, not tattoo 'em," the maritime man said, sounding like he was bound for Davy Jones's locker, the grave for drowned sailors.

There were eighteen characters in the first sentence, counting the spaces. The first line was closest to Esther's collarbones—*I care for myself.* The second line, still above her breasts, also had eighteen characters—*The more solitary,* ending with a comma. The next two lines—*the more friendless, the more unsustained*—would wrap around her rib cage. These two were the longest lines; they each had twenty characters. The shortest line—the *I am,* only five characters—was just above Esther's navel. The last two lines were below her belly button—both *the more I will* and the *respect myself.* Each line had fifteen characters. It was a lot to say on one torso, even a long one, but Esther was assured the tattoo would fit, and she liked leaving her breasts untattooed—as did Dr. Larch.

"An eight-letter word would be two inches long," the tattooist told Esther. In the font size he recommended, each letter was between half an inch and an inch tall. "It's not too big, young lady, but it's big enough to read—even the wrong way, in a mirror," Anchor Al told her.

Larch wanted the Winslows to know Esther was determined to get the *Jane Eyre* tattoo. Esther was determined to go to Jerusalem, too. And after she met the rabbi at Shaarey Tphiloh—after she saw her passport and her mother's—Esther was determined to go to Vienna. After all, it was where she came from—she was born there. "And she wants to learn German, the language her mother and father spoke—their first language," Dr. Larch went on to the Winslows.

"Of course she does—what a good girl she is!" Constance cried.

"Right you are, Connie," Thomas said.

Then they were distracted by the incantations above Dr. Larch's office. The boys were repeating by rote what they knew they should say, but their hearts weren't in it. "Let us be happy for Esther Nacht—Esther has found a family," the boys intoned, sounding more like a dirge than a celebration.

"Good night, Esther!" one boy wailed.

"Good night, Esther!" the boys cried in chorus.

"Mercy me!" Edna declared.

"Don't tell them to be happy, Wilbur," Angela said to Dr. Larch.

There was a thudding sound, like something heavy being dragged downstairs one step at a time. "That sounds like Esther's rucksack—it weighs a ton," Edna explained to the Winslows.

"It sounds like she's stuffed one of the boys in her rucksack. I wonder which one!" Larch exclaimed.

"You know what she's stuffed in her rucksack, Wilbur. The poor girl is taking too many books—there's no room for her clothes," Angela said.

"She doesn't care about her clothes," Larch wearily said; from the doctor's casual attire, the Winslows could see he felt similarly.

"We live in a school town with a good bookstore. We can provide Esther with any book she wants—and Connie is a librarian," Thomas Winslow reminded Dr. Larch.

"Esther wants her own copies of the books she's marked—the passages she rereads to herself. I'm surprised there's only one tattoo she wants," Larch whispered. They could hear how close Esther was; her heavy breathing reached them from the hall.

"What a good girl she is," Constance repeated, very quietly.

"Right you are, Connie," Thomas whispered.

They now heard Esther huffing as she hoisted the books, wrestling her way into the shoulder straps of the rucksack. Yet the Winslows were unprepared for the tall, broad-shouldered girl in the doorway of Dr. Larch's office. In spite of the disarming frankness of the doctor and his nurses, and their admirable attention to detail, the Winslows had underestimated Esther Nacht. The child's yellowing passport (and her mother's) had been issued by the Austro-Hungarian Empire, but the old coat of arms had faded; even the script of Franz Joseph's name looked old and tired. In Larch's office, there were five of them waiting for Esther. They all looked old and tired and small, compared to the resolute young woman towering in the doorway.

Esther Nacht was fourteen going on twenty-four. In the direct way she spoke to the Winslows, looking straight at them, there was no doubting her sincerity. "I'm sorry I've kept you waiting, but I'm still learning how to say goodbye. Maybe there's no good way to do it," Esther told them. The Winslows would have reason to remember this, but Esther had already moved on. She was looking straight at Dr. Larch when she spoke to him—no less directly.

"You know I would give my right arm for you—you know this, don't you?" Esther asked Dr. Larch.

"And you know you should try to *hold on* to your arms—*both* arms, Esther!" Larch told her.

"Wilbur," was all Nurse Angela could say; then she started crying.

"I'll check on our bed-wetter—we have a poor boy who wets his bed when Esther gets him overexcited," Nurse Edna told the Winslows. Edna turned away from Esther before speaking to her. "If I give you a hug, Esther, I'll never let you go. You know this, don't you?" Edna said.

"I know," Esther said, as Edna left the office. Esther was looking straight at the Winslows again. "The next train is usually on time. We should get going," Esther told them. Angela lay facedown on the examination table, sobbing. Dr. Larch had turned away from all of them; that way, they couldn't see him crying.

"You Winslows are getting the best one," Larch said.

"We thank you for her," Thomas told him.

"You know where I am, Esther—if you're in trouble," Larch said.

"You know me—I'll get myself in and out of trouble," Esther told him. All the while, her eyes remained steadfastly on the Winslows.

"We're ready when you are, Esther," Constance said to her.

Thomas withheld his *Right you are* refrain. Those Winslows had never felt less ready for anything.

Dr. Larch still wouldn't look at anyone. "Esther, if you run into the stationmaster, just be thankful it's the last time you'll see him—just try not to kill him," Larch told her.

"You know me—I keep trying," Esther said to him. She was already leaving with the Winslows. As Larch and his nurses knew about Esther, there would be no looking back.

Outside, in the darkness, the hoarfrost was slippery on the rutted dirt road. The Winslows were in no danger of falling—not with Esther between them, not the way the tall girl had hold of their upper arms. The strength of her grip would bruise them, but the Winslows felt safe in Esther's hands. It was keeping Esther safe that worried the Winslows. They were educated, they were privileged, they had good intentions, but once again the Winslows were aware of what they didn't know. The Winslows weren't Jewish. How could they help a young Jew find herself?

Esther must have known the Winslows were worrying; maybe she could feel them trembling in her strong hands. "Don't be afraid," Esther told the Winslows, giving their arms a painful squeeze. "I know what my job is. I'm giving Honor all I've got—that girl is going to get everything I can give," Esther assured them.

"We don't doubt you, dear girl—we're just afraid we can't give you enough," Constance told her.

"Right you are, Connie!" Thomas declared. "What we're afraid of, Esther, is that we don't know enough to help you with the Jewishness," Thomas said to her.

"That's not your job," Esther told the Winslows; she squeezed their arms affectionately, but more painfully. "You're giving me an education, you're making me smarter—my learning how to be a Jew is my job," Esther assured them.

Then she saw the stationmaster standing on the platform. He sternly watched her and the Winslows; he wasn't looking up the track in the direction the train would be coming from.

"Oh, great—it's this guy," Esther quietly said. "He hates me," she told the Winslows.

"It's the Judgment Day man, Connie," Thomas whispered.

"I *know*, Tommy," Constance said, more loudly than she meant to.

"He likes mail-order catalogs—undergarment catalogs, the ones advertising bras and girdles. He especially likes the women wearing nursing bras," Esther whispered to the Winslows.

"Nursing bras!" Thomas tried to say quietly, but they were all on the station platform now. The stationmaster had heard him.

"You're taking *her*—you're taking the *Jewish* one?" the disapproving stationmaster asked the Winslows. Everyone could hear the train coming, but no one looked up the track.

"We're taking the *best* one—she's the *best*," Constance told the stationmaster.

"The Jewish one is the best one," Thomas said to him.

"'I care for myself,'" Esther recited to herself, as if Jane Eyre's words were already tattooed on her torso.

Then Esther and the Winslows got on the train—not looking back at the unmoving stationmaster, who was standing like a sentinel on the platform. The stationmaster might have been imagining those women in nursing bras. Yet in his uniform, with its glinting hardware, he appeared to be eternally disapproving.

Once onboard, Esther found four seats together—one for her rucksack. They were the only passengers who got on in St. Cloud's; they sat on the opposite side of the train from the station platform. They couldn't see the stationmaster, but everyone in their passenger car could hear him. "She's *Jewish*—they took the *Jewish* one!" the disapproving stationmaster shouted as the train pulled away from the platform.

Only the Winslows looked at Esther. Their fellow passengers focused their scrutiny on the Winslows. Anyone could see the orphan was a young woman, merely a girl. As everyone knows, orphans don't get to choose who they are or where they come from. But who would choose to adopt a Jew? That was the way the Winslows' fellow passengers looked them over.

The stationmaster's shouting was farther away, but it was not out of hearing. Esther and the Winslows heard him clearly. "She's a *Jew*—they took the *Jew*!"

"Don't be afraid—this is just how it is," Esther said softly to the Winslows, as if they were children. "The hatred isn't usually this overt, but the covert kind of hatred is still hatred, isn't it?" Esther asked them. The Winslows nodded their assent. They realized Esther was an adult; the Winslows knew they would learn a lot from her.

The tall girl must have been tired—given all the books she packed, and all the goodbyes. Esther slept so soundly that she didn't wake up at the stops along the way. She somehow managed to sleep in two seats with her long arms hugging her rucksack. Once, in her sleep, the Winslows heard Esther reciting (like a prayer) the passage she loved in *Jane Eyre*. "'The more solitary, the more friendless, the more unsustained I am,'" Esther murmured, "'the more I will respect myself.'"

"The tattoo she wants won't work with a bra, Tommy," was all Constance said.

"Right you are, Connie," Thomas told her.

Thus, before they brought their tallest orphan home, those Winslows knew there wouldn't be a bra for Esther.

9.

A Preexisting Idea

Fifteen years later, the Winslows were still learning from Esther Nacht. The Winslows would continue to feel safe, if a little bruised, in Esther's hands. Honor was fourteen, almost fifteen now—the same age Esther was when the Jewish one had joined the Winslow family.

Prudence, who'd been only eleven when she first met Esther, was twenty-six now. She was finishing her master's in organic chemistry and applying to medical school. A young man had proposed to her. She was too busy to get married, Prudence told him—this was after she'd asked Esther how she should reject him.

"For starters, just say you're too busy—but if he keeps proposing, you'll have to hurt his feelings more," Esther advised Prudence.

Hope had been thirteen when Esther moved in with the Winslows; she was a year and a half younger than Esther. Faith was only a few months older than Esther; through high school, they would be in the same grade together. Now Hope was twenty-eight and Faith was thirty; they were married and starting families of their own. Faith had a three-year-old and a one-year-old, and Hope was expecting.

"If Esther were staying around, I would have a bunch more kids," Faith told everyone.

"Me, too!" Hope said. Esther had found the time to look after Faith's little ones—to give Faith and her husband an occasional night off. Esther volunteered to be on hand when Hope had her newborn.

If Esther had stayed around looking after Honor, Prudence joked that she could have married the guy who proposed to her and also gone to med school. This was Prudence's way of saying she shared her older sisters' esteem for Esther. Even the townspeople of Pennacook knew enough to know that Prudence would never have married that guy. He was beneath the Winslows' standards in terms of higher education.

In 1934, James Winslow wasn't even born. He wouldn't be a student abroad for almost thirty years. Sooner than that, Thomas and Constance Winslow would realize that their grandchild Jimmy was already a preexisting idea. But in 1934, when Esther first told the Winslows she was going to Vienna, Honor Winslow and Esther just seemed unusually dedicated to each other. After all, Esther had moved on (and come back) before. "Esther and I have made a pact—she'll be back when the time is right," Honor told her mother, with Esther's capacity for self-determination.

"My goodness—a *pact*," was all Constance could say. At fifteen, her fourth daughter was as articulate and confident as Esther had been at that age. Constance couldn't help wondering what those kindred spirits were cooking up. The bond between Honor and Esther seemed inseparable

Whenever the Winslows were feeling anxious about Esther's consuming interest in the exile of the Jews from the Land of Israel—Esther was obsessed with the Jewish Diaspora—they would seek reassurance from Daniel and Naomi Rosenthal. The Rosenthals weren't so young anymore, and although they'd decided not to have children, for the past fifteen years, they had served as a surrogate Jewish family for Esther. For those Jewish boys who were students at the academy, Daniel and Naomi Rosenthal had provided a home away from home. Most of the Jewish students at Pennacook came from New York, and there were some from Boston.

The nearest synagogue to Pennacook was in Portsmouth; Temple of Israel had set up shop in the former Methodist Church on State Street. A Conservative Jewish congregation, Temple of Israel wasn't relaxed enough for those nonobservant Jewish boys from Boston and New York. Maybe no synagogue could be nonobservant enough for Esther Nacht—or for the Rosenthals.

In the Puddle Dock area near the waterfront, there were a couple of kosher butcher shops, a Jewish bakery, and some Jewish grocery stores. The food was of more interest to Esther than the synagogue; the food was also of more interest to the Pennacook Academy Jews, including the Rosenthals.

Esther wanted to learn Hebrew—to really learn it, to actually speak it. The Rosenthals knew the Hebrew school at Temple of Israel wouldn't work for Esther. "It's just a joke for Esther to go to Hebrew school— it's like a Jewish Sunday school," Naomi Rosenthal explained to the Winslows.

"The way Esther will learn to speak Hebrew is in Jerusalem," Daniel Rosenthal told Thomas and Constance. This was when the Winslows knew Esther really would be going to the Land of Israel—first to Vienna, then to Jerusalem. True to her word, Esther kept her Jewish business to herself.

As for learning German, Esther didn't need to wait until she got to Vienna. French was not the only foreign language taught in the Pennacook public high school. The Pennacook Academy boys could choose to study French, Spanish, or German. Isaac Drucker, the senior member of the Pennacook German Department, was a Viennese Jew. Like Esther's parents, Isaac had emigrated from Austria with his wife, Bluma, before World War I. Both Bluma and Isaac had been teachers in Vienna, but there were no women on the Pennacook faculty.

The Druckers were an endearing couple on the academy campus, beloved by the students and faculty alike. The Jewish boys loved to hear Bluma bemoan her fate: "a female tutor marooned on an island of pubescent boys!" Bluma said (in English, German, and Yiddish). Isaac laughed along with the boys.

As a couple, the Rosenthals would agree that Naomi was the dramatic one. Naomi told Bluma about Esther—a Viennese-born Jew who grew up in an orphanage in Maine, her mother murdered by anti-Semites in Portland! (This was what Esther told everyone she met about herself; her story didn't need Naomi's dramatizing.) The Rosenthals knew that Esther's story would resonate with the Druckers. It was a sore point with Bluma that the Druckers' only child had given them no grandchildren. She would be the one to teach Esther German.

"At last, I have a student—one without a penis!" Bluma rejoiced just in English; only Isaac and Naomi were there to hear her. Isaac saw fit to explain to Naomi that the word for *penis* was the same in German. Naomi already knew this, but she pretended to be surprised. Bluma refrained from reciting a bunch of Yiddish vulgarisms for penis. (Probably Naomi knew them all.)

One warm day, when the Rosenthals went with Esther and the academy's Jewish boys to Temple of Israel in Portsmouth, the Rosenthals allowed the teenagers to take a walk—provided they stayed together and returned to the synagogue at a designated time.

They were walking on Marcy Street, near the river. The Jewish boys were teaching Esther the etymology for *penis,* just the words with Yiddish roots. Of course Esther knew the *schlong* word—from the Yiddish word *shlang,* meaning a hose or a snake or a penis.

"Ew!" Esther said. In the distance, she saw a navy guy; he was headed their way. The Portsmouth Naval Shipyard (called the Portsmouth Navy Yard) was on Seavey's Island, in the middle of the Piscataqua River—between Portsmouth and Kittery, on the southern boundary of Maine. Both Kittery and Seavey's Island belonged to Maine—hence the Portsmouth Navy Yard was considered part of Kittery. The weird geography made no sense to the Jewish boys from New York and Boston.

"It should be called the Kittery Navy Yard," one of the Jewish boys had reasoned.

"Or Seavey's Island should be part of New Hampshire," another boy from New York or Boston asserted.

"Tell me more Yiddish words for *penis*," Esther urged them. She didn't care about the boring boundary dispute.

"There's a shvantz and a schmeckel," one of the boys said, as the sailor was getting closer.

"A shtickl is a small one," a boy explained to Esther.

"A petzl is a dirty one," another boy told her.

"Yuck!" Esther said. "Don't tell me there's no Yiddish word for female genitalia—don't lie to me," Esther was saying, when the sailor was close enough for them to see his short-sleeved shirt and his tattooed arms.

"You have a shmoonda or a shmoochky!" one of the Jewish boys cried.

"Nobody's getting in my shmoonda or my shmoochky until I say so," Esther told the Jewish boys. With all the boys laughing around her, she felt safe to speak to the navy guy. "Excuse me—did you get your tattoos around here?" Esther asked him.

"I got tattooed in New York—I don't know any tattoo shops in Kittery or Portsmouth," the sailor answered. On one forearm was the U.S. Navy eagle, clutching an anchor in its talons. On his other forearm, a bleeding heart was pierced with a dagger; the name *Alice* was dripping blood.

"Are you still seeing Alice?" Esther asked him.

"Every now and then," the sailor said with a shrug. Right now, the Jewish boys could see, the sailor had eyes only for Esther.

"Nobody's getting in my shmoonda or my shmoochky until I say so," Esther told the navy guy—just to see if she could say it right.

The U.S. Navy's oldest shipyard, the Portsmouth Navy Yard had been around since 1800. They started building submarines in 1917; they would be building them for years.

"Are you on a submarine?" one of the Jewish boys asked the sailor—just to change the subject from Esther's shmoonda (or her shmoochky).

"Not right now," the navy guy answered him, walking on.

"I'm in no hurry for my tattoo—I can wait," Esther told the Jewish boys, as they were walking back to the synagogue. She meant that her Jewishness came first—her learning German and Hebrew, her going to Vienna and Jerusalem. Esther's Jewish identity took precedence over her *Jane Eyre* tattoo.

The Winslows were relieved to hear that Esther was willing to wait for her tattoo, their reverence for *Jane Eyre* notwithstanding. "Right you are, Esther—Jane would be the first to understand!" Thomas Winslow told her. The ladies of the town had put a bug in Constance Winslow's ear about Jews and tattoos. It was just like those ladies to hide their thoughts in what sounded like an innocent question.

"Is it true that Jews can't be buried in a Jewish cemetery if they're tattooed?" one of the ladies of the town asked Constance. Of course Constance didn't know, and she was afraid to ask Esther. Having been denied a Jewish childhood, Esther will want a Jewish burial, Constance was thinking. Esther didn't get to begin her life with other Jews; surely she'll want to end her life with her people, Thomas thought.

As the Rosenthals knew, the Winslows were always worrying about Esther; the Rosenthals were always reassuring them. "There is no prohibition—Esther can be buried in a Jewish cemetery even if she is tattooed with the entire text of *Jane Eyre*," Daniel Rosenthal said to the Winslows.

"There's a taboo about tattoos in Orthodox communities, but even they don't have a problem with burying someone who's tattooed—the burial thing is a myth," Naomi told the Winslows. As the Winslows would learn, there were many myths about the Jews. The townspeople of Pennacook had heard the myths; they remembered the strange-sounding ones.

By World War II, the Jewish community in Portsmouth had grown. The name of the congregation would one day be shortened to Temple Israel. Long before then, Esther had stopped going to any synagogue—as had the Rosenthals, who were as nonobservant as Esther. A younger faculty couple now accompanied the academy's Jewish students to the Portsmouth synagogue.

The public library in Pennacook (because of Constance Winslow) and the Pennacook Academy library (because of the Rosenthals and the Druckers) had books on the Jewish Diaspora and the emergence of modern Zionism in Central and Eastern Europe in the late nineteenth century. It was because of the Druckers and the Rosenthals that Esther had heard of a homeland for the Jewish people in Palestine—formed in reaction to the rising anti-Semitism in Europe and the anti-Jewish pogroms in the Russian Empire. It would be because of Bluma and Isaac Drucker that Esther was quoting Theodor Herzl's *Der Judenstaat* (*The Jewish State*), in German and in English, at a preternaturally young age.

At a time when many Jews were getting out of Europe, the Winslows were frightened that Esther was going there. "Esther has a history of going against the grain, Thomas," Daniel Rosenthal reminded him.

"Remember Wellesley, Tommy," Constance said.

"Right you are, Connie," Thomas told her. Wellesley College was Constance's alma mater; Faith, Hope, and Prudence would be Wellesley girls, like their mother.

Thomas Winslow was a Boston University boy—BU had been his backup when he didn't get into Harvard, and he had loved it. The Winslows' earlier au pair girls—their first three orphans, as the townspeople of Pennacook called them—were BU girls, both as undergrads and in graduate programs. But Esther was such an exceptional student, Constance encouraged her to try Wellesley. Constance couldn't be faulted for dramatizing when she wrote her alma mater, recommending Esther Nacht. Constance quoted Naomi, who'd merely repeated (in an exclamatory way) what Esther nonchalantly told everyone she met about herself. (The part about her being "a Viennese-born Jew who grew up in an orphanage in Maine, her mother murdered by anti-Semites in Portland!")

Not only did Esther get into Wellesley; she captured the attention of the Wellesley Students' Aid Society.

"Deservedly so, Connie—way to go, Esther!" Thomas told them.

Furthermore, there were Jewish girls at Wellesley—not only from Boston and New York. For occasional long weekends, or the shorter of the college's vacations, Esther brought some of her new Jewish friends to Pennacook to meet the Winslows. Thomas and Constance adored these smart girls, not least for how they gave Honor their utmost attention. For years after Esther's one year at Wellesley, the Winslows would remember the names of these Jewish girls. Esther had seemed so happy at Wellesley.

Faith Winslow was a first-year student at Wellesley College when Esther started there. "No one ever had so much fun her freshman year," Faith would later say of Esther. Esther had already decided what her major would be—zoology and physiology. Esther was also dedicated to improving her German. And a course of study called Biblical History, Literature and Interpretation attracted her.

"I don't know if I like the sound of that one, Connie," Thomas Winslow said.

"You don't know everything, Tommy," Constance told him.

For what would be her second year of college, Esther transferred to Boston University. She cited Wellesley College's motto as inspiring her: Non Ministrari sed Ministrare—Not to Be Ministered unto, but to Minister.

"I'm having too much fun—I'm not going to school to have a good time," was the way Esther put it. She'd decided she was going to be a nurse.

After this utilitarian-sounding (and disappointing) news, the Winslows were over their heads as they tried to follow the complicated path of Esther's extensive training to become a nurse. She ultimately earned a BS from Boston University and got further training in the nursing school at the New England Hospital for Women and Children.

What the Winslows would understand of all this was that Esther had a bachelor's degree in nursing—"a BSN, or the equivalent thereof," was the way Esther put it. What the Winslows would struggle to comprehend was what Esther had done all this for. It seemed Esther needed a BSN from an accredited program—or the equivalent thereof—to qualify for the U.S. Army Nurse Corps.

"She's going into the *army,* Tommy!" Constance exclaimed.

"Attagirl, Esther!" Thomas Winslow cried.

Pity the Druckers; they had to explain the Jewish Diaspora to the Winslows—the dispersion of Israelites or Jews out of their ancestral homeland (the Land of Israel) and their resettlement in other parts of the world. Pity the Winslows; the exile of the Jews wasn't foremost in Thomas and Constance Winslow's consciousness. Isaac Drucker skipped over several centuries, choosing to begin with the increasing migration and resettlement in the Middle Ages, dividing the Jews into two geographical groups—the Ashkenazi Jews of Northern and Eastern Europe, and the Sephardic Jews of Spain, Portugal, North Africa, and the Middle East.

"Both the Ashkenazim and the Sephardim suffered many of the same expulsions and persecutions and massacres," Bluma Drucker wanted the Winslows to know. "And Isaac left out the pre-Roman Diaspora. The Jews were always being defeated or overthrown—then we were sold into slavery," Bluma continued with the Winslows, while Isaac skipped over the First Jewish-Roman war, ending in the siege of Jerusalem and the burning of the Temple. Isaac ignored all the Byzantine, Islamic, and Crusader business. Notwithstanding the atrocities Isaac left out, the Winslows were getting the picture. Bluma understood why her husband hurried over the history. The Winslows were worried about Esther. Isaac Drucker was a purposeful teacher. Isaac was leading the Winslows to the Zionist "negation of the Diaspora," because Isaac knew and understood why Esther was seriously intent on going there.

Esther was of an age and disposition to make up for lost time. She wanted to be the best Jew she could be—to Esther's thinking, this meant the most committed to being Jewish. The differing waves of

Zionism meant that Zionism was ever-changing—or so the Druckers wanted the Winslows to know. "Bluma and I are old, Tommy," Isaac told Thomas Winslow. "Esther is young, and she's naturally rebellious. Of course Esther would dedicate herself to a fundamental premise of Zionism—what Bluma might say is the most radical and didactic presumption of Zionism," Isaac added. (Indeed, Bluma said this.)

It alarmed the Winslows that Esther wanted to be part of the Jewish immigration to Palestine. Esther believed the Jews would never be free from discrimination and persecution in exile—not in Europe, not in the United States. "Look what happened to Esther in Maine! Did Esther's mother find tolerance and assimilation in Portland?" Isaac asked the Winslows.

"Esther doesn't want to be persecuted *or* assimilated, Connie," was the way Bluma put it to Constance.

It further alarmed the Winslows that Daniel and Naomi Rosenthal were much more wary of Zionism than the Druckers. The ancestry of most American Jews went back to the Ashkenazi Jews, the ones who began immigrating to the U.S. in the nineteenth century. As Daniel and Naomi told the Winslows, American Jews were the most assimilated; there were lots of mixed marriages between Jews and non-Jews.

"Many American Jews don't see themselves as *in exile,* Tommy— Naomi and I don't see ourselves as part of the Jewish Diaspora, not anymore," Daniel Rosenthal told Thomas Winslow.

"Esther definitely sees herself as making aliyah—she believes that immigrating to the Land of Israel is the only solution for her," Naomi told the Winslows, who (of course) were clueless about *making aliyah.*

A basic tenet of Zionism, making aliyah is "the act of going up"— from the Hebrew word *aliyah,* which means "ascent." As the Rosenthals would struggle to explain to the Winslows, aliyah is the opposite of the Hebrew word *yerida,* which means "descent"—namely, the emigration of Jews from the Land of Israel.

As politically aware as the Winslows imagined they were, they didn't know how harshly the United States had restricted immigration in 1921—despite the persecution of the Jews in Europe. The Winslows were barely aware that Mandatory Palestine was under British administration. The Winslows were completely unaware of the Fifth Aliyah; the fifth wave of Jewish immigration to Palestine began in 1929. Hitler's rise to power in Nazi Germany would lead to mass migration between 1933 and 1939; in those years, as many as 55,000 Jews from Central Europe immigrated to Mandatory Palestine. Without Esther—meaning without the Druckers or the Rosenthals—what would the Winslows have known about the Arab riots there, or the British White Paper, which sharply cut Jewish immigration?

The Winslows were over their heads trying to understand Esther's terms of engagement with the U.S. Army. Neither the Druckers nor the Rosenthals could help the Winslows comprehend how Esther "deferred" her active service in the U.S. Army Nurse Corps—"pending other plans of engagement," as Esther vaguely put it. (After all, what did the Druckers or the Rosenthals know or care about the military or an army nurse's service?)

What the Winslows would slowly understand was that the Druckers felt more empathy for Esther's inclination to Zionism than the Rosenthals did. Isaac and Bluma were Viennese-born Jews. The Rosenthals had been born in New York; their parents had emigrated from Europe, but the Rosenthals were more assimilated than the Druckers. Isaac and Bluma knew they were living in the privileged seclusion of an all-boys' private school—an ivory tower of academia, where they were accepted and felt safe to be Jewish. Yet they were aware that the Jews in Vienna weren't safe.

What the Winslows didn't know—what not even the Rosenthals knew—was that Isaac and Bluma Drucker had already put Esther in contact with some old Social Democrats, now members of the Austrian Resistance in Vienna. When Esther told the Rosenthals, the Winslows were further alarmed that the Rosenthals were alarmed.

"You can't blame Esther for making things happen," Isaac told the Winslows.

"Isaac wishes we made more things happen," was all Bluma said to the Winslows and the Rosenthals.

Both the Winslows and the Rosenthals thought the Austrian Resistance sounded dangerous. By now they all knew danger didn't deter Esther Nacht.

But hadn't the aging Druckers been away from Vienna too long? How old were their old friends in Vienna—Social Democrats, now reputed to be in the Austrian Resistance? In 1934, when Esther was on her way there, the fascists had taken charge of Vienna; the Austrian fascists had designated the Social Democrats as an illegal political party. Many socialist leaders had left Austria for Czechoslovakia. According to Isaac and Bluma Drucker, many of their Jewish friends from Vienna were also exiles in Czechoslovakia.

"You can get a new passport made in Brno," Isaac said.

"Bernard and Joanna Morgenstern will look after Esther—they've not left Vienna," Bluma told the Winslows and the Rosenthals.

"Not yet," Isaac added—ominously, the Winslows thought.

The Rosenthals knew what the Winslows were thinking. To Thomas and Constance, with their lofty literary standards, all this intrigue sounded like an espionage novel—a tacky thriller. Trains back and forth between Brno and Vienna, Austrian Jews and socialists in exile in Czechoslovakia—fake passports and crossing borders in secret.

The Winslows could understand why Esther wanted to learn German and be in Vienna—her birthplace, in the country her parents had emigrated from—but why did Esther need to be involved with old socialists in the Austrian Resistance? This was where Esther's commitment to "making aliyah" mattered. Esther's embrace of Zionism was met with *much* more empathy from the Druckers than the Rosenthals.

Vienna was a necessary stepping-off place for Esther, who was on her way to the Land of Israel, which she believed was the rightful homeland of the Jewish people. More Jews would be (and should be) leaving Europe, Esther believed—not only leaving Austria. Fascism was ramping up in Europe, not only in Austria—or so the Druckers told the Winslows and the Rosenthals.

Honor seemed to know more about Esther's Jewish business than the rest of the Winslows. It was Honor who told her parents how Esther had deferred her active service in the U.S. Army Nurse Corps. In truth, Esther declined her enlistment into military service. As Honor said to Thomas and Constance, instead of enlisting in the U.S. Army Nurse Corps, Esther chose to immigrate to her Jewish homeland in Palestine.

"It sounds like Esther's move to Palestine is *permanent*," Thomas Winslow told his daughter.

"I thought you and Esther had a *pact*—you said she'll be back when the time is right," Constance said to Honor.

"She'll be back just once—Esther is going to have a baby for me," Honor told her parents. "Esther will be back when she's pregnant, but the baby will be mine—all mine. That's our pact," Honor said. That was when Thomas and Constance Winslow realized that their grandchild Jimmy—who wasn't yet conceived, much less born—was already a preexisting idea.

10.

The Two-Moms Idea

The townspeople of Pennacook were counting on Honor to be the black sheep in the Winslow family. After all, she was reputed to be an unplanned child, a suspected child of passion, and Honor was a lot younger than her three sisters. The ladies of the town were waiting for Honor to cause a rift among those Winslow girls. Was something missing in Honor? Was there a hole in her?

"Whoever heard of four daughters who uncritically love and support one another?" those ladies of the town would ask themselves.

Thomas and Constance Winslow weren't surprised that Faith, Hope, and Prudence already knew about Honor's pact with Esther. The three elder sisters were all in favor of the plan Honor and Esther had cooked up together. As the eldest, Faith spoke first; she put it as plainly as possible to her parents. "Honor wants to have a baby—she knows she wants to raise a child—but Honor doesn't want a penis poking around in her vagina."

Not to be outdone, Hope put her heart into the childbirth business. "Honor wants to be a mother—she just doesn't want something the size of a baby's head pushing its way out of her vagina," was how Hope explained it.

Prudence had waited for her turn. She'd clearly composed her thoughts on the unusual terms of her younger sister's adventure in motherhood. "We all know Honor will be a wonderful mom, and of course we'll help her. Given what Esther is offering to do, there's no reason Honor's vagina needs to be involved. Nobody gets in, nobody comes out," was the way Prudence put it.

"Well, really!" Constance exclaimed.

Thomas Winslow didn't say a word. Notwithstanding that he was the father of four daughters, the vagina wasn't his area of expertise. In the novels of the nineteenth century, vaginal matters weren't brought to light. *Honor's child will have two moms;* this was all Thomas thought.

The senior Winslows were similarly unprepared for what this plan meant for Honor's secondary education. With Esther off to Vienna, Constance had considered sending Honor to Abbot Academy, Constance's alma mater. The all-girls' prep school would be more challenging for the good student Honor was, at a time when Honor might be missing Esther. Abbot offered a rigorous college-preparatory program—English, foreign languages, math, science, history, and Bible study.

"Honor shouldn't waste her time with Bible study, Connie," Thomas complained.

Constance refrained from comment, although her memory of Abbot's constitution lingered on. Written in 1829, now more than a century ago, the words tormented Constance—"to regulate the tempers, to improve the taste, to discipline and enlarge the minds and form the morals of youth." *Oh, dear!* Constance Winslow was thinking. *What would the framers of Abbot's constitution make of the two-moms idea?*

For a private all-girls' school, the Great Depression of the 1930s was a tough time. In the academic year of 1933–34, there were only 71 boarders at Abbot—down from 135 in 1929–30. Constance had thought she would lend a hand to her struggling alma mater and send Honor there. But it wouldn't work out for Honor to go to Abbot. As it happened, the two-moms idea took precedence over the senior Winslows' ambitions for Honor's education, and she went to the public high school in Pennacook. Honor was such an overqualified student there, she took all the advanced courses and increased her course load by a third. She would graduate a year and a half ahead of time, with flying colors—with the highest grades and the utmost esteem of her fellow students.

"And with no Bible study, Connie!" Thomas exulted.

His worries were focused on what would happen to Honor's higher education. He'd had lofty dreams for his fourth and youngest daughter. Honor was the best fiction reader among his children. When she was only thirteen and fourteen, Honor was already reading (and loving) those nineteenth-century novels her daddy loved. In a liberal arts program at a college or university, Thomas had imagined her majoring in literature. Too bad for Abbot Academy, but it was okay with Thomas that Honor chose to speed up her time in high school; he hadn't realized why she was in a hurry.

Esther had her own timeline; she knew when she wanted to get pregnant and have the baby. Esther's plans left her ample time to get pregnant, but it was a short time for Honor to complete her higher education.

"Esther is thinking about how old she'll be when the baby is born," Faith told her mother and father.

"If Esther waits till 1942, she'll be thirty-seven—I wouldn't want to have a baby when I was that old," Hope said.

"Thirty-seven sounds like almost *forty!*" Prudence declared.

"Thirty-six sounds better, like you're just over thirty-five—Esther says her baby will be born in 1941," Faith explained to her parents.

"Early in 1941—the earlier, the better," Hope had added.

"That's why Honor is in a hurry—she wants to be finished with nursing school before she has a child," Prudence told the senior Winslows, who'd not seen the nursing school coming.

Given Honor's adoration of Esther, Thomas and Constance had worried that Honor would seek to imitate Esther; it was only natural that Honor would want to follow in Esther's footsteps. Of course

Honor had wanted to be Jewish, but Esther didn't hesitate to put a stop to that idea.

As Esther told Thomas and Constance Winslow, "My job is to look after Honor, to protect her. There's no protecting anyone who's Jewish—I should know, right?" Not even the Druckers or the Rosenthals knew how Esther had worded her argument to Honor, but Honor stopped asking to be Jewish.

It was Esther's idea that Honor should go to nursing school at the New England Hospital for Women and Children—a teaching hospital, where women could study and practice medicine, where women and children were treated by female doctors. Only women physicians were on the full-time staff; the patients were exclusively women and children. What Esther called an "all-women's hospital" was the first hospital in the country to have a school for nurses.

Esther's *all-women* designation made Constance question if Honor "liked" women.

"Not in the way you mean, Mommy—Honor doesn't like men *or* women. She's *asexual,*" Faith said.

Trying to steer the conversation to what Honor would be studying, Hope mentioned obstetrics, pediatrics, and gynecology—in that order. In her summary way, Hope tried to tell her parents that Honor was mostly interested in obstetrical nursing, hoping to work with obstetricians and midwives. "As for the pediatrics part," Hope hurried on, "Honor will be studying prenatal development, and I suppose there'll be other stuff—like pediatric primary care."

Thomas Winslow was relieved Hope didn't elaborate on the gynecology part of the nursing program. He was determined to change the subject, but he should have known Prudence would want to weigh in. How her mother had questioned if Honor liked women probably annoyed Prudence. "Honor is studying gynecology, Mommy—Honor isn't attracted to anyone's vagina or penis!" was how Prudence put it.

"I understand—I was just *asking!*" Constance cried.

"I want to know what the two moms are thinking about the father," Thomas Winslow interjected. "What qualities are under consideration for the father of Esther's baby—the would-be father of Honor's child?" Thomas had asked.

The three elder Winslow daughters didn't look at one another; their heads were bowed. Constance had bowed her head as well. Faith spoke first. "He should be short, Daddy," was all she said.

"He certainly shouldn't be as tall as Esther—she's too tall to be a Winslow!" Hope had cried.

"Ideally, to offset how tall Esther is, he should be a little guy," Prudence added. She was the only Winslow daughter who would go to med school; Prudence knew better than to promise that height was genetically controllable.

"Winslows are rather small, Tommy—we don't want Honor's child to feel like a giant in our family," Constance told him. She raised her head and looked tenderly at her husband, the little doll.

"I was thinking of other attributes, of more fatherly qualities than his size!" Thomas Winslow exclaimed. His family knew he wasn't sensitive about his small stature; Thomas honestly didn't care if Honor's child looked like a Winslow.

"Esther likes men, but they have to respect her—she won't tolerate a guy who pushes her around," Faith said.

"The would-be father will have to be as dedicated as Esther is—he'll have to be a hard worker," Hope pointed out.

In the spirit of offsetting one of Esther's characteristics, Prudence suggested that the father of Honor's child should be disinclined to hurry. "We all know Esther is making up for lost time, but it might be better if her baby's dad is a cautious kind of guy—if he goes slowly, if he takes his time," as Prudence tentatively put it.

Thomas Winslow was suddenly stricken with the vision of a persevering but uninspired student—a struggling plodder. He'd had many such students, the ones who were diligent but fell behind. Thomas both admired and pitied them. "I'm getting the picture—the two moms are looking for a short guy who's a dogged plodder!" Thomas declared.

"Mercy me, Tommy!" Constance cried.

They could all hear Honor laughing from the next room; they hadn't known she was there, listening to them. When Honor joined them, they were relieved to see how composed and confident she was—and what a well-spoken teenager she was. "Esther is aware of trying to offset her impulsiveness—she's looking for a little guy who's the epitome of deliberation," Honor told them. Even the youngest Winslow daughter knew that a deliberate little guy would touch a chord in the hearts of her mother and father. If something was missing in Honor, it wasn't her heart.

"He should also be fair-minded, Honor," Thomas told her.

"Fair-minded most of all, Daddy," Honor answered him.

Most of all, maybe, the townspeople of Pennacook hated the unanimity of the Winslows, who were in agreement about the name for Honor's child. If Esther had a girl, the baby would be another Esther. The Winslows were smart enough to know there would be no keeping the two-moms idea a secret from the townspeople of Pennacook; the ladies of the town would be among the first to know, or those ladies would presume they knew.

This prompted Thomas Winslow to a tirade worthy of Dr. Larch. Even if Honor went to Palestine for a whole year, and she came back to Pennacook with her child, the terrible ladies of the town would somehow know whose baby it was. When Esther was pregnant, when she was really showing, she might as well show herself to the entire town; she might as well give birth to her baby in Pennacook Hospital. "We tell the truth, we have nothing to hide—we simply tell the townspeople of Pennacook whose baby it is, and whose child," Thomas Winslow told his family. The Winslows were even in agreement about the townsfolk. You knew what they said about you was nothing they would say to your face; you knew their anti-Semitism wasn't always the silent kind, but they would never speak of Esther's Jewishness to Esther or the Winslows.

And what if Esther had a baby boy? Thomas Winslow was partial to the name *James*. All the Winslow women loved the pet name *Jimmy*. The Winslows were unanimous again. A baby boy would be both a Jimmy and a James. Then what were the Winslows worried about? Even the townspeople of Pennacook could tell the Winslows were worrying about something. And where did the Jewish one go? the townsfolk were wondering. The Jew didn't hang around as long as those earlier orphans, the ladies of the town thought to themselves. (Not even the Winslows had learned that Esther would make looking after Honor a lifetime's work, or that—in Esther's mind—taking care of Honor included looking after Honor's child.)

It was Honor who gave voice to the troubling question the Winslows were worrying about. "How old do you think my child should be when we tell him or her the whole story?" Honor asked. Heads nodded in assent to the pertinence of the question. All the Winslows knew the answer—Honor, too. We should tell your child before some kid in school blabs the whole story, Faith felt like saying, but she didn't say it. The birth-mom story should come from us, together with all we know about the father! Hope struggled not to say. We tell your kid before one of the ladies from the town says something about it! Prudence refrained from screaming.

"Your child hears everything from us first—from all of us, Honor," Constance assured her daughter.

"Right you are, Connie—from all of us!" Thomas cried.

Given where Esther was, and where she was going, there was no doubt the baby's father would be Jewish. The Winslows all knew the day would come when Honor's child would wonder if he or she should be Jewish. Esther had already told Honor what to say to her child. "For your own sake and mine, you should not be Jewish, but you better stand up for Jews," Honor Winslow would tell her child. Of this the Winslows were most certain: Esther's baby would stand up for Jews.

There would be more things to worry about, the Druckers wanted the Winslows to know. The way things were going in Europe, and in Mandatory Palestine, Esther's timeline might be at risk. Neither the Druckers nor the Rosenthals were thinking about Esther's plans to get pregnant. Esther's travel plans were what worried them.

They didn't doubt that Esther would somehow manage to leave Austria and arrive at the port of Haifa or Jaffa. It was a time when many Jews were getting out of Europe and finding their way to Palestine. But how did Esther imagine she was going to get from one of those far-off Mediterranean ports to the United States? Wouldn't she have to land at a port or two in Europe before she sailed across the Atlantic? Even if Esther got all the way to London—and, from there, found her way to the U.S.—how pregnant would she be by the time she got to Pennacook? She wouldn't want to be too pregnant—not with such a long ocean voyage ahead of her.

If Esther got pregnant in late June or early July of 1940—if she sailed from Haifa or Jaffa at the end of that summer, or in the fall of 1940—she would certainly be showing when she was in Pennacook for Christmas. Then Esther's baby would be born in March of 1941. Even if all that went according to plan, how would Esther get back to Mandatory Palestine in the spring of 1941?

"Esther will have to make herself indispensable to the Yishuv, even if this means making herself of use to the British," Isaac Drucker told the Winslows.

Yishuv means "settlement" in Hebrew, Bluma explained, but Isaac meant it in the Zionist way. The Yishuv was the Jewish population in Mandatory Palestine, the community of Jews who immigrated to the Land of Israel.

At the moment, how Esther might make herself indispensable to the Jewish population in Palestine was not explained to the Winslows. As for the part about Esther making herself of use to the British, Constance knew how her Tommy felt about them. Diehard Yankee that he was, Thomas Winslow distrusted the British more than he did the people of Maine.

Thinking of Maine, Thomas was reminded of his ongoing (if intermittent) correspondence with Dr. Larch—how Larch had written that Esther was clearly motivated to be "of use." She was making herself of use to Bernard and Joanna Morgenstern in Vienna.

Those two outlawed Social Democrats were helping other Austrian Jews and socialists in exile in Czechoslovakia. They wrote the Druckers about their high esteem for Esther; she was a willing and crafty courier, of both verbal messages and documents. With her American passport, Esther could get away with pretending to be a tourist. For how long was the question. It was noted in Esther's passport that she'd been born in Vienna. At the border crossing between Brno and Vienna, the guards would one day realize they'd seen her—again and again. They must have known *Nacht* was an Ashkenazi Jewish name.

On her way back from Brno, Esther made sure she wasn't followed from the Bahnhof in Vienna. She knew better than to lead someone to the Morgensterns. "You'll know when you're being followed," Joanna Morgenstern assured Esther.

"That's the day you'll be on your way to Haifa or Jaffa," Bernard Morgenstern told her. But before she was followed from the Bahnhof in Vienna, Esther had a more pressing reason to get out of Austria.

"Esther has met someone, and he's in trouble—his name is Moshe Kleinberg," Honor told her sisters and her parents. *Moshe* is the Hebrew name for *Moses*, Honor explained—and *Kleinberg* (in German) means "Little Mountain." "When Esther writes me, she calls him Moses Little Mountain—just to be funny," Honor elaborated.

"It's not funny that Mr. Little Mountain is in trouble, is it?" Thomas Winslow asked his fourth and youngest daughter.

"Are you saying Esther has met someone in the romantic way?" Faith was the first to ask Honor.

"Does Little Mountain have *father* potential?" was the way Hope asked the same question.

"The Little Mountain man sure sounds like he might be *small* enough!" Prudence cried.

"Girls, girls—let Honor tell the story in her own way!" Constance cried. Like Esther, Honor could keep her mom business to herself.

"All I care about is the trouble," Thomas told them.

Born in Vienna in 1906, Moshe Kleinberg was a year younger than Esther. When he was sixteen, his mother died and his father met a woman in Munich. Moshe wanted to move in with his aunt Reva, his mom's sister, but his father made him move to Munich. "That boy should have moved in with me—he wanted to, and I wanted him!" a distraught Reva, who would never marry, told the Morgensterns. Esther met Reva at the Morgensterns'. Before Esther met Moses Little Mountain, she'd heard all about him.

At seventeen, Moshe joined a Munich sports club—part of a German sports association. Since he was small, the fact that wrestling had different weight classes might have appealed to him. Esther didn't know or care why Moshe chose Greco-Roman wrestling instead of freestyle. She couldn't be bothered to know what Moshe's actual weight class was. She'd mastered German, but Esther would never make the move from pounds to kilograms. She didn't know or care if Moshe weighed in at sixty or sixty-two kilograms. She didn't trouble herself with kilograms.

"Moshe weighs about a hundred and thirty pounds—I weigh more than Moshe, but he can pick me up and I can pick him up," Esther wrote to Honor. Furthermore, Esther couldn't be bothered to measure Moshe to see how tall he was. Instead, she sent Honor an awful photograph. It was apparent that neither Aunt Reva nor the Morgensterns were gifted photographers.

"You can't see Moses Little Mountain at all!" Faith lamented. His face was pressed to Esther's chest; the bridge of Moshe's nose was aligned with her sternum, perfectly between Esther's unnoticeable breasts.

"If Esther had bigger boobs, Little Mountain couldn't breathe," Hope observed. Esther was smiling at the camera, her big hand holding the back of Moshe's head.

"Moses has no neck, but he has pretty big shoulders for a little guy," Prudence said. And Moshe's upper arms looked strong. His arms were wrapped around Esther, but you couldn't see where he'd locked his hands—maybe around Esther's waist, or around her hips. Esther's waist was below the bottom of the photo.

"If Moshe is lifting Esther up, he might be bending his knees—he might not be as short as he appears," Constance cautioned her family.

"Right you are, Connie," Thomas told her, but everyone could tell he was anxious to hear about the trouble.

"Whether Little Mountain is bending his knees or not, he more than offsets how tall Esther is—he's certainly short enough," Honor wanted her family to know.

Of more relevance to the trouble Little Mountain was in, he had made a name for himself in Greco-Roman wrestling, competing against other sports clubs and wrestling in the lightweight class. "Moshe is a Leichtgewicht—that's all you need to know about his weight class," Esther wrote to Honor.

Before he and Esther met, Moshe Kleinberg had won some medals and trophies. At that time, the trophies in Greco-Roman wrestling looked like Greek statues—maybe they were meant to evoke the ancient Olympian wrestlers. Moshe had sent photos of his trophies to Aunt Reva, who'd shown them to Esther. Reva took a picture of Esther, sending the photo to Moshe. "Look at this statuesque beauty—you should come back to Vienna and meet her!" Reva wrote to her beloved nephew.

"Did you tell Moshe how tall I am?" Esther asked Aunt Reva.

"I may have exaggerated a little, dear—Moshe always looked twice at the tall girls," Reva told Esther. (Liebe Esther was what Reva usually called her—dear Esther.)

"So Little Mountain had already seen Esther—he was smitten with her before they met!" Faith interjected.

"Little Mountain is a father waiting to happen!" Hope shouted.

"Esther will have to watch herself, or she'll have Little Mountain's baby too soon," Prudence put in. Thomas and Constance wrung their hands, beseeching Honor to tell them about the trouble.

In an all-German wrestling tournament in 1931, Moshe Kleinberg had been impressive. Esther said he'd received "some kind of recognition certificate." The certificate had been signed by Hindenburg, then president of the German Reich. Moshe had sent Aunt Reva a photo of the certificate with Hindenburg's signature. Esther sent Honor a photo of the photo. The photographs were black and white; there was the German eagle and what looked like a raised seal. The lettering was capitalized, larger and more legible than Hindenburg's signature.

RINGEN: LEICHTGEWICHT

KLEINBERG

Ringen was German for "wrestling," Esther had explained. Hindenburg was already in his eighties when he signed the certificate. The former field marshal, and a World War I hero, Hindenburg was president of the German Weimar Republic from 1925 until his death in August of 1934. Upon Hindenburg's death, Hitler became president of Germany and then swiftly abolished the office of president and declared himself "Führer of the German Reich and People." But even before then, with the rise of the Nazis in 1933, many Jews in Germany were persecuted. With the Morgensterns' guidance, Esther saw how Moshe's success as a wrestler led to his persecution. In what would be his last wrestling tournament in Germany, Moshe had lost a close match to the German Greco-Roman champion.

"The more successful Jews are more persecuted—the better we do, the more they hate us," Esther wrote to Honor. Esther said Moshe

Kleinberg's name was written on "some kind of blacklist." The warning was unclear, but he'd been told he had to be careful. With the Nazis in power, the activity of Jewish athletes in Germany would be restricted.

The Morgensterns had time to arrange Moshe's immigration to Israel in 1934, when Moshe was twenty-eight. His devoted aunt Reva would go with him, but the Morgensterns were worried about them. "The two of them are like children—they have little awareness of what's going on around them," Joanna Morgenstern told Esther.

"For different reasons, Reva and Moshe are the last to catch on politically," Bernard Morgenstern said. Esther agreed. Reva was a loving aunt; she doted on her nephew to the exclusion of the outside world. Moshe was a different kind of horse with blinders; he was dedicated to wrestling, and to his training, but he was lost in real-life situations.

"Moshe is the sweetest guy—you would love him," Esther wrote to Honor. Esther reiterated that Little Mountain was a Pferd mit Scheuklappen—German for "horse with blinders."

Constance saw what was coming. "Esther should go with Little Mountain and Aunt Reva—those two need help, and Esther is good at looking after someone!" Constance cried.

"Of course Esther is going with them, Mommy—Esther is on her way there anyway," Honor explained to all of them.

In the Fourth and Fifth Aliyahs, many Jewish immigrants came to the port of Haifa. The British had developed the port as a hub for oil. Esther hadn't planned to stay in Haifa; she was on her way to Jerusalem. Moshe and Reva had other ideas. When their ship landed in Haifa, they decided they had traveled far enough; they weren't moving on. Naturally, Esther would stay with them in Haifa—at least until those two children were settled in.

Esther was the one who found the other wrestlers living in Haifa. The European wrestlers who made Haifa their home were from Germany, Austria, Czechoslovakia, and Hungary. "Maybe wrestlers don't like to move on," Esther wrote to Honor.

There were almost three times as many Arabs living in Mandatory Palestine as there were Jews. The Jewish wrestlers in Haifa found a job for Moshe, and a place for him and his aunt to live. The wrestlers even found a job for Reva in a Hebrew kindergarten. Esther wrote that Reva was learning "kindergarten Hebrew."

In 1935, the Jewish wrestlers gained access to a sports hall in a school in Haifa, where they assembled a competitive wrestling team. The Haifa wrestling club was the only one in the country equipped and managed at a level equivalent to the European clubs.

The Haifa wrestling club was supported by an Israeli Jewish sports association called the Hapoel—Hebrew for "The Worker." The Hapoel crest was a proletarian variation of the Communist hammer and sickle, encircling a boxer. Esther needed to assure Moshe that Hapoel's ties to socialist workers were okay with her.

By 1938, there would be 48,000 Jews (and 51,000 Muslims and Christians) living in Haifa. A new wrestling club was up and running in Tel Aviv. The best competitions were between the wrestling club in Haifa and the one in Tel Aviv, with Moshe Kleinberg winning most of his matches in the lightweight class. There were also wrestling competitions between the Haifa wrestling club and the British military's Eighth Army—stationed in Haifa.

In the summer of 1939, with the beginning of World War II, a few of the wrestlers in the Haifa club were recruited by the British military—Moshe among them. "Do it, work with the British—for now, the British are our friends," Esther told Moshe. In Haifa, Esther had made friends among the British military; they'd tried to recruit her, too. Perhaps the British military's Eighth Army had recruited Esther as a nurse, but Esther was vague about it.

"I'm keeping my contacts with the British military open, but—for now—they know I'm up to my own business in Jerusalem," was all Esther wrote to Honor about the British.

Thomas and Constance Winslow were frustrated that Esther was more specific about Moshe's business than she was about her own. Esther was determined to be vague about what she was up to, but she'd been vague before. In 1939, Esther was thirty-four.

Esther's long-range plan worried Thomas. Real life was not a nineteenth-century novel. Those novels managed the passage of time; long jumps in time were one of the things those novels did best. Maybe Moshe was smitten with Esther when they first met in 1934. But what a long courtship Esther was trusting in. "Little Mountain might meet another woman before Esther's ready to get pregnant—maybe there are lots of women wrestling fans!" Thomas told his family. "Little Mountain might get married! Esther's good at taking charge, but only a novel can control what time can do," Thomas said.

"You should write to Esther, Daddy—Esther is good at keeping a promise, and she's good at getting a guy to keep his promise to her," Honor told her father. (There was obviously something she wasn't saying.)

"Esther should tell you herself, Daddy—you won't believe us if we tell you," Faith jumped in.

"Little Mountain made a deal with Esther—even if he has a wife and children, he'll knock Esther up when she wants him to," Hope said to Thomas and Constance.

"Well, *really*!" Constance exclaimed.

"Any guy would make that deal, Mommy," was how Prudence put it.

"Right you are, Prudence," Thomas said, quickly adding, "not that I would make such a deal, Connie—not if I were with you!"

"You *are* with me, Tommy," Constance reminded him. In truth, Constance included, all the Winslows knew Little Mountain wasn't the only guy who would make such a deal with Esther.

11.

An Old Testament Girl

Thomas Winslow was further frustrated that Esther's addresses were always in care of someone else. In her brief time in Vienna, she'd been in care of the Morgensterns—in Haifa, in care of Moshe Kleinberg. And now, whatever her business was in Jerusalem, Esther was living with one stranger after another—not strangers to Esther evidently, but unknown to the Winslows. And not all of Esther's addresses were in Jerusalem. Thomas Winslow would write to Esther at one address. When she wrote back to him—not such a long time later—she was writing from a different address.

"Isn't Esther living like an itinerant—what can she possibly be doing?" Thomas asked his family.

"More to the point, Daddy, did Esther convince you that Little Mountain will get the job done?" Honor asked her father.

Esther could convince anyone to get her pregnant, on her terms, Thomas Winslow was thinking—he didn't doubt the wrestler was committed. Moses Little Mountain would keep his promise to impregnate Esther when she wanted him to.

As for what Esther could possibly be doing in Mandatory Palestine, the Druckers seemed determined to be as vague as Esther. Isaac, newly retired from Pennacook Academy, and Bluma were in close contact with her.

"It's possible that protocol prevents Esther from making public statements about her Haganah activities, especially in writing," Isaac told the senior Winslows. This was the first they'd heard of Esther's involvement with the principal Zionist paramilitary organization there. (Honor must have known and kept quiet, her sisters thought.)

Haganah is the Hebrew word for "The Defense"—its purpose was to protect Jewish settlements from Arab attacks. The Winslows were surprised to hear how many such attacks there'd been—like the riots of 1920, 1921, and 1929 (not to mention the 1936–1939 Arab revolt). The Winslows were confused by the word *Havlagah* (meaning "The Restraint"), the official policy of Haganah—a policy of moderation, at least until the end of World War II.

To left-wing supporters of the Zionists like the Druckers, Havlagah was a morally superior policy—to abstain from taking revenge on Arabs (by not attacking innocent Arab civilians) was a way to stay friends with the British, and it didn't hurt to give the rest of the world a positive impression of the Zionist ideology.

Yet the Winslows were further confused by the two words themselves—*Haganah* and *Havlagah* sounded too much alike. "Defense and restraint sound potentially contradictory to me," Thomas Winslow would say to the Druckers, who said nothing. Isaac and Bluma knew how contradictory Haganah and Havlagah could be. As long ago as 1931, there already was a split in Haganah; the more militant Haganah fighters had objected to the policy of Havlagah. To many Haganah fighters, it seemed defeatist not to initiate counterattacks against Arab gangs—or against their communities.

Neither the Winslows nor the Druckers imagined Esther was a soldier. Given her training as a nurse—and, as time went on, her age—Esther most likely was a medic. Many female Haganah recruits served as medics. What the Winslows and the Druckers would leave unsaid was foremost on Honor's mind, and on her sisters' minds. Everyone knew that restraint didn't come naturally to Esther.

But Esther Nacht knew how to bide her time—she was planning ahead. By showing restraint, Esther would make herself indispensable to the British. The British didn't officially recognize Haganah, but British security forces cooperated with the group. During World War II, about four thousand Haganah women volunteered for service in the British assisting forces. In 1941, to prevent a possible Axis invasion of Palestine through North Africa, of course Haganah cooperated with the British.

The Palmach, the elite fighting force of the Haganah, was established in May 1941. With Israel's independence in 1948, the Haganah would become the core of the Israel Defense Forces, with Palmach members constituting the IDF's high command.

"The Haganah, the Palmach, the Israel Defense Forces—there are too many names to remember, Connie," Thomas would say.

"I suppose they all need nurses, Tommy," Constance told him.

This echoed what Isaac Drucker, in his vague way, offhandedly said. "It doesn't matter what you call them, Tommy—the military probably has a use for nurses."

Honor Winslow had her own way of saying this. "You can't be a soldier forever, Daddy, but you can be a nurse as long as you want—Esther will always be looking after *someone*."

Whatever Esther was up to in the Land of Israel, she was keeping an eye on Moshe Kleinberg. Moses Little Mountain was married, and his new wife was pregnant, when it was time for him to impregnate Esther. The Rosenthals had been somewhat aloof from the Zionist and Haganah conversations. On the subject of Little Mountain knocking up Esther, though, the Rosenthals, the Druckers—not to mention all the Winslows—were on the same page. Esther was uncharacteristically restrained; she didn't say how many times she and Little Mountain had sex.

Years later—long after Jimmy Winslow was Honor's child—those Winslow daughters would carry on about Esther and Little Mountain in their own vernacular. "The pregnant wife was a promising sign," Faith would say first.

"We knew Moses was carrying a loaded gun," Hope usually added.

"We knew Little Mountain wasn't shooting blanks," Prudence liked to put it.

"Girls, girls—no guns and blanks around Jimmy!" Constance said.

The Winslow grandchildren who were old enough to be in school—including the little ones, who were only in kindergarten—were on Christmas vacation when Esther came "home," as she called Pennacook. It was the end of December 1940; Esther wasn't due for another two months. She'd not wanted to risk miscarrying at sea. Esther was as tall and slim as ever, but she didn't hesitate to show anyone her small but growing baby bump. Esther wanted everyone to know she was expecting.

In regard to the Rosenthals, the Druckers, and the Winslows, Esther wanted them to know that her feelings about the British had changed. In 1939, the British White Paper had harshly curtailed Jewish immigration to Palestine, pissing off the Zionists. In Esther's opinion, the Zionist leaders weren't pissed off enough. Ben-Gurion had said: "We shall fight in the war against Hitler as if there were no White Paper, but we shall fight the White Paper as if there were no war."

That didn't sound sufficiently pissed off to Esther, who would one day be in favor of Haganah's sabotage activities against the British. Esther would support Haganah's assistance in bringing Jews to Palestine in defiance of the British. And after World War II, when Haganah was bombing British bridges, rail lines, and ships—the ones used to deport illegal Jewish immigrants—Esther would be in favor of the bombing, too.

"It's like when the Arabs attack us—we're going to fight back," Esther told the Rosenthals, the Druckers, and the Winslows. "When Jews want to come to Palestine, they must be allowed to come—if the British don't let Jews in, we will drive the British out," Esther said. (To a New Englander like Thomas Winslow, driving out the British wasn't a bad idea.)

Esther was no less outspoken on the subject of the United States not yet taking up the fight—she meant "the war against Hitler," as Ben-Gurion had called it.

"Why has the U.S. not entered the war—are we waiting for someone to attack us first?" Esther asked. (The Winslows would remember this the next December, when the Japanese attacked Pearl Harbor—and, following Japan, Germany and Italy declared war on the U.S.)

But when she was pregnant that Christmas of 1940, Esther just told the Winslows her thoughts on the burning of the Fasanenstrasse Synagogue in Berlin. The liberal Jewish synagogue had been closed by the Nazis in 1936. The synagogue was burned during Kristallnacht in 1938. The name meant "Crystal Night," as Esther would explain—in reference to the shards of broken glass littering the streets, after Jewish shops and synagogues were smashed. Now the Night of Broken Glass had forever marked the name of *Nacht* or *Nachtman*—any Jewish name with *Nacht* in it was a reminder of Kristallnacht.

"I'm keeping my name—I'm a Nacht, and I always will be," Esther told the Rosenthals, the Druckers, and the Winslows.

"Not vague anymore, Tommy—our Esther is back," Constance said.

"Right you are, Connie—I was worried about the vagueness," Thomas told her. What still worried those two was Honor's vagueness.

Of more interest to Honor and her sisters was Esther's news about Little Mountain's wife—she'd had a baby boy.

"Maybe Little Mountain makes boys," Faith was the first to say.

"It would be a little different for this family to have a boy around," Constance ventured in her cautious way.

"A *James* Winslow has a nice ring to it, Connie," Thomas said.

"If he's a James, he'll be a *Jimmy*," Hope insisted.

"I'm betting Little Mountain makes a Jimmy!" Prudence cried.

The talk about Hitler's war had worried Honor. If the United States were in a war, the young men would be in it, she was thinking. Maybe Faith's husband was too old, and he had trouble with one knee, but

Hope's husband might be young and healthy enough. *Maybe I don't want a boy,* Honor was considering. What if her child was a young man when the U.S. was in a war? she was worrying, but—for the time being—she was silent.

All Honor would say was ventured as cautiously as her mother might have said it. "I just want to have a child—I'll be a good mom to an Esther or a Jimmy," Honor told her family, with noticeable uncertainty.

It was the Winslows' public certainty (not to mention Esther's) that confounded the townspeople of Pennacook. The publicness of their certainty was most confounding to the ladies of the town. For two months and counting, Esther took her baby bump all over town.

"It's my baby, but he or she will be Honor's child," Esther liked to say for starters. "If he's a boy, he'll be a James or a Jimmy, but if she's a girl, she'll be an Esther—like me!" Esther always added. There were no rings on her long fingers. Not only did Esther make it clear that she wasn't married; she expressed her doubts that she would ever marry. "Marriage and motherhood aren't in the cards for me—I don't want to be a wife or a mother," Esther frankly said. "I just want to see what being pregnant and giving birth is like—I just want to try it," she added.

To the townspeople of Pennacook, particularly the ladies of the town, Esther was a brazen hussy, but she was unashamed. As all the Winslows knew, she came naturally to being radical. The Rosenthals were reminded of when Esther had gone to synagogue, just to try it—not because she would ever be an observant Jew, or necessarily go to synagogue again. And no one knew Esther as well as the Druckers did. As they understood, marriage and motherhood were not among the reasons Esther felt compelled to move to Jerusalem—to make the Land of Israel her permanent home. What made Isaac and Bluma stand apart from the townspeople of Pennacook went beyond the Druckers' Jewishness. As Isaac and Bluma were smart enough to know, what Esther did with her vagina was strictly Esther's business. Or as Esther would say to anyone, "I'm not making a career of breastfeeding—I'm just trying it!"

That late December of 1940, and the first two months of 1941, when Esther wasn't with the Winslows, she was visiting the Beaudettes. During Esther's Pennacook years, Josephine and Antoine had been a second mom and dad for her, and those Beaudette girls were a lot of fun. To an orphan like Esther, it was a wonderful thing to have too many sisters to count.

Beaudette girls were "too well-endowed for their own good," Constance Winslow had said, as if those girls' breasts had precipitated their renowned procreation. And Thomas and Constance couldn't help upholding their love of higher education; the senior Winslows mainly wished those Beaudette girls would go to college before they had babies.

When the townspeople of Pennacook condemned the Beaudettes for overbreeding, Thomas and Constance would stand with the Beaudettes. All the Winslow daughters had loved those Beaudette girls, and the Beaudettes were nice to everyone. It wasn't lost on Thomas Winslow why the Beaudettes and the pregnant Jewish one were the best of friends. To the ladies of the town, the Beaudettes were typical French-Canadian Catholics who had too many children. Esther was an unmarried Jew who was having a baby for someone else!

"The townspeople of Pennacook don't like anyone who's different, Tommy," Constance told her husband.

"Right you are, Connie. Attagirl, Esther! Way to go, all you Beaudettes!" Thomas said.

Honor Winslow knew she was always welcome to visit the Beaudettes. She hadn't held a baby in a while—except the way you hold a baby when you're a nurse. The way mothers held their babies was different, Honor knew. That winter of 1941, Faith's two children were ten and eight. Hope had only one kid, who was already six. Honor knew those Beaudette girls always had babies around.

"I held you not long after you were born," Josephine Beaudette told Honor. "I'd baked a blueberry pie for your family—not knowing

Esther was a pro at baking blueberry pies, and she was only fourteen!" Josephine said, laughing. Esther didn't laugh.

"I learned to bake a blueberry pie in the kitchen of the dining hall at St. Cloud's, where I also learned to read—and to hold a baby," Esther began, but her voice trailed away.

Honor hugged Esther first. Honor knew the story, as did all the Beaudettes, who hugged Esther, too. As much as Esther loved Dr. Larch, she'd not wanted to have her baby at the orphanage, where the way those babies cried when they needed to be held was different. Those babies' mothers had left them, taking their breast milk away. In the old days, not all of those crying babies would survive. Now that there was baby formula, made from evaporated milk, newborn babies who weren't breastfed thrived. Nevertheless, Esther's pregnancy gave her bad dreams of the way those abandoned babies had cried.

James Winslow would be born at the New England Hospital for Women and Children on March 2, 1941. It was a time when many American baby boys were circumcised—to prevent, or make more treatable, some sexually transmitted diseases and urinary tract infections. As Constance Winslow would unwillingly discover, there was a litany of dubious reasons. Honor Winslow had beseeched her mother to stock up the Pennacook Public Library with medical journals. Esther was uncharacteristically more specific. "In the area of medical history, Connie, we're looking for a timeline of circumcision—the pros and cons," as Esther put it. Constance Winslow's master's degree in library and information sciences was put to the test. Thus did the Pennacook Public Library become a trove of penis-cutting history. To Constance's dismay, her sacred library was where Honor and Esther argued about the benefits and cruelties of circumcision; they seldom agreed.

In 1855, the English physician Jonathan Hutchinson published an article claiming circumcision prevented syphilis—based on his studies of venereal-disease cases among Jewish and non-Jewish men.

"Bullshit," Esther said.

Honor had argued that venereal diseases could thrive under a foreskin. "Not in the library—no talking about foreskins here," Constance told them.

Those two also disagreed about the relevance of clitoridectomies to male circumcision. In the late 1850s, clitoridectomies were introduced as a treatment for hysteria, epilepsy, masturbation, and other so-called nervous diseases in women. Honor maintained that male circumcision was different.

They did agree on one point, at least. In the 1850s, James Copland popularized the idea of circumcision as a way to discourage boys from masturbating. "There's nothing wrong with beating off!" Honor cried, while Esther nodded her head like someone crazy.

In an 1860 article in *Lancet,* Athol Johnson said circumcision was a cure for masturbation in boys. *Asshole* Johnson, both Honor and Esther called him. "Not in the library," Constance repeated. Somehow curing boys of masturbation by circumcision would become medical dogma in Britain for a century—in the U.S., for 150 years.

In 1865, William Acton referred to the foreskin as a "source of serious mischief."

"I think the foreskin is the most sensitive part," Esther said. Honor didn't know how she felt about this. Constance knew it was not library talk. In 1870, Lewis Sayre, a New York orthopedic surgeon, introduced circumcision as a cure for paralysis, epilepsy, *and* masturbation. "There are no words," Esther said.

As for universal circumcision as a preventive health measure, there would be more hysteria by the 1890s, when physicians linked the foreskin to insomnia, chronic indigestion, asthma, bedwetting, erectile dysfunction, skin cancer, and insanity. Honor Winslow knew all this was truly insane.

Esther championed Eugen Levit, a Jewish doctor in Vienna; in 1874, he published a pamphlet urging Jews to abolish circumcision and replace it with an uninjurious rite. Esther quoted a London doctor, Herbert Snow, who, in 1890, deplored the spread of circumcision—calling it a "barbarity." Circumcision history was not on Esther's side, though. By 1900, Honor Winslow was winning the argument. E. Harding Freeland published an article in *Lancet,* declaring male circumcision would reduce the incidence of syphilis by 49 percent.

In 1914, in the *Journal of the American Medical Association,* Abraham Wolbarst, a Jewish doctor in New York, enraged Esther by urging universal male circumcision as preventive of syphilis, cancer, and masturbation. "The 'and masturbation' ruins everything else he says," as Esther put it. In 1932, the same Dr. Wolbarst claimed that smegma under the foreskin caused cancer of the penis, but Esther had stopped reading what he wrote.

Earlier, in 1928, a U.S. doctor (Thomas Bolling Gay) recommended routine infant circumcision to prevent phimosis. Honor was horrified that boys could suffer from a foreskin that was too tight to pull back. Nor was Honor's foremost belief in male circumcision—to make sexually transmitted diseases more treatable—eased by Esther's labeling. "Your penile hygiene fixation," Esther called it.

"What did your Dr. Larch do about it?" Honor asked Esther.

At St. Cloud's, Esther remembered the nurses checking the baby boys to see how their little penises were healing from the obligatory circumcision. In those days, all the boys born at St. Cloud's were circumcised—because Dr. Larch had experienced some difficulty treating uncircumcised soldiers "for this and for that" in World War I. Esther just gave up arguing.

"I know what the 'for this and for that' was—sexually transmitted diseases!" Honor Winslow had cried. Everyone in the library heard.

Esther said she felt better about a medical circumcision than she did about a bris ceremony. "If someone's going to cut my baby's foreskin, I want a doctor to do it—not a mohel, not a ritual circumciser," Esther said. She was particularly put off that the foreskin was buried. "If they think a foreskin is important enough for a burial, I think they shouldn't cut it off to begin with!" Esther maintained.

Constance couldn't stop reading everything about circumcision history in the damn medical journals, until she read one that stopped her. In 1935, in the *British Medical Journal,* Dr. R.W. Cockshutt stated that all boys must be circumcised as an incentive to chastity. Constance was so upset, she talked to Naomi Rosenthal about it. "His name really is Cockshutt!" she said.

"Circumcision got going with Abraham—blame him, not Cockshutt," Naomi Rosenthal bluntly said. "When it comes to the circumcision covenant between God and Abraham, Esther is about as nonobservant as a Jew can be—I love this girl!" Naomi cried.

When Jimmy Winslow came home from the hospital, Esther was still breastfeeding. Honor was the one who changed his diaper and looked after his little penis. "That's a mother's job—I'm not into tiny injured penises," Esther said. She was stalling about ending the breast-feeding. What the Winslows were thinking was that Esther would move on, and they'd never see her again after Jimmy started drinking from a bottle.

The Druckers were stalling, too, or Isaac was—he held back news about the Morgensterns. They'd saved so many Jews, but Bernard and Joanna Morgenstern had stayed in Austria too long; they'd not saved themselves. After Esther went back to Palestine, Isaac told the Winslows about the Morgensterns, who'd been "taken away"; either Isaac didn't know where they'd been taken, or he didn't say. "The Nazis are hunting Jews—they're rounding us up," was all Isaac could say.

"You're not saying everything you said to me, Isaac—you should tell the Winslows what you told me," Bluma told her husband.

"One day, Esther will be hunting Nazis—if anyone is hunting Nazis, Esther will be," Isaac told the Winslows.

At that time, with what was known about Hitler's war, Thomas and Constance couldn't imagine Esther as a Nazi hunter. Thomas thought old Isaac was growing senile; the retired faculty aged more quickly. Soon Isaac and Bluma would be slipping away to the retirement home favored by the elderly faculty needing care. It was named The Meadow, which was not everyone's name for it.

The townspeople of Pennacook called it The Marsh. The retirement home's location, on the saltwater side of the town, was more of a marsh than a meadow. "The Wetlands," the ladies of the town had named it. The Squamscott was a saltwater river; at high tide, the river valley was waterlogged.

The residents of The Meadow had their own name for the place— The Last Faculty Meeting. This was the name that resonated with the faculty who were still teaching at Pennacook Academy—and with their wives. (A final faculty meeting was indeed where they were headed.)

The Winslows' four daughters weren't looking as far ahead as The Meadow. Unlike their parents, those four could easily envision Esther hunting Nazis.

"Our Esther isn't a New Testament girl—she's not buying the Sermon on the Mount, she's not a Gospel of Matthew kind of girl," Faith announced.

"No 'turn the other cheek' shit for our Esther—she's an 'eye for an eye' kind of girl!" Hope declared.

"Our Esther comes from the Esther in the Old Testament. Because Haman is plotting to destroy the Jews, the original Esther doesn't hesitate to wreak vengeance on Haman," Honor said, reminding her sisters she was a good reader. The Esther Honor knew and loved was an Old Testament girl.

Honor moved on quickly, making herself busy with the more immediate business at hand. It was in her nature to be a painstaking mother. The day after the circumcision procedure, a yellow film thinly covered the wound. A nurse showed Honor how to put the petroleum jelly and the gauze on Jimmy's sore penis. "If the gauze sticks, soak the gauze with warm water before you take it off," the nurse said, making Honor cry. In three or four days, Jimmy's penis felt better—he no longer cried when he peed. Thomas Winslow thought that being a good mom and being a good reader were both about attention to detail. Honor would be a meticulous mom, in the same way she applied herself to taking care of Jimmy's penis. In a week or ten days, Jimmy's penis wasn't red and swollen, but for a while longer, Honor saw her son's red and swollen penis in her sleep—as she told her mother.

"There's such a thing as too much attention to detail, Tommy," was all Constance said about Honor's fixation on Jimmy's penis.

"Right you are, Connie," Thomas knew enough to say.

As a little boy, James Winslow would have no lack of attention. With those Beaudette girls around, they even took turns changing Jimmy's diaper. As Josephine Beaudette herself would say, "You know, Honor, we don't get to see many *little* penises."

Josephine and Antoine had only girls, who mostly had more girls. Of Josephine's four grandsons, Arnaud Beaudette was born almost exactly one year after Jimmy Winslow. After each of their circumcisions had healed, their little penises were a great relief and a small miracle to look upon—for both Josephine Beaudette and Honor Winslow.

If Honor ever felt guilty for having Jimmy circumcised, it must have been a comfort to her that Josephine Beaudette—who wasn't Jewish, and who'd had so many children—also believed in male circumcision. Was old Antoine Beaudette circumcised? Thomas Winslow certainly was, but he and Constance didn't talk about it. Constance wondered if her daughters even knew their father was circumcised. Notwithstanding all they'd read about the history of male circumcision, Honor Winslow never asked her mother if Thomas was circumcised—or how Constance felt about foreskins.

"It's just a penis—don't think too much about it," was all Esther said.

12.

Children Hear You

In December 1942, a presidential executive order closed voluntary enlistment for all men between the ages of eighteen and thirty-seven. These men would now be drafted into enlistment. Honor saw how relieved Hope was—her husband was thirty-nine, almost forty, and he'd separated the same shoulder twice. The young man who'd proposed to Prudence went to the war. For disqualification purposes, Honor would remember, separated shoulders were good. Prudence, now a doctor, told Honor that a bad knee injury was better. Honor would remember this, too.

In his infant years, whenever James Winslow couldn't sleep—or something scary had woken him up—his mom would soothe him with a song. It wasn't really a song, but Honor sang it like a song. "No war, no war, no war," she whispered in her little boy's ear like a lullaby, but it was a bewitching incantation.

"How long will it be before Jimmy starts to remember what he's heard or seen?" Honor asked her sisters.

"Before Jimmy's three, he'll be repeating words he's heard," Faith said first, but she didn't sound sure.

Hope had only one child; she sounded more uncertain than Faith. "Around four or five, Jimmy will develop something like a linear memory—he'll see the storyline, he'll start putting things together," Hope had said.

Prudence had no children, but she was a doctor; she spoke an incomprehensible kind of language. "Verbal and visual recognition are different cognitive processes," Prudence started to say, but she just stopped—she knew when no one in her family was listening.

Thomas Winslow was beside himself with anguish over such a woeful lack of specificity. As an English teacher and a reader of those plotted novels of the nineteenth century, Thomas was all about being specific.

In September 1947, Jimmy Winslow would be six and a half—to Constance Winslow's thinking, this was a year older than he needed to be to go to kindergarten. As a librarian, Constance was no less enamored of specificity than her husband. Jimmy would be an old kindergartner, in his grandmother's opinion, but his enrollment was put off until Arnaud Beaudette, Jimmy's frequent playmate, was due to start school.

In a well-meaning way, the Winslows were specific regarding when Jimmy should hear the story of his birth mother—undoubtedly before kindergarten, where another child could speak to him, or he might overhear kids talking.

"Saying 'the orphan's kid,' or worse," Faith suggested.

"Maybe 'the *Jewish* orphan's kid' is worse," Hope had said.

"Just 'the Jew' would be bad enough for Jimmy to hear some kid say, because you know it would be said in a hateful way," Prudence piped up.

"Right you are, Prudence—we tell James who he is before our dear boy hears something hateful," Thomas said.

"Or the first time our dear boy hears anything—we tell him then!" Constance cried.

But the drawn-out way the war was ending would test the Winslows' best intentions. The townspeople of Pennacook had never seen so much news about what was happening (or had happened) to the Jews. Before the end of World War II, Allied forces were uncovering the magnitude of the Holocaust. The Allied advance into Germany shed more light on Nazi forced-labor facilities and concentration camps. There were sixty thousand prisoners at Bergen-Belsen when it was liberated in April 1945. American troops found Dachau, where they made the remaining SS guards gather up the bodies and put the corpses in mass graves. That same spring of 1945, the Dachau death train was discovered—a train of forty or fifty freight cars, transporting four thousand prisoners from Buchenwald to Dachau. More than half the inmates starved to death en route; the train was traveling for three weeks. That same April, the Americans liberated Ohrdruf, a subcamp of Buchenwald, as well as Dora-Mittelbau and the Flossenbürg concentration camp. Not even the townspeople of Pennacook could avoid seeing the newsreels and the photographs in the Western media, though what they saw wouldn't deter a few townsfolk from denying the Holocaust happened. The publicizing of the atrocities in the Nazi death camps made almost everyone aware of the systematic extermination of the Jews. For a small New Hampshire town, there was a lot of talking about Jews.

In the fall of 1945, one of the ladies of the town spoke to Constance, who heretofore would have pegged this woman as one of Pennacook's silent anti-Semites. Yet the woman sounded sincere when she inquired of Constance, in a tremulous voice, if Esther was "all right." Obviously, because the Jews were in the news, there was more talk about Jews. This made Constance worry more about what Jimmy might hear.

"Children hear what adults talk about to other adults, Tommy—children might not listen to you when you tell them what to do, but children hear you," Constance told him.

"Right you are, Connie, and children repeat what they've heard. Nowadays, what another child could say to our dear James might not be hateful—it could be innocent or sympathetic," Thomas said.

The Winslows foresaw how the horrors of the Holocaust might make some of the townsfolk feel sympathy for the Jews—not to mention the news of the Nazi and fascist war criminals who were already fleeing Europe. Not even the townspeople of Pennacook wanted the war criminals to get away.

"Rattenlinien," old Isaac Drucker would say in German, in reference to the ratlines, the escape routes for Nazis and other fascists seeking safe havens in Latin America. There were two main ratlines. One went from Germany to Spain, then to Argentina; the other went to Rome and Genoa, then to various countries in South America. There were Vatican ratlines, supported by some Catholic clergy. Isaac and Bluma Drucker hated Bishop Alois Hudal, an Austrian Catholic and Nazi sympathizer who was rector of a Roman seminary for Austrian and German priests. Bishop Hudal helped wanted Nazi war criminals escape, including Franz Stangl, the commanding officer in Treblinka, and Adolf Eichmann, who fled to Argentina. (Joseph Mengele fled to Argentina, too—then to other countries, dying in Brazil.)

In March 1946, a Haganah team of Palmach fighters assassinated Gotthilf Wagner, the leader of the German Templer colonies in Palestine. In her letter, Esther was a little vague, calling Wagner "a former (maybe active) member of the Nazi party."

"Perhaps the parentheses are deliberately contradictory, Connie—or some vagueness remains in our Esther," Thomas said.

"Esther's Jewish business is her business—not ours, Tommy," Constance reminded him.

In 1948, there were more assassinations intended to drive the Germans out of Palestine. Long before then, the British authorities had called the Templers "enemy nationals"—arresting and deporting many of them to Australia. There'd been Templer colonies in Haifa, Jaffa, Jerusalem, and Sarona—now a neighborhood of Tel Aviv. The Templer colonies would be resettled by Jews. With Israeli independence in 1948, the State of Israel was most specific about the Templers. There'd been pro-Nazi sympathizers in the Templer colonies. Israel wouldn't permit ethnic Germans who'd been sympathetic to the Nazis to return to Israel or stay there. The Templers who'd been deported weren't allowed to come back; the ones who'd remained in Israel had to go.

In 1946, Esther's letter didn't have much to say about the German

Templers. Without comment, Esther had enclosed an old photo of the Haifa wrestling club with the wrestlers from the British military's Eighth Army. Honor was repulsed by the muscular men in their absurd singlets—she seemed reluctant to pick out Moses Little Mountain among the wrestlers. The other Winslows were more interested in the photo. Some of the wrestlers were tattooed, including Moshe Kleinberg.

"Do wrestlers like tattoos?" Thomas asked Honor.

"I don't know, Daddy—Esther didn't tell me," Honor told her father.

"Haifa is a seaport—I suppose you can get tattooed in a seaport," Thomas ventured to say.

"I don't know, Daddy," Honor repeated.

When Esther was showing everyone her baby bump, the senior Winslows had noticed she'd still not been tattooed. They'd wondered if Esther had changed her mind about the *Jane Eyre* quotation.

"Is Esther ever going to get her *Jane Eyre* tattoo?" Constance asked Honor.

"Esther said she'll get that tattoo after her stretch marks have faded," Honor told her mother.

With the outbreak of World War II, the Templer colony in Sarona became a detention camp. After the war, the fortified camp became a military base for the British. One day, after the British Mandate had ended, the old Templer houses and the army barracks would become Israeli government offices—including offices for the IDF and the intelligence services.

But this was where the Winslows would get lost—even Honor, who was in the closest contact with Esther.

Did Esther really write that Ben-Gurion changed the name of Sarona to Kirya? Honor thought so, but she couldn't find the letter where Esther wrote this.

And what about the Israeli intelligence services?

As Israel's first prime minister, Ben-Gurion set up the Mossad. Yet nowhere in Esther's letters to Honor—not once, not ever—did Esther mention the Mossad. Not that the Winslows knew or would remember, but Ben-Gurion put a former foreign ministry adviser, Reuven Shiloah, in charge of the Mossad.

On March 2, 1951, Ben-Gurion ordered Shiloah to take over all overseas operations. Not that the Winslows knew or would remember—after all, it was Jimmy's tenth birthday.

Over the years, in regard to what the Mossad's operations would be—beyond Israel's borders—these would certainly include covert intelligence-gathering and pursuing Nazi war criminals. Not that the Winslows would know—nor would Esther write about it to Honor. In Hebrew, *Mossad* meant nothing more than "institute."

Two months after Jimmy Winslow's tenth birthday in 1951, the State of Israel was just three years old. Yet concerning the Mossad, it didn't take long for there to be grumblings of discontent. The negative comments would one day include calling the governance of Israel a secretive state with unauthorized powers operating independently of the country's legislators. These criticisms were driven by the belief that Mossad operated as a kind of shadow government. It was Ben-Gurion's intention that Mossad should be accountable only to the prime minister—not to the Knesset, the legislators of Israel. Some American Jews, the Rosenthals included, would occasionally complain about Mossad's tactics.

By the time the Mossad was operating beyond Israel's borders, Isaac and Bluma Drucker had moved to The Meadow. It was all due to a kitchen mishap: a potholder had burst into flames on the stove, setting Bluma's hair on fire. Isaac just happened to have a full glass of orange juice in his hand; he doused Bluma's head with it. The episode spelled the end of their self-confidence. The Druckers were a welcome and likable addition to The Last Faculty Meeting, but they could be volatile—especially old Isaac. In his Zionist way, he was a passionate advocate for Israel. Isaac would not countenance any criticism of the Mossad. "I don't care about Mossad's tactics! It doesn't matter where you catch the Nazis, or how you kill them!" Isaac would tell his clueless colleagues at The Meadow, where the Winslows were frequent visitors, along with the Rosenthals.

If Esther's ever-changing addresses told a story, Esther wasn't saying. For a while, in 1951, Esther's address was on HaYarkon Street in Tel Aviv—Mossad's office was originally there. "That could be a coincidence," was all Isaac Drucker said. Mossad's headquarters later moved to the Foreign Ministry offices in Sarona, which Esther called the Kirya; it could have been a coincidence that Esther also had an address there.

Kirya in Hebrew is a female name meaning "town" or "settlement," but in her letters Esther referred to the Kirya interchangeably as "the camp" or "the compound," as if the name (or the purpose) of the place didn't concern her.

Honor noted: "It's as if nursing doesn't matter to Esther anymore— she never mentions it."

Of the Haganah, the Palmach, and the Israeli Defense Forces, Constance remembered saying, "I suppose they all need nurses, Tommy."

"The military probably has a use for nurses," the Winslows remembered Isaac Drucker saying, in his vague way. Not now—not anymore. Once, when the Winslows were visiting the Druckers at The Meadow, Isaac even said: "The Mossad doesn't have much use for nurses, Tommy."

"If our Esther's working for the Mossad, she's not nursing, Connie," Bluma added. For the Druckers, they were being dramatically more specific than usual.

Constance found Esther's obdurate lack of specificity annoying. When the senior Winslows were alone, she even said: "There's more than a certain vagueness in Esther. She has embraced being vague, Tommy."

"Esther's Jewish business is her business—not ours, Connie," Thomas reminded her.

But as the years went by, it was Honor who reminded both her parents: "When it comes to looking after me, there's nothing vague about Esther." Maybe Honor had *embraced being vague,* Constance thought.

Despite the Winslows' best intentions, when Jimmy Winslow had just turned six, the story of the boy's "other mother" slipped out during a playdate. Before then, of course, James Winslow had asked about his father. Who was he? Why wasn't he around?

Naturally, Honor had thought about what she would say; she knew Jimmy was going to ask questions. "Your father lives far away, in another part of the world. We'll never see him, Jimmy," Honor said.

"Does he think about me?" James Winslow asked his mom.

"I don't know—he has another life now, he has other children," Honor told him. She'd rehearsed what she would say with her sisters.

"It doesn't matter what you say, Honor. Jimmy will keep asking you," Constance said.

"He'll want to know what his father looks like," Thomas told them.

"You're the one who wants to know what he *looks like,* Daddy. You never stop looking at those old photos," Honor reminded him. This was true. Thomas Winslow would search for signs of Moshe Kleinberg in his dear James. In the photos Esther sent, most of the wrestlers had overdeveloped upper bodies in comparison to their legs. In Little Mountain's case, his muscular torso was longer than his stumpy legs. Thomas could only hope the singlet exaggerated the length of Moshe's torso and the shortness of his legs.

"Do I look like him?" James Winslow would ask his mother.

"It's too soon to know exactly, Jimmy, but you're going to be handsome—that's all I can say," Honor answered her child. She promised to tell him more about his father. "When you're older, Jimmy," Honor kept telling him.

Jimmy's all-important playdate was with Arnaud Beaudette. Chantal Beaudette was Josephine's youngest daughter—her last child. Chantal was a precocious eight, but she often played with Jimmy and Arnaud.

It was already funny that Arnaud was only a few years younger than Chantal, who was his aunt—not to mention that Chantal was smaller than Arnaud. (It was not lost on Josephine or Honor that Chantal Beaudette was the same small size as Jimmy Winslow.)

Because Honor and Josephine were talking in the Beaudettes' kitchen, they didn't hear what Arnaud asked Jimmy. Chantal clearly heard her nephew ask if what happened to the Jews made Jimmy sad. (No doubt Chantal could tell that Jimmy didn't understand the question.)

"Arnaud means if killing the Jews makes you sad because of your other mother," Chantal explained to Jimmy.

James Winslow wasn't the only six-year-old who didn't know what had happened to the Jews, but he might have been a minority in Pennacook because he didn't know he had two moms. "What other mother?" Jimmy asked Arnaud's aunt Chantal.

"*Your* other mother—the *Jewish* one!" Chantal had cried. This was what Honor and Josephine overheard; they both knew Chantal and Arnaud loved Jimmy, and Jimmy loved them. As Honor and Josephine also knew, there were always adults talking in the Beaudettes' kitchen. (In the Beaudette household, there were always children listening, too.)

At the moment, all Honor and Josephine could do was hug each other, but they surely understood what had to happen next. From now on, there would be no holding back—it all had to come out. This was when James Winslow had to hear the whole story, when he'd just turned six—when parts of his story would be hard for him to grasp.

"For a six-year-old, Esther's story can be confusing," Constance cautioned Honor.

"As a three-year old, Esther's story was already confusing, Connie. Just ask Dr. Larch!" Thomas cried.

Those Winslow girls were a well-rehearsed chorus; when they told Jimmy his birth mom's story, those daughters didn't shirk from the details. "Esther was the mom who got pregnant, Jimmy—your mom didn't do the pregnant part," Faith said first. (The *pregnant* part would take some explaining.)

"Esther was the mom who carried you inside her, Jimmy," Hope told the boy, holding her stomach in a way that suggested the *inside her* part.

"Esther gave birth to you, Jimmy," Prudence said. (Thomas couldn't watch how Prudence enacted the *giving birth* part, but James Winslow never took his eyes off her.)

"Esther gave you to me, Jimmy. You were her gift to me, because Esther knew how much I wanted you," Honor told her child. If James Winslow thought about being a present to the only mother he knew, the boy didn't say.

All the explaining could be confusing. All the roads led Jimmy back to his father. The boy seemed to accept Esther's story, even the part about her not wanting to be a mother to him. But James Winslow kept asking why his father didn't even want to see him, not even photos.

"He doesn't even know what I *look like*, Grandpa!" the indignant boy told Thomas. (Jimmy told his mother how he wished Grandpa Tommy were his father.)

"We should show our dear James the photos of his father. Little Mountain might inspire the boy to be a wrestler," Thomas told his family. (Those photos of Moshe Kleinberg and his fellow wrestlers in their singlets made Thomas imagine his grandson as a future wrestler.)

The Winslow women were appalled at the very idea of their darling Jimmy as a wrestler. "Honestly, Tommy, we should show the dear boy photos of his birth mother. Jimmy's going to have Esther's hands," was all Constance could say.

This was why six-year-old James Winslow saw the photos of his biological father and mother, while Honor and her sisters did their best to guide the boy through the biological parts of being a father and a mother. Naturally, all the Winslows did their best to ease the burden of too much information on the boy—though sparing Jimmy the impregnation parts of the reproductive process could later be confusing. Constance, in her resolve not to talk about sexual reproduction, hurried what she wanted to say about Esther's hands. (In the photos Esther sent, you could see the long fingers on her big hands.)

"You have Esther's hands, Jimmy," Constance said, pointing to one of Esther's photos. (Constance shouldn't have hurried; she should have said Jimmy was going to have hands *like Esther's.*)

The six-year-old looked horrified. "Does Esther have no hands now, Grandma?" Jimmy asked, staring at his hands.

When that confusion was cleared up, there would be other pitfalls for the young James Winslow—beginning with his dawning awareness of where he came from. As he was aware, his hands were comparatively bigger than the rest of him. If the boy's disproportionate paws came from the tall woman who'd given birth to him, Jimmy wondered what he was going to inherit from his father.

Like his granddad, James Winslow was transfixed by the photos of Moses Little Mountain; the boy seemed determined to be a wrestler. Jimmy wished he could wear a singlet, like the wrestlers wore. "I don't know if they make singlets for children, honey," Honor told him.

That fall of 1947, when James Winslow and Arnaud Beaudette started kindergarten together, Arnaud's aunt Chantal may have been only two years older than Jimmy, but she was way wiser. Naturally, the Beaudettes had seen Moshe Kleinberg's photos—Chantal, too. In her small, pretty hands, Chantal squeezed Jimmy's noticeably bigger hands.

"You will have Esther's hands, Jimmy, but you'll look more like Little Mountain than you'll ever look like Esther. You're going to be small, Jimmy—maybe we'll always be the same size," Chantal told the boy.

In one of the photos Esther sent, young James had noticed Moshe Kleinberg's cauliflower ears. "Am I going to have his ears?" Jimmy asked Arnaud's aunt. The boy whispered in Chantal's ear, because he didn't want his friend Arnaud to hear him.

"Look at your ears, Jimmy—you don't have ears like Little Mountain.

I think the wrestling messed up his ears," the wise girl whispered back. (Chantal Beaudette was way wiser than most children her age, too.)

Unbeknown to his family, Thomas Winslow would seek out the wrestling coach at Pennacook Academy. For as long as Thomas could remember, the academy had a wrestling team, but Coach Ted (as everyone called him) was brand-new. In the wrestling world, Thomas would learn, Coach Ted was already well-known.

He'd been a two-time Big Ten champion at Illinois when James Winslow was still a newborn. Coach Ted was twice an All-American, too—placing third and second in the national championships in 1941 and 1942. In 1945, Coach Ted moved to New Hampshire, where he became the coach at Pennacook Academy. Though no one would think Coach Ted seemed dissatisfied, everyone thought he was overqualified for the job. (His teams would dominate wrestling in New England prep schools for more than thirty years.)

What mattered most to Thomas Winslow, when the two men met, was that he could rely on Coach Ted's discretion from the start. Since Thomas began with the story of his dear grandson's biological father, this was essential. Coach Ted, of course, confirmed the cause and authenticity of Moshe Kleinberg's cauliflower ears from the photos. Little Mountain's mangled ears were the result of repeated rubbing—not only from rubbing on the mat, but wrestlers' heads were always rubbing together, the coach explained.

Thomas Winslow would ask if Coach Ted believed a predisposition to wrestle was hereditary.

"Sons of wrestlers are more inclined to wrestle—younger brothers of wrestlers are also more inclined to wrestle," Coach Ted began, in his measured way. "But this inclination is a matter of growing up around wrestling—not anything hereditary, as you say," the coach told Thomas. English teacher that he was, Thomas admired Coach Ted's specificity as much as the man's discretion. And Thomas was excited by the prospect of his grandson growing up around wrestling; to introduce Jimmy to the sport, Thomas proposed bringing the boy to the next wrestling meet at Pennacook. "Not so fast. Take it easy," the coach said. "In a couple more years, I'll have a better team, Tommy—not to mention that your Jimmy will be old enough to sit still at a wrestling meet," Coach Ted told him. In Thomas Winslow's estimation, Coach Ted would turn out to be both prescient and specific.

In the winter of 1950, Ted's wrestlers were winning most of their matches. By then, Thomas and James Winslow were riveted spectators. Thomas never saw Jimmy sit as still as the boy did when he watched wrestling. Arnaud Beaudette came to the wrestling meets with them; the wrestling totally engrossed Arnaud, too. Sometimes Arnaud's aunt watched the wrestling; Chantal was an animated spectator. She shut her eyes, she winced, she was judgmental of the referees. Chantal knew which referees she liked, and the ones she didn't. Once, when the ref warned a Pennacook wrestler for stalling, Chantal screamed at the ref. "The *other* guy is stalling!" Chantal shouted.

Thomas and James preferred watching the lightweight wrestlers to the heavier weight classes, not only because it was evident that Jimmy would wrestle in one of the lighter weight classes. The lightweights were quicker, and they made more moves. "The little guys are more fun to watch," Chantal observed. It was evident that Arnaud Beaudette was destined to be one of the bigger wrestlers. (Coach Ted and Thomas Winslow were already looking into a scholarship for Arnaud at the academy.)

"I know you guys are best friends, but it's not likely you'll be work-out partners—you'll be in different weight classes," Thomas told them.

"If Jimmy and Arnaud are best friends, it's just as well they won't be workout partners," Coach Ted told Thomas.

In 1950, James Winslow was nine. Arnaud's aunt was eleven. "We're still in the same weight class, you know," Thomas overheard Chantal telling Jimmy.

That same year, Moshe Kleinberg was forty-four; he won a medal in the national Hapoel championships. Little Mountain would be one of the wrestlers chosen to represent Israel in the Third Maccabiah Games—"like the Jewish Olympics," Esther wrote—where Moses won another medal. "They weren't gold medals, maybe just silver or bronze ones," was all Esther wrote Honor about Moses. Esther sent no photos.

In 1954, Moshe Kleinberg had stopped competing as a wrestler while Arnaud Beaudette and Jimmy Winslow couldn't wait to start. Little Mountain was refereeing and coaching wrestling at forty-eight. Again, Esther sent no photos.

Chantal Beaudette was fifteen in 1954; she stopped coming to the wrestling meets. "When you two are wrestling, I'll come watch you," Chantal told Jimmy and Arnaud.

Jimmy Winslow would notice that Chantal now wore the baggy blouses and sloppy sweaters of her older, bigger sisters. "Chantal doesn't want anyone to know she has breasts," Arnaud confided to Jimmy, who was already smitten with Chantal. At thirteen, James Winslow couldn't imagine confiding his feelings for Chantal to Arnaud. Yet not to tell Arnaud how he felt about Chantal made Jimmy feel he was disloyal to his best friend.

13.

To Take a Chance on Love, or Not

I n March 1956, for Jimmy Winslow's fifteenth birthday, his grand-father gave him a copy of *Great Expectations*—the next to last novel Charles Dickens finished. "We're going to read this novel aloud to each other, James—I'll read the odd chapters, you'll read the even ones," Thomas told his grandson. Both Thomas and Constance admired Jimmy's determination to read the emblematic novels of the nineteenth century, the ones his granddaddy taught at the academy. But James Winslow was a slow reader; his lips moved when he was reading a book. "It's as if the boy is writing every word, Connie," Thomas told his wife.

Constance knew her husband had another reason for reading *Great Expectations* aloud with his dear James. The Pennacook Academy faculty were not allowed to teach their own children (or grandchildren) in the classroom. The English Department had overruled Thomas Winslow's request to make an exception in Jimmy's case. Thomas was generally considered the Dickens man in the department; Constance understood that her Tommy believed he owned the teaching rights to *Great Expectations*.

"If dear James can hear the novel out loud, Connie, it will help him as a reader," Thomas told her.

"Just don't lecture Jimmy to death, Tommy," was all Constance could say about it. She'd heard his lectures on *Great Expectations,* all good ones. He believed that *Great Expectations* was the most empathetic and perfectly plotted novel in the English language.

"And it sublimely illustrates the one thing people most dislike about Dickens," Constance had heard her husband say. "Dickens intends to move you emotionally, more than he cares about persuading you intellectually," Thomas always said. "In *Great Expectations,* my dear James, you will love the characters you're supposed to love, and you'll hate the ones you're supposed to hate," Constance would overhear her husband say to their grandson. "You cannot encounter a lawyer of Mr. Jaggers's terrifying ambiguity and ever again put yourself willingly in a lawyer's hands. Jaggers, although only a minor character in *Great Expectations,* is arguably the novel's foremost indictment of living by abstract rules," Thomas Winslow would lecture. As a teacher, he didn't overlook the money problems of Dickens's father—or that Dickens, at age eleven, was a child laborer. Dickens knew social evil firsthand; at fifteen, he left school. (It wasn't lost on Constance that Jimmy would be fifteen and a half when he started at Pennacook Academy in the fall of 1956.)

Constance was exasperated with her husband's lecturing; he just went on and on. "You'll notice how Dickens's lush language grows thinner as the plot progresses," Constance overheard him telling Jimmy. "Both in the lushness of his language, when Dickens means to be lush, and how spare he can be when he simply wants you to follow the story, he is ever conscious of his readers," Thomas went on. "And Dickens overpunctuates! He makes long and potentially difficult sentences slower but easier to read; his punctuation is a form of stage direction," Thomas Winslow was saying; he didn't know that Honor was listening to him, alongside her mother.

"*Fuck* Dickens's punctuation, Daddy!" Honor shouted to her father.

"For pity's sake, Tommy—just read aloud to each other!" Constance told him.

Because Thomas was reading all the odd-numbered chapters, he was the one who started. It seemed to Constance and Honor that he gave special emphasis to the second sentence of the second paragraph of that first chapter. "As I never saw my father or my mother, and never saw any likeness of either of them (for their days were long before the days of photographs), my first fancies regarding what they were like were unreasonably derived from their tombstones."

Both Constance and Honor wondered if Thomas was trying to make Jimmy feel better about his own circumstances. (At least the boy had seen photos of Esther and Moses Little Mountain—they weren't *tombstones*.)

For similar reasons, Constance and Honor thought, Thomas purposely paused before reading aloud that ominous passage in Chapter Seven when young Pip is contemplating how a man might freeze lying out on the marshes. "I looked at the stars, and considered how awful it would be for a man to turn his face up to them as he froze to death, and see no help or pity in all the glittering multitude." Was this Thomas Winslow's way of assuring his grandson that James would never be without help or pity, because the boy came from an adoring family? (By now, whenever Thomas and James read aloud to each other, they had the whole family for their audience—not just a couple of eavesdroppers in an adjacent room.)

And what a long pause there was, after young James read that most declarative first sentence in Chapter Fourteen. "It is a most miserable thing to feel ashamed of home." James Winslow was overcome with emotion; the dear boy needed a minute to collect himself before he could continue reading. It meant the world to all the Winslows that Jimmy didn't feel ashamed of home; the idea of that was repugnant to them.

It was only when Thomas read aloud that passage near the end of Chapter Nineteen—just before what Dickens calls "THE END OF THE FIRST STAGE OF PIP'S EXPECTATIONS"—that Constance would realize why her Tommy chose to read the odd chapters. (It was as deliberate a choice as the rest of her husband's teaching process; he wanted to give voice to those passages that illuminated Dickens's intention to move readers emotionally.) "Heaven knows we need never be ashamed of our tears, for they are rain upon the blinding dust of earth, overlying our hard hearts."

Constance and her daughters were not surprised when Thomas histrionically enacted Miss Havisham's "passionate whisper" in Chapter Twenty-nine, when she tells poor Pip "what real love is." (In this respect, Constance understood, her husband and Dickens were kindred souls; their hatred of Miss Havisham knew no bounds.) On the subject of "real love," neither Thomas Winslow nor Miss Havisham held back. "It is blind devotion, unquestioning self-humiliation, utter submission, trust and belief against yourself and against the whole world, giving up your whole heart and soul to the smiter—as I did!" Thomas Winslow as Miss Havisham cried.

Honor Winslow was projecting her own fears about "real love" onto her darling Jimmy. Her father's rendition of Miss Havisham's condemnation of love might make James Winslow never take a chance on love, as Honor never did. Of course Honor couldn't help projecting her own fears about love onto Jimmy. (What kind of mother wouldn't want her child to take a chance on love, even if she herself didn't?)

Constance knew her husband well, especially his teaching methods. Constance was waiting for the teaching lesson that remained, concerning the two endings of *Great Expectations*. Before Thomas read the last chapter, Chapter Fifty-nine, he asked young James to read Dickens's original ending—Pip's final meeting with Estella, his old heartbreaker. Somehow we're supposed to believe Pip can see in Estella that "suffering had been stronger than Miss Havisham's teaching"—it's even harder to imagine that Estella has a heart! Pip believes that Estella will somehow "understand what my heart used to be." (If you know Estella, good luck with that idea!)

Thomas Winslow and his grandson agreed about the original ending. The tone is self-pitying, hence more modern than Dickens's romantic revision. "There is a contemporary detachment in the original ending—

even a smugness, and it isn't like Dickens to be smug," Thomas told young James. "What's worse, Pip is moping, and Dickens didn't mope!" Thomas exclaimed. Then he read the last chapter (the revised ending) aloud—reading tearfully when he got to the part about Pip and Estella ending up together.

"I saw no shadow of another parting from her." These are Pip's last words, his declaration of eternal love for Estella—his eternal tormentor. Constance marveled at what her husband had pulled off; he'd praised the new ending as the right one for the novel, while he'd given Jimmy justifiably grave doubts about Estella.

"I don't have a good feeling about Pip and Estella as a couple," Jimmy told his granddad after they'd finished reading *Great Expectations* to each other.

Constance knew where this would go; she'd heard her husband's lecture before, one of his best ones. How Pip's expectations had been dashed before; how we've come to believe his expectations weren't so great to begin with. As we know, Pip has heard Estella is "leading a most unhappy life"; the husband she'd separated from "had used her with great cruelty." (Honor Winslow would be unhappy with herself for thinking of Estella as used or damaged goods.) Of falling in love, Pip observes: "How could I, a poor dazed village lad, avoid that wonderful inconsistency into which the best and wisest of men fall every day?" As Pip bluntly states, when he encounters Estella later (when they're both older): "The freshness of her beauty was indeed gone."

"It's the right ending for the novel, my dear James, but it seems to me that Pip is asking for trouble when he sees 'no shadow of another parting from' Estella," Thomas told young James.

"I would be running away from her, as far as I could get!" Jimmy Winslow cried.

"What a wily old fox you are—as a teacher, Tommy!" Constance told her husband. Thomas Winslow would be right; hearing *Great Expectations* out loud did indeed help young James as a reader.

What Thomas Winslow didn't expect was that reading *Great Expectations* aloud made Jimmy Winslow want to be a writer—but only if he could be a novelist like Charles Dickens, as young James would tell his grandfather.

Thomas never meant to burden the boy with such an outdated desire; to be a novelist like Charles Dickens struck Thomas as a dinosaur of an ambition, and Thomas truly loved Dickens. Yet he was aware that many of his colleagues thought teaching Dickens was old-fashioned. He knew that most of his students detested Dickens. As a would-be writer, wasn't James Winslow doomed to be out of date before he began—condemned to obscurity before he started? *What havoc have I wreaked (or wrought)?* Thomas Winslow (ever the English teacher) was worrying. Thomas regretted his role in encouraging his beloved grandson to become a nineteenth-century novelist; he'd just been trying to help the struggling boy as a reader.

As his grandfather had feared, James Winslow would be a struggling student at Pennacook Academy. The boy could hold his own in history class and in English; he was still a slow reader, but a conscientious one. Thomas noticed that young James's written work was meticulously rewritten, not to mention overpunctuated to a fault. Thomas blamed himself for his grandson's obsessive rewriting. In an academically demanding school, there was never enough time to rewrite everything. Jimmy Winslow would fall behind in math, and in all the sciences. He would fail to grasp a foreign language, too—not for want of trying. His granddad had recommended Spanish. (Thomas's colleagues at the academy told him Spanish was the easiest foreign language.) Yet young James had taken to heart where his biological mom and dad came from. When he was just starting prep school, Jimmy Winslow was already dreaming about going to Vienna; he imagined taking a junior year abroad in his university years. The only foreign language James Winslow wanted to learn was German.

Of course Thomas admired his grandson's perseverance. Charles

Dickens was the dear boy's hero; young James saw for himself how his hero had rewritten the ending of *Great Expectations*. Unfortunately, three years of the same foreign language was a graduation requirement at Pennacook Academy; three years of math were also required. James Winslow would need five years to pass three years of German, and it took him five years to pass three years of math.

It was a small humiliation for Jimmy, not to graduate with the class of 1960—when his best friend, Arnaud Beaudette, would. All the Beaudettes were there, Aunt Chantal included. Because he was in love with her, young James tried not to stare at Chantal, but the boy was aware of how she watched him; Chantal was wise to be worried about him.

Coach Ted was wise, too. After the graduation ceremony, people were milling around, but Coach Ted took Jimmy aside. "It doesn't matter when you graduate, Jimmy. All that matters is to get where you're going," Coach Ted told the boy. "Besides, a fifth year won't be all bad. It just means you have another year of wrestling ahead of you," the coach said.

Being a fifth-year wrestler in prep school was of some consolation to James Winslow, who would never win a New England championship. Like Little Mountain, Jimmy was in the running for a title a few times; in the championship tournament, he placed fourth once and third twice. He was a rewriter as a wrestler, too; he was what Coach Ted called methodical. Ted had taught him to be technical—to be defensive from the start, to be a counterpuncher. Jimmy's first moves weren't fast enough, or sufficiently explosive. James Winslow won wrestling matches by countering the first moves of his more athletic appointments. To finish fourth in New England wasn't bad—to take third twice was in the category of pretty good. But Jimmy wasn't much of an athlete; his superior hand strength was his only natural advantage. He indeed had Esther's hands; he could control his opponents' wrists and ride their ankles. He would beat some better athletes with his hand control and his methodical technique, but Coach Ted didn't mislead him. Beyond the schoolboy level, the coach was frank about Jimmy's future prospects as a wrestler. Not bad or pretty good wouldn't cut the mustard at the next level, Ted told the boy. At Arnaud's graduation, Coach Ted encouraged James Winslow to start thinking about actually *being* the writer the boy wanted to become.

"When you move on from here, Jimmy, and you will, stick to the writing—stick to being a writer, in the way a wrestler would keep wrestling," Ted said. "Here comes someone you should talk to, Jimmy. Listen to Chantal." It wasn't lost on James Winslow that the people who were worried about him had talked to one another. He knew it was Chantal's turn to take him aside.

Unlike all the other Beaudette girls, Chantal started college before she had a baby. As far as Arnaud and Jimmy knew, Chantal had never had a boyfriend. As the Winslows had observed, the townspeople of Pennacook were not as accustomed to French Canadians as people were in northern New Hampshire. Most French Canadians in Pennacook didn't speak French; it would just make them stick out more. Chantal Beaudette *wanted* to stick out more than she already did.

Chantal was a French major at the University of New Hampshire. She'd hoped to have a junior year abroad in Paris, where she could learn to speak French the way natives did. But she had to change her plans. She wasn't going to Paris, but instead was staying home to help her mom; Josephine Beaudette was too old and tired to be looking after all her grandkids. Chantal was commuting every day to the University of New Hampshire. She said it took only twenty minutes—"at the speed limit, maybe half an hour"—to drive from Pennacook to Durham, but James Winslow certainly knew enough to know that Durham wasn't Paris. (Arnaud had told Jimmy that his aunt wasn't just majoring in French; Chantal was on course to get a master's degree so she could teach French at a college or university.)

Yet at Arnaud's graduation from the academy, Chantal was focused on Jimmy's future. "There are two novelists in the English Department

TO TAKE A CHANCE ON LOVE, OR NOT

at UNH," Chantal told Jimmy. "You can show your writing to other writers. That's what matters the most to you, right?" she asked him. "It doesn't matter that UNH doesn't have a wrestling team, Jimmy. No more weighing in for you," Chantal told him. "If you want to keep wrestling, you can find a workout partner in the academy wrestling room, where you can help Ted with the coaching, too," Chantal said. "We can commute to Durham together, sometimes," she added.

James Winslow had a history of driving to Durham with Chantal—a fond memory of his and Arnaud's formative adolescence. When those boys were growing up in Pennacook, before Chantal was old enough to have a driver's license, the only movies they saw were the current American films; the local movie theater didn't show any foreign films. But Durham was a college town; the Franklin Theatre was more of an art house. The Franklin not only showed the acclaimed foreign films but also revived some great older movies.

When they were younger, Arnaud and Jimmy saw a couple of classic Westerns at the local movie theater in Pennacook. They saw *High Noon* twice in 1952, when Jimmy was eleven; they saw *Shane* three times the year after. As Chantal would remember, Arnaud and Jimmy were only eleven and twelve when the Winslow girls snuck those boys and Chantal into the Pennacook movie theater to see *From Here to Eternity*—a little too young, in Chantal's opinion, though she herself was only fourteen. She still remembered all the explaining she had to do, because Arnaud and Jimmy were way too young to understand the adultery part—not to mention the prostitution part.

Chantal's dismay at those kids seeing *From Here to Eternity* was on her mind three years later, in 1956, when she drove those two teenagers to Durham, where the Franklin Theatre was showing a Carol Reed revival, *The Third Man*. The boys were fourteen and fifteen when Chantal took them to see the wet sewers under postwar Vienna, where Harry Lime (Orson Welles) pays for his terrible crimes. Harry Lime is crippling or killing children with diluted penicillin.

If Arnaud and Jimmy had recovered from their exposure to adultery and prostitution, surely those boys wouldn't flinch from film noir when they were older—or so Chantal thought. But she could see that the melancholic music (Anton Karas on a zither) made both boys anxious from the start. Chantal saw that a doomed love story might adversely affect young James or Arnaud, who'd not yet been on a date with a girl. And she should have known that those two teenagers would be smitten with the character of Anna (Alida Valli), Harry Lime's lover. At the end of the film, as Anna leaves the cemetery where Harry Lime has been buried, she gives the cold shoulder to Holly (Joseph Cotten). His heart is breaking—he is hopelessly in love with Anna. Holly is a hack fiction writer; he writes Westerns.

Anna is a sophisticated European, and Holly is a naïve American, James Winslow was thinking; he was just trying to imagine himself meeting an older woman like Valli in Vienna.

Chantal saw that both boys were heartbroken; they were expecting Anna and Holly to end up together. "Don't you see?" she asked the boys, as they were leaving the Franklin. "She was in love with Harry! Holly is just so *out of it,* and Anna has seen everything!" Chantal told them. Compared to adultery and prostitution, Chantal was thinking, maybe pessimism, fatalism, and menace are harder for boys to understand.

As Thomas Winslow would point out to young James, the screenplay of *The Third Man* was written by Graham Greene—a novelist. Jimmy just nodded. Until now, he'd thought of Arnaud's aunt Chantal as his foremost fixation on an older woman—not imagining there might be older women like Valli in Vienna. As for Coach Ted's advice that Jimmy should "stick to the writing," Thomas Winslow was already worried about his grandson's single-mindedness. The boy was always writing fiction; young James was making up stories when he should have been doing his schoolwork. As a budding storyteller, James Winslow seemed to be living in a parallel universe. Jimmy was a daydreamer; he was more in touch with the world of make-believe than he was with reality. In Thomas's opinion, his grandson needed no encouragement to immerse himself in his writing.

James Winslow would be twenty before he graduated from prep school; his writing was partly to blame. (And to think his grandmother once thought Jimmy would be an old kindergartner.)

Meanwhile, Honor Winslow was driving Coach Ted crazy; she kept asking Ted to tell her what the worst wrestling injuries were. Naturally, the coach thought he was dealing with another anxious wrestling mother; Ted just tried to reassure her. "In wrestling, if you get injured, your injuries are usually the kind that heal," the coach told her.

"But what are the *worst* ones, the kind that *don't* heal—not completely?" Honor had insisted.

Thomas Winslow wasn't worried about his grandson's wrestling injuries; the writing worried him more. In writing, Thomas was thinking, if you don't make it as a novelist, maybe you never heal. Why would Thomas think twice about Honor's obsession with the worst wrestling injuries that might befall her dear child? Honor was just being a good mother, expressing her worst fears—or so Thomas thought.

What's more, Jimmy had made his birth mother proud; he'd already demonstrated his readiness to stand up for Jews. Honor hadn't hesitated to tell Esther the whole story. The starting 115-pounder on the academy wrestling team was one of Pennacook's nonobservant Jews from New York. Jonah Feldstein was one grade below his teammates Jimmy and Arnaud, but Jonah was arguably more sophisticated than both of them. For such a small boy, he had the savvy of a big city about him.

An air of self-assurance radiated from little Jonah; this was what got him in trouble, along with the yarmulke. Neither Arnaud nor Jimmy had ever seen Jonah wear the skullcap; he was not an Orthodox Jew, and he wasn't on his way to a synagogue. It was a Sunday, and Jonah went to the only convenience store in downtown Pennacook that was open on a Sunday.

"Cover your head," the Talmud says, "in order that the fear of heaven may be upon you." Jonah wasn't devout; he was not inclined to be prayerful. But Jonah was praying that his older sister, Sarah, wasn't pregnant. It was out of respect for Sarah that Jonah was wearing a yarmulke—to send her his blessings.

The academy students were cautioned to stay away from Morrison's; the convenience store was a hangout for local ruffians. Morrison's was in the Mill Street part of Pennacook, across the river from the town's textile mill. If academy students ventured there, they were advised not to be alone. Jonah was alone in his yarmulke when he encountered the Duval brothers—no one could tell those two thugs apart. Marcel and Marceau were not twins, but they were inseparable. They not only looked alike; they exhibited the same bullying behavior. Jonah was leaving Morrison's store when the brothers accosted him on the Mill Street sidewalk. "Hey, Jew boy—you don't belong here," one of the brothers began.

"No Yids allowed," either Marcel or Marceau said.

"You can't wear your kike hat here," one of the Duvals told Jonah, reaching for the yarmulke. That's how it started. Jonah wouldn't have been beaten up as badly if he hadn't taken down the Duval brother who grabbed him by the yarmulke.

In wrestling terms, the 115-pounder got the first takedown, but he lost the match to the two bigger Duval brothers on the Mill Street sidewalk. The Pennacook police seemed to think it was sufficient to give the Duval brothers a warning. It was inaccurate of the police to call the beating up of Jonah Feldstein a first-time offense for those brothers; Marcel and Marceau had roughed up other academy students before.

"Maybe I'm the first Jew the Duvals have beaten up—maybe that's what the cops mean by the first time," Jonah told his teammates. This was only one aspect of Jonah's worldliness among his wrestling teammates. The Jewish boy from New York was not only acutely aware of anti-Semitism; he was used to it.

Marcel and Marceau weren't the only boys in the Duval family. The Duvals had boys the way the Beaudettes had girls. At an early age, those Beaudette girls were told to keep their distance from the Duval boys. It didn't help that both families lived in the Mill Street part of town. It was Jimmy's idea that Arnaud should rough up Marcel and Marceau in the way those Duval brothers had beaten up Jonah Feldstein. Arnaud took some teammates with him; they were mostly wrestlers in the upper weight classes, but Jimmy Winslow went with them. The way it worked was straightforward. All the wrestlers restrained Marcel or Marceau while Arnaud beat the crap out of the other brother; then it was Marcel or Marceau's turn to be beaten up by Arnaud.

The Pennacook police gave Arnaud Beaudette and Jimmy Winslow a warning; this time, it was accurate of the police to call the beating up of the Duval brothers a first-time offense for Arnaud and Jimmy. For no clear reason, the police didn't mention the other wrestlers. (They were boarding students, but this was no reason to absolve them.)

The Disciplinary Committee at Pennacook Academy gave all the wrestlers involved a warning, with one faculty member going so far as to refer to them as "vigilantes." Warnings were all that came of it, but the Feldsteins in New York were appreciative of Jimmy and Arnaud's vigilantism.

After one Thanksgiving break, Sarah Feldstein drove Jonah back to Pennacook Academy. She was a college student somewhere in the Boston area. Jonah led Sarah all around the academy campus until they found Arnaud and Jimmy. "My sister wants to give you a hug and kiss," Jonah said matter-of-factly when he found them; Jonah looked away when Sarah hugged and kissed them. Arnaud and Jimmy had never been hugged and kissed the way the dark and smoldering Sarah hugged and kissed them. More older-women material—this was the way James Winslow (the writer) would one day think of it.

In his fifth year at Pennacook Academy, young James and Jonah Feldstein were best friends. With Arnaud away in college, Jonah was the one Jimmy hung out with. Jonah confided to Jimmy that he had a crush on Arnaud's aunt Chantal, too.

As for Chantal, she was true to her word—she went to all of Jimmy's wrestling matches at the academy. She continued to drive him to the Franklin Theatre in Durham, even after he had his driver's license. Certainly the highlight of those foreign films he had seen with her and Arnaud was Ingmar Bergman's *The Seventh Seal*. Chantal had a lot of explaining to do on this one; she began with the story of the medieval knight returning to Sweden from the Crusades, the easy part for those boys to understand. On a winter night in New Hampshire in 1958, the Black Death—a bubonic plague in the middle of the fourteenth century—was harder for those boys to grasp. How the knight meets the personification of Death and the high stakes of the chess game between them were perfectly clear to Jimmy and Arnaud, as was the knight's encounter with the caravan of actors—and how the knight distracts Death long enough for the young couple to escape with their child. Both boys understood how this "one meaningful deed" stands as an act of redemption for the knight.

The going got harder for Chantal when she tried to address how "the silence of God" is such a big deal to the knight. Chantal realized that God's silence was the norm for Arnaud and Jimmy; those boys weren't remotely religious.

Then Chantal got bogged down with the biblical quotation (Revelation 8:1) that begins the film and is repeated near the end. She skipped "the seventh seal" part and hurried her delivery of "there was a silence in heaven for about half an hour," which made both boys laugh.

"There was silence for *only* half an hour?" Arnaud asked, dissolving into uncontrollable laughter.

"I thought there was *always* silence in heaven," James Winslow said more seriously to Chantal, who decided not to mention the final scene in the film—the knight and his companions in a Dance of Death.

She would spare the sixteen- and seventeen-year-old a reminder of the universality of death, Chantal (who was only nineteen) decided. No *Danse Macabre,* no *Totentanz,* for Arnaud and Jimmy. Not even the townspeople of Pennacook were as preoccupied with the inevitability of death as people were in the late Middle Ages, Chantal was thinking.

It turned out that Jonah Feldstein had not only seen *The Seventh Seal;* he'd seen other Bergman films. (Of course he had; Jonah lived in New York, where there was more than one movie theater like the Franklin.) But Jonah and Jimmy agreed that seeing *The Seventh Seal* was one of the experiences that had "formed" them. Death would forever have a human face—the moonlike face of Bengt Ekerot, a Swedish actor.

The two boys disagreed about Dickens. Jonah accepted that *Great Expectations* had been formative for Jimmy; in turn, young James conceded that the portrayal of Fagin in *Oliver Twist* was anti-Semitic.

Where the two boys bonded, incontrovertibly, was with *The Diary of a Young Girl.* The boys hadn't yet met when they each read Anne Frank's diary. For Jonah, *The Diary of a Young Girl* was the *Great Expectations* in his life. It was the book that made him want to be a writer—not a diarist, but a novelist, a storyteller. For young James Winslow, *The Diary of a Young Girl* was the first book that made him cry that *wasn't* a novel; it affected him emotionally, like the nineteenth-century novels he loved.

Anne Frank's diary was first published in English in 1952, when Jimmy was eleven and Jonah only nine. Both the Winslow and Feldstein families thought those boys were too young to read it then. The Winslows allowed Jimmy to read *The Diary of a Young Girl* the summer before he started at Pennacook Academy, when he was fifteen— Anne Frank's age when she wrote her last diary entry. (She died at Bergen-Belsen three months short of turning sixteen.) Jonah read the book around the same time, when he was still in middle school; he was only thirteen—the same age Anne Frank had been when she was given her diary.

Both in their lives before and after wrestling, Jonah and Jimmy would suddenly remember and recite passages from Anne Frank's diary—with disturbing spontaneity, depending on the passage. As young writers, both boys liked reminding each other of one of the earliest diary entries—"it seems to me that later on neither I nor anyone else will be interested in the musings of a thirteen-year-old schoolgirl." A long time after the two friends were schoolboys, whenever Jonah and Jimmy were drinking beer together, they would interject a solemn toast to each other—two lines Anne added as a comment in her diary in 1942. "I'm terrified our hiding place will be discovered and that we'll be shot. That, of course, is a fairly dismal prospect." (The short version of Anne's comment was reverently repeated as a refrain by those two friends—just "a fairly dismal prospect.")

But before those two ever met—the summer Jimmy was just fifteen, when he first read *The Diary of a Young Girl*—the boy was already reciting the passages he'd memorized to his mother. There was a diary entry from October 1942 that young James casually repeated to Honor one night when they were doing the dishes. "Our many Jewish friends and acquaintances are being taken away in droves." Honor had been taken aback; at first she'd thought that Jimmy was just making conversation.

When Honor wrote Esther, telling her how much Jimmy revered Anne Frank, she cited some of her son's favorite quotations. Esther wrote back, asking Honor to share her own list of favorites with Jimmy—beginning with "there are no greater enemies on earth than the Germans and the Jews."

Honor wasn't surprised that Esther liked the last line of a January 1944 diary entry. "If only I had a girlfriend!"

Young James felt a closeness to his birth mother when Esther quoted a long passage from Anne Frank's April 1944 entry. "In the eyes of the world, we're doomed, but if, after all this suffering, there are still Jews left, the Jewish people will be held up as an example. Who knows, maybe our religion will teach the world and all the people in it about goodness, and that's the reason, the only reason, we have to suffer. We can never be just Dutch, or just English, or whatever, we will always be Jews as well. And we'll have to keep on being Jews, but then, we'll want to be."

Like Esther, Jimmy was also moved by Anne Frank's final diary entry in August 1944—her desire to "keep trying to find a way to become what I'd like to be and what I could be if . . . if only there were no other people in the world."

Thomas and Constance Winslow would keep to themselves their thoughts about the end of Anne's diary—"if only there were no other people in the world." To those two, who knew Esther so well, this sounded more like Esther than Anne. And why had Esther stopped sending photos? the senior Winslows wondered. Was she trying to disappear?

For a fifth-year student at Pennacook Academy, there were few photographs of James Winslow in his school yearbooks—not a single photo of his struggles with German, no record of his falling behind in other courses. There was not one photo of Jimmy writing, which the Winslow family would best remember the boy doing—his head bent over a desk or a table, just writing away.

Of course there were wrestling photos of James Winslow in those five yearbooks, including photos of Jimmy in competition as a wrestler and in posed photos of the academy wrestling team—where Jimmy was seated or standing alongside the lightweights. The singlets the schoolboys wore were not the low-cut kind that Moshe Kleinberg and other international wrestlers wore.

Thomas Winslow wondered why the wrestlers in New England wore tights under their singlets; their legs were covered. Was it a matter of American propriety that the wrestlers weren't as exposed, or did they simply prefer to wear more clothes? Constance wondered. This wasn't a question for Coach Ted—not really a wrestling question, Thomas decided.

Moshe Kleinberg was fifty-five in 1961, when he was a referee at the Sixth Maccabiah Games in Israel. Esther sent a photo of his referee certificate. This was prompted by Jimmy's wrestling photos, which Honor had been sending to Esther. "Except for how short he is, Jimmy looks more like me," was all Esther had written about the photo of Moshe's referee certificate. Honor was glad to get a look at Moses Little Mountain's cauliflower ears, and she was delighted to show them to Jimmy. Diligent nurse that she was, Honor drained and attended to her son's cauliflower ears each time he got one.

"Little Mountain's ears look like animal droppings," Faith said, staring with disgust at his referee certificate.

"I've seen some stuff in the kids' diapers that looks like this guy's ears," Hope told everyone.

"We should call Little Mountain 'Dog-Turd Ears,'" was what Prudence had to say about it.

His two moms had made him who he was, James Winslow firmly believed; he saw nothing of himself in his father's referee certificate. (It was like a passport photo; you couldn't see how short Moses Little Mountain was.)

There was a foreignness inside him, Jimmy believed, and it didn't just come from Esther's decision to move to her Jewish homeland. The two-moms idea was part of Jimmy's intrinsic foreignness, or so the boy believed.

Why wouldn't James Winslow believe that giving birth to a child and being a mother were two separate choices? And Jimmy understood what was the same about his two moms: they would never be committed to a lifelong partner. Of course young James thought this lack of commitment to a partner was natural. Why wouldn't Jimmy believe this was also part of his intrinsic foreignness?

James Winslow would love foreign films, as if films with subtitles were natural. It didn't hurt that he saw these films with Arnaud's aunt Chantal. During his last semester of high school, Jimmy was alone with Chantal when she took him to the Franklin to see Godard's *Breathless*—a crime drama with a doomed love story.

In February 1961, Chantal was twenty-one and Jimmy nineteen; they had all the makings of their own doomed love story. Not that Chantal ever encouraged young James to imagine that their seeing foreign films together even remotely resembled a love story. (Jean-Luc Godard and the film's story writer, François Truffaut, were French, and Chantal took her French very seriously.)

That same school year, Thomas Winslow had given his grandson a book—*Four Screenplays of Ingmar Bergman*. It's enough to say that Jimmy Winslow was sufficiently informed of love and doom before his twentieth birthday.

James Winslow had just turned twenty-one in March 1962, his freshman year at the University of New Hampshire—what should have been Chantal's junior year abroad. This time Jimmy called Chantal and invited her to the Franklin, where Truffaut's *Jules et Jim* was playing. "It's probably another doomed love story," he said.

"I know what it is, Jimmy," Chantal told him. It was more of a doomed love story than young James had heretofore imagined. At the end of the movie, when Catherine asks Jim to get in her car, saying she has something to tell him, she also tells Jules to watch them. Jules watches Catherine drive the car off a ruined bridge into a river—killing herself and Jim. Then there's just Jules, attending to their cremation.

Chantal sobbed throughout the film, holding Jimmy's hand during the car scene. Young James realized she'd seen the movie already, maybe by herself or with a date—it didn't matter. Jimmy didn't know what to say, so he just started speaking for the sake of saying something.

"This was almost like a date," Jimmy began. "You cried, you held my hand. . . . I don't really know what I'm saying," he admitted.

"No, this wasn't *at all* like a date, Jimmy," Chantal told him rather crossly. "You weren't pawing my breasts while I pushed you away, you weren't sticking your tongue down my throat while I tried to bite it off," Chantal said, with a certainty similar to the way Jeanne Moreau drives her car off the bridge.

"Oh," was all Jimmy could say. That same year, in 1962, Moshe Kleinberg died of prostate cancer at the age of fifty-six. Esther wrote to Prudence, since she was the doctor in the family. Prudence told Jimmy not to worry about it; she said she would keep an eye on his prostate. Jimmy didn't know how to mourn someone he'd never known; there were characters in novels he had mourned, but he'd known those characters.

When his father died, James Winslow was reading Shakespeare's *Hamlet* for the second time—in freshman English at UNH. He had already read some Shakespeare at Pennacook Academy. "To be, or not to be, that is the question," Hamlet muses to himself.

Jimmy wasn't fooling around when he said to Chantal: "To take, or not to take, a chance on love—that's the question!"

"That's just awkward, Jimmy," Chantal told him. But Jimmy sincerely wondered if he would *ever* take a chance on love.

Like the only mother Jimmy knew and loved—like his birth mom, too, from what he'd heard about Esther—young James Winslow had grounds to doubt he would fall in love. He believed that Moses Little Mountain, his departed birth father, would not have blamed him for having doubts.

14.

Like You

A further thought that Thomas Winslow would keep to himself concerned the Jonah for whom Jonah Feldstein was named— the Hebrew prophet in the Tanakh (the Hebrew Bible), and in the Book of Jonah in the Christian Old Testament. This is the same Jonah who is swallowed by a huge fish. Jonah spends three days and nights in the fish's belly, praying. Then God tells the fish to vomit Jonah out. When Jonah Feldstein was losing a wrestling match, the boy looked like someone who'd been swallowed by a fish and vomited out. Or so Thomas thought; he knew better than to say this, except to his wife.

"Don't tell the Feldsteins, Tommy—they'll think you're anti-Semitic," Constance told him.

Thomas doubted that anyone would think he was anti-Semitic for imagining Jonah Feldstein as the Jonah in the Hebrew and the Christian Bibles, but Thomas didn't say anything to Coach Ted about it. Being swallowed by a fish and vomited out weren't wrestling techniques, Thomas decided.

Being swallowed by a fish and vomited out weren't the kind of wrestling injuries Honor Winslow was obsessed with—she was interested only in the worst ones. What no one knew was that Honor believed the worst wrestling injuries were the best ones. In this respect, Honor Winslow was ahead of her time; she was already looking for an untouchable draft deferment for her dear James. Honor wanted Jimmy to be reclassified 4-F—"registrant not acceptable for military service due to physical, mental, or moral defect." The physical defect was the one Honor was aiming for. Being swallowed by a fish and vomited out might lead to a mental defect—probably not a moral one. Honor Winslow even knew the knee surgery she was imagining for Jimmy.

In the 1970s, when arthroscopic partial meniscectomy (or meniscal repair) began to displace open meniscal surgery, a torn meniscus was no big deal. Nowadays, arthroscopic surgery for a torn meniscus is one of the easier knee surgeries you can have. Not in the 1960s, when the Smillie knife was used in an open manner to remove the entire meniscus—as Honor Winslow was aware.

A no-holds-barred meniscectomy was the way they did it in the 1960s. On her desk, Honor Winslow kept a photo of the Smillie cartilage knife. The handle of the instrument looked like the letter *T,* and the working end was shaped like a spatula—to make cuts into the menisci in the knee. Not that Jimmy Winslow had the slightest idea what the instrument was. All Jimmy knew was that his mother was an OB-GYN nurse; he wasn't going to ask her what that instrument was for.

Whatever Esther was up to, in her secretive way, she'd been trained as a nurse. Honor wrote Esther about the "usefulness" of a certain kind of wrestling injury for her dear James; an injury requiring open meniscal surgery would be "desirable," Honor wrote. Greco-Roman wrestlers weren't as prone to knee surgeries, Esther wrote back.

Esther knew some Greco-Roman guys in the Haifa wrestling club who'd had the "Smillie surgery" (as she called it). "We'll keep our boy out of a war," Esther assured Honor. "Nearer the time, let's hope we find a better option than Smillie." To Honor, there was no better option than Smillie. That surgery did real damage; in a loving mother's mind, that surgery had 4-F written all over it.

James Winslow knew his mom and Chantal Beaudette were seeing more of each other, just the two of them, but why would the boy think twice about it? Arnaud told Jimmy that his aunt Chantal admired Jimmy's mom. Maybe Honor Winslow was a beacon of independence for a young woman like Chantal, who'd stayed aloof from anything resembling a relationship. (Chantal's closeness to his mother made Jimmy more conscious of the doomed nature of his infatuation with Arnaud's alluring aunt.)

And why would Coach Ted think twice when Honor Winslow asked him if the worst wrestling injuries happened in a match—not in practice? Ted told her it made no difference. If you were wrestling, you could get injured—in a match or in practice. In a match, a referee might stop a situation that looked "potentially dangerous," Coach Ted explained. In practice, no ref was watching. Ted thought Honor looked somehow relieved to know this; there was no fathoming what went on in the minds of wrestlers' mothers, the coach knew. It didn't occur to Coach Ted that Honor Winslow *wanted* Jimmy to get one of the worst wrestling injuries—meaning one of the best ones.

Now that Jimmy was a student at UNH, he was no longer competing as a wrestler. Honor had imagined he was less likely to be injured, because Jimmy was just working out with the Pennacook Academy wrestlers. Honor was indeed relieved to know that he was no less likely to be injured in practice.

James wondered why his mom and Chantal Beaudette still attended the academy wrestling matches. Jimmy was just helping with the coaching. He definitely knew those two women weren't there to watch him wrestle.

The way his mother explained it to Jimmy was that Jonah Feldstein was still competing as a wrestler. "Jonah is your new best friend, Jimmy, and I just love that little boy!" Honor declared. James Winslow was certainly aware of how much his mom loved hugging Jonah. "Jonah's so small, he reminds me of hugging you when you were little," Jimmy's mother told him. Why wouldn't this seem plausible to Jimmy?

When Jonah got injured one day, Honor and Chantal were watching the match, but those two were also talking. Coach Ted and Jimmy were sitting beside each other; before Jonah screamed, they both saw the injury coming. "That does it," Ted said. "A twisting force on a loaded leg—that'll do it, Jimmy," the coach told him. It was a twisting knee injury. Jonah's leg was rotated when the boy's weight was stuck on the mat on that same foot—a sickening injury to see, but Jimmy's mom and Chantal kept talking till Jonah screamed.

"Let the trainer immobilize Jonah's knee before we move him," Coach Ted told Jimmy. Once Jonah's knee was immobilized, but before they moved him, Jimmy's mom was out on the mat, hugging Jonah like she was Jonah's mother.

"Your mom was imagining you were injured, Jimmy," Chantal told him later.

There was a half-truth to this cover-up, young James Winslow would realize—long after the fact of Jonah Feldstein's knee injury. (The whole truth was that Honor Winslow wished her son was the one with the twisting knee injury.)

In his post-op state of mind, Jonah Feldstein wouldn't remember how his orthopedic surgeon described the "injury mechanism" that led to Jonah's meniscectomy—his Smillie surgery. (Jonah just said that Coach Ted's description of the injury was easier to understand.)

James Winslow wasn't paying attention when his mom described the strategy of Jonah's surgery. "Beginning with the anterior horn, the surgeon cuts the body of the meniscus from the capsule and displaces it in the middle of the knee," Honor Winslow recited to her son. "Lastly, the posterior horn is cut free and the entire meniscus is removed." (She didn't tell Jimmy that Jonah was lucky; Jonah's meniscus didn't break, which would have led to more invasive surgery.) "They'll put Jonah in a cast—this allows scar tissue to fill the void left from the meniscectomy," was how Jimmy's mom explained it. Honor knew when her son wasn't really listening. Budding writer that he was, the word *void* didn't get Jimmy's attention.

When Jonah's cast came off and the stitches were removed, James

Winslow would remember the fuss his mother made. There was quite a scar on Jonah's knee from the incision made by the scalpel. Honor Winslow was impatient for the scar to heal sufficiently for her to start massaging it. Jimmy couldn't watch the way his mom massaged Jonah's scar. Honor would bear down with her index finger; the muscles of her forearm were tensed as she followed the scar made by the scalpel. "You should do this yourself, Jonah—you can't overdo it," the good nurse told the boy. "The more you massage it, the less it will stand out."

"I don't care if the scar stands out—it's on my leg. It's not like everyone will see it," Jonah said. He was wincing in a way that made Jimmy think you could definitely overdo the massaging of a scar. (Jimmy had no doubt that his mom was overdoing it.)

Jonah Feldstein wasn't worrying about the adverse side effects of his Smillie surgery. He'd been warned that he might not be able to run, Jonah told Jimmy. "We're going to be *writers,* Jonah—the only injuries we have to avoid are *writing* injuries," Jimmy told his new best friend. Honor could hear those two boys laughing.

You won't get reclassified 4-F for *writing* injuries, Honor Winslow was thinking. She'd already written Esther about a more pressing problem. Her dear James had studied German for five years, but Jimmy's German was a struggle. He spoke the language hesitantly, in a faltering voice; when spoken to, he strained to understand. James Winslow would take two more years of German at the University of New Hampshire, enough to satisfy the university's requirement for a foreign language. The year abroad in Vienna was what Jimmy and his mom worried about.

At the time, the study-abroad program was called the Institute for European Studies. IES accepted James Winslow to their program in Vienna. They assured him that he'd had more German than many of their students; Jimmy would be in an advanced German class. Jimmy felt somewhat reassured, but not his mother. Honor had already written Esther, asking if she knew any German tutors.

"Don't worry! A young Jewish woman will watch over our boy—she's a guard dog!" Esther wrote back. This worried Honor more.

James Winslow would be twenty-two when he went to Vienna. His mom didn't think he needed a young Jewish woman guarding him. "Jimmy just needs a German tutor," Honor wrote to Esther.

"This woman knows Vienna—she's an Israeli, but she knows German," Esther wrote. Now the Rosenthals were worried, too.

"An Israeli isn't in Vienna to be a German tutor," Daniel Rosenthal told Honor. Yes, of course there was an Israeli Embassy in Vienna, but there were also some serious Nazi hunters around. As Naomi Rosenthal pointed out, Simon Wiesenthal opened the Jewish Documentation Center in Vienna in 1961. Wiesenthal had survived the Nazi death camps and his documentation of Holocaust crimes assisted Mossad agents in the capture of Nazi war criminals.

One of Wiesenthal's more current cases was Karl Silberbauer, the Gestapo officer who'd arrested Anne Frank. Silberbauer was working as a police inspector in Austria in 1963 when Wiesenthal identified him to the Vienna police. Silberbauer would be suspended, but the Austrian government let him off the hook. This happened in November 1963, when James Winslow was a student in Vienna, but his tutor never mentioned it, and Esther didn't write a word about it. The Austrian government stated that Anne Frank's arrest didn't warrant Silberbauer's arrest or his prosecution as a war criminal. And Otto Frank, Anne's father, testified that Silberbauer had "behaved correctly" and "only done his job." The police review board exonerated Silberbauer of guilt; the Vienna police gave him a desk job.

Honor Winslow was weirdly reminded of the time she wrote Esther about how much she and Jimmy liked *High Noon,* the Western with Gary Cooper and Grace Kelly. It was 1952; Jimmy was only eleven. When Esther wrote back, she told Honor to take Jimmy to the movie again. Fred Zinnemann was the director; his parents were Austrian Jews who'd been murdered in the Holocaust. Like Billy Wilder, Zinnemann was a European Jew who had a wonderful influence on American movies. "Fred Zinnemann made a Jewish Western," Esther wrote.

All the Winslows went to see *High Noon* again; the first time they saw it, they hadn't realized they were seeing a Jewish Western. They didn't get what was Jewish about it the second time, either. "Maybe you have to be Jewish to get what's Jewish about it," Constance Winslow said. But the Rosenthals saw *High Noon* a second time, too; they knew Fred Zinnemann's story and what Esther thought of the film.

"The Grace Kelly character is a Quaker and a pacifist—she certainly isn't Jewish," Daniel Rosenthal said.

"Maybe you have to be *Esther* to get what's Jewish about *High Noon*," Naomi said.

The folks in the small town in New Mexico Territory, the ones who won't support the town marshal, reminded Thomas Winslow of the townspeople of Pennacook. "Maybe Esther thought the townspeople in *High Noon* were like anti-Semites, Connie," Thomas said.

"I think that's your idea, Tommy—not Esther's *or* Fred Zinnemann's," Constance told him.

The following year, Fred Zinnemann directed *From Here to Eternity.* Strangely, Esther didn't write to tell everyone to see it. Thomas and Constance learned their daughters snuck Jimmy into the theater, along with Arnaud and Chantal, to see the film. Like Chantal, the senior Winslows doubted those boys were old enough to watch it. They needn't have worried. Young James was bored, Honor told them. It was no *High Noon;* there was nothing as good as the gunfight, or Tex Ritter's singing "Do Not Forsake Me, Oh My Darlin'."

Thomas Winslow was serious when he asked the Rosenthals if they'd seen anything Jewish in *From Here to Eternity.* "Jews don't have sex outdoors—especially not on a beach, Tommy," Daniel told him. Constance and Naomi laughed, but Thomas was speechless with embarrassment. "I was just kidding, Tommy," Daniel Rosenthal said.

Esther wasn't kidding when she wrote the Rosenthals and the

Winslows advising them to ignore what Freud had called the Austrian novelist and playwright Arthur Schnitzler. Esther explained that Freud and Schnitzler were fellow residents of the Leopoldstadt district of Vienna. Freud called Schnitzler a "colleague" in the study of the "underestimated and much-maligned erotic."

"Believe me—the erotic has nothing to do with why I want the kid to read Schnitzler's *The Road into the Open* before he gets to Vienna. The rest of you will hate it—especially you, Tommy," Esther wrote. She did not mention modernism, a literary movement Thomas Winslow loathed, but Esther knew an oppressive novel about a Christian aristocrat whose principal friendships are with Jewish intellectuals in pre–World War I Viennese society—at a time when anti-Semitism is on the rise—would not be Thomas's cup of tea.

Der Weg ins Freie, the German title, was first published in 1908—the English translation in 1913. Esther praised Schnitzler for his prescience of the anti-Semitism to come. In what she wrote to the Rosenthals and the Winslows, she emphasized that *Judenhaß*—the word for anti-Semitism in German—means "hatred of the Jews."

Schnitzler's books were banned by the Nazis in Austria and Germany. Hitler called Schnitzler's writing "Jewish filth." In 1933, when Goebbels was organizing book bannings in Berlin, Schnitzler's books were burned with the works of other Jews—Einstein, Marx, Kafka, Freud, and Stefan Zweig.

But this wasn't what Esther wanted Jimmy to notice about *The Road into the Open.* "The kid has to read it to the end—then he'll see it's not just a novel of manners, then he'll know what this novel is really about," Esther wrote.

Thus challenged by his birth mom "to read it to the end," Jimmy Winslow would read the novel very carefully; he also read everything he could find about Arthur Schnitzler's life. Schnitzler had studied medicine at the University of Vienna; he worked at Vienna's General Hospital before he stopped practicing medicine in order to write. Schnitzler would separate from his wife; they had a daughter who committed suicide when she was nineteen. He himself died in 1931.

James Winslow was twenty-two in March 1963, when President Kennedy reintroduced draft deferment for men who had children. JFK's Executive Order No. 11098 stated that any man, married or single, could be classified 3-A if he maintained "a bona fide family relationship" with a child or children—"registrant deferred by reason of extreme hardship to dependents." Honor Winslow was paying attention; she kept watch on Kennedy's increasing involvement in Vietnam. (In 1961, JFK sent four hundred Green Berets to train South Vietnamese soldiers.)

But Jimmy Winslow was up to his ears in Schnitzler's Vienna; he couldn't have told you what a 3-A draft classification was. Jimmy hadn't noticed the 1961 test runs of the U.S. herbicidal warfare program in South Vietnam. (In 1962, Operation Ranch Hand and Operation Trail Dust began; U.S. planes would spray herbicides and defoliants over South Vietnam until 1971.)

Thomas Winslow knew his grandson was no Renaissance man. Young James was a dreamer. A writer in the making is a novel in progress, Thomas thought. Jimmy was focused on Baron Georg von Wergenthin, the standoffish Christian aristocrat in Vienna. For a main character, Georg is not very likable—or so Jimmy complained to his grandfather. The baron confesses to feeling consoled by his lack of closeness to other human beings. He mocks Willy Eissler, a Jewish friend, for Willy's seeming oversensitivity to anti-Semitism. Georg von Wergenthin believes he has no grudge against Jews; yet he complains that he only encounters Jews who are ashamed of being Jewish, or those who are proud of being Jewish but afraid you'll mistake them for Jews who are ashamed of it.

"It helps to be Jewish to get what anti-Semitism is," Thomas told his grandson. In *The Road into the Open,* they were both confused by the apparent anti-Semitism among the Jewish characters. And there was so much contradictory dialogue about Zionism, it was hard to know what

Schnitzler thought about it, but Jimmy and his grandfather agreed that Schnitzler probably sided with Herr Ehrenberg, who admits he'd like to see Jerusalem before he dies.

"Me, too, Grandpa—I want to see Jerusalem," Jimmy said.

"Dear boy, that would make your mother worry *more*," Thomas told him. "The problem with *The Road into the Open* is that there's too much dialogue—this is to be expected when a playwright writes a novel," Thomas Winslow said, changing the subject. Thomas was not only reverting to being an English teacher; he knew the two-moms idea didn't include the possibility that James Winslow would go to Jerusalem.

Their quibbles with Schnitzler's writing left both James and Thomas Winslow unprepared for the death of Baron von Wergenthin and Anna Rosner's child—a boy, strangled at birth by his umbilical cord. The doctor leaves Georg alone with his dead child, who strikes the Baron as a creature of undreamed-of perfection—destined to pass from one darkness to another.

Anna Rosner and Georg von Wergenthin aren't married. The death of their child absolves the baron of whatever sense of duty would have compelled him to marry Anna. Georg's friends feel no pity for the child who never lived; they believe Georg and Anna are fortunate to have avoided a questionable marriage. Yet Georg and Anna are devastated by the death of their child; their relationship is over because Anna won't undergo the agony again. The baron wonders if an unborn child can die of insufficient love; he wonders if his child has died because no one truly longed for it to be born. At the same time, Baron von Wergenthin realizes (more deeply than ever) how much he wants to be free.

As Esther had known Jimmy would see, a *wanted* child really matters. Both Jimmy and his grandfather were distraught. The child who never lived made James Winslow aware of how much his two moms had longed for him to be born.

"Esther was always a good reader, Tommy," Constance reminded her husband.

"Right you are, Connie—I didn't see the dead child coming," Thomas admitted.

What both senior Winslows *did* see coming was that Chantal Beaudette and Honor were cooking something up together. After all, Thomas and Constance were very much aware of what their fourth daughter had cooked up with Esther.

"It looks like another kind of two-moms idea to me, Tommy," Constance said. Thomas argued that Honor had the only child she wanted, and—to Thomas's thinking—what set Chantal apart from the rest of those Beaudette girls was that Chantal wanted nothing to do with boys or babies. (Especially nothing to do with *babies,* Constance thought to herself.)

"So it appears, Tommy, but when I see two women talking this exclusively and intently to each other, I think they must be talking about sex or childbirth—or both," Constance told him. She knew Thomas Winslow would have been happier defending Modernism as a literary movement than he would willingly talk about sex or childbirth—God forbid both.

In May 1963, the Buddhists were demonstrating in South Vietnam—not that Jimmy Winslow appeared to care. As he told Chantal, he was more concerned that Arnaud never answered his letters or made only the most cursory replies.

"Arnaud isn't a writer, Jimmy," Chantal told him. "When Arnaud is with you, he's totally there—when he's away, he's totally gone."

"I saw you talking to Chantal. Do you find her attractive?" Jimmy's mom asked him.

"Do I find her *what?*" Jimmy exclaimed.

"Jimmy, I'm just asking if you think Chantal is sexually attractive. I'm just asking, honey," his mother said.

"I think Chantal is very attractive, but she's Arnaud's aunt," Jimmy pointed out.

"You and Chantal—you're just the same!" Honor declared. "What does Arnaud have to do with it?"

In June 1963, a protesting Buddhist monk burned himself to death in Saigon; there were photos of the monk's self-immolation in U.S. newspapers. As young James Winslow told Chantal, he was more interested to know what his mother was thinking.

"Just imagine that you get me pregnant, Jimmy," Chantal began. "We get married, or not—or we get married and divorced—but the custody of our child is entirely yours," Chantal told him.

"It's like you do an *Esther,*" Jimmy said. (He was only beginning to get the picture.)

"If you're the single parent of our child, you don't get drafted, Jimmy," Chantal explained. "We don't have to live together, or have a real relationship," Chantal told him—as if a real relationship were the worst thing she could imagine.

"Arnaud will go bananas," was all Jimmy could think of saying.

"If I knew I could keep Arnaud out of a war, I would have *his* baby—Arnaud will go bananas either way!" Chantal told him.

"*I'll* go bananas either way!" Jimmy exclaimed.

"You're going to Vienna, Jimmy—maybe it's better if you knock up a European girl," Chantal suggested.

If Isaac and Bluma Drucker had been alive, they would have been too old to know what Esther was arranging in Vienna. Only the Rosenthals had noticed the German tutor's name—die Hauslehrerin, "the private tutor," was a certain Fräulein Annelies Eissler.

"Annelies Marie Frank was Anne Frank's full name," Naomi Rosenthal told the senior Winslows.

"And you remember Schnitzler's Willy Eissler, Tommy—the oversensitive Jew who thinks 'every ambiguous smile' is anti-Semitic," Daniel said.

"You're saying Fräulein Eissler has a made-up name—she's not a coincidence?" Thomas asked.

"She sounds fictional—it's a name an operative would have," Daniel answered.

"An *operative*—you make Fräulein Eissler sound like a secret agent!" Constance exclaimed.

"We know Esther has Mossad connections, Connie," Naomi reminded her.

"We know the Mossad operates beyond Israel's borders—that's no secret," Daniel said.

"But we're just guessing, Daniel. No one knows exactly how Esther and Fräulein Eissler are connected," Naomi said.

"Yes, we're just guessing," Daniel told the Winslows. "No one knows what Esther's connections really are—we just think Esther and Fräulein Eissler are working together."

The senior Winslows would tell the Rosenthals that Honor had recently written Esther, inquiring if Fräulein Eissler knew any wrestlers in Vienna. Was there a wrestling club, a gym where Jimmy could continue to work out with other wrestlers?

What were those two moms cooking up together *now*? both the Rosenthals and the senior Winslows were wondering. If Honor Winslow wanted her dear James to keep wrestling, she'd not given up on the Smillie surgery. And if Chantal Beaudette was reluctant to do an *Esther,* maybe Annelies Eissler knew a European girl Jimmy could knock up.

His grandfather was right: James Winslow was a dreamer, in the way young writers in the making are. Yet Jimmy had read *The Diary of a Young Girl* and *The Road into the Open* very carefully; Jimmy knew where Annelies Eissler came from. At first, he'd imagined that his birth mom might be his German tutor—he'd hoped that Esther had made up Annelies Eissler to disguise herself. But Jimmy was told that his tutor was a "young" woman; he knew his birth mother's story.

Esther was fifty-eight in 1963. It was nonetheless encouraging to young James Winslow to believe his birth mom must have had a hand in choosing his Jewish German tutor, not only her name. Jimmy wanted to write Esther and thank her for not naming his tutor Anna

Rosner—Baron von Wergenthin's unmarried lover, the woman whose baby dies in childbirth—but Jimmy guessed that writing to his birth mother wouldn't be welcomed or allowed.

Jimmy was satisfied with whispering to Esther as he fell asleep. "Like you, I'm going to Vienna first—then to Jerusalem," he whispered. "Like you." And during the day, unconsciously, he would sometimes say it out loud. "Like you."

15.

Over the Phone

Thomas Winslow couldn't have known that his beloved grandson was already reimagining him as the main character in what would be the young man's first novel. That summer of 1963, before young James left for Europe, Thomas gave him Henry Fielding's novel *The History of Tom Jones, a Foundling,* a picaresque comedy written in the eighteenth century. It was a bildungsroman with a romantic ending.

"Oh, Tommy—a foundling for the child of a foundling!" Constance told him, bursting into tears. Thomas was crying, too. They were good grandparents, who only sought to protect their grandson; yet their Jimmy's belief in his intrinsic foreignness was unshakeable. He was determined to see himself as an orphan. All Thomas and Constance could do for the boy was to give him an orphan's story with a happy ending.

While young James was immersed in his summer reading, Honor Winslow was worrying about her son's unpacked steamer trunk. No one in the Winslow family had ever packed for a year abroad. Jimmy's mom was exasperated with him; he demonstrated no interest in selecting his winter clothes, nor the ability to do so. Honor had written Esther and asked her about winters in Austria. "His clothes for winter in New Hampshire will work," was all Esther wrote back. Esther had more to say about the wrestling gym in Vienna.

The Greco-Roman wrestlers Esther knew from the club in Haifa recommended a gym, Turnhalle Leopold, on Währinger Straße. Esther asked Fräulein Eissler about the gym. As it turned out, Leopold Spiegel, who owned the gym and coached a Greco-Roman team there, was a friend of Fräulein Eissler's. "Leo is a former Greco-Roman wrestler, a little guy," Fräulein Eissler wrote to Esther.

Fräulein Eissler knew the differences between Greco-Roman and freestyle wrestling and she knew Jimmy Winslow was a freestyle wrestler, not a Greco guy. There were no holds allowed below the waist in Greco-Roman wrestling. Freestyle wrestlers are catch-as-catch-can guys; the Greco guys like body locks and arm drags and upper-body throws. Freestyle wrestlers were welcome at Turnhalle Leopold, but there wasn't a team for them. There were only four freestyle wrestlers who worked out regularly, two Israelis and two Soviets. Only one Israeli and one Soviet were in James Winslow's weight class. "Leo tells me those two workout partners will be good enough," Fräulein Eissler wrote to Esther.

The Greco-Roman wrestlers Esther knew from the club in Haifa spoke of Leopold Spiegel in reverential tones. *Spiegel* means "mirror" in German. Leo was called Kleiner Spiegel ("Little Mirror") because he imitated the moves his opponents made. Then Leo did what they did better. The little guy was a suplay master. You didn't go chest to chest with him, or he would throw you on your head.

Fräulein Eissler knew the two Israeli wrestlers. "A couple of Haganah graybeards," Esther called them. Fräulein Eissler said the Israeli wrestlers were in their late thirties now.

Jimmy Winslow asked Coach Ted if he thought the graybeards were too old to be wrestling. "If the Israelis are European-trained, they could still be pretty tough," Ted said.

According to Fräulein Eissler, the Soviet wrestlers were in medical school in Vienna. "Two former Red Army wrestlers, likely working for the KGB," was all Esther said about the Soviets. Fräulein Eissler added that the Russians were older than the average med student, but she confirmed they were in medical school.

As Coach Ted would tell Jimmy, if the Soviets had wrestled for the Red Army team—as CSKA Moscow, a Russian sports club, was referred to in the West—the Soviets were probably pretty tough. To young James Winslow, his wrestling workout partners in Vienna just sounded old.

That summer of 1963, Arnaud Beaudette was back home in Pennacook. He and Jimmy hung out together, trying to be best friends again. As always, Arnaud was more resolute and unwavering about his plans than Jimmy ever was. Having graduated college, Arnaud would soon be headed to Fort Benning, Georgia—to the U.S. Army Officer Candidate School. "OCS is the way to go, Jimmy—it's better to be an officer," Arnaud said.

"You're going to Vienna, Jimmy—maybe it's better if you knock up a European girl," Arnaud's aunt Chantal had told young James. Now he felt embarrassed and ashamed; he couldn't tell Arnaud the truth, but the prospect of knocking up a European girl was far more appealing to him than the very idea of officer candidate school.

Jimmy tried to engage Arnaud in other areas of conversation. He told his friend that he had a Jewish German tutor, just to see what Arnaud would say. Arnaud disappointed him. "That's exactly what the Nazis deserve, after what they did!" Arnaud said. Arnaud was laughing; he must have thought it would be funny to have a Jewish German teacher.

James Winslow would change the subject to Arnaud's aunt Chantal. "What do you suppose Chantal really wants—what do you think her hopes and expectations are?" he asked Arnaud.

To Jimmy's surprise, Arnaud kept laughing. "Chantal imagines herself married to a Frenchman and living in Paris—only the two of them, no kids!" he said. "Just imagine a Frenchman in Paris being happy with *only* Chantal!"

Young James knew how many babies' butts Chantal had wiped in the Beaudette household. No kids for Chantal made sense to Jimmy, who could imagine being happy with *only* Chantal—even in Pennacook. This wasn't a conversation Jimmy could pursue with Arnaud. (Or with Chantal.) From such a watershed moment—the recognition that his best friend in childhood and adolescence was lost to him—young James sought solace in the packing of his steamer trunk.

Whether or not Chantal Beaudette had big breasts, or only a *onesie*, she was no dummy. "You and Arnaud are very different young men, Jimmy—you're not the boys you were," Chantal said. "What would be the point of your telling Arnaud you want to be a novelist like Charles Dickens? Arnaud doesn't *read* novels anymore!"

An unexpected bond between Chantal Beaudette and Jimmy was their mutual interest in male circumcision, which Constance Winslow would see for herself in the Pennacook Public Library. She'd expected her grandson to be curious about the subject one day; between nakedness in shower rooms, or when wrestlers weigh in, Constance knew Jimmy would have seen uncircumcised penises. Then there was the day when Chantal and Jimmy asked for the same issue of the same medical journal; as Constance had foreseen, it was only a matter of time before they discovered their mutual interest in circumcision history.

In 1941, 75 percent of boys born in urban hospitals in the U.S. were circumcised. In 1942–43, following the Battle of Guadalcanal, there was mass circumcision of U.S. soldiers in the Pacific—due to "an outbreak of phimosis and paraphimosis." (The soldiers' foreskins were so tight they cut off circulation to the tips of their penises.) After the war, former military circumcisers promoted circumcision to the masses—in both medical and popular journals. And after U.S. troops landed in South Korea, in 1950—during the subsequent U.S. occupation, boyhood circumcision became a near-universal practice in South Korea. By 1955, the rate of routine circumcision in Australia peaked at 90 percent. Given Jimmy's and Chantal's interest in penis cutting, Constance again succumbed to the subject.

Both Chantal Beaudette and Constance Winslow would notice that after World War II, there was scant mention of the Italian and German soldiers, who had uncut penises. Jimmy had exhibited no interest in *uncut* penises until that day in the Pennacook Public Library when Chantal said: "Frenchmen, Jimmy—the ones in France who are your age and mine—are *uncut.*" Constance hadn't known this; she would have been embarrassed to ask Chantal which issue of what journal told her about uncut Frenchmen. Jimmy remembered thinking there might one day be a lucky guy in France.

As for the steamer trunk, James Winslow wouldn't remember later if it was shipped ahead of him to Vienna, or if it traveled with him on the ship that sailed from New York Harbor to Europe. As a writer in the making, Jimmy was more alert in his imagination than he was attentive to the details of his own life. He would remember little of getting to Vienna, but he'd already imagined himself *being* there—a foreigner in a foreign city.

The students at the Institute for European Studies sailed on the *Queen Elizabeth,* a virtual hotel. There were German classes onboard. For the most part, James Winslow was relieved to find that though his German wasn't very good, almost no one knew any German at all. They showed movies on the ship, too. All Jimmy would remember of his transatlantic voyage was Tony Richardson's film of *Tom Jones*— Jimmy thought it was wonderful. The boy wouldn't remember where the *Queen Elizabeth* first docked in Europe—maybe Cherbourg. Somehow the IES students crossed the English Channel. Jimmy remembered nothing of London, or whether the IES students were taken to Oxford or Cambridge—it was one or the other. And did they go to Scotland— to Edinburgh, maybe? James Winslow would have no idea. There were lots of lectures wherever the IES students went. (The lectures made Jimmy feel like a tourist; he tuned them out.)

James Winslow would remember Bruges, in northwestern Belgium. (Perhaps the ship from Scotland had landed in Oostende?) Bruges was a medieval city; there were lots of canals. Young James was excited to be around people who weren't speaking English. He tried to talk to a young chambermaid who spoke Flemish; they discovered they both spoke bad German. She was pretty, but she was missing an eyetooth. (To a New Hampshire boy, this made her look like a pretty hockey player.) They kissed on a bridge over one of the canals. That was all, only a kiss. Jimmy Winslow would remember Bruges and the Flemish chambermaid who kissed him—his first foreign experience in a foreign country.

The IES students traveled along the Rhine. The historical river came with consequences—lots of cathedrals, many lectures, more tuning-out. Did they travel by boat, by train, by bus—all three? James Winslow wouldn't remember. On their way to Vienna, Jimmy made two friends among the IES students. One was a handsome and entertaining Jewish boy from Chicago. The other was a Cornell student who'd grown up in Ithaca; like Jimmy, he wanted to be a writer. Their German was better than Jimmy's; he would learn from them. Two American friends were enough, Jimmy decided.

The Institute for European Studies arranged for their students to board with families in Vienna. James Winslow wanted to distance himself from his fellow American students. He wanted to meet his family and see where in the city he would be living. Most of all, he was looking forward to meeting his Jewish German tutor. Regarding how to contact Fräulein Eissler, Esther had been unusually explicit to Jimmy's mother. "Tell the kid to call Annelies as soon as he has settled in with his family in Vienna," Esther had written.

As a writer in the making, James Winslow had written Fräulein Eissler's phone number everywhere. He'd even carved her phone number with a knife on the case carrying his portable typewriter. The IES students had teased Jimmy about lugging his old Underwood with him, but you wouldn't ship a typewriter in a steamer trunk, would you? And if young James bought a new portable typewriter in Vienna, wouldn't it have a German keyboard? (Such was the would-be writer's thought process that led him to tote the battered typewriter through Europe.)

Along the Rhine, Jimmy wrapped a leftover chunk of sausage in wax paper. He saved the sausage in the Underwood—in the hollowed-out area where the typewriter's keys were nestled closely together. (The bratwurst in Germany may have made a more enduring impression on him than the lectures.) The smell of sausage would linger eternally on the keys of James Winslow's little typewriter. He believed that once he was settled in with his family in Vienna and arranged his things in his room, he would find a way to deodorize the Underwood. He didn't anticipate how long it would take him to get accustomed to Frau Holzinger's family in the widow's apartment on the Schwindgasse. Jimmy's sausage-smelling typewriter would wait. And young James didn't know he would be sharing the Holzingers' apartment with two other students—not fellow Americans, not from the Institute for European Studies. They were foreign exchange students, studying at the University of Vienna— a young woman from the Netherlands, a young man from France.

Jolanda Lammers was from Amsterdam. A tall, thin girl—her angular face was handsome in a boyish, defiant way. A breakup with her girlfriend had precipitated Jolanda's coming to Vienna. (Jolanda was very attractive to Jimmy, in her unapproachable way.) Claude Guilbert was from Paris, where he'd tired of his aristocratic family's matchmaking. Claude's parents, in league with his uncles and aunts, were always introducing him to the marriageable daughters of other Parisian aristocrats. (Jimmy tried to refrain from suggesting Claude should meet Chantal Beaudette.) Naturally, Claude and Jolanda were fluent in German; their classes at the university were in German. And those two spoke excellent English. To young James, Jolanda and Claude were models of European sophistication. They shared a pair of rooms adjacent to the Holzingers' kitchen. There was no door between their two rooms—just a narrow doorway, with a curtain. Jolanda had the room with the window, overlooking the Schwindgasse sidewalk. She was trying to give up smoking, Jolanda explained. "When I need a cigarette, I exhale out the window," she told Jimmy.

"I can still smell the smoke through the curtain," Claude said.

"I can hear you when you beat off, Claude," Jolanda told him.

"I hear *you* sometimes, Jolanda," Claude said.

"I hear Claude *every* time," Jolanda told Jimmy.

Claude and Jolanda had been in residence with the Holzingers for only a week before James Winslow arrived, yet those two already resembled a long-married, contentious couple. In one area, Claude and Jolanda were united; they agreed about the dysfunctional nature of the Holzinger family, and they'd learned the house rules. (Jimmy thought Claude and Jolanda were the best thing about his year abroad, so far.)

"We foreign students are allowed to make local calls from the landlady's phone in the living room," Claude told Jimmy.

"Frau Holzinger usually hangs around and listens to your call," Jolanda added. Claude nodded.

Frau Holzinger didn't speak or understand a word of English, as young James discovered when he asked her if he could use her phone in the living room to call Fräulein Eissler. Jimmy confused the word for "private tutor" (*Hauslehrerin*) with the word for "landlady" (*Hausbesitzerin*). He'd asked his landlady if he could use her phone to call his landlady. After this confusion was cleared up, Frau Holzinger lingered in the living room during Jimmy's first conversation with Fräulein Eissler, who spoke English with precise deliberation and a strong Austrian accent.

"We will spend six tutorial hours a week together—three times a week, two hours at a time," Annelies Eissler began. "It will work best for you if we do it three days in a row," she said.

"Three days in a row," young James repeated. He was already infatuated with Fräulein Eissler's voice.

"That way, it's more intense," she said.

"More *intensive*?" Jimmy asked her—what he thought she meant.

"More intensive *und* more intense," Annelies Eissler insisted. Her voice was giving him a hard-on in his landlady's living room, where

Frau Holzinger frowned at him—as if she doubted this was a local call. She was a doomed-looking widow, James Winslow was thinking—the way he would describe her in writing, he thought. Evidently, Frau Holzinger didn't like her foreign students to make complicated calls—not even locally.

"And where would our tutorials take place—where would I meet you?" Jimmy asked his Jewish German tutor.

"Where you sleep," Annelies answered. Her voice had a possibly derisive tone—as if she'd said, *In your dreams,* James Winslow was thinking (or writing). Was Fräulein Eissler mocking him, or had he just misheard her? "You have a room, don't you? I presume you sleep somewhere," she said.

Jimmy was watching the widow Holzinger. The Frau was fussing with the ancient and soiled antimacassars on the arms and headrests of the sofas and chairs. No one liked the living room. Jimmy and Claude and Jolanda were welcome to use it, but up to now the foreign students went there only when they needed to make a call. Frau Holzinger herself didn't appear to like the living room, although she was often in it, despairing over the shabby furniture—or despairing over Irmgard, her unmarried daughter.

The daughter was a single mother who seemed angry and depressed. She was often sleeping on one of the sofas, lying on her back in such splayed disarray that Jimmy more than once imagined she'd been raped and murdered there. Her five-year-old son, Siegfried, sadistically slaughtered his armies of plaster soldiers on the living room rug. Young James and his fellow students would be wary of new casualties during their discomforting phone calls—their discomfort caused by Frau Holzinger's impatience for the calls to be fertig ("finished").

Across the hall from Jimmy's bedroom was a bathroom, which he shared with Jolanda, Claude, and Siegfried. Siegfried's depressed and angry mother bathed him in the bathtub. As the widow Holzinger had explained, the foreign students' bathroom was the only one with a tub.

The Frenchman was morbidly afraid of Siegfried. In addition to the ceaseless carnage caused by the boy in the living room, the foreign students found his decapitated (or otherwise amputated) soldiers in their bathtub. The enterprising child used a garlic press to maim his soldiers. For some reason, the garlic press made Jimmy more afraid of Siegfried's unmarried mother, Irmgard.

There was a toilet, solely a water closet, farther along the hall from Jimmy's bedroom. James, Jolanda, and Claude were allowed to make coffee or tea in the Holzinger family's kitchen, where they also kept beer in the fridge. Where the Holzingers slept was off-limits to the foreign students, who knew there was another bathroom in the Holzinger apartment. But the students never saw it; they only knew it didn't have a tub.

As a foreign student, Jimmy was allowed to have visitors in his room. "Up to a point," as the Frau had told Claude and Jolanda. But young James was uncomfortable at the prospect of having his German tutorials in his bedroom. Jimmy asked Annelies Eissler if she thought the institute had a classroom to spare—a room at IES. But she refused to set foot in the Institute for European Studies—at that time in Dr.-Karl-Lueger-Platz.

Jimmy had just arrived in Vienna; he didn't know who Karl Lueger was. Der schöne ("the handsome") Karl, once mayor of Vienna, was a former leader and the founder of the Christian Social Party. Karl Lueger's populist and anti-Semitic politics were praised in Hitler's *Mein Kampf.* In Fräulein Eissler's opinion, Lueger's Christian Social Party had been an influence on Germany's National Socialism. "The handsome Karl was a model for the Nazis," was the unambiguous way Jimmy's Jewish German tutor put it.

"Der schöne Karl has a square named after him—fuck Lueger-Platz!" Fräulein Eissler cried. Although Frau Holzinger didn't understand a word of English, the eavesdropping widow could hear Jimmy's tutor screaming on the phone. There was a statue of the handsome Karl in Lueger-Platz, and a section of the Ringstraße was named for the Judenhasser—the "Jew-hater," as Annelies called him. She wasn't equivocal in her remarks.

The historian William L. Shirer would write of Karl Lueger: "His opponents, including the Jews, readily conceded that he was at heart a decent . . . tolerant man." Annelies Eissler *conceded* no such thing.

She cited two Jewish writers who sounded equivocal about Lueger. Amos Elon noted: "Lueger's anti-Semitism was of a homespun, flexible variety—one might almost say gemütlich."

Fräulein Eissler translated *gemütlich* as "good-natured."

Stefan Zweig, who grew up in Vienna when Lueger was mayor, had this to say: "His city administration was perfectly just and even typically democratic."

Fräulein Eissler loathed Lueger, unequivocally.

"He voted for a bill to restrict the immigration of Russian and Romanian Jews—how 'perfectly just' and 'typically democratic' is that?" Annelies asked. "Und Lueger created a pun, in reference to all the Jews in Budapest—he called the Hungarian capital *Judapest*. How 'flexible' and 'good-natured' is that?"

All this was said before Jimmy met Fräulein Eissler in his bedroom on the Schwindgasse. James Winslow was a young American writer who hadn't written anything yet. He was just a kid. Like a kid, he was falling in love with his Jewish German tutor over the phone.

16.

Bad Paintings over Bullet Holes

In 1963, Jolanda and Claude were more aware of President Kennedy's escalation of American military personnel in South Vietnam than James Winslow ever was. Vietnam wasn't on Jimmy's horizon.

"Your JFK has a bug up his ass about stopping Communist expansion—a Cold War thing Kennedy got from Eisenhower, Jimmy," Jolanda said. The Dutch girl's idiomatic English was better than Jimmy's.

"American imperialism won't work in South Vietnam. French colonialism failed, you know," Claude told Jimmy, who didn't know. (This was before November, when South Vietnamese President Diêm would be shot and killed in a CIA-backed coup d'état.)

Jimmy was mulling over why he'd never had a girlfriend. It was embarrassing to be a twenty-two-year-old virgin—especially in Europe; the foreign cinema he'd seen gave James Winslow the idea that European women were more sexually experienced at a younger age. Sex and depression went together in those women Jimmy remembered most vividly from those films. Jolanda's gloom about the breakup with her girlfriend made her more attractive to Jimmy.

Weren't writers predetermined to be attracted to depressed women? young James was thinking. As a writer, Jimmy believed in destiny. Weren't gloomy girls his destiny? Weren't the great love stories the doomed ones? he was wondering.

Besides, Jimmy was in Europe. The female American students at the

Institute for European Studies didn't strike James as inclined to sex, or to depression. Those young women were more determined to have a good time *socially*, as many American students tend to be—whether they're studying at home or abroad. Furthermore, in the novel of his life, James Winslow was imagining he was supposed to meet a tormented *European* woman. He hadn't come to Vienna to engage in a doomed relationship with a melancholic American—not that Jimmy could have found one.

He was seeking experience and cynicism. European women were supposed to be experienced and cynical. Or was this only what a young and naïve American thought? In Frau Holzinger's Schwindgasse apartment, Jimmy didn't have far to look for an angry and depressed young woman. Irmgard, the five-year-old Siegfried's unmarried mother, was certainly experienced and cynical.

She'd had the sadistically inclined Siegfried; there'd been no mention of Siegfried's father, no hints of a virgin birth. And the way Irmgard slept (or hurled herself) on the largest of the living room sofas—lying on her back with her knees splayed apart—young James couldn't help but imagine her as inclined to giving herself over to moments of unrestrained abandon.

Irmgard was not a morning person. She slept in. She couldn't have had a job, Jimmy thought. He rarely saw her when she was sufficiently dressed to go out. Irmgard virtually lived on the living room sofa, always wearing one of several well-worn dressing gowns.

Frau Holzinger made Siegfried's early-morning Frühstück—the boy's "breakfast." Then the Frau marched the five-year-old off to kindergarten. On occasional afternoons, James Winslow would see Irmgard wearing normal clothes—a young mother, not much older than he was, walking Siegfried on the Schwindgasse sidewalk. Did Irmgard attract Jimmy? Yes, in her lawless way. And Irmgard was a big girl—her size attracted him, though she wasn't big in a healthy way but in an unruly way. It was Irmgard's sadness that affected Jimmy most deeply—as much as her underlying anger made him wary of her.

Jimmy didn't once see Irmgard strike Siegfried, or lash out at him in a physical way, but when she stepped barefoot on one of the boy's plaster soldiers, she would utter Siegfried's name with frightening vehemence and condemnation. This happened a lot. Irmgard was always barefoot, and the garlic-pressed soldiers were everywhere, not only in the living room but in the crowded kitchen, or in the narrow hall that led to the foreign students' bathroom. (Irmgard not only bathed Siegfried in this bathtub; she often took a bath with him.)

"Siegfried!" Irmgard would cry or hiss, whenever she trod on a beheaded or amputated plaster soldier. Sometimes she would encounter one of the military casualties while lolling or trying to sleep on the living room sofa. "Siegfried!" Irmgard would moan, as if she were reliving the pain of childbirth—or the anguish of whatever led to Siegfried's birth.

The only TV was in the living room. Afternoon and night, it was on the movie channel, as if there were no news, no sports, no weather—as if in Austria there were only old movies, always in German or dubbed in German. In Austria, why was every movie that wasn't made in the German language dubbed in German? Why had no one told James Winslow? Jimmy was a boy who loved subtitles—he'd grown up on subtitles. He'd imagined he would improve his German by watching American movies and reading the German subtitles. Not in Vienna.

Yet it was old American movies on Austrian television that brought Irmgard and Jimmy together, in a misleading and unsatisfying fashion. Maybe their tortured relationship was born of mutual misunderstanding. This could have led to shame or self-loathing. But in the beginning, it didn't appear that their confusion amounted to more than a language problem. James thought Irmgard's English—her vocabulary, in particular—was pretty good. Her English was better than his German, though there was something willfully wrong with her word order. Jimmy suspected Irmgard was deliberately speaking English with German word order, but it wasn't always accurate German word order. Was she being obstinate, or trying to be funny? Was she baiting him to correct her? (He didn't take the bait.) It was just awkward, at first, but Jimmy made the mistake of imagining there was something romantic about the awkwardness.

Disquietingly, Jimmy's bedroom door had an elliptical panel of frosted glass. The bottom of the glass panel was waist-high to the average adult. When little Siegfried was passing Jimmy's bedroom in the lighted hall, Jimmy couldn't see the top of the boy's head in the egg-shaped panel, but Siegfried would hold his hand above his head, scraping one of his plaster soldiers (or the garlic press) against the glass. Even when Jimmy wasn't looking at the door, he knew when the little executioner had passed. If Jimmy didn't see the small hand clutching the condemned soldier or the makeshift guillotine, Jimmy heard the plaster or metal scraping against the glass.

Frau Holzinger was a squat, blurry presence when she was shuffling in her slippers past Jimmy's panel of frosted glass. His fellow foreign students passed as quickly and were as easy to recognize; they went briskly about their business, spending as little time as possible in the Frau's Schwindgasse apartment. Claude passed furtively, as if the French aristocrat had stolen something and was fearful of being caught. The very tall Jolanda—too tall for her head to appear in the frosted-glass panel—seemed more depressed and more defiantly lesbian when she was headless, and she struck Jimmy as even thinner and more physically fit without her head. Jolanda was a cyclist. She said her bicycle pump had been stolen too many times; she no longer left it attached to her bicycle. A machinist in Amsterdam made a protruding hand grip for the pump—a pistol grip. Jolanda carried her bicycle pump in a holster for a handgun, hanging from the belt on her jeans. Through the frosted-glass panel on Jimmy's bedroom door, he could tell if Jolanda was wearing her bicycle pump in the holster or not.

As for Irmgard, there was no mistaking her for anyone else. Irmgard wasn't as tall as Jolanda; only the very top of Irmgard's head was above the panel of glass. And Irmgard always paused at Jimmy's door; she squared her broad shoulders to the egg-shaped panel and leaned face-first against the door. When she opened her mouth, her breath fogged the glass. The first time this happened, James expected her to say something or to knock on his door, but she didn't. Before Irmgard moved on, she turned her body in profile to the glass oval, where she paused again. Notwithstanding the loose fit of Irmgard's dressing gown, the contours of her big breasts were clearly defined through the frosted glass.

What was James Winslow to make of this? Naturally, it aroused him, while at the same time Jimmy could imagine Irmgard as akin to the witchlike Valkyries—the scary maidens of Odin who select the soldiers to be slain in battle and escort them to Valhalla.

And from the beginning, Irmgard used the *du* word with the foreign students. *Sie* was the formal or more respectful word for "you"—*du* was more familiar, or the word one would use to address a child. Because he'd heard her say "du" to Claude and Jolanda, Jimmy didn't think Irmgard was being either disrespectful or flirtatious when she said "du" to him.

It was late one night when Jimmy saw her big body pressed against the oval panel on his bedroom door; he watched her out-of-focus face come into view, her breath fogging the frosted glass. "Schläfst du?" Irmgard asked, surprising him. ("Are you sleeping?")

"Nein, ich schreibe," Jimmy answered. ("No, I'm writing.")

"Möchtest du mit mir ins Kino gehen?" Irmgard asked. Before he could reply, she translated herself into English, being weird about the word order. "Would you like with me to the movies go?"

"Ja, gern," Jimmy said quickly. ("I would like.")

"Jetzt," she said, standing up straight and showing him her breasts in profile before moving away. ("Now," she'd said.) At first, Jimmy had thought Irmgard meant going out to the movies, not watching a movie on TV.

"Ich komme gleich!" Jimmy called to her, hastily getting dressed—not knowing what was proper to wear to see a movie on one of his landlady's living room sofas. ("I'm coming at once!" he'd told her.) He put on clean sweatpants, a clean T-shirt, some white athletic socks. The socks, he hoped, would protect his feet from Siegfried's stray soldiers, but he took them off. Irmgard, he knew, would be barefoot. James Winslow would be brave and barefoot, too. He would let the T-shirt and the sweatpants suffice. Even through the frosted glass, he'd noticed that Irmgard was wearing one of her usual dressing gowns; her idea of going to the movies didn't entail going out or dressing up. Before Jimmy could get to the living room, he could hear Tex Ritter singing over the opening credits of *High Noon—12 Uhr mittags,* in German. The bad guys were gathering in black and white, before riding into town. Mercifully, they'd not dubbed Tex Ritter; James Winslow was relieved that a substitute for Tex wasn't crooning away in German.

What could be more perfect? The great Fred Zinnemann, an Austrian, had directed *High Noon.* Jimmy was imagining himself telling Irmgard that Fred Zinnemann was one of the wonderful European Jews who had transformed Hollywood. Zinnemann had a law degree from the University of Vienna *and* his parents were killed in the Holocaust. Jimmy was happy he had something to contribute to the conversation he imagined with Irmgard.

Jimmy padded barefoot down the hall to the living room, wary of brutalized plaster soldiers or their sharp little body parts, while Tex Ritter repeated, "Do not forsake me." And there was Irmgard lying full-length on the sofa—one languid arm fallen to the floor, the fingers of her hand trailing on the rug. In the context of the killers getting ready to ride into town, Irmgard made Jimmy think of a shoot-out victim.

Without lifting her head from the sofa cushion, Irmgard indicated the empty sofa parallel to hers. Lying down on it, Jimmy was discouraged by the coffee table between them. Irmgard was too far away to touch. The opening credits rolled, while the killers rode into town.

"Wait along . . ." Irmgard sang in chorus with Tex. Jimmy took this to mean that Irmgard, like him, had seen *High Noon* before. (It was 1963—the film had been made more than a decade ago.)

"Fred Zinnemann," Jimmy said tentatively, only a few minutes into the movie. "Er ist Österreicher." (This wasn't offered as an opinion. "He is Austrian" was a fact.)

"Gary Cooper ist Amerikaner," Irmgard said. "He American is," she added, translating herself.

Jimmy didn't know the word for *director* in German. He could only try to explain himself in English. "Fred Zinnemann is the director," Jimmy told Irmgard. "He directed *High Noon*. He's Austrian. His parents died in the Holocaust—he's Jewish," Jimmy said, just to be clear. "Fred Zinnemann has a law degree from the University of Vienna," young James babbled away.

Irmgard thought this over, but she kept her eyes on the movie. When Grace Kelly appeared, Irmgard pointed at her. "Grace Kelly ist Amerikanerin—she American is," Irmgard told him. "Keine Jüdin— not Jew is," Irmgard added, just to be clear.

"Ich weiß—I know," James Winslow said.

Now Gary Cooper was on the small screen—the German he was speaking was not in sync with his lips. "His parents in the Holocaust didn't die," Irmgard pointed out. "Not a lawyer from Vienna is," she added, sounding pretty sure of herself.

"Ich weiß," Jimmy could only repeat. It was not quite the conversation he'd expected; they'd not explored film as art. (Even James Winslow would wonder if Irmgard was putting him on, from the beginning.)

At the end of the movie, when Grace Kelly hears the gunfire and gets off the train, she runs to the marshal's office—a great camera angle, as she comes into frame with the holstered revolver hanging from a peg. Jimmy stole a look at Irmgard, her breasts rising and falling on the sofa. "I this part love," she told Jimmy, not looking at him. When Grace Kelly shoots one of the bad guys through the window, she gets him in the back. "She a Quaker no more is," Irmgard pointed out.

"I know," James said.

"Wait along . . ." Irmgard sang together with Tex, as the marshal and his bride are leaving town.

"I like watching movies with you," Jimmy said to Irmgard, hopefully.

"In winter, the living room colder is—better on one sofa movie to watch," Irmgard told him. Jimmy couldn't tell if the look she gave him was suggestive—if this was a promise. The looks Irmgard gave James Winslow were obdurately neutral; she gave nothing away. Naturally, James thought he understood something about unwed mothers. Considering the mother he knew and loved—not to mention Esther— Jimmy remembered how those two could hold things back.

In the first letter she wrote her dear James in Vienna, Honor Winslow held nothing back. "Forgive me for putting this in writing to you, honey, but maybe it's easier for both of us," Jimmy's mom began. James Winslow was grateful to Chantal for their earlier conversation; he was prepared for the gist of his mother's idea. It began with his getting someone pregnant. He needed to be what his mom called "a bona fide father" to a child. Being a father was the best way not to be drafted into what she called "another misguided war." Naturally, there was mention of Chantal's reluctance to be the birth mother. "As you say, Arnaud wouldn't understand!" Honor wrote, with irritation.

Even Jolanda, who was very tall and lesbian, was a better idea than Irmgard, Jimmy considered. It seemed safer to show his mom's letter to Claude and Jolanda together. This way, it wouldn't look like Jimmy was proposing anything—or so he thought. Yet this entailed his having to tell them the two-moms story—so that Claude and Jolanda could understand the origin of his mother's plan. (Getting pregnant for the purpose of giving a baby to someone else wasn't a new idea in the Winslow family.)

"Wait, wait!" Claude cried. "Is Chantal *your* aunt?" he asked Jimmy.

"Remain calm, Claude. Chantal isn't Jimmy's aunt," Jolanda said.

But this entailed Jimmy's saying more about Chantal than he meant to—her uniqueness among the Beaudette women of childbearing age, her smallness in her bigger sisters' hand-me-downs.

"You should never have mentioned the cruel speculation that Chantal might have one big boob instead of two," Jolanda told Jimmy later. "Claude will never let go of the horror that she has a *onesie*."

"Wait, wait! Poor Chantal!" Claude had cried. "A *onesie* is so sad!"

"It's not *sad,* it's just a cruel thing to say. No one has a *onesie*—you idiot, Claude!" Jolanda had told him.

Now both Claude and James Winslow were remembering the reason Jolanda broke up with her girlfriend. She'd told Jolanda she wanted to try having sex with a guy. "I just want to *try it* once—I know I'm going to like it with you better!" the girlfriend had said. (This did not go over well with Jolanda.) Jimmy was hoping Claude would be intrepid enough to ask Jolanda if her girlfriend might be interested in *trying it* with Jimmy. It was probably safest to leave the part about getting pregnant for a second question, James Winslow was thinking—just when Claude, in his intrepid but bumbling way, posed an onslaught of questions.

"Your girlfriend's name is hard to say, Jolanda—if you're not Dutch," Claude began. "MEE-kuh, MEE-kuh, MEE-kuh," he chanted.

"You got it, Claude—that's how you say Mieke," Jolanda told him.

"If Mieke wants to *try it* with a guy, she could try it with Jimmy—with you there. You could hold her head, or talk to her, the whole time," Claude went on. Claude kept looking at Jimmy—not at Jolanda, who was speechless. "It wouldn't be like Mieke was having an affair—she would just be *trying it.*"

"Stop it, Claude!" Jolanda cried. "I never want to *try it* with a guy, but I would rather *try it* with Jimmy than hold Mieke's head while she's *trying it*!"

"But do you or Mieke want to try the getting-pregnant part?" Claude asked Jolanda. "That's the more complicated part," he said.

"You idiot, Claude—we *know*!" Jolanda cried.

Young James apologized to his newfound friends; he hadn't meant to cause any strife between them. His problem, or his mother's plan, was not their problem. He had no expectation that Jolanda or her girlfriend would be interested in having sex with him, or in having his baby. "I understand—it's okay," Jimmy told Jolanda.

"No, it's not okay," Jolanda said. "Now we'll never be friends—not with your wanting me all the time." Jimmy hoped she was kidding.

"Jimmy never said he *wanted* you, Jolanda," Claude pointed out.

"I can tell that Jimmy wants me, Claude—like I can tell you *don't,*" Jolanda said. Jimmy still didn't know if Jolanda was kidding.

"It's true, I don't—I want someone *smaller,* because I'm small. But I *like* you, Jolanda," Claude told her, looking like he would burst into tears. Then they both hugged; things were all right between them again.

"I like you both," Jimmy told them; they hugged him, too. Claude and Jolanda were very clear with Jimmy that he shouldn't *try it* with Irmgard, who seemed entirely capable of watching a movie while she got pregnant.

"It's not Siegfried's fault that he's Siegfried," Claude strangely said. Jolanda and Jimmy knew what Claude meant. The boy's pent-up frustrations were understandable. Siegfried was blond and blue-eyed, a pale wraith of a boy; his mother and grandmother were heavyset, with brown hair and eyes. Siegfried must have wondered where he came from, or where he belonged.

"It's too bad you can't adopt Siegfried, Jimmy—it would be a way out for both of you," Jolanda said. At the time, the idea of anyone adopting Siegfried seemed unlikely to James Winslow—if not as far-fetched as Jimmy knocking up Mieke while Jolanda held Mieke's head and talked to her.

At night, Jolanda locked her bicycle to a rack in the enclosed courtyard of the Schwindgasse apartment building. Jimmy and Claude could tell that Jolanda liked carrying her bicycle pump with the pistol grip like a six-gun in a holster. "The pump extends, you know—it's like a club that gets longer," Jolanda explained. "It works well as a weapon. First you go for his eyes, and when he raises his hands to protect his face, you kneecap him—or you go for his balls," Jolanda said. She talked tough, but Jolanda was an inscrutable girl; Jimmy couldn't tell if she was speaking speculatively or from experience. When they were alone, Jimmy and Claude talked about it.

"I'm betting 'from experience,' as you say," Claude said.

Sometimes, when he was half-asleep, Jimmy thought he smelled Jolanda's cigarette smoke all the way from her balcony window, even when Jimmy thought his balcony window was closed. The Holzingers' apartment was on the second floor. In the event of a fire, the Schwindgasse sidewalk wasn't far below. Jolanda worried that someone could climb into her balcony window from the sidewalk. "A guy could reach the balcony if he sat on another guy's shoulders, or he could stand on the seat of a motorcycle parked on the sidewalk," Jolanda told Jimmy and Claude.

"I think I would hear you being raped, Jolanda," Claude assured her. "I would go get Jimmy, who's a wrestler. Jimmy would wrestle the guy into submission. Then you could beat him to death, or destroy his balls, with your bicycle pump," Claude elaborated.

"Don't try to make me look forward to it, Claude," Jolanda said.

Most mornings, James Winslow would walk with Claude to a streetcar stop on the Opernring, but Claude and Jimmy took the Straßenbahn in opposite directions on the Ringstraße. One afternoon, walking home alone, Claude had encountered some troublemakers—when he was crossing the Karlsplatz, near the Technische Universität. It was unclear to Claude if they were students at the university.

They were young men with an Austrian predisposition to xenophobia, and Claude was small and furtive. Claude may or may not have looked like a Parisian aristocrat, but he didn't look Viennese. Claude's German was good, but when he spoke, you could hear his French accent. From one of the aggressive young men, Claude had heard the

Ausländer word. (In Vienna, "foreigner" wasn't said in a nice way.) One of the young men asked Claude if he was jüdisch, another one asked if he was homosexuell.

"The standard questions, the usual xenophobes," Claude said.

Jimmy and Jolanda were very fond of Claude, but he was anxious all the time—for good reason. As time went on and the weather got colder, Frau Holzinger started turning the heat down at night when she and Siegfried went to bed. Claude, Jimmy, and Jolanda then went out together, usually to a Kaffeehaus on the corner of the Schwindgasse and Argentinierstraße. The foreign students needed a warm place to do their homework, or for James Winslow to write. Jolanda toted her bicycle pump with the pistol grip in her six-gun holster. She said Claude shouldn't go out alone at night.

"I hope you're not writing about my rejecting you, and how you want me all the time," Jolanda said, whenever she saw Jimmy writing.

"That's the ending—I'm not there yet," the young writer replied. Now that Fräulein Eissler was Jimmy's German tutor, he was wanting her all the time—he wasn't wanting Jolanda the way he used to. (Jimmy still thought of Irmgard as a more realistic possibility.)

James Winslow's first tutorial with Fräulein Eissler, in his bedroom at the Schwindgasse apartment, had caused quite a stir. Fräulein Eissler had insisted on two-hour sessions on the late afternoons and early evenings of Tuesday, Wednesday, and Thursday. This meant that Jimmy's tutorials chaotically coincided with the preparation and serving of Siegfried's supper, where the mother and grandmother ate their fill along with the murderous five-year-old. Siegfried rarely relinquished his grip on the garlic press, not even when he was eating. At 4 P.M., when Fräulein Eissler arrived, the narrow hall outside James Winslow's bedroom already reeked of frying bratwurst; the sauerkraut was reheated, every night, in a double boiler on the stove. "A bit early for Abendessen, isn't it?" Fräulein Eissler asked Jimmy, on her first visit.

"There's a five-year-old," young James explained.

"Yes, I've just met Siegfried, and his garlic press," Fräulein Eissler replied.

She was looking around Jimmy's bedroom; she'd not yet taken off her coat. "Do the mother and grandmother always eat with the boy?" she asked. James nodded. "Does the mother ever get dressed?" Fräulein Eissler asked.

"Not usually," Jimmy said. He was looking at his tutor's small, pretty feet; she was barefoot and her toenails were painted a magenta color. Frau Holzinger made everyone leave their shoes or boots on the over-large doormat at the entrance to the apartment.

"I'll ask you to let me wear a pair of your socks, preferably white, while I'm here," Fräulein Eissler told Jimmy. She kept her coat on, still looking all around. There was a queen-size bed with an ornate headboard, like one belonging to someone of Jimmy's grandparents' generation. There was an enormous wardrobe closet, with floor-length mirrors on the double doors—perhaps intended for a fashion-conscious woman who changed her clothes four times a day. There was a desk heaped with Jimmy's homework and his writing notebooks. (When he wrote at night, he was afraid the tapping of his typewriter's keys would wake up Claude or Jolanda.) At the desk by the balcony window was a rigidly upright wooden chair. Last, Fräulein Eissler assessed what she called the "settee" or the "love seat"—a straight-backed sofa for two, with uncomfortable wooden arms. By the uninviting sofa was a glass-topped table, too slippery for Jimmy's writing notebooks and poorly lit.

Fräulein Eissler sighed, finally taking off her coat, which she put on the bed. Pointing to the settee and the glass-topped table, she said: "We'll try doing this on the love seat, but I have my doubts."

They'd no sooner sat down on the love seat than Fräulein Eissler noticed the large painting on the wall, to one side of the bed's headboard. This was a cheap painting you could buy in a tourist shop, a stylized rendition of the white Lipizzaner stallions in the Winter Riding School in the Hofburg—Vienna's Spanish Riding School for classical dressage.

(The Lipizzaner stallions and their riders were a tourist attraction—one the IES students would go see, but James Winslow wasn't interested in.)

"There must be something behind that awful painting—something Frau Holzinger is trying to hide," Fräulein Eissler said. She got up and peeked behind the painting. "Bullet holes," she said, showing him the holes. "The Schwindgasse was in the Russian sector of occupation, after the war. Was Frau Holzinger's late husband a soldier? They were probably Nazis. I have friends I can ask," Fräulein Eissler told young James. "Sehr wienerisch, very Viennese—bad paintings over bullet holes!" she exclaimed.

Was this a common occurrence in the Russian zone of occupation? James Winslow would ask his German tutor. There was something merely teacherly, even perfunctory, in Fräulein Eissler's answer. In 1945, the Allies had determined the four zones of occupation in Vienna. The Americans and British chose the best residential sections in the city. The French occupied the shopping areas. The Soviets took the industrial neighborhoods, where the workers were, but they also settled themselves around the Inner City—near the embassies and government buildings, including the Schwindgasse. Fräulein Eissler gave Jimmy the impression that it didn't matter anymore, since the occupation was over.

The bullet holes hidden by the Lipizzaner stallions were the reason James Winslow and Annelies Eissler were standing next to his bed when they heard the knocking on Jimmy's door. Jolanda and Claude usually didn't knock. One of them would quietly open Jimmy's door, which had no lock, and wiggle the fingers of one hand. If Jimmy was asleep, or writing at his desk by the window, he never saw the inquiring hand. Jolanda or Claude would quietly close his door and go away. If Jimmy was naked, he would say, "Just a minute!" If he was available and presentable, he invited them in. Now he recognized their figures behind the frosted glass—the headless Jolanda, the wraithlike Claude. Young James understood the unaccustomed formality of their knocking on his door. Those two must have wanted to get a look at his Jewish German tutor.

"Come in!" Jimmy called to them. When the door opened, Jolanda made herself appear taller by standing on the threshold. Claude hung back, taking refuge behind Jolanda's hip—the hip with the holstered bicycle pump. As usual, the heel of Jolanda's right hand rested on the pistol grip of the pump handle—as if every situation might require a quick draw, and the bicycle pump was her Colt .45.

"Your roommates, I presume," Fräulein Eissler said to Jimmy. She took off her cashmere cardigan and put it on his bed; she was wearing a matching short-sleeved sweater under the cardigan. The tucked-in sweater was a light-gray color, accentuating her dark hair and dark eyes. Her small breasts were very noticeable in the sweater, as were her small but shapely hips in her fitted slacks.

"Annelies," she said, coming forward and shaking Jolanda's hand, as Jolanda mumbled her own name.

"Claude!" Claude blurted out, bumping against Jolanda's jutting hip. Claude reached for the small, pretty hand with the silver thumb ring. When Fräulein Eissler said something in French to him, Claude's reply made him sound as if French were his second (and much neglected) language. Jolanda, holding tight to the pistol grip of her bicycle pump, whacked her elbow against the doorjamb.

"Ouch," Annelies said. She smiled at Jolanda and Claude, who had now retreated into the odors of frying sausage that were overwhelming the narrow hall.

Annelies and Jimmy tried sitting beside each other on the love seat. She'd put her cardigan back on, but she left it unbuttoned. That was when she asked young James if Jolanda was a "potential girlfriend." Was it a young writer's inclination to tell the whole story? Telling Annelies that Jolanda was a lesbian would have been sufficient, but Jimmy opened the whole can of worms. The "potential girlfriend" might be Mieke, who wanted to *try it* with a guy. Fräulein Eissler was repelled by the thought of Jolanda holding Mieke's head.

"There's a more natural way to get a girlfriend pregnant, Jimmy,"

Annelies told him. "Finding a girlfriend who'll *give* you her baby is the unnatural part," Fräulein Eissler added.

"I guess you know what my mom and Esther want," Jimmy said.

"Don't look at me! I'm not a potential girlfriend, Jimmy Winslow," Fräulein Eissler told him. Then she moved on; the girlfriend subject was this quickly passed over. "Every week, there will be four days in a row when you don't see me," Annelies announced. She told James to write down, in English, every sentence he wished he could say "in perfect German." (Jimmy was already writing down these instructions.) "Eventually, you won't have to write down *everything*," she said, sighing.

"Werden wir nur sprechen?" ("Will we only speak?" he'd asked her.) Jimmy doubted he would ever say anything in perfect German.

"Das Bett," she said, pointing to the bed. "When you're not writing things down, when we're only speaking, the bed will be more comfortable than this misnamed love seat," Annelies said. "Let me hear you say, 'more comfortable'—bequemer," Fräulein Eissler said.

"Bequemer," James said, trying not to look at (or think about) the bed. He stared under the glass-topped table at Fräulein Eissler's feet in his white athletic socks. "Bequemer," Jimmy repeated, because Annelies was shaking her head.

"Again. Noch einmal," she said.

"Bequemer," Jimmy said again.

"Noch einmal und noch einmal," Annelies intoned. He kept saying the word, until he got it right. "Repetition is the key to language. Aren't you a Ringer—you're a wrestler, right?" she asked him. "Isn't there repetition in wrestling? Isn't anything you get good at *repetitive*? Like sex, I suppose," Annelies said, offhandedly, as if James Winslow knew anything about sex—having not had sex, not once.

"Bequemer," Jimmy repeated, as if he were having sex with her and it would never stop.

"Das reicht," she said, softly. ("That's enough.") She was distracted.

"Siegfried's mother—I've seen her before. I just can't remember where I saw her," Fräulein Eissler said, sighing again.

"You mean Irmgard?" Jimmy asked.

"The one who is not dressed, whatever her name is," Annelies said; she was impatient with distractions and already moving on, in her authoritative way. "I don't know what I think of this perfume—it's new, and it's in conflict with the cooking smells. Do you like it?" she asked, pointing to the side of her throat as she turned her face away from him—entreating him (and showing him precisely where) to sniff her neck. It was intoxicating to inhale her. It took more self-control than young James thought he had, but he somehow managed to restrain himself. He didn't kiss her throat. No doubt the look on Jimmy's face, after he'd breathed her in, gave him away.

"Don't fall in love with me, Jimmy—there's no future in it," Annelies said. James Winslow knew her warning had come too late. (Fräulein Eissler must have known this, too—she just looked away.)

Jimmy was reminded of Irmgard's unreadable utterance, her weird word order and the rest. He would never forget what Siegfried's unmarried mother said, or how she'd said it: "In winter, the living room colder is—better on one sofa movie to watch." It wasn't yet winter, but the living room was already colder, and he'd not been invited to watch another movie with Irmgard—not on separate sofas or the same sofa. As for what Irmgard meant, she'd promised Jimmy nothing beyond sharing a sofa. Irmgard's expressions revealed her anger and her depression. In the other expressions Jimmy saw on the tired face of Siegfried's unmarried mother, he could not discern the difference between baleful and indifferent.

It was a little after 6 P.M. on her first tutorial visit when Fräulein Eissler left. She'd pointed out to Jimmy that Jolanda and Claude had interrupted them. Otherwise, she said she would have left "on time." James Winslow was as unaccustomed to his attraction to Fräulein Eissler as he was to her exactness. In their two hours together, he'd noticed those moments when Annelies had glanced at her wristwatch. When she checked the time, Jimmy looked at her breasts in her tucked-in sweater.

Meanwhile, Irmgard and Frau Holzinger had thoroughly examined Fräulein Eissler's boots on the doormat at the entrance. Jimmy's landlady said it was ungewöhnlich ("unusual") that his tutor didn't wear socks in her knee-high winter boots.

This didn't seem strange to Irmgard, because the German tutor's boots were lined—as Irmgard told her mother and Jimmy.

"Trotzdem ungewöhnlich," Frau Holzinger said. ("Still unusual.")

"The lining like flannel or fleece felt," Irmgard further explained to Jimmy, in her out-of-order English. She'd *felt* the insides of Fräulein Eissler's boots? Jimmy was thinking, when Irmgard added, "The Jew her toes paints."

"Annelies paints her *toenails*," Jimmy corrected her.

"Wer ist Annelies?" Frau Holzinger asked. ("Who is Annelies?" the Frau had asked.) She'd not heard Fräulein Eissler's first name before.

"Die Jüdin—the Jew," Irmgard answered her mother. "Your tutor a Jew is, you know," Irmgard told Jimmy.

"Ich weiß," he said, as he was always saying to Siegfried's mother.

The next night, Jimmy went out with Jolanda and Claude to their local Kaffeehaus. They had their own name for that café, calling it the "Kaffeehaus Nachtmusik," though it had another name—since forgotten. Yes, the café played Mozart's "Eine kleine Nachtmusik," repeatedly, but they played other music no less obsessively. There was a fanatically limited but eclectic list.

At the café, Jimmy was trying to explain why Siegfried's before-bedtime bath disturbed him—that Irmgard took a bath with Siegfried was the issue. "How much longer will it be appropriate for a five-year-old's mother to take a bath with him?" he asked Claude and Jolanda.

"It's not appropriate *now*," Claude said, shivering at the mere thought of Irmgard naked in a bathtub.

"Fuck what's 'appropriate'—it's a whale with a herring situation," Jolanda said. "That little boy could drown in a tub with her—the cow!"

"And the cow wraps herself in *all* the towels afterward, while poor Siegfried is *dripping* in the hall!" Claude said, his teeth chattering.

They were listening to a Johann Strauss II waltz. "Vienna Blood Waltz" wasn't everyone's favorite. The TV at the bar was on a news channel with the sound off, as always. (For the patrons of the Kaffeehaus Nachtmusik, what was happening in the news was a matter of guesswork.)

As for Mozart's "Eine kleine Nachtmusik," the foreign students thought the usual English translations were a little misleading. "A Little Night Music" or "A Little Serenade," they'd heard people say in English, but Jimmy and Claude liked what Jolanda called it. "A Little Frivolous," Jolanda had labeled the only Mozart the café ever played. The three foreign students certainly didn't feel *serenaded* by the music they played (again and again) at the Kaffeehaus Nachtmusik.

"Your Jewish German tutor," Jolanda said, enunciating each syllable—as slowly but succinctly as a death knell. "Fräulein Eissler is about a decade older than we are, but she dresses like a middle-aged woman. She must buy her clothes in a thrift shop—an expensive thrift shop, in a neighborhood where well-off divorcées move to die," Jolanda told Jimmy and Claude.

"Annelies is *beautiful!*" Claude exclaimed; he was still shivering.

"Your Annelies, Jimmy, is the kind of woman who's always having her period—if you know what I mean," Jolanda said.

"What do you *mean?*" Claude blurted out; his teeth were chattering to beat the band. Young James wasn't sure what Jolanda meant, either.

"For Christ's sake, Claude, we come here to get warm—stop the teeth and the shivers!" Jolanda shouted at him. A passing waiter, elderly and disapproving, was shakily carrying a tray of water glasses; the glasses were too full and kept spilling. Whenever Jolanda raised her voice, which was often, all the old waiters shook and scowled. The foreign students had blamed the ancient waiters for the oft-played selections of classical music.

In the kitchen, young people were working; only young people could be blamed for the contemporary music selections, which were random and startling (and no less repetitive). There were some good choices, more not. Perhaps made by an unseen sous-chef, or the tattooed woman dishwasher the foreign students had seen smoking in an alley off the Schwindgasse—where the garbage was collected and there was a sad-eyed German shepherd on a chain. Everyone smoked in the Kaffeehaus Nachtmusik, including in the kitchen. Maybe the tattooed woman dishwasher wanted to keep the dog company, or the sad-eyed German shepherd was her dog.

Jimmy thought against telling Jolanda and Claude about his prospects of sharing a sofa with Irmgard—more moviegoing in the semidarkness of the increasingly cold living room. Besides, Jolanda had worked herself up to explaining what she'd meant by saying Annelies was "the kind of woman who's always having her period"—the prospect of which had made Claude's teeth chatter more. "I forgot, for a second, that I'm talking to a couple of sexual beginners," Jolanda began, putting Jimmy and Claude in their respective places. She'd already made compromising remarks about their respective penises.

"I'm not trying to be a sexual beginner—it just works out that way," Claude protested. Jolanda sighed, moving on to Jimmy.

"Fräulein Eissler is the kind of woman who tells you she's having her period when she doesn't want to get laid. When Annelies doesn't want to do it with you, she'll blame her period," Jolanda told Jimmy.

"Oh," Claude and Jimmy said in unison. James Winslow realized that a wrestling teammate had explained this to him before, even in Pennacook.

"What a couple of choirboys you two are!" Jolanda declared.

There'd been an awkward moment in the hall outside the bathroom—Claude and Jimmy with just towels wrapped around them. Claude had taken a bath; Jimmy was waiting his turn. When Jolanda tried to slip past them in the hall, she'd brushed against them and their towels fell off. Before they could cover themselves, Jolanda had noticed what was different about those boys. Jimmy was circumcised; Claude wasn't.

"Wait, wait, *wait!*" Jolanda cried. "You guys have *different* penises!"

Typical of Jolanda, this led to a closer inspection in Jimmy's bedroom. "This might be my only time to see a penis—not to mention *two* penises!" Jolanda explained. Claude and Jimmy had already had a brief conversation concerning circumcision. Jolanda thought both penises were unappealing, but in different ways. "Jimmy's is smaller—it's almost *cute,* but it looks like a misconceived clitoris," Jolanda declared. "Claude's is like a horse's dick, or a big dog's dick!" she exclaimed.

In the café, the three foreign students were listening to the second of the two Johann Strauss II waltzes—the more familiar one, "The Blue Danube Waltz." (These were the only two Strauss II waltzes in the unfathomable repertoire of the Kaffeehaus Nachtmusik.)

And Claude said, for the hundredth time, "I wonder why the younger Strauss wrote waltzes—he was reputed to be a terrible dancer."

Jolanda replied, as she usually did: "If someone had kneecapped him, he might have stopped writing waltzes." Jimmy just thought he should go back to his bedroom at Frau Holzinger's. Although the Frau had turned down the heat, maybe he could get in bed and try writing under the covers. The café wasn't hopping at night; they gave the three foreign students a table for six, so they had room for their homework and Jimmy's writing notebooks. The Kaffeehaus Nachtmusik was busier in the daytime hours, but the foreigners didn't know who the few bookish-looking daytime customers were—perhaps from the Polish Reading Room, also on the Schwindgasse.

Jimmy was on the verge of leaving, but the prospect of the nighttime chill in the Holzinger apartment made him linger at the café with his newfound friends and the repetitive music. Then the music changed— in its often jarring, always illogical fashion—and Jimmy decided to brave the chill in his bedroom. It was October; the nights were beginning to get colder. It was best to get used to the cold, James was thinking, while the only Elvis Presley they ever played in the Kaffeehaus Nachtmusik assaulted them—making the elderly waiters tremble and causing Claude to close his eyes. Claude hated to see how "It's Now or Never" always made Jolanda bend her teaspoon into a U-shaped bracelet, which she put around her wrist like a handcuff.

"I would like to see Elvis try to move his hips after I kneecap him," Jolanda murmured, as if she were praying. She hated Elvis. Jolanda believed the Elvis selection was the tattooed woman dishwasher's fault. As Elvis kept crooning, Jolanda said she wanted to kneecap the ink addict. When the tattooed woman dishwasher was smoking in the garbage alley, she had an Elvis-like, now-or-never look about her. Yet Claude and Jimmy saw how Jolanda had looked at the ink addict. It wasn't a *kneecapping* look. The look Jolanda gave the woman was more of a *girlfriend* look. Claude and Jimmy thought the tattooed woman dishwasher was Jolanda's kind of girl.

Jimmy bid his friends good night. He returned to the Schwindgasse apartment, where he gave writing under his bedcovers a try. He was wearing a T-shirt and a pair of sweatpants under the covers, and the same pair of white athletic socks Annelies had worn. Jimmy heard Jolanda and Claude come home from the café; they took their turns in the bathroom across the hall from Jimmy's bedroom. He was still trying to write under the covers when the big, blurry figure pressed herself against his door—first her breath fogging the frosted glass, then showing him her breasts in profile.

"*Verdammt in alle Ewigkeit*—in all eternity damned," Irmgard said. Did she mean this should happen to students with Jewish German tutors?

All Irmgard meant was that *From Here to Eternity* was badly translated in German. "Burt Lancaster, Deborah Kerr, Frank Sinatra, Montgomery Clift, Donna Reed," Irmgard named the cast—her voice trailing away as she went down the hall to the living room, where the movie was starting. "Jetzt!" she called. ("Now!") When Jimmy hurried after her, he kept his socks on. Naturally, Jimmy couldn't part with the socks, now that Fräulein Eissler had worn them.

James Winslow knew perfectly well it was another Fred Zinnemann movie in black and white, but he knew better than to try to remind Irmgard that the director was an Austrian-born Jew. Jimmy didn't care about *From Here to Eternity.* On his way to the living room, Jimmy was rehearsing how he should say to Irmgard that there'd been a change in the weather. He needn't have bothered. Jimmy saw her sprawled on the sofa, beckoning him with both arms. "It already colder is—better on one sofa movie to watch," Siegfried's unmarried mother said.

Lying on top of Irmgard, between her legs, which she wrapped around him, with his head pillowed between her big breasts, represented the height of James Winslow's erotic experience thus far. And she was very clean, albeit smelling slightly of baby powder. She'd probably sprinkled the baby powder on herself and Siegfried after their nightly bath. Yet the way Irmgard made herself comfortable under Jimmy—the way she purposely arranged him between her legs and breasts to suit herself—gave Jimmy the feeling that he was being used as a blanket. She seemed not in the least sexually interested in him. And inconceivably, to Jimmy, Irmgard was as riveted to *Verdammt in alle Ewigkeit* as she'd been to *12 Uhr mittags.*

"Burt Lancaster," Irmgard told him, pointing to the small screen, which Jimmy knew would soon give him a crick in his neck—unless he removed his face from Irmgard's mountainous bosom, which he wouldn't have dreamed of doing. "Burt not a Jew is—Montgomery Clift *und* Deborah Kerr also not are," Irmgard asserted, sighing.

"Ich weiß," Jimmy said, also sighing.

"Frank Sinatra Italian is. Er ist wahrscheinlich katholisch." ("He almost certainly Catholic is," Irmgard had added.)

"Ich weiß—Frank is probably Catholic," Jimmy agreed.

"Ja, wahrscheinlich—yes, probably," Irmgard replied. She'd shifted herself under him, pushing Jimmy's head to the snug hollow between her left breast and her armpit, where he couldn't see the screen at all. He was more interested in Irmgard's underarm deodorant than he was in *From Here to Eternity*. Jimmy had seen the spray deodorant in the bathroom with the tub. He should spray Irmgard's deodorant in his typewriter, Jimmy thought. Her deodorant could kill the sausage smell.

"Ernest Borgnine is probably also Catholic and Italian," Jimmy told Irmgard. (She'd not mentioned Ernest Borgnine with the rest of the cast.)

"Fatso?" Irmgard asked. Jimmy nodded his head, trying not to disturb her bosom or her armpit area. "Wahrscheinlich auch katholisch und italienisch," Irmgard agreed.

He'd fallen asleep when he heard her say something curious about Donna Reed. "Donna not a real prostitute is," Jimmy thought Irmgard said. Did she mean that, in real life, Donna Reed wasn't a prostitute, or was Irmgard venturing into the field of film criticism—was Irmgard saying that Donna wasn't convincing as a prostitute in *From Here to Eternity*? But this question was beyond Jimmy's capabilities to say in German. He needed more tutorials with Fräulein Eissler before Jimmy could sort out what Irmgard meant by saying Donna Reed wasn't "a real prostitute."

Besides, he was too comfortable lying in Irmgard's less than erotic but warm embrace. He'd never slept with his face buried in a woman's bosom, and Jimmy's feet were very cozy in the socks his Jewish German tutor had worn.

James Winslow was not aware when Irmgard left him alone on the sofa. He presumed she was tired and had gone to bed. He thought it was only in his dreams that he smelled a more womanly perfume than baby powder. And Jimmy must have been dreaming when he imagined Irmgard dressed as he'd never seen her before. In his dreams, Irmgard was a sensual woman in beautiful clothes—as if she were going out for the night.

Jimmy woke up at the end of the movie, when the unfaithful wife (Deborah Kerr) and the prostitute (Donna Reed) are onboard the ship—just before the end credits roll. Jimmy must have dreamed that Irmgard said something during the love scene on the beach—when Burt Lancaster and Deborah Kerr are wet and lying on the sand. Oh, the things you imagine when you're sleeping, for the first time, on a woman's breasts! Yet, in Jimmy's dreams (*if* he'd been dreaming), it sounded like something Irmgard could have said.

"You will sand in your vagina get—if you on beach fuck," Irmgard said. But what did Jimmy know? He would have sworn he was asleep.

17.

A German Shepherd Named Hard Rain

November 22, 1963, was a Friday—the first of four consecutive days when James Winslow wasn't scheduled to see Fräulein Eissler.

It was 12:30 P.M. in Dallas when JFK was shot—and around 8 P.M. in Vienna when it was announced on Austrian television that President Kennedy had died. At their table for six in the Kaffeehaus Nachtmusik, Jolanda, Claude, and Jimmy were conducting their usual business. It was earlier in the evening than 8 P.M. when the foreign students noticed that the black-and-white TV above the bar was drawing a crowd. Despite the unusual interest in the news, the sound (as usual) remained off. Jimmy was always imagining things. Did he only imagine that a few customers swiveled on their barstools to give him a quick look? Then they as quickly looked away. Did the elderly waiters ramp up their shaking when they tottered near the foreign students' table? The spilled water glasses overflowed the trembling waiters' trays.

Now that the weather had turned reliably colder, Jimmy and his "roommates" (as Annelies called Claude and Jolanda) were an almost nightly presence. Usually, those three were the only ones speaking English in the café. The ancient waitstaff knew Jimmy was the sole American in the place, as did Dagmar—the attractive but reserved manager. Dagmar was a widow—the age of Jimmy's mom, he would have guessed. Dagmar had made a point of inquiring about the foreign students' respective nationalities; she was always welcoming to them, in her aloof way.

"Dagmar doesn't choose the music—she looks like she doesn't even *hear* the music," Jolanda had told Jimmy and Claude. Jolanda was steadfast in seeking to correctly attach the blame for the café music selections.

"Dagmar looks like she's in mourning, or she's on the verge of a nervous breakdown," Claude said to Jimmy and Jolanda.

"You keep repeating 'poor Chantal' in your sleep, Claude—*you* are on the verge of a nervous breakdown," Jolanda told him.

"This might be why I recognize Dagmar's symptoms," Claude said.

"Dagmar is pretty, but she seems sad." Jimmy regretted saying this as soon as it left his mouth. Jolanda bent a teaspoon into one of her U-shaped handcuffs, causing Claude to close his eyes.

"Get over your attraction to *sad*, Jimmy—especially to older women who are sad," Jolanda told him.

"Annelies isn't sad, and I'm attracted to *her*," Jimmy declared.

"Annelies is beyond you—you should get over her, too," Jolanda said.

Dagmar was watching the TV over the bar; she only once interrupted her gaze at the screen to look at Jimmy. "Dagmar doesn't even *notice* the music," Jolanda was complaining to Claude and Jimmy. The music at this moment was Bob Dylan. James Winslow was thinking that he couldn't get enough of Bob Dylan—not in Vienna. Claude silently mouthed the words to "Blowin' in the Wind," which Claude (like everyone, of a certain age) knew by heart. Jimmy saw Dagmar whisper to one of the old waiters; it looked like she was sending him to the kitchen, but before the waiter tottered through the swinging doors, the old guy gave Jimmy a despairing look.

"Dagmar may not even *notice* the music," Claude observed, "but she has noticed what's on the news tonight. It looks like the U.S. and the

Soviets have launched their missiles, and we have only minutes—maybe only seconds—left to live."

"For Christ's sake, Claude!" Jolanda started to say, but she stopped. The three friends saw the shaking waiter; he'd almost immediately emerged from the swinging doors with the tattooed woman dishwasher. Dagmar was leading the muscular dishwasher to the students' table. "That the ink addict likes Bob Dylan somewhat redeems her," Jolanda was saying.

Everyone crowded around the TV at the bar had turned to look at the foreign students. Dagmar's hand signal to the bartender was clear; she drew her index finger across her throat, and the bartender killed the music. This was the first time Jimmy didn't hear "Blowin' in the Wind" to the end.

"Washington and Moscow are gone," Claude announced. "Paris, London, New York—all obliterated. We're only alive because Vienna isn't a strategic target. We're going to die slowly, from the nuclear fallout!" Claude cried, giving a stricken look at the darkened windows. "The radioactive particles are already in the atmosphere."

"Jesus Mary Joseph, Claude—you doom fucker!" Jolanda said.

When the widow spoke, she looked at Jimmy. "You should know something," Dagmar said. All Jimmy could think was how Irmgard would have said this. ("You something know should," in Irmgard's word order.)

"Es ist etwas passiert." ("Something happened," the tattooed woman dishwasher told James Winslow.)

"Wo?" Claude cried, jumping to his feet. ("Where?")

"Not in France," Dagmar assured him.

"In Dallas—to your president," the ink addict told Jimmy.

The way the widow whispered made her hard to understand. "Er wurde erschossen," Dagmar said.

"Kennedy is shot?" Jimmy asked; he couldn't think.

"Er ist tot," Dagmar whispered.

"JFK is dead?" Jimmy asked; he could barely speak.

"Ja, tot. Es tut mir leid," Dagmar confirmed, in her managerial fashion. ("Yes, dead. I'm sorry," she'd said.) "Hildegund speaks better English than I do," Dagmar told Jimmy, pushing the tattooed woman dishwasher closer to the foreign students' table.

"How can one person, the *same* person, like Bob Dylan *and* Elvis Presley?" Jolanda asked Hildegund. Jolanda had stood up to make sure Hildegund knew how tall she was, but Claude and Jimmy noticed that Hildegund was almost Jolanda's height. Hildegund's tattoos were of gargoyles and other demons.

"I like the Beatles, too," Hildegund told Jolanda.

"We've noticed," Jolanda said. "How can anyone like Elvis *at all*?" Jolanda asked her.

"I only like 'It's Now or Never'—just one song," the dishwasher said.

"It's definitely a theme with you," Jolanda told her.

Claude and Jimmy could see where this was going—no knee-capping.

"The dog in the alley—the German shepherd you smoke with," Jolanda was saying. "That's your dog, isn't it?" she asked Hildegund.

Jolanda had never wanted to kneecap the ink addict—only sleep with her. "She's my dog—for now, anyway," the tattooed woman dishwasher told Jolanda, as Claude and Jimmy made their way to the bar.

"What's her name?" Jolanda asked Hildegund.

"Hard Rain—it's from the Bob Dylan song," Hildegund said.

"I know where it's from," Jolanda told her, but Claude and Jimmy were caught up in the news from Dallas. On the black-and-white TV above the bar, they kept showing the footage of JFK's motorcade approaching Dealey Plaza and the chaos that ensued after the shooting; there followed footage of Parkland Hospital, where the president was pronounced dead.

James Winslow knew he should call his mother, but it was his grandfather Jimmy wished he could talk to. When the roommates got back to Frau Holzinger's apartment, Jimmy didn't call home; he didn't want to talk about JFK. The living room was in darkness, the TV turned off.

"Irmgard must have gone to bed," was all Jimmy could say.

"Or she went out," Jolanda said. "You can still smell her perfume."

"Irmgard wears perfume?" Claude had asked.

"When she goes out, Claude. I've seen her all dolled up when she was going somewhere," Jolanda said. "I've smelled her perfume before."

That was when James Winslow knew he'd seen Irmgard "all dolled up, when she was going somewhere"—he'd smelled her perfume before, too. (He hadn't just dreamed this when he slept through *From Here to Eternity*.)

"Once, when I had to get up to pee at night, a woman's clothes were strewn in the hall, and the smell of perfume was very strong, and someone was taking a bath in the bathtub—not Siegfried, not at two or three in the morning. It must have been Irmgard!" Claude declared.

"I don't like to think of you getting up to pee at night, Claude," Jolanda told him. But that was when Jimmy realized he'd heard someone taking a bath in the middle of the night before; he hadn't just imagined he heard the bathtub filling or draining in the early-morning hours.

"There are bullet holes in my bedroom wall," Jimmy said to Jolanda and Claude. "Fräulein Eissler showed me. The bullet holes are behind the ugly painting. Maybe the Soviets shot someone against the wall when they occupied this district."

"For Christ's sake, *show* us the wall!" Jolanda cried.

"Maybe all three of us shouldn't be in one bedroom—not at this hour of the night," Claude said, for no discernible reason.

"We're Jimmy's roommates, Claude—we're not visitors, we *live* here!" Jolanda cried. "We three could fuck one another in the same bed, if we wanted to!"

"I wasn't thinking of *that*—I was just *speculating*!" Claude cried. The friends took a long look at the bullet holes. There were only three holes, close together, in a diagonal line; the holes were of a circumference slightly bigger than a pencil, maybe more between a pencil and an adult index finger. The holes were chest-high to Jimmy, but he was thinking the bullets would have struck Jolanda in her lower abdomen. There was no imagining what Claude was *speculating*. The concept of the three of them fucking one another in the same bed must have been more disturbing to Claude than the bullet holes, which he appeared to be examining closely. "They look like bullet holes, but if someone was shot against this wall, where's the blood?" Claude asked. "If a person had been shot here," he speculated, standing in front of the holes, "wouldn't the bullets have passed through the body? Wouldn't the wall be spattered with blood?"

"Maybe they wallpapered over the bloodstains, Claude," Jolanda said.

"Then wouldn't they have bothered to put some plaster in the bullet holes? Wouldn't they have wallpapered over the bullet holes, too?" Claude kept speculating, in his irritating way.

"Are you saying someone just shot the wall, Claude?" Jolanda asked him. "Why would *anyone*, even a trigger-happy Soviet, just shoot a wall?"

"I'm just saying that's what it *looks like*," Claude protested. From this impasse, the foreign students' conversation degenerated.

Jolanda complained it was impossible for her to have sex with Hildegund. There was simply nowhere they could do it. Hildegund had told Jolanda that the dishwasher's place was off-limits for their sleeping together. Hildegund lived with "a bunch of barbarians," or so she'd told Jolanda.

"Do you think you should have sex with someone who lives with barbarians?" Claude asked Jolanda, who ignored him.

"On the other hand, if Hildegund comes here, what do we do with her dog?" Jolanda asked. "Where does Hard Rain go?"

"Do you mean the dog will be with you and Hildegund? Do you

mean Hard Rain is in the same room where you have sex?" Claude asked Jolanda.

"Jesus Mary Joseph, Claude—I mean, does the Frau allow dogs *at all*? And if I ask the Frau, and she says no—*then* what?" Jolanda cried.

"Well, in the first place, the dog should *not* be in your room when you and Hildegund have sex! Hard Rain should *not* see that—the poor dog shouldn't *watch*!" Claude declared.

"For Christ's sake, Claude! Dogs don't care if people have sex—dogs aren't interested in people fucking!" Jolanda said.

"The poor dog!" Claude cried. "I'm still adjusting to a German shepherd named Hard Rain," he said, for no known reason.

"We can chain the dog to the bicycle rack in the courtyard. It's enclosed and Hard Rain will be safe," Jolanda reasoned.

"The poor dog!" Claude cried. "The courtyard is cold—Hard Rain will be abandoned with a bunch of bikes!"

"Hard Rain is abandoned in an alley with a bunch of *garbage*!" Jolanda shouted. "Maybe the dog could stay in one of your rooms when Hildegund is visiting me," Jolanda said.

"I've never slept with a German shepherd," Claude told them.

"You never cease to surprise me, Claude," Jolanda said.

"I just mean that Hard Rain is a *big* dog," Claude pointed out.

"What if Hard Rain has to pee or something?" Jimmy asked.

The only issue was thunderstorms, or so Jolanda was told.

When there was thunder and lightning, Hildegund had said, Hard Rain cowered in a bathtub, where she would shit her brains out. As Jolanda put it to Jimmy and Claude: "In a thunderstorm, it's best to leave the bathroom door open—to be sure Hard Rain has access to the Holzingers' only bathtub."

"Wait, wait, *wait*!" Claude said to Jolanda. "Your new girlfriend lives with a bunch of barbarians, and her dog has diarrhea in a bathtub during thunderstorms?"

The *new girlfriend* designation was a hard one for Jolanda to hear. It was clear to Jimmy and Claude that Jolanda was still missing Mieke.

"Winter is just beginning. Winter takes four months, or more," James Winslow reminded his roommates. "Thunder and lightning aren't the usual winter weather," he said. He knew nothing about the winters in Vienna. James Winslow couldn't have explained why the idea of hiding a German shepherd in the Holzingers' apartment appealed to him.

"I usually break up with a new girlfriend before two or three months," Jolanda told Jimmy and Claude. "I just never expected to break up with Mieke, but I had no idea she wanted to *try it* with a guy!" Jolanda lamented. The three friends agreed that it wouldn't work to chain Hard Rain to the bicycle rack in the courtyard. Hard Rain was a friendly dog, but she was still a German shepherd. People are afraid of German shepherds.

Therefore, Jimmy and Claude said they would take turns concealing the German shepherd while Jolanda was having sex with Hildegund. This is the kind of thing roommates do for one another when they're in their twenties—when thunder and lightning might be months away, a remote possibility.

After Claude and Jolanda had gone to their rooms—likely long after they were asleep—Jimmy was still writing, under his bedcovers. In the novel he was beginning, the easy part was reimagining his grandfather as the main character. Thomas Winslow's benevolence as a teacher extended beyond the classroom; he was a good teacher as a father and a grandfather—he was always teaching. In James Winslow's first novel, the character of the beloved English teacher is a confirmed bachelor. In an all-boys' school, there are some faculty wives and students who think such men must be nonpracticing homosexuals. In the novel Jimmy was writing, there would be no evidence to support such knee-jerk homophobia. The bachelor English teacher is as asexual as Honor Winslow. In the novel, he's called Tom or Teacher Tom. He seeks out the students who are lost or depressed. He saves them with Dickens. Teacher Tom knows which Dickens novel will lift their spirits.

That night, under his bedcovers in Vienna, young James settled on the title for his first novel—*The Dickens Man,* he'd decided to call it. Then Jimmy had gone to the WC down the hall; later on he'd washed his face and brushed his teeth in the bathroom across the hall from his bedroom. He was in bed with his lights off, but he was wide awake when Irmgard came home. She'd turned on the hall light; her big body was recognizable through the panel of frosted glass on Jimmy's bedroom door. He could see she was undressing herself in the hall. She was not stripping for him—he could tell. She was just getting undressed before she went in the bathroom, where Jimmy could hear her drawing a bath. He got out of bed and quietly opened his door, just a crack—enough to get a look at the pile of clothes in the hall. The clothes were redolent of the overpowering perfume Irmgard had been wearing; there was not a trace of baby powder in the strong fragrance.

Jimmy waited in his room, in the dark, until he could hear the bathtub draining. Then he turned on the lamp on his writing desk, by the window. When Irmgard emerged from the bathroom, wrapped in towels, Jimmy opened his bedroom door and saw her. She was picking up her clothes.

"Can I ask you about something? I must show you," he told her.

"Ask me what—show me what?" she said, stepping into his room.

Jimmy was wearing just a T-shirt and some sweatpants when he struggled to remove the bad painting from the wall beside the headboard of his bed. Irmgard had to help him with the painting.

"Oh, the bullet holes. Is that all?" Irmgard asked. She'd thrown her clothes on his bed. She'd told him most of the story before Jimmy realized there was nothing wrong with her word order in English. "Never rent a room to a Russian, unless you have rats and you want to get rid of them," was the way Irmgard began the story. The Russian was kept awake because there were rats crawling between the walls. There were rats all over the neighborhood; the rats had overrun the apartment building when Irmgard was a little girl. "I was not much older than Siegfried when the Russian was living here," Irmgard told him in perfect word order.

"The Russian shot the rats through the wall?" Jimmy asked her.

"Of course not! The Russian made three perfectly placed bullet holes," she told him.

"Why didn't he use a drill?" young James asked her.

"This is a family without a father, Jimmy—fathers are the ones who have tools. The Russian had a gun; that's how he made the bullet holes," Irmgard explained. The Russian inserted some tweezers in two of the holes; the third hole was used to insert what looked like a sugar cube, which was held by the tweezers. The sugar cube was actually rat poison. "You knew when the rats had taken the poison, because the tweezers fell back inside the bedroom," Irmgard explained.

"Did the rats die between the walls?" Jimmy asked her.

"Of course not! The rats would have smelled awful. The poison made the rats thirsty. When the rats went outside to drink some water, they exploded in a puddle—they died outdoors," Irmgard told him, while she was gathering up her clothes.

"Your word order is perfect. It wasn't perfect before," he pointed out.

"I'm tired of playing games, Jimmy—my English isn't bad," Irmgard admitted. "Your mother called earlier, to speak to you. She said my English was pretty good. Your mother asked me if you were going to the gym. She wanted to know if you were wrestling. I said I didn't think so, but I didn't really know. Your mother wants you to keep wrestling, you know," she added.

"Ich weiß. I know," Jimmy said. "I thought she might have called because Kennedy was killed. That would have been a better reason for her to call me."

"Your mother asked me if you ever thought about Vietnam—she said you *should*, now that Kennedy is gone," Irmgard told Jimmy. "I said

I didn't think so, but I didn't really know," she added. Jimmy couldn't think of what to say, as he and Irmgard struggled to put the painting back on the wall over the bullet holes. "Your mother asked me if you had a girlfriend, Jimmy," Irmgard told him.

"And you said you didn't think so, but you didn't really know," Jimmy ventured to say.

"Your mother asked me who I was, and I told her what my circumstances were—Siegfried, and so forth," Irmgard said, pausing there. She was picking up her clothes again—this time, from Jimmy's bed.

"I hope my mom didn't ask you if *you* would be my girlfriend, and if you would consider getting pregnant again and giving me your baby," young James asked Irmgard.

"I just said I didn't think so, Jimmy," Irmgard told him.

"I'm so sorry, Irmgard. My mother is determined to keep me from being a soldier—she's completely obsessed about it," Jimmy said.

"I don't blame her, Jimmy, but it can't be me," Irmgard told him. She stopped in the hall, looking back at him—not a warm or welcoming look.

"Thank you—I guess now I know everything," Jimmy said to her.

"No, you don't know everything, Jimmy, but you know enough," Irmgard said. Once more, there was nothing amiss with her word order. She was done playing games with him; there would be no more movie-going in the living room, Jimmy could tell.

Back in his bedroom, Jimmy saw her black bra; it had fallen from her armful of clothes at the foot of Jimmy's bed. He'd had limited experience with bras. There was a distinct plunge between the cups, and a push-up aspect to the cups themselves. He could feel there was some underwiring involved in the uplifting. It suffices to say that Irmgard's bra was no mere undergarment. It was a bra that was meant to be seen, a bra you were supposed to see someone take off—or so Jimmy imagined.

James Winslow was tempted to take her bra to bed—its fragrance, its feel, inspired fantasies. But if Irmgard was done playing games with him, as she'd put it, Jimmy sincerely tried to be done with her and her Judenhass. Irmgard's hatred of Jews—her anti-Semitism, or whatever you called it—made Jimmy hate her. He was deeply ashamed of his ongoing desire for her, which seemed to contradict his hatred.

Irmgard had turned out the light in the hall, but there was sufficient light from Jimmy's bedroom for him to see where her black bra ended up—where he threw it, in the hall, halfway between the bathroom and the WC.

18.

Sharing a Bed

It hadn't occurred to Jimmy that Claude would step barefoot on the bra in the dark—on his way to take a whiz in the WC—or that when Claude turned on the hall light and saw what he'd stepped on, the sight of such a salacious brassiere would cause him to piss in his pajamas. (Jimmy and Jolanda slept soundly through Claude's traumatic encounter.)

On Saturday morning, either Frau Holzinger or Siegfried was the first to find the fallen bra. Surely the Frau would have known whose bra it was. She'd no doubt returned it to its rightful owner. Even Claude could tell it was way too big a bra to be Jolanda's.

The commotion Jimmy heard in the hall, the dialogue he woke up to, was not about the bra. "Nicht Dienstag, nicht Mittwoch, nicht Donnerstag," Frau Holzinger was saying. ("Not Tuesday, not Wednesday, not Thursday," the Frau was bitching.) "Samstag ist ungewöhnlich," she complained. ("Saturday is unusual.")

"Kennedys Tod ist auch ungewöhnlich," Jimmy heard Annelies say to his landlady. ("Kennedy's death is also unusual.") Jimmy could see Annelies in the panel of frosted glass on his bedroom door.

"Trotzdem ungewöhnlich," he heard the Frau say, but he couldn't see her; she was probably preparing Siegfried's Frühstück in the kitchen. ("Still unusual," the widow Holzinger had said about Fräulein Eissler's impromptu visit to the Schwindgasse on a Saturday morning.)

Annelies pointed to herself in the oval of frosted glass. "Ich bin ungewöhnlich," she said, referring to herself. ("I'm unusual," she said, opening Jimmy's door.) She stuck one bare foot in his bedroom, wiggling her painted toenails. "Are you decent?" Annelies asked. It was an old-fashioned thing to say—like something Jimmy's grandmother might have said, though Constance wouldn't have wiggled her toes.

"Yes! Come in!" Jimmy cried. He got out of bed in the T-shirt and sweatpants he'd slept in. He was worried that his breath was bad; he hadn't brushed his teeth. And Jimmy could see himself in the double-door mirrors on his wardrobe closet; he looked terrible.

"You've had a visitor—her perfume is furchtbar," Fräulein Eissler said, shutting his bedroom door in the Frau's inquisitive face. Annelies opened the balcony window. "That means 'terrible,'" she told him.

Jimmy hoped the terrible smell was just Irmgard's perfume, and not the result of his spraying her underarm deodorant on his typewriter keys—the unwise commingling with sausage smells from the enduring bratwurst. Jimmy simplified his explanation of Irmgard's visit—her overpowering perfume, her account of the phone call from Jimmy's mom—but he got bogged down in Irmgard's story about the bullet holes. In citing the moral of the story, Jimmy quoted what Irmgard had said to him: "Never rent a room to a Russian, unless you have rats and you want to get rid of them."

"That's not the moral of the story, Jimmy," Annelies said. "The moral of the story is that every household should have a drill." She was sitting on his bed, pointing to her painted toenails. "Socks, please," she said to him, as if she'd decided to stay awhile. "You seem okay," she told him, while he fetched the socks. "It's not every day your president is assassinated," she went on. "Right now, you're the only American I know in Vienna—I thought I'd check to see how you were doing."

"I'm fine," Jimmy told her, but that was when they both realized he was kneeling on the floor by his bed, where he was putting a pair of his white athletic socks on her pretty feet.

"This is strange, Jimmy—the kneeling is more than a little subservient for the usual student-tutor relationship," Fräulein Eissler said.

"I'm okay with it if you are," Jimmy told her.

Of course Annelies knew all about Honor Winslow's hopes to extricate her dear James from the draft, thus saving him from the war in Vietnam. Esther must have informed her of the pregnancy plan. Jimmy's German tutor already knew he was supposed to knock up *someone*.

"Leave your bedroom door open, Jimmy," Annelies told him when he went to the bathroom to brush his teeth and wash his face. When he came back, she'd gotten under his bedcovers and was lying with her head on his pillow—as if she'd taken off all her clothes. After Jimmy closed his bedroom door, Annelies got out of bed—with all her clothes on, he noticed. Annelies told Jimmy she just wanted to be sure the Frau had seen her in his bed. "Let the old Judenhasser imagine what she will," Annelies said. He'd already told Annelies what a Jew-hater Irmgard was.

"I hate Irmgard for hating you," he'd said to Annelies, but she surprised him.

"You shouldn't hate her. Siegfried's mother is a sad story," Annelies told him. "The Judenhass comes from Frau Holzinger's generation— hate the Frau, not Irmgard," his Jewish German tutor said.

Annelies was thinking ahead, but where she was going wasn't evident from where she began. For example, she suddenly said: "When the Institute for European Studies asks you if you're sleeping with me, please tell them the truth—say you aren't. But leave out how I tricked Frau Holzinger into thinking we were sleeping together." Annelies took off his socks. It was clear she was leaving, her mission accomplished.

"Okay," Jimmy said. The interrogation she predicted would happen before Christmas. The dean of students at IES—Jimmy liked her, but he could never remember her name—called him in to discuss the issue. Jimmy had followed Fräulein Eissler's instructions. He'd pointed out to the dean that Frau Holzinger and her daughter ("an angry unmarried mother") were Jew-haters, which Annelies also told him to say. After all, there were Jewish students in the Institute for European Studies. What if one of the IES Jewish students had been a boarder in the Holzinger apartment?

Naturally, the dean pointed out that Frau Holzinger had seen Fräulein Eissler in Jimmy's bed, under the bedcovers, but Annelies had prepared him for this line of questioning. Jimmy told the dean how the Frau turned down the heat at night, and she often left it turned down on weekends. Jimmy wrote under his bedcovers at night, he told the dean. On the Saturday morning after JFK was killed, it was cold in Jimmy's bedroom; Annelies got under the covers because she was cold. "And when Fräulein Eissler visits me, for our tutorials, she always puts on a pair of my socks," he said to the dean. (Jimmy left out the kneeling, and the fact that he put the socks on his Jewish German tutor's feet.)

It got a little warmer in the Schwindgasse apartment in the evenings after that. The Frau still turned down the heat, but only a little, and she did not leave the heat turned down over the weekend. Jimmy's friendship with Jolanda and Claude was steadfast; they still went out together in the evenings to the Kaffeehaus Nachtmusik, but Jimmy didn't have to write under his bedcovers anymore. Fräulein Eissler had made her point. The Judenhass was still palpable in the Schwindgasse apartment, especially on Tuesdays, Wednesdays, and Thursdays—before, during, and immediately after his tutorials with Annelies—but the *Jew* word was scarcely mentioned. Neither Frau Holzinger nor Irmgard uttered "die Jüdin" as a virtual synonym for Fräulein Eissler's name; their Jew-hatred was held back.

"There's still something I need to show you," Annelies told Jimmy. "One night, we'll go out together. It'll be late."

"How late?" Jimmy asked her, but Fräulein Eissler was moving on.

"As late as it is when Irmgard goes out at night, whenever she goes out—as late as that, or later," Annelies answered.

"Okay," Jimmy said. His tutor didn't wait to change the subject.

The wrestlers at Turnhalle Leopold were wondering where he was, she now told Jimmy. Leo ("Little Mirror") himself had asked her about him. The freestyle wrestlers, the two Soviets and the two Israelis, had been looking forward to meeting the American. Solomon was the Israeli in Jimmy's weight class. He used to compete at sixty-two kilos (136.6 pounds), Annelies told Jimmy, but she said the former Haganah fighter was heavier than that now. ("So am I," Jimmy told her.) Jimmy had been waiting for the Christmas break before he ventured to the gym on Währinger Straße, he explained to Annelies. Claude and Jolanda would be going home for Christmas, and Jimmy's fellow IES students were spending the holiday in Kaprun—a ski resort in the Austrian Alps. Young James would be alone in Vienna for half of December—a good time to work on his novel, and to meet his fellow wrestlers, he told Annelies.

Fräulein Eissler didn't think the freestyle wrestlers would be going anywhere for Christmas. The other Israeli was Simon; the bigger of the two Haganah graybeards had to weigh at least seventy-five kilos, she told Jimmy (more than 165 pounds). Simon's only workout partner was Sergei, the bigger of the two Soviets. The former Red Army wrestler in Jimmy's weight class was Zander, Fräulein Eissler said.

The Christmas part of their conversation prompted an anti-Christmas diatribe from Annelies. Austria was a Catholic country, and a socialist one; Christmas was both a religious and socialist excuse not to work, she said. Furthermore, Annelies knew that Jimmy's mom was writing him. But what was the point of paying extra for airmail if the Austrian postal workers were off because of Christmas? Fräulein Eissler told Jimmy she would continue their tutorials during the Christmas holidays, except for Christmas Day—unless Jimmy was too busy writing and wrestling.

"Did Esther tell you my mother was writing me?" young James asked Annelies, but she didn't respond to the *Esther* part of Jimmy's question.

"Your mom is writing you a Vorschlag, Jimmy," Annelies told him—a "proposal." She wouldn't say what it was. She'd detected a new fragrance in his bedroom and had opened his balcony window to the cold. "You're not seeing Irmgard, are you?" Annelies had asked him. "Has she changed her perfume? It's not much better. Immer noch furchtbar." ("Still terrible.")

"I'm not seeing Irmgard," he told Annelies. She'd caught a whiff of Hard Rain. Jimmy didn't know what his Jewish German tutor might think of sharing a bed with a German shepherd. The dog-sitting schedule was still new. Claude and Jimmy were taking turns, but Claude had nightmares that made him whimper in his sleep. This made Hard Rain whimper and whine with him, which gave them both nightmares.

"It really shouldn't be that complicated to sleep with a dog, Claude," Jolanda had told him, but both Jimmy and Claude were sensing that Jolanda was finding it complicated to sleep with Hildegund, her tattooed dishwasher. Jolanda had provided no details; she just blamed the "bunch of barbarians" Hildegund lived with.

As for Hard Rain, Jimmy and Claude loved her. They'd never had a dog or slept with one; they didn't know if Hard Rain's habits were all her own or common to other German shepherds (perhaps to all dogs). It wasn't Hard Rain's fault that she smelled slightly like garbage; the poor dog was chained in the alley where the café's garbage was collected. And that Hard Rain had a smoky smell was Hildegund's fault—she was a smoker.

It didn't escape Jimmy and Claude's attention that Hildegund's smoking had reignited Jolanda's smoking habit.

"Whoever she is, Jimmy, her perfume is putrid, and she smokes, but if she lets you knock her up, she serves a purpose," Annelies told him.

"She's a German shepherd. I'm hiding her—what amounts to three or four nights a week," Jimmy admitted.

Fräulein Eissler was unshockable. "I trust you will explain," she calmly said. He did. No doubt Jimmy's fondness for Hard Rain was evident.

"She doesn't shed much," young James told his tutor, pulling back his bedcovers to show Annelies the sheets.

"No, not much," Annelies said, shrugging. Jimmy loved the way she shrugged—her small shoulders rolling forward, her breasts shifting slightly when she sighed. "A symbolic breed—it's not the fault of the dog who their masters were or are," Fräulein Eissler mysteriously said. James Winslow was baffled by her reference to German shepherds. It made him hesitate to tell Annelies what the foreign students were warned about Hard Rain—her alleged overreaction to thunderstorms. Jimmy saw no signs, in the Hard Rain he was getting to know and beginning to love, that this was a dog who would shit out her brains in a bathtub at the onset of thunder and lightning. Jimmy and Claude didn't trust anything Jolanda's tattooed woman dishwasher had told her; they hated Hildegund.

What if Hard Rain had a onetime diarrheic episode in a bathtub? What if she'd eaten some tainted dog food, and the thunder and lightning were merely coincidental? Who were the so-called barbarians Hildegund said she lived with? In what way were they barbarians?

Jimmy could tell Claude really liked Hard Rain, even though they gave each other nightmares. "She's a good girl," Claude said. "I don't believe she shits out her brains in a bathtub every time there's a thunderstorm. If Hard Rain ever shit in a bathtub, she would be embarrassed about it," Claude maintained. "She's even embarrassed when she farts, isn't she?" he asked Jimmy, who thought she was—or she looked more sad-eyed than usual after she farted. When Hard Rain farted, she wagged her tail—a little uncertainly, as if seeking approval. As for her being a bathtub shitter, the evidence against Hard Rain was "strictly hearsay," Claude concluded.

It was also unrealistic for the foreign students to imagine they could keep the door to the bathroom open—in case Hard Rain had to jump in the bathtub, at the first flash of lightning or a distant rumble of thunder. Jimmy and Claude couldn't be expected to make sure Hard

Rain had access to the bathtub—certainly not when Irmgard was taking baths in the wee hours of the morning. All Jolanda would say about Hard Rain's reputation as a bathtub shitter was: "She farts a lot." Surely Jolanda knew she would see Mieke back in Amsterdam during Christmas break. Jolanda was already feeling guilty about having sex with Hildegund.

Jimmy told Annelies about the night Irmgard must have heard him talking to Hard Rain, who was biting his toes under the bedcovers; she wasn't biting hard, just being playful. "No biting—be a good girl," Jimmy was telling her. She thumped her tail under the covers. "What a good girl you are," Jimmy told her, and she wagged her tail harder; then she snorted or sneezed, thrashing her head all around. Sometimes she sounded more like a pig than a dog, especially when she was under the bedcovers.

That was when he saw Irmgard's big and blurry body pressed against the frosted glass; she was wrapped in towels, fresh from her bath, steaming up the glass oval on his bedroom door.

"I hear you talking to someone, Jimmy," Irmgard said. "Is your German tutor with you?"

"Not the tutor," Jimmy said, but Irmgard opened his bedroom door, her body filling the doorway.

In the early-morning darkness, when Hildegund left Jolanda's bed, the tattooed dishwasher came into Claude's room or Jimmy's—to take Hard Rain home with her, back to the barbarians. Hard Rain didn't like to leave with Hildegund, faced with venturing into the cold and darkness at such an early hour of the morning. She always cowered under the covers.

"What's the matter with her—is she just shy?" Irmgard asked now. There was a single thump of the tail from Hard Rain, like the twitch of an arm or a leg. This was followed by a bed-shaking snort—a violent, strangled sneeze. Then Hard Rain rolled over on her back, poking up the bedcovers with her forepaws.

"She's just shy, and she has a cold," Jimmy explained to Irmgard. "And she's naked—she doesn't want you to see her," he added.

"I hope she's not underage, Jimmy. She's not underage, is she? We don't want the Polizei coming here," Irmgard told him.

"No police—I promise. She's not underage," Jimmy said to Siegfried's angry and depressed mother. Hard Rain was arching her back and scratching herself under the covers; she was also gnawing on Jimmy's wrist, in her gentle way. "She just *acts* underage," Jimmy tried to assure Irmgard, but Irmgard was leaving—abruptly closing his door behind her.

Before Irmgard turned off the light in the hall, Jimmy heard her say: "I'll know how old she is when I get a look at her."

"Whatever Irmgard thought, she couldn't possibly have imagined *you* were under the covers," Jimmy told Fräulein Eissler. He expected her to be amused by the story, but she was not in the least amused. She looked worried or distracted, or both.

"I said you shouldn't hate Irmgard, and you shouldn't," Annelies said, "but you also shouldn't get too close to her, Jimmy. It's safer to sleep with the German shepherd." Jimmy thought so, too, but Fräulein Eissler was already moving ahead—this time, to the 1964 Winter Olympics. Everyone was talking about how the Austrians would do in alpine skiing. At the end of January, through early February, the 1964 Winter Games would be held in Innsbruck. Austrian television would air all the skiing, but Irmgard would probably be watching the movie channel. Jimmy, Claude, and Jolanda were counting on Dagmar at the Kaffeehaus Nachtmusik, who had told the foreign students that the TV in the café would be showing the Olympics. When the Austrians were skiing, Dagmar even said, she'd turn on the sound. Fräulein Eissler, who didn't ski, just said she was "dreading" the Olympics. "It brings out nationalism, which doesn't have a good history in this country," she said. But Jimmy, Claude, and Jolanda were looking forward to watching the skiing in their local café, where they did their homework—and Jimmy tried to write, or to believe in himself as a future writer—where at least they were warm, and they didn't have far to go when they were tired and wanted to go to bed.

Claude said the French had some good downhill skiers. Even Jolanda was somewhat interested in the Winter Games. "The Dutch skate—not me, but other Dutch people do," she said, sighing. Jimmy and Claude were worried about Jolanda. They could see it wasn't going well with Hildegund. While Jimmy and Claude had grown attached to Hard Rain, Jolanda had lost interest in her tattooed dishwasher. What would happen to Hard Rain when Jolanda dumped the dishwasher? (This is what Jimmy and Claude were also worrying about.)

It was Claude's turn to have nightmares with Hard Rain. Jimmy was alone in his bed when he woke up knowing it was preternaturally cold in his room; he could feel a draft from the balcony window by his writing desk. There was a nearby streetlight on the Schwindgasse. Jimmy could see the ghost sitting at his writing desk—she was smoking, blowing her smoke out the window, which was open a crack. Maybe other bullets had been fired in Jimmy's bedroom; perhaps this young woman, the smoker, had been a victim. Jimmy just watched her for a while. She was a young ghost, lost in her thoughts. Jimmy just felt sorry for her. It was hard to tell how tall she was when she was sitting down, but Jimmy eventually recognized her. Not wanting to startle her by saying her name, he rolled over in bed to get her attention.

"I'm sorry I woke you up," Jolanda said; she flicked her cigarette into the street and closed the window.

"I thought you were trying to quit smoking," Jimmy told her. Jolanda was cold and shivering when she got into bed with him. Jimmy knew nothing sexual was desired or intended. Jolanda just wanted to get warm, and she didn't want to go back to her room—to her tattooed dishwasher.

"I'd almost stopped smoking before you and Claude met me, but the smell of smoke on Hildegund and Hard Rain makes me miss smoking," Jolanda told Jimmy. "Now I'm smoking again, and I *hate* Hildegund. She's cruel, and she makes love like she's washing dishes—like she's just doing it to get the job done. That said, I usually have better reasons when I dump someone," Jolanda added.

"Those are good reasons," Jimmy told her.

"I always need *better* reasons!" Jolanda cried. "And if I dump the dishwasher, we lose the dog. I *love* the dog! It's Hildegund I want to dump, not Hard Rain," she said.

"I love Hard Rain, too," Jimmy told Jolanda. They were lying in bed, hugging each other, when Claude came in; he had Hard Rain with him. The dog jumped on the bed and burrowed her way under the covers, inserting herself between Jimmy and Jolanda. Claude told them he'd first thought Jolanda was Fräulein Eissler.

"For Christ's sake, Claude—Annelies is small, and I'm big! She's also pretty, and I'm not," Jolanda said.

Jimmy guessed it wouldn't be a good time for Jolanda to hear he'd first thought she was a ghost.

"It's really cold in here," Claude told them, shivering, "and Hard Rain and I have been frightening each other like crazy."

"For Christ's sake, Claude—if you're cold, get in bed with us!" Jolanda told him. All three of them were under the covers with Hard Rain when Hildegund barged into the bedroom, looking for her dog— or looking for her dog and her girlfriend, and finding all of them. "I don't like you anymore," Jolanda told the dishwasher. As usual, Hard Rain didn't want to get out of bed and venture into the cold and darkness. Why would she? The dog didn't make a move toward Hildegund. Hard Rain put her forepaws on Claude's chest, with her long nose poking in Claude's ear on the pillow.

"You don't love her enough," Claude said to Hildegund. Under the circumstances, Claude could have meant Jolanda, but both Jolanda and Jimmy knew what Claude meant: Hildegund didn't love Hard Rain enough. The tattooed dishwasher didn't deserve to have a dog like Hard Rain.

"Ausländer," Hildegund said, with her middle fingers raised to Claude and Jimmy. ("Foreigners," she'd called them.) "Ausländerin," said the tattooed dishwasher, pointing only one index finger at Jolanda— a "female foreigner." Hildegund held out the short leash and harness to Hard Rain, who reluctantly got out of bed and allowed Hildegund to hook her up—the same short leash and harness used for a Seeing Eye dog. When Hard Rain was hooked up, she didn't look happy.

"Typisch ausländisch," Hildegund told them as she left, leaving Jimmy's bedroom door open. ("Typically foreign," she'd called them.)

"You xenophobic asshole!" Jolanda called after her. To be *foreigners* was a bad thing to the Viennese, as the foreign students were learning.

"Das geht bei uns nicht," Frau Holzinger would say to Jimmy or Claude or Jolanda—if one of them left an opened bottle of beer in the fridge, or an unrinsed coffee cup in the kitchen sink. ("That doesn't go with us," the Frau would tell the foreign students.)

Fräulein Eissler told Jimmy that anti-Semitism in Austria was part of "a larger xenophobia." She'd also teased the foreign students, in a nice way, about their habit of hanging out at the Kaffeehaus Nachtmusik. "No one goes to that dreary café. Not even the Polish Reading Room types," Annelies said. She'd meant this as a joke. (No one was ever seen entering or leaving the Polish Reading Room on the Schwindgasse; no one saw who went there.)

Jimmy, Claude, and Jolanda lived within walking distance of the Kärntner Straße, Annelies had reminded them. They should be hanging out at the Café Hawelka; they should go have fun at the Augustinerkeller. "You should go where other young people go!" Annelies urged them. Naturally, Claude was afraid of being beaten up; places where other young people went had not been kind to him. As for Jimmy and Jolanda, they had little confidence in their ability to meet other young people—or little desire to. Besides, they had homework to do. You couldn't do your homework, or try to write, at the Café Hawelka; too many people were talking and having a good time there. Jimmy and Claude and Jolanda needed a lugubrious place, where the only conceivable conversation concerned the insanely limited but randomly heterogeneous music selections.

Fräulein Eissler had also exhorted the foreign students to "make an effort to save Siegfried." They could have "an international influence" on the isolated boy, she'd said. The xenophobic Judenhass of Siegfried's mother and grandmother would either stop with Siegfried or be continued by him, Annelies had told them. "You could inspire this kid to think globally," she had assured them. But what could *they* do? the foreign students were wondering. Jimmy loved Annelies, and his roommates were increasingly impressed by her. Yet saving Siegfried seemed beyond them; the atrocities he'd committed with the garlic press might have marked the child as a future war criminal. Siegfried seemed a sullen, uncommunicative five-year-old. What if Irmgard's anger and depression had been passed down to the boy? How could three foreign students save Siegfried?

On the morning when Jimmy and his roommates were left together in his bed, with Jimmy's bedroom door flung open—the cold, dark morning when the tattooed dishwasher had labeled them "typically foreign" and taken Hard Rain away from them, back to the barbarians—Jimmy, Claude, and Jolanda had fallen into a deep and despondent sleep. They'd wasted the first three months of their study-abroad year; they'd failed to engage very much with anyone other than themselves.

James Winslow was most of all embarrassed by what made him unique in Fräulein Eissler's eyes, and in the eyes of his two roommates—his mom's commitment to keep him out of Vietnam, which included his knocking up someone. More embarrassing, the best option of *that* happening (in Jimmy's mind) was Claude's idea that Jimmy should impregnate Mieke—the girlfriend Jolanda had broken up with—while Jolanda held Mieke's head and talked to her. No wonder Jimmy was embarrassed! In such confusion and despondency, Jimmy, Claude, and Jolanda were lying asleep in one another's arms, with his bedroom door wide open, when Frau Holzinger made her early-morning march to the kitchen to prepare Siegfried's breakfast. The Frau didn't wake them; she'd surely given them a disapproving look in passing. Those three didn't hear what she'd muttered to herself, the usual admonition: "Das geht bei uns nicht." The first thing the students heard was the harsh sound of Frau Holzinger grinding her coffee beans. In the foreign students' bedrooms, even if their doors were closed, the coffee grinder was their wake-up call. The Frau did fuck all for Siegfried's Frühstück until she got the coffee going.

Claude was whimpering when Jolanda kicked him under the covers. "It sounds like Siegfried is grinding his soldiers with the coffee beans," Claude said, moaning. But when the three had opened their eyes, they saw Siegfried standing beside the bed, just staring at them. The boy was doubtless unfamiliar with seeing three adults in bed together. He stood as resolutely as a soldier—the garlic press held tightly in one little hand. In his other hand, the silent soldier was holding what looked like an airmail letter.

"Guten Morgen, lieber Briefträger," Jolanda addressed the child. ("Good morning, dear letter carrier.")

"Ist Post für mich da?" Claude asked him. ("Is there any mail for me?")

"Nein, nur für Yimmy," Siegfried said, handing Jimmy the letter. ("No, only for Yimmy.")

19.

Der Vorschlag

There were additional postage stamps on the airmail letter; it felt like there was a photograph enclosed. Knowing his mom, Jimmy thought she might have included a photo of Chantal.

"It's from your mother, right?" Jolanda asked.

"Der Vorschlag!" Claude cried, startling Siegfried, who dropped the garlic press on Jolanda's knee. ("The proposal!" Claude had cried.)

"Don't scare Siegfried, Claude—you idiot," Jolanda said. She gave the garlic press to Siegfried, saying something soothing, to mollify the anxious child. "Nur von Yimmys Mutter," Jolanda told the boy, pointing to the letter. ("Only from Jimmy's mother.")

"When you read us the letter from your mother, Jimmy, you should try to sound as much like your mother as you can," Claude began. "After all, she *is* your mother, but Jolanda and I don't know her at all," Claude said.

"Jesus Mary Joseph, Claude! You're not exactly brimming with girlfriend experience, but you sound as lacking in mother experience," Jolanda told him. "Jimmy doesn't have to *act out* his mom for us!"

"My mother is always trying to marry me off, Jolanda," Claude said.

James Winslow would realize—but not until a few years later, when he was finishing his first novel—that this was a writing lesson. Albeit inadvertently, he'd compounded the problem; his roommates (right now, his bedmates) were poised to hear him read aloud the proposal his mother was making to safeguard his passage through the Vietnam War. And what Honor Winslow was proposing had preoccupied Jimmy's Jewish German tutor. When Jimmy managed to open the envelope, he saw that Siegfried was poised to listen to the proposal, too. The little soldier was still standing at the bedside; he didn't understand English, but Siegfried wasn't moving on.

"Poor Chantal," Claude uttered like a prayer, when he saw the photo. Naturally, the photo was the first thing out of the envelope— the first thing everyone saw. For once, Chantal was wearing a sweater that fit her. Jimmy recognized the sweater—an old-fashioned cashmere cardigan his mom used to wear. It fit Chantal perfectly, although the sweater made her look a little older than she was. Even Siegfried looked closely at the photo. The foreign students should have realized that Siegfried thought the photo was of Yimmy's mother.

Someone should have spoken up before Claude started improvising.

When Claude began to speak to Siegfried—in overcareful German, as if Siegfried had not yet learned to talk in any language—Jolanda and Jimmy just thought Claude was trying to get the child to leave. But knowing Claude and his baffling bad timing, they should have been prepared for Claude to bewilder the boy with whatever lay lurking in Claude's subconscious. "What do you think of dogs, Siegfried?" Claude asked the boy. He spoke with an exaggerated slowness; the question seemed a matter of grave concern.

When Siegfried answered Claude, the boy understandably spoke as slowly as he'd been spoken to; Siegfried probably imagined that Claude had the mental capacity of a two- or three-year-old. "I don't know any dogs," Siegfried said in German even Jimmy could understand.

"But would you like to have a dog, Siegfried—a *female dog*?" Claude emphasized, in an unnatural way.

The word for a female dog in German (*Hündin*) is different from the word for a male dog (*Hund*). Claude obviously felt it was necessary to specify the sex of the dog. It's a wonder Claude didn't tell Siegfried that Hard Rain was spayed. The gender-related part of having (or not having) a dog clearly caused Siegfried some consternation. As Jolanda would say—thankfully not then, but later—the females in Siegfried's family might not have predisposed the boy to wanting a female dog. Claude's question (Would Siegfried like to have a Hündin?) caused Siegfried to wave the garlic press around, as if he were conducting an unseen and unheard orchestra.

"For Christ's sake, Claude," Jolanda said, kicking him under the covers. "Siegfried!" Jolanda suddenly said to the boy, startling him. "Wouldn't you rather have breakfast?" She spoke quickly to the child— that is, she spoke naturally—in her not-messing-around German. Jolanda spoke in German to Siegfried the same way she would have spoken to Claude or Jimmy in English.

"Ich möchte lieber . . ." Siegfried started to say. ("I would rather . . .") When Siegfried spoke again, there was no question that he meant what he said. "I would rather have a dog," Siegfried told them—a Hündin, a female dog, the boy had distinctly said.

"What's your follow-up, Claude?" Jolanda asked their improvisational roommate. Claude deserved credit; he'd started something with Siegfried, but at the time no one understood what had been set in motion.

"Siegfried! Frühstück!" Frau Holzinger hollered, and Siegfried darted away; that the boy would rather have a female dog did not deter him from running to his breakfast. Naturally, Siegfried took the photo of Yimmys Mutter with him to show his grandmother. The Frau brought the photo back to Jimmy's bedroom. She was clearly disapproving of the three of them in one bed; she didn't linger, and Jimmy couldn't understand what she'd said about the photo, which she returned to him.

When the Frau went back to the kitchen, Jolanda got out of bed to close the bedroom door. She was wearing an oversize T-shirt that hung to her knees, and when she got back in bed, she kicked Claude again—her long legs could have reached him anywhere. Claude was just staring at the photo of Chantal, which he'd taken from Jimmy. In the sweater that fit her, it was clear—even to Claude—that Chantal wasn't a *onesie*. "Everyone has two, Claude—you idiot," Jolanda was saying. The Frau had said Yimmys Mutter was very pretty; she'd wondered how long ago the photo had been taken. Jimmy's mom looked so young, the Frau had added.

"Chantal *is* very pretty, *and* she looks so young!" Claude was saying.

"Chantal is only two years older than we are, Claude. Chantal *is* young, you idiot," Jolanda told him.

"Just start reading, Jimmy. We'll catch on," Claude said. Jimmy knew his mother was good at beginnings; when Honor Winslow had determined what she wanted, she knew how to set something in motion.

"Honey, you know I wouldn't say (or even think) any of this, except for your own good—don't you?" the letter from Jimmy's mom began.

"Wait, wait, *wait*—the 'honey' is already complicated!" Claude cried. "Does your mother call everyone 'honey,' or only you?" Claude asked Jimmy.

"If your mother calls everyone 'honey,' that's a different kind of story. That's not *this* story, Claude," Jolanda said.

"You have a classification problem, honey," Jimmy's mom went on. "Right now, your draft deferment is 2-S—that's your classification. The student deferment gets you through college, but what happens then? I didn't go through what I endured to have you, only to lose you in a misbegotten war!"

"I like your mother," Jolanda said. Claude made a panting sound—something he'd picked up from Hard Rain.

"It's too bad you're not wrestling, honey—the right kind of knee injury could be useful," Jimmy's mother had written. "A 4-F deferment is ideal. You know, 'unfit for service' sounds fine to a mom like me! But you can't count on the right kind of wrestling injury, can you?"

Claude shook his head in the insane way Hard Rain shook hers—hard enough to make her ears flap. Jolanda kicked Claude under the covers.

"That's why I like 3-A, 'married with child'—the dependency defer-ment," Honor Winslow called it. "But you haven't met someone you can knock up—have you, honey?"

What a scornful look James Winslow got from Claude and Jolanda. Claude was shaking his head like Hard Rain again. Jimmy was think-ing of the girls he knew at the Institute for European Studies, but he couldn't think of one who would go out with him.

"Generally, you have to meet a girl and go out with her a few times before she'll consider getting knocked up by you," Jolanda was saying, as if she'd been reading Jimmy's mind under the covers.

"Poor Chantal. I can see Chantal coming!" Claude cried despairingly.

"Ideally, honey, you should start knocking someone up this spring—like in March or April," Jimmy's mom asserted.

"Why does your mother think you should 'start knocking someone up this spring'—you don't have to do it more than once to knock some-one up, do you?" Claude asked.

"Usually, Claude, you and the person you're knocking up *like* doing it more than once," Jolanda had pointed out to him. But the three of them saw Chantal coming. They knew Chantal was where Jimmy's mom was going.

"You have JFK to thank for 3-A, honey, but now that he's gone, you can't count on 3-A always being there," Jimmy's mother wrote to him.

"What about Dagmar? Is she still young enough to get knocked up?" Claude suddenly asked. Jimmy had told Claude and Jolanda that he thought the widow manager of their nighttime café was attractive.

"Jesus Mary Joseph, Claude! Dagmar must be in her forties. Why would Dagmar want Jimmy to knock her up?" Jolanda asked Claude.

"I was just wondering if Dagmar was still young enough to get knocked up," Claude said, sorrowfully.

Dagmar was probably still young enough to have children, Jimmy thought. He guessed the widow was about his mom's age, around forty-four.

"Chantal can come to Vienna in March or April. Chantal will do this for me—she'll do this for *us,* honey," Jimmy's mother wrote. "I think Chantal is realizing that she'll never meet a Frenchman who doesn't want to have children—someone who wants *only her.*" If Jimmy had seen *that* coming, he might have stopped reading the letter aloud to his roommates. Jimmy thought he could have done a better job of preparing Claude for *that.*

"Wait, wait, *wait*! What, what, *what?*" Claude had cried.

"I could have told you Claude never wants to have children, Jimmy," Jolanda would say later. "We could have both done a better job of preparing Claude," Jolanda said.

When he sat bolt upright up in bed, Claude unintentionally whacked Jolanda in her mouth with his elbow. "Chantal doesn't want *children?*" Claude babbled in prayer mode. "Chantal wants to meet a Frenchman—someone who wants *only her?*" he asked, clutching Chantal's photo. Claude's eyes never left her.

"Don't wreck the photo, Claude—for now, it's as close as you're getting to Chantal," Jolanda told him. She'd bitten her tongue when Claude hit her in the mouth. Jolanda was exploring her mouth, checking to see if her teeth had been loosened.

If he'd been alone, Jimmy might have stopped reading his mother's proposal, but even a beginning writer knows the story gathers momentum when you have an audience. "I know you like Chantal, honey, and that's okay—that makes it easier, doesn't it?" Jimmy's mom had written.

"Wait, wait, *wait*! Do you have the hots for Chantal?" Claude asked Jimmy in a muffled voice. He'd crawled back under the covers to escape Jolanda's glowering face; her tongue was bleeding.

"Is that what your mom means when she says you *like* Chantal?" Jolanda asked Jimmy, who just kept staring at his mother's letter; he couldn't look at Jolanda. "Holy shit—you have the hots for her," Jolanda concluded.

"No, no, no," Claude moaned, shaking his head under the covers—the way Hard Rain would have done it. Jolanda kicked him.

"You know, Claude, I'm not relaxed in bed with you—not with you thrashing around under the covers like a dog," Jolanda said.

"We're an unconventional family—aren't we, honey? We can do this, can't we?" Jimmy just kept reading. "Look at it this way, honey," Honor went on. "When you want to marry someone, you'll be a single father who doesn't have a first wife or an ex-wife. You'll have *no* wife, just a wonderful kid! Ideal first marriage, if you ask me, honey!" Jimmy stopped reading to Claude and Jolanda. He let the letter fall on the bed; they knew that was the end of it.

Claude had emerged from under the bedcovers. "Your mom's not kidding, is she?" he asked Jimmy. "But she means well, doesn't she?"

For once, Jolanda didn't kick Claude or hit him; she just hugged him. "Holy shit," Jolanda said softly.

"No, she's not kidding—yes, she means well," was all Jimmy could say.

Claude didn't ask any questions. Even Jolanda had nothing to say. The foreign students lay in bed like invalids, trying to imagine how Jimmy's mom and Chantal might have foreseen the potential child's formative years. If only to each other, Honor Winslow and Chantal Beaudette must have acknowledged that Jimmy's child would grow up as their child, too. James Winslow wouldn't be an absent father; he would have to maintain a bona fide family relationship with his child. But for how much longer would Jimmy be a student? When or if Jimmy wanted to marry someone, how would his mother and Chantal explain such sexual hippieness to Jimmy's child—even if, by then, the child was a teenager or a young adult? And what would James Winslow's child make of his or her status as a ticket out of Vietnam?

In such a stupor, Jimmy and his roommates were lying silent and unmoving—as if they'd been poisoned, or they'd been murdered in bed—when they saw Siegfried's little hand in the frosted glass of the bedroom door. They heard the garlic press grate against the glass. The boy held something aloft in his other hand—what looked like a photograph, which he pressed against the glass oval above his head.

"Was zu sehen," the five-year-old enunciated, slowly enough for Jimmy to understand him. ("Something to see.")

"Herein!" Jolanda called to the boy, and he came in. ("Come in!" Jolanda had said.) Siegfried was eager to show them the photo. It was a faded black-and-white photograph; the edges were crumpled and torn. Maybe Siegfried had used undue force, or the garlic press, to free the photo from an old picture frame. Jimmy's mistaking Jolanda for a ghost misled him again, but he wasn't looking at Siegfried's long-dead ancestors. The young mother, who resembled a slimmer Irmgard, was Frau Holzinger. Because she was smiling, Jimmy, Jolanda, and Claude needed a second to recognize her. Her pretty preteen daughter took them a second to recognize, too. They'd never imagined that Irmgard might have been pretty, although she once was a pretty little girl. What gave Irmgard away was her evident anger and depression—even when she'd been ten or eleven, and very pretty.

The dog, of course, was why Siegfried had wanted to show them this family photograph. The German shepherd sat at attention between the Frau and Irmgard. The dog's ears stood straight up, as if the photographer had just given the command to *sit*! Whatever command got the shepherd's attention appeared to have frozen Frau Holzinger and Irmgard. If the Frau and her daughter had ears like a German shepherd, their ears would have stood straight up, too.

"Eine Hündin?" Siegfried asked the students. ("A female dog?")

"Eine Möglichkeit," Jolanda answered. ("A possibility.")

Given Irmgard's age, the photo was taken not long after the war— when the Schwindgasse was in the Soviet zone of occupation. If the photo was taken by a soldier, he was likely a Soviet soldier. The German shepherd might have been the soldier's dog. The photographer could have been the Russian with the gun, the Russian who'd shot Jimmy's bedroom wall. (Not Siegfried's father, James Winslow was thinking.)

Claude torturously asked the five-year-old who'd taken the photo, but Siegfried just shrugged; he didn't know. The German shepherd in the photograph was the only dog the boy knew, and this dog might have died before Siegfried was born.

"Siegfried!" Frau Holzinger was calling again.

"You should put this back in the picture frame," Jolanda whispered in German to the child, handing him the photo. With a nod, Siegfried acknowledged her advice; he slipped the photo inside his shirt and ran out of the bedroom. With hindsight, your fate is delineated; looking back, you can see where your fate began. But fate doesn't tell you when it's getting started. Siegfried's fate was just starting.

That night, when Jimmy, Jolanda, and Claude were trying to recover from the sequence of music at the Kaffeehaus Nachtmusik, Jimmy showed his roommates the postcards he'd written to his mom and Chantal. There was no significance intended by the photograph on the two postcards, which he'd bought in a tobacco shop. The postcards were identical, a photo of the Karlskirche—St. Charles's Church, the baroque church in the Karlsplatz, where Claude had been harassed by the xenophobes. (St. Charles Borromeo was a counter-reformer in the sixteenth century, not to be confused with another Karl—the anti-Semitic mayor of Vienna, Karl Lueger, whom Annelies Eissler loathed.)

The messages on Jimmy's postcards made no mention of the fact that Hedwig Eva Maria Kiesler, at age eighteen—before she became the American movie actress Hedy Lamarr—married a thirty-three-year-old munitions manufacturer and Austrofascist in the Karlskirche in 1933. The messages on Jimmy's postcards weren't about Hedy Lamarr.

"Dear Mom: Chantal should meet a Frenchman I know in Vienna. Claude is from Paris, and he doesn't want children. Chantal should come to Vienna and hang out with Claude, not with me! Love, Jimmy."

"Dear Chantal: I'm friends with a Frenchman from Paris who never wants children. You should come to Vienna to meet Claude—not to get pregnant! Love, Jimmy."

The way Claude kept looking at the picture of the Karlskirche, Jimmy thought the Frenchman was recalling the xenophobes he'd encountered in the Karlsplatz, but—pointing to the church—all Claude said was, "Hedy Lamarr married an Austrofascist arms dealer there."

Back-to-back selections of Schubert's "Ave Maria," Bob Dylan's "Girl from the North Country," and Wagner's "Liebestod" (from *Tristan und Isolde*) had Jolanda overwrought. The death of Jolanda's love for her dishwasher was more to blame than Wagner, but the love-death music didn't help.

At a nearby table was a couple with a well-behaved beagle. Dogs were welcome in many cafés and restaurants in Vienna. Whenever Claude saw a dog, he questioned why Hard Rain couldn't hang out in the café instead of being banished to the garbage alley. This was a murky matter to Jimmy and Jolanda. Maybe Hard Rain refused to hang out in the café when her owner was in the kitchen washing dishes? (No one knew if there were restrictions regarding dogs in restaurant kitchens.)

Jolanda was complaining that she hadn't officially broken up with Hildegund, and it didn't feel right that Hildegund hadn't officially broken up with her. Jimmy and Claude told Jolanda that the breakup seemed official to them. She'd called Hildegund an asshole. Hildegund had called them foreigners, in the superior-sounding way the Viennese say the word. This was a breakup—official enough for Claude and Jimmy. Jolanda was in search of a bigger reason, or more reasons. The Beatles' "Love Me Do" was of no help to Jolanda, who was in knots over the death of love.

When the couple with the beagle left, the students were surprised to see Dagmar with Hard Rain. The widow manager was table-hopping, introducing the café customers to the German shepherd—as if Hard Rain were her dog. When Dagmar got to the students' table, the widow was taken aback by how happy Hard Rain was to see them. Dagmar was less aloof than they'd ever seen her; she sat down at their table with them and told them how happy she was that she'd finally fired her "evil dishwasher." The widow manager had wanted to fire Hildegund for a long time; she'd kept the evil one in the kitchen only because she was worried about what would happen to Hard Rain. This resonated with Jimmy and his roommates—not least with Jolanda, who started to sob.

Dagmar then told them that the evil dishwasher's husband and his gang of thugs were "a bunch of barbarians." Dagmar further explained this was why Hildegund brought Hard Rain to the café—because her husband and his pals abused the dog. It had been Hildegund who wouldn't allow Hard Rain to hang out in the café; she'd told Dagmar that the café life would spoil the dog.

"Hildegund has a *husband*?" Jolanda blubbered. Hard Rain put her head in Jolanda's lap to console her. Jimmy and Claude did their best to explain the situation to Dagmar, who—only that day—had seen Hildegund with Hard Rain in the alley when Dagmar was taking out the garbage. Hildegund was beating Hard Rain with the short leash; this was after the evil one had chained up the poor dog.

"Hildegund probably thought we were spoiling Hard Rain to let her sleep in a bed!" Claude cried. Jolanda was still sobbing. Liszt's *Liebesträume* might have had something to do with it. Jolanda was in no mood for love dreams, not after the Beatles' "Love Me Do."

Dagmar had not only fired her dishwasher; she'd taken Hard Rain away from Hildegund. Dagmar sent Hildegund home with the chain—telling the bitch to chain up her barbarians. Dagmar told Hildegund she would report her to the police for animal abuse if the dishwasher didn't leave Hard Rain in the Kaffeehaus Nachtmusik.

"I had to wait for the beagle to leave before I showed Hard Rain around," Dagmar told the foreign students. "Hard Rain doesn't like male dogs. She hates dogs with balls."

"I can relate to that," Jolanda said, sounding like herself again; Jimmy and Claude hoped her breakup with Hildegund was now official. Surely Jolanda thought the husband was a big enough reason.

The anger Hard Rain felt for dogs with balls made her less than ideal for a dog who hangs out in a café, Dagmar admitted. It was awkward to warn dog owners of dogs with balls, but the real problem was that Hard Rain always knew which dogs had them. Dagmar speculated that Hard Rain must have had a traumatic experience, "perhaps a dog with balls who was trying to hump her." One look at Jolanda told Jimmy and Claude that Jolanda could relate to this, but Jolanda didn't say anything. Jimmy, Claude, and Jolanda knew there might be another factor that made Hard Rain less than ideal for a dog who hangs out in a café. If Hard Rain had a thunderstorm issue, this could amount to a bigger problem than dogs with balls. There was no bathtub at the Kaffeehaus Nachtmusik, where the foreign students were listening to Hard Rain's song—Bob Dylan's "A Hard Rain's A-Gonna Fall." The three friends hoped the timing of the Dylan song wasn't prophetic.

Dagmar was being candid with the students about her situation; she lived with her mother (like Dagmar, a widow) and her mother's aged schnauzer. The dog was an old male with balls. "There's no cutting his balls off, short of killing him," Dagmar explained.

"Hard Rain can sleep with us," Claude said immediately.

"But there's something you should know about the dear girl," Jolanda began, uncharacteristically taking Dagmar's hand.

"It may be hearsay," Claude interjected; he was scratching Hard Rain behind her ears. This was when the foreign students brought the widow manager into their confidence, because she had confided in them. No doubt Claude was starved for optimism, because he instantly and stupidly became overly optimistic. There's no other explanation for why he grasped Dagmar's other hand, the one Jolanda wasn't holding. "I'm sure you don't think of remarrying. I can't imagine why anyone would want to!" Claude suddenly said to the widow manager. "But have you ever thought of just *doing it* with a younger man—maybe even having his child?" Claude asked. Poor Dagmar. She withdrew her hands from Claude and Jolanda.

246

"I'm just a dog person, Claude—I don't do children," Dagmar said. "Let's just do the best job we can with Hard Rain."

Not only was the widow his mother's age, but Jimmy saw something of his mom's aloofness in her. Dagmar had a similar opaqueness, and an obdurate nature—not unlike Honor Winslow, who was very resistant to change.

Dagmar continued her table-hopping, but she'd left Hard Rain at the foreign students' table. Hard Rain's head was back in Jolanda's lap. Jolanda was bent over her, kissing her, while the shepherd's big tail thumped the floor. "No dishwasher will touch you again—I promise," Jolanda told the dear girl. "You hear thunder, you see lightning—you come find me. Forget about the bathtub," Jolanda said to Hard Rain. "And what's all this about balls?" Jolanda asked Hard Rain, who wagged her tail harder. "Don't pay any attention to dogs with balls—just ignore those dogs, and their balls," Jolanda advised the German shepherd. Jimmy and Claude didn't think that ignoring dogs with balls was advice Hard Rain would be likely to follow. "If those dogs mess with you, bite their balls off," Jolanda went on saying to the dutiful-looking dog. "But try ignoring them first."

Jimmy and Claude just wished they knew what Hard Rain would do with respect to thunder and lightning or dogs with balls. She was a German shepherd of a certain age, and with a complicated history. The business at hand would determine what Hard Rain would do. Jimmy watched Dagmar, who was still table-hopping. Jimmy saw that Claude was back to staring at the postcards of the Karlskirche, where the young Hedy Lamarr married an Austrofascist. And Jolanda, Jimmy and Claude could see, was engaged in assembling her own and Hard Rain's future—after their evil dishwasher. Jolanda held Hard Rain's big head in her hands.

As an emerging writer, James Winslow understood this moment in the story. What Hard Rain would do was out of Jolanda's hands. Like the widow manager, making her rounds—like Jimmy's mom, hell-bent on saving her only child—Hard Rain would do what she was inclined to do. You couldn't reconstruct her. Hard Rain would tell her own story.

"Der Vorschlag, the proposal—whatever you call it, it's not entirely in my mother's hands," Jimmy told Fräulein Eissler, when he met with her. He'd shown her his mom's letter. He'd described for her the duplicate postcards of the Karlskirche, his messages to his mother and Chantal. (He'd already airmailed the postcards to New Hampshire.)

Fräulein Eissler read Honor Winslow's letter twice. She nodded, as if in agreement, when he told her what he'd written on his postcards, but she wondered why he had chosen to send them pictures of the Karlskirche. "Hedy Lamarr was married there," Jimmy said, as if Annelies didn't know.

"Everyone knows," she told him.

Jimmy wished his tutor would say something, now that he'd shown her everything he knew, but she sat beside him on the settee—their love seat by the glass-topped table—as if she were waiting for him to show her more. Jimmy was staring at her feet in his white athletic socks when he said: "It comes down to how determined my mother is, when there's something she wants, or it's something she believes in, and how Esther always goes along with it—whatever it is."

Annelies made no response; she waited, as if she knew that Jimmy had more to tell her. James Winslow was aware of what he didn't say. He'd learned something from his mother's letter; he hadn't known why his mom wanted him to keep wrestling, how "the right kind of knee injury could be useful." Jimmy was considering that Esther must have known this. And if Esther knew, wouldn't Fräulein Eissler know, too?

"What it comes down to, Jimmy, is how much you want to control your own destiny," Annelies said. "We should revisit the idea of Mieke, Jolanda's former girlfriend—the lesbian who wants to *try it* with a guy."

Naturally, Jimmy remembered how repelled Annelies had been by the thought of Jolanda holding Mieke's head. ("There's a more natural way to get a girlfriend pregnant, Jimmy," Annelies had told him.) Now, given the dearth of potential girlfriends, it seemed Fräulein Eissler was considering an unnatural solution to Jimmy's predicament. But she didn't linger over Jolanda and Mieke; in her fashion, Fräulein Eissler just moved on.

There was the "ordeal" of Christmas in a Catholic country to get through, Annelies reminded Jimmy. And before Christmas, she told him, she had to "suffer through" eight days of fried food. She meant Hanukkah, Fräulein Eissler explained. Before Christmas, there were eight days of Hanukkah—commemorating the Maccabean Revolt and the rededication of the Temple in 164 B.C., following its desecration by the Greeks. "This is how Jewish people have a good time, Jimmy," Annelies told him. "We celebrate our survival after someone has desecrated us."

20.

Not Like Donna Reed

Relationships, real or what-if, haunt you—not only what happens between two people, but also what might have happened. James Winslow fell in love with Fräulein Eissler. At the same time, Jimmy and his roommates were in a complicated relationship with Dagmar, the widow manager of the Kaffeehaus Nachtmusik. Sharing a German shepherd wasn't the only complicated part. It wasn't helpful how Claude asked Dagmar if she'd ever thought of "just *doing it* with a younger man—maybe even having his child." At first, Dagmar didn't realize Claude was asking on *Jimmy's* behalf. Claude was a small, awkward French boy; he'd not appeared to be aroused by her before. It made no sense to Dagmar that Claude wanted to knock her up. When she asked him to clarify things, he sent her down a different but no less confusing path. "I was asking for Jimmy—he's the one with an urgent need to knock someone up," Claude told her in his offhand, witless way. This made more sense to Dagmar, who was aware of how Jimmy looked at her. All of this went over Jimmy's head.

"Dagmar's flirting with you, Jimmy. You get it, don't you?" Jolanda asked him, one night at the café. He'd noticed that Dagmar had been behaving strangely, but he hadn't picked up on the flirting part. Claude only then confessed what he'd told Dagmar.

"You told Dagmar I want to knock her up?" Jimmy asked Claude.

"I expressed it as a *need,* not a want," Claude insisted.

Jimmy thought it was strange when Dagmar said to him, out of the blue, "I do everything *except* children, Jimmy. You can have fun *not* having children, you know," the widow manager had said—somewhat ambiguously, he thought. Dagmar was not as aloof as usual; he'd noticed this much.

James Winslow wondered if the foreignness inside him—a foreignness that was *in* him, a part of who he was—made him deaf and blind to Dagmar's flirting with him. Or was it because Dagmar was his mom's age, and Jimmy was afraid of finding out what it would be like to sleep with an older woman? (Was he so conventional, and such a New Hampshire boy, that Jimmy imagined he was supposed to sleep with someone his own age first?) He was attracted to the widow manager, who reminded him of his mother; this alone was complicated enough. And didn't Dagmar live with her mom, and her mom's old schnauzer? He pictured the two widows in a small apartment, somewhere near a Straßenbahn stop. At night, you could hear the streetcars on the rails. The aged male schnauzer was sensitive to the screech the Straßenbahn made when it stopped. The screeching, throughout the night, made the old dog bark—his balls retracting with every woof.

Jimmy found Dagmar desirable, but he tried to suppress his attraction to her by picturing the possible horrors of a sleepover at her place. He was determined not to meet Dagmar's mother, or her mother's dog. Besides, Jimmy and his roommates were committed to sleeping with Hard Rain. "If you sleep with Dagmar, just don't come home smelling like a dog with balls," was the way Jolanda put it. Claude just shook his head insanely, the same way Hard Rain did.

It never occurred to Jimmy that resisting Dagmar was good practice for resisting Chantal, if it ever came to that. "Would it be characteristic of your mom, or not—to have Chantal just show up unannounced in Vienna?" Annelies had asked Jimmy.

"I don't know," he'd admitted.

Jimmy's beloved grandfather sent him a black-and-white postcard—

a forbidding one, from a long-ago production of *King Lear*. The stage direction reads: ENTER LEAR, WITH CORDELIA IN HIS ARMS—ACT 5, SCENE 3. In a world of bad moments between parents and their children, a howling father holding his dead daughter is one of the worst, but Jimmy knew that Thomas Winslow didn't know about his fourth daughter's manipulations. The histrionic English teacher (like his hero, Charles Dickens) was being sentimental about Christmas. All Thomas had written on the postcard was: "Christmas won't be the same without you, my dear boy!" Thomas wasn't referring to Honor Winslow's plot in progress; to have Jimmy knock up Chantal Beaudette was the farthest thing from Thomas Winslow's mind. Jimmy knew *King Lear* wasn't a reference to knocking up anyone.

Honor Winslow was harassing the local Pennacook draft board. She crammed her message on a plain postcard, one without a picture. "If you don't knock up someone in Europe, we'll shoot you in the patella when you come home. Or we can cut off the index finger of your dominant hand—also known as your trigger finger. It would be easier and more fun to just fool around with Chantal, honey." There was no room for "Love, Mom."

Claude found a photo in one of the newspapers in the Kaffeehaus Nachtmusik—a U.S. helicopter strike against Viet Cong guerrillas in the Mekong Delta. In the aerial photograph, a U.S. serviceman is watching ground movements of enemy troops below. By 1963, almost sixteen thousand American military personnel were deployed in South Vietnam.

Jolanda found a photo in another newspaper—of firebombs falling in a village on the outskirts of Hue. In the foreground of the photo, houseboats glide down the Perfume River; the incendiary bombs cause clouds of smoke to darken the lighter gray of the sky. There were other napalm pictures in the news. "Your baby would have a whole bunch of moms around, honey!" Jimmy's mother wrote on a napalm-bombing picture postcard.

"Chantal just showing up in Vienna would be like a napalm bomb," Jolanda said to Jimmy and Claude.

"No, no, *no*—poor Chantal!" Claude moaned.

"You should forget about the Chantal Vorschlag—I'm not knocking up Chantal," Jimmy told them.

The three roommates tried to move on from the firebombing situation, but they couldn't escape the constant evidence of the mutilations of war in the Schwindgasse apartment—Siegfried's slaughtered armies, his toy soldiers' scattered body parts.

"Immigrate to France—no one wants children in Paris!" Claude cried.

"Straight Dutch girls carry condoms, Jimmy," Jolanda said.

Yet this kind of carnage was what would come of Jimmy's not knocking up Chantal—or of his not allowing his mother and aunts to mutilate him. The three roommates had discussed the pros and cons of a bullet in the patella versus an amputated index finger. Jimmy's trigger finger was also the index finger on his writing hand; he preferred being shot in the knee, he told Claude and Jolanda. They weren't writers; they said they could do without an index finger on their dominant hand.

Napalm was in the news and in the mail. Jimmy was unnerved by what Irmgard said one evening. He was writing in his bedroom; he'd not accompanied Claude and Jolanda to their complicated café.

"Death," he heard Irmgard say. From his writing desk, at the balcony window, Jimmy could see her inimitable shape pressed against the frosted glass. He'd not heard of a film called *Tod,* but *Death* didn't sound like an American movie, either. "It's almost over, if you're interested," Irmgard told him, moving away from Jimmy's bedroom door.

Jimmy found Irmgard on her usual sofa in the living room, watching Bergman's *The Seventh Seal,* which had been dubbed into German like everything else. The German title was *Das siebente Siegel*—not *Tod.* Death himself was the main character, in Irmgard's estimation and Jimmy's, and *Tod* was what Irmgard called the film—even if Bergman and the Germans didn't. Jimmy curled up with her on the sofa for the final chess game. (He'd read the screenplay so many times in English, he didn't need to understand Swedish or the incessant German dubbing.)

"It is your move, Antonius Block," Death tells the knight, but we can see the alarm in the knight's eyes. Block wants the juggler, with his young wife and their child, to escape Death.

"Nothing escapes you—or does it?" the knight asks Death.

"Nothing escapes me. No one escapes from me," Death replies. (Death's answer sounds a lot longer in German.)

Then the knight pretends to be clumsy; he knocks over the chess pieces with the hem of his coat. Of course Block tells Death that he's forgotten where the pieces go, but Death hasn't forgotten. "You can't get away that easily," Death tells the knight, laughing. In this one instance, the knight distracts Death—the juggler, with his young wife and their child, will get away. Antonius Block, with his wife and the rest of his companions, will die.

"God, You who are somewhere, who must be somewhere, have mercy upon us," the knight prays—his last words. While the end credits rolled, Irmgard went on holding Jimmy on top of her—his head held fast between her breasts.

"Speaking of death, how's it going with your mother's plan? Are you going or not going to Vietnam?" Irmgard asked him. "Not going sounds smarter to any mother, Jimmy," Irmgard said.

That was when James Winslow knew he was wrong to judge his mother for committing herself, and including Chantal, to save him from a wrongheaded war. The war had more wrong with it than Honor Winslow's unconventional proposal. Just then, Jolanda and Claude came back from the Kaffeehaus Nachtmusik, finding Jimmy transfixed in Irmgard's embrace—her legs wrapped around his waist, her heels digging into the backs of his thighs. "It's not what you think," he tried to tell his roommates, but his voice was muffled—speaking, as he was, between Irmgard's breasts.

"I'm just trying to tell him not to go to Vietnam—he should listen to his mother," Irmgard said to Jolanda and Claude. (James Winslow wondered if explaining the entire situation to Hard Rain would have been easier.)

Fräulein Eissler just sighed when Jimmy told her everything; he also showed her the postcards he'd received. There was no comprehending the picture postcards Jimmy sent in return. The one of the Soviet War Memorial in the Schwarzenbergplatz seemed especially ill-suited to the issue under consideration, but it was in Jimmy's neighborhood—at one end of the Schwindgasse. The Heldendenkmal der Roten Armee, the "Heroes' Memorial of the Red Army," was built to commemorate the seventeen thousand Soviet soldiers killed in action during the Vienna Offensive in World War II. German prisoners of war and Austrian construction workers built it. Over the years, increasingly, the monument would be attacked by acts of politically inspired vandalism, but James Winslow would send the same picture postcard to his mother and to Chantal.

"I think I see your point about there being no end of moms around," Jimmy wrote to Honor. "And I appreciate your offer to maim me— I may take you up on it," he wrote to her.

"Please don't come here to get knocked up—just come here to meet Claude," Jimmy wrote to Chantal.

Given the context—such a solemn postcard of the Soviet War Memorial—James Winslow shouldn't have sounded so cavalier. And he would worry that the monument to the slain Soviet soldiers somehow suggested, falsely, that Jimmy had a newfound affinity for becoming a soldier.

With Claude and Jolanda going home for Christmas, it was no wonder Jimmy started wrestling again. There were too many unanswered questions: to sleep or not sleep with Dagmar; to knock up or not knock up Chantal; to submit or not submit to his mom's mutilations. At least the wrestling would be familiar, or so Jimmy thought. He wondered how Leo Spiegel at the Turnhalle Leopold had befriended Fräulein Eissler, or how she knew the two Israeli freestyle wrestlers. "We're Israelis, Jimmy. I knew Sol and Simon in a previous life," was all Annelies had said.

Fräulein Eissler didn't say how she knew about the Russians' knees. Little Mirror must have told her; Leo would know. The Soviet wrestlers were familiar with the Smillie knife, and not only because they were med students; they'd both had the surgery.

As Annelies explained, the gym was a short walk from the Medical University of Vienna, and the medical library, where there was a complex of clinics and pharmacies. With the university students around, that part of Währinger Straße had some coffeehouses; there was also an Italian restaurant and a Hungarian one. From the street, the gym didn't look like a gym. It was actually in the basement of a hairdresser's shop. Helene, the hairdresser, was tired of being asked where the gym was.

"Unten," Helene told Jimmy, when he first inquired. ("Downstairs," she'd said, pointing to the basement stairs.) Helene and her team of hairdressers gave wrestlers the evil eye. It was a grievance to the hairdressers and the wrestlers that they shared the washing machines and the dryers, which were in the basement with the wrestling mats.

Downstairs, the cement walls were heavily padded. The showers, the lockers in the changing area, the urinals, even the crapper stalls—were not enclosed. The Turnhalle Leopold was one giant room. The washing machines and the dryers were set apart from the mats at the far end of the basement, away from the stairs. You had to walk across the wrestling mats to get to them. The hairdressers resented that they had to take off their shoes when they walked on the mats. The wrestlers disliked having hairdressers in their wrestling room—especially the hairdressers who watched them take showers, or stand at urinals, or sit in crapper stalls. The naked wrestlers weighing themselves were also exposed to the hairdressers.

Kleiner Spiegel, the eponymous Leopold, weighed only fifty-eight kilos, not quite 130 pounds. Leo wasn't competing anymore, but he'd kept himself in shape. Greco-Roman wrestling was better known in Austria than the freestyle kind, but any kind of wrestling was unpopular in Austria, and not only with Helene and her hairdressing gang. For Jimmy's sake, since his German was subpar, he and the four other free-style wrestlers at the Turnhalle Leopold spoke English to one another. As a minority, those five sought to assert themselves for having chosen, in their minds, the superior style of wrestling. To freestyle wrestlers, no holds below the waist, no trips, no leg dives—no legs at all—was an absurdly limited or restricted way to wrestle. When they were with one another—when there were no Greco-Roman wrestlers around—the two Israelis, the two Soviets, and Jimmy called the Greco-Roman guys "wrestlers without legs." Fräulein Eissler didn't approve.

"You make the Greco-Roman wrestlers sound like amputees, Jimmy," Annelies told him. When he'd referred to her as his German tutor, the Israeli wrestlers, Sol and Simon, just looked at each other in disbelief. Even the former Red Army wrestlers, Sergei and Zander, seemed to know more than Jimmy concerning Annelies Eissler's line of work.

"We bet the Eissler is working for Wiesenthal, or for the Mossad," Sergei said; he and Zander looked at Simon and Sol for confirmation, not at Jimmy. Sergei and Zander didn't say they'd ever seen Fräulein Eissler entering or leaving the Jewish Documentation Center in Vienna.

"Most Israelis stand with Simon Wiesenthal—we're all Nazi hunt-ers, in our hearts," Sol said; he didn't mention the Mossad.

"We assume you and Zander are working for the KGB, when you're not too busy with your medical studies," Simon told Sergei, who was his workout partner. Sergei and Zander just laughed; they'd heard they were supposed to be working for the KGB before. Even Helene and her hairdressers had accused them.

As Jimmy had expected, the former Red Army wrestlers were in a league of their own; they were technically superior to him. Fräulein Eissler had been right to say they were older than the average med students. Like the Haganah graybeards, Sergei and Zander were in their late thirties. Who knew what their previous commitments to the Red Army had entailed? And Annelies had been right to say they were still in shape. From the start, those two took it easy on Jimmy. He just drilled moves with Sergei, the bigger one—no live wrestling. Sergei was a gentle bear. And when Jimmy wrestled with Zander, he could tell Zander held himself back. The Russians warned Jimmy to be wary of Leo, the little Greco coach and the owner of the gym. Little Mirror liked to invite the new guys in the wrestling room to do some pummeling and hand-fighting with him.

"It doesn't end there. After the pummeling and hand-fighting, Leo locks up, chest to chest or chest to back, and he throws you on your head," Zander warned Jimmy.

"The Greco guys call him a Wurfmeister. Leo is a 'throw master,' and Leo is a kidder, Jim—he just likes to fool around," Sergei said.

"Er wirft. 'He throws,' Jim," Zander told him. "Leo is a compulsive thrower—he can't help it. Throwing is just fooling around to Leo."

Therefore, Jimmy politely declined Leo's invitations to do some pummeling and hand-fighting with him. Once or twice, Little Mirror surprised Jimmy. Leo slipped behind Jimmy and locked his hands low on Jimmy's waist, at his hips, lifting him off his feet before returning him to the mat and letting him go. "You see? No suplay. Kein Werfen. 'No throwing,' Jim," Little Mirror said, smiling.

"Du wirfst. 'You throw,' Leo—I know you do," Jimmy told Leo.

"Ich werfe. 'I throw,' it's true—but not you, Jim!" Kleiner Spiegel said.

"You can trust Leo, Jim," Sol said. "When Kleiner Spiegel saw you in the shower, he saw your Jewish penis." Jimmy liked the Jewish-penis jokes.

"Leo knows your heart is in the right place, Jim," Simon said. Jimmy liked how the wrestlers called him Jim; it made him feel like a grown-up.

When Jimmy complained to Zander about his limitations as a

wrestler, Zander would say: "We're just ex-wrestlers, Jim—we're all the same." But in the Turnhalle Leopold, the wrestlers weren't all the same. There was Leo, born to throw, and there were the two Red Army wrestlers; those three knew what they were doing. The rest of them were "all the same."

The Israeli wrestlers were no better, technically, than Jimmy, but they were strong and super fit. Even in his late thirties, Sol could outlast Jimmy.

From their first workout, Jimmy made sure he knew which knee was Zander's bad one. Jimmy was certainly familiar with the scar from Zander's meniscectomy. Sergei had two bad knees; both had the Smillie resection scars.

"I know twice as much about the Smillie knife as Zander knows, Jim," Sergei said, smiling at Zander. The Soviets definitely knew more than James Winslow did—not only more about wrestling and knee surgeries.

Leo Spiegel had introduced the Israeli and Russian freestyle wrestlers to the Café Meisel on Währinger Straße, where all the wrestlers went after practice. The Greco-Roman guys weren't much fun to socialize with. The wrestlers who were competing had to weigh in, so they weren't drinking. Leo was more fun; he always went to the Meisel after practice. Even the wrestlers who weren't competing or weighing in drank only beer, and not a lot. But two beers were enough to make Little Mirror tell funny stories. The beer drinkers laughed; the water drinkers were determined to be bored.

"When I was competing, I drank coffee—too much coffee," Leo said. "It made me want to throw everyone—anywhere, all the time!" This seemed entirely plausible to the Soviet and Israeli wrestlers and Jimmy. They were glad Leopold Spiegel had switched to beer; they wouldn't have wanted to socialize with him when he was wired on Viennese coffee. The ambiance at the Café Meisel was much improved by the wrestlers who drank beer.

Sometime before the new year, Zander and Sergei said they would take Sol and Simon and Jimmy to a nightclub they knew in the Favoriten district, near the Wien Südbahnhof—the Vienna South Station. Favoriten was the tenth district of Vienna—formerly in a Soviet-occupied sector, a workers' district. The nightclub was called Die Ägypterin. "The Egyptian" referred to the nightclub's belly dancer. Zander and Sergei doubted that she was Egyptian—she was Turkish, the Soviets said. Belly dancers had used the stage name "Little Egypt" since the 1890s, but this belly dancer was too big to be called little.

"Calling the belly dancer 'The Egyptian' gives the girl some degree of anonymity," Sergei said. The Favoriten district had a higher-than-average Muslim population for Vienna.

"The so-called Egyptian is Turkish," Zander insisted. The Favoriten district had a sizable Turkish population. The former Red Army wrestlers had spotted some wrestlers' mangled ears on the Turkish men watching the belly dancer. The Turks were good wrestlers, the Russians had told Jimmy.

Sol and Simon asked about the ambiance at Die Ägypterin. "Maybe a belly-dancing club in the Favoriten district isn't the safest place for a couple of Jews," Sol said—no Jewish-penis jokes now.

"We're just ex-wrestlers, Sol—we're all the same," Zander told his workout partner. It was exactly what the Soviet had said to Jimmy.

"How big is the belly dancer?" Simon asked about The Egyptian.

"She's in our weight class," Sergei told his workout partner. A big girl, seventy-five kilos or 165 pounds. The Israelis said they'd test the ambiance.

Meanwhile, Hard Rain had improved the ambiance at the Kaffeehaus Nachtmusik. Dagmar said her clientele loved having the good-natured dog visit their tables. Dagmar's disposition was also improved by her new dishwasher. In his late thirties, and missing one ear, Walter was an inventive handyman. He sized up the situation with Hard Rain and built a doghouse in the alley. The shelter for the shepherd was enclosed in a pen—at some distance from the garbage cans, and large enough to contain a bathtub. Walter was a fix-it man with a just-in-case mindset. He said he didn't want Hard Rain to be embarrassed; in the event of thunder and lightning, Walter wanted her to have a place to go.

Hard Rain liked her doghouse, and she preferred her pen to being chained up. The German shepherd smelled better, because she was no longer sniffing around garbage cans. Dagmar took her to a pet-grooming place on Argentinierstraße, where Hard Rain had a dog shampoo, and she had her ears cleaned and her toenails clipped; she even got her teeth brushed. Yet Hard Rain stared with uncertainty at the oddly disconnected bathtub in her pen—that is, when she chose to look at the tub at all. At times, the shepherd seemed to purposely overlook or ignore the bathtub.

Jolanda and Claude and Jimmy could tell that Hard Rain was anxious about the bathtub in the Schwindgasse apartment. When the roommates would sneak the dog along the hall, on their way in or out of the apartment, the door to the bathroom was usually open; the glance Hard Rain gave to the bathtub was both ambiguous and disconcerting. "If only the poor girl could tell us her thoughts," Walter said.

Walter had been "a child soldier," Dagmar told the foreign students. He'd been captured by the Americans and had spent the end of the war in an American POW camp. "Lucky Walter," Dagmar had said. Like Hard Rain, Walter couldn't (or didn't) tell anyone his innermost thoughts—nor did the new dishwasher speak of his missing ear.

Claude couldn't stop obsessing about how Hard Rain would react to a thunderstorm. "For Christ's sake, Claude—we'll find out when it happens! There are worse places to shit than in a bathtub, you know," Jolanda said.

"It might be the mildest February in sixty years," Claude warned them. "The thunder and lightning might not wait for spring—there could be a thunderstorm this winter! I just was thinking: What if *Hil-*

degund is the one who shits her brains out in a bathtub? What if *Hilde-gund* wanted us to keep the bathroom door open for *her*, not for Hard Rain?"

"There are no words for what a diehard optimist you are, Claude," Jolanda told him.

That said, Claude had spontaneously set something in motion with Siegfried—he'd kindled in the five-year-old a burning desire to have a dog. This hadn't escaped the attention of Irmgard or Frau Holzinger. The boy had been talking in his sleep about a Hündin—specifically, a female German shepherd—and Irmgard had discovered that Siegfried was sleeping with the family photo of that other German shepherd. The Frau was worried that Siegfried had somehow sensed the restless ghost of that long-dead dog in the Schwindgasse apartment.

"You and your ghosts," Irmgard said to her mother.

"That German shepherd was a female," the Frau reminded her daughter. Jimmy had understood only this much of their German.

It was difficult for Jimmy to understand Frau Holzinger and Irmgard when they were arguing, but Claude and Jolanda translated what Irmgard told the Frau: "Siegfried doesn't want *that* German shepherd—he doesn't want your old, dead dog! Siegfried wants a new, alive Hündin!"

It was dinnertime in the Holzinger household. Jolanda, Claude, and Jimmy were pussyfooting their way in and out of the kitchen. Siegfried wasn't contributing to the conversation; the five-year-old was silently eating his supper. That was when Irmgard stepped in front of Claude, stopping him from leaving the kitchen. "Siegfried says *you* gave him the idea of having his own dog," she said to Claude. Siegfried, mouth full, just pointed the garlic press at Claude and continued eating.

With agonizing slowness, Claude began speaking his German for toddlers. "When I was a boy, I wanted a dog—not just any dog, but a female German shepherd," Claude began, in such a desperate-sounding voice that Siegfried stopped eating. "If I'd been allowed to have a dog, I might have turned out differently!" Claude cried, while Jolanda seemed to choke back a sob. Jolanda was gagging, or suppressing vomit, or perhaps she was acting. This may have been a more emotional moment than the Holzingers were used to having in their kitchen. There was a respectful (or utterly disbelieving) silence. Jolanda was still recovering from the strained sounds she'd made; Siegfried had resumed eating. The widow Holzinger was seeing her old, dead dog—the German shepherd in the photo Siegfried slept with. Irmgard, Jimmy could tell, wasn't troubling herself to imagine how Claude might have turned out differently if he'd had a dog. Yet Irmgard Holzinger stood stone-still. Claude had given her the idea that things might turn out differently for Siegfried if the five-year-old had a female German shepherd.

"Hausaufgaben," Jimmy said, excusing himself as he left the kitchen. "Homework," he'd said, taking hold of the choked-up Jolanda by her hand. Claude—clutching the neck of his beer bottle, as if he were strangling it—followed them. They'd gone to the kitchen only to get some beer from the fridge; normally, the foreign students knew better than to invade the Holzingers' space during the supper hour.

That night, the roommates took Fräulein Eissler's advice: they went to the Augustinerkeller and tried to have fun, instead of doing their homework. But three guys were looking over Jolanda in an uncomfortable way; she thought she recognized them. Jolanda said she might have seen them with Hildegund. "Those guys are friends of the dog beater—of the ink addict's asshole husband," was the way Jolanda put it. The roommates left the Augustinerkeller and went to the Café Hawelka. It seemed to suit them: to leave a bigger, noisier place for a smaller, quieter one. They also liked the smaller, quieter street where the Hawelka was—the Dorotheergasse—although, when they were walking home, Claude claimed he saw the three guys from the Augustinerkeller. Maybe those guys were following the foreign students, or so Claude feared, but Jolanda and Jimmy didn't see them.

The roommates felt good to have ventured out of their neighborhood, into the Inner City—die Innere Stadt. It made them feel like they were more than students. So much was up in the air. Jimmy had the feeling that the stage was set, but set for what? There were too many things that might (or might not) happen. It made Jimmy think of how his mom must have felt when she knew she wanted to be a mother, but she wanted Esther to have the baby for her. It was a kind of up-in-the-air moment.

James Winslow should have remembered that there was something Fraülein Eissler wanted to show him. Hadn't she told him they would go out together very late one night?

It was late enough—after the last call at the Kaffeehaus Nachtmusik. Hard Rain was sleeping under the students' café table, with her heavy jaw resting on Claude's foot. Claude was startled to see Annelies standing at their table; he jumped to his feet, tripping over Hard Rain's big head. Dagmar tried to tell Annelies that the café was closing, but the tutor pointed to Jimmy. "There's something he should see, and I'm taking him to see it," Annelies said, holding out her hand to Hard Rain's inquiring nose.

Annelies led Jimmy past the Staatsoper, along the Kärntner Straße. In those days, the first-district prostitutes hung out on those side streets off the Kärntner Straße—on Johannesgasse and Annagasse, Jimmy might one day remember, and there was a hotel on Krugerstraße, where the women took the men they picked up. He'd seen the prostitutes around the Westbahnhof and the Südbahnhof; in the vicinity of those train stations, the prostitutes weren't as young or as pretty as the women working in the first district. Jimmy was standing with Fräulein Eissler on the Krugerstraße—diagonally across the street from "the whore hotel," as the IES students called it.

"If we wait here long enough, you know who we'll see, don't you?" Annelies asked Jimmy.

That was when Jimmy knew, but not until then. "Yes, if you mean Irmgard," James Winslow managed to say.

"That's why you should have sympathy for her, Jimmy," Fräulein Eissler told him. "And if we wait until we see her, she'll see us, you know—you better think about that, too."

Jimmy certainly didn't want Irmgard to know he was onto her being a prostitute, but Annelies and Jimmy had already been standing on the Krugerstraße too long.

Even a first-timer could see the way it worked at the whore hotel. A prostitute arrived with her client, but the client left alone. The prostitute stayed longer, to fix herself up. By the time the prostitute left, she'd found another prostitute in the hotel; the two women left the hotel together. When Irmgard came out of the hotel, she was with another prostitute—a prettier one, though not necessarily a younger one. Naturally, Irmgard saw Jimmy standing there with Fräulein Eissler.

"We were just passing by," Jimmy stupidly said to Irmgard, in English.

"This is the student I told you about," Irmgard said to the prettier prostitute, also in English. "His family pays his education-related expenses—his mother told me," Irmgard added. The way the prettier prostitute smiled made it clear she understood English. "We don't count as education-related expenses, I guess," Irmgard carried on, in English.

"If he's a virgin, we should count—if he's a virgin, we're definitely education-related," the prettier prostitute said; her English was as good as Irmgard's. When she spoke, Jimmy could see there was something wrong with her upper lip; a small scar appeared to pull her lip askew, but you saw the slight disfigurement only when her lips moved.

"I'm guessing Jimmy is definitely a virgin," Irmgard said, smiling.

"Nice to meet you, Jimmy—I'm Berta," the prettier prostitute said.

"And this is Fräulein Eissler—die Hauslehrerin, the one I told you about," Irmgard said to Berta, interjecting the German term for *private tutor*.

"Tell me why you two would ever be 'just passing by' the Krugerstraße!" Irmgard suddenly said to Annelies.

"A vocabulary lesson, Irmgard," Fräulein Eissler answered her. "We walk everywhere, and I point to things. Jimmy has to tell me what the things I point to are—in German."

Irmgard pointed to herself and Berta, but she looked only at Jimmy. "Prostituierte," Irmgard said. That was when Jimmy knew what Irmgard had meant—when they'd been watching *From Here to Eternity* and Irmgard had told him that Donna Reed wasn't a real prostitute. "We're not like Donna Reed, Jimmy—we're the real ones," Irmgard said. To make herself perfectly clear, she more emphatically pointed to herself and Berta.

"Ich weiß," Jimmy said, as he was always saying to Irmgard. The two prostitutes linked their arms together, the way European women do when they're walking. Irmgard and Berta were ready to move on.

"You know where to look for me," Berta told Jimmy.

"Ich weiß," James Winslow repeated.

But Berta had more to tell him. She touched the scar on her upper lip. "I was a child, at a family picnic—I was running with a mayonnaise thing in my hand," Berta told Jimmy. "How do you say a stupid mayonnaise *thing* in English?" Berta asked Fräulein Eissler.

"A jar—a mayonnaise *jar*," Annelies answered her.

"Ja, a mayonnaise *jar*. I fell, my lip was cut. Now I kiss a little funny," Berta said, smiling.

James Winslow walked with Annelies to her Straßenbahn stop on the Opernring. "It would have been better if I'd just told you, but I thought you should see Irmgard for yourself," Annelies said. Jimmy wouldn't recall how it came up, but both of them were impressed by how familiar Irmgard and Berta were with English. "I'm sure they pick up a lot of English-speaking tourists in the first district," Fräulein Eissler told Jimmy.

There was something Jimmy wanted to ask Annelies, but he didn't dare. Hadn't she tricked Frau Holzinger into thinking he was sleeping with his Jewish German tutor? Didn't Irmgard find Jimmy in bed when there was *someone* under Jimmy's bedcovers? Then why did Irmgard sound so sure of herself when she told Berta that Jimmy was *definitely* a virgin? Was Jimmy's pathetic inexperience obvious, not only to a prostitute? But Jimmy was afraid of what Fräulein Eissler might tell him. Besides, her streetcar was coming, and she had more to say.

"You know—don't you, Jimmy—what Berta was doing when she told you about her lip?" Annelies asked, as her Straßenbahn came screeching into the streetcar stop. "You know she was trying to make you more attracted to her, don't you?"

It had worked, James Winslow wanted to say. Jimmy was dying to know what would be *funny* about kissing Berta. But all he said to Annelies was the usual: "Ich weiß!" He had to raise his voice to be heard above the train braking on the tracks.

"And there's something else you should know," Fräulein Eissler said, as she was getting on the Straßenbahn. "Prostitutes usually refuse to kiss their clients!" she called to him, in English. Her fellow riders on the train surely heard her, but it was late at night. At that hour, it's not likely there were any English-speaking tourists or first-district prostitutes taking the Straßenbahn. In the passing windows of Fräulein Eissler's departing streetcar, Jimmy saw no hint of a face as pretty as Donna Reed's. Annelies must have taken a seat on the far side of the train.

21.

Not an Egyptian

Honor Winslow would have liked how the Soviet med students worked together to drain her son's cauliflower ear. Zander drew out the fluid with the needle; Sergei applied the gauze with wet plaster to fit the configurations of Jimmy's ear. Jimmy had told them his mom was a nurse, and how she'd always drained his cauliflower ears. All of his fellow wrestlers had very noticeable cauliflower ears. Jimmy didn't tell his newfound teammates how his aunts had compared cauliflower ears to animal droppings, like dog turds.

"You should try to do what your mom wants, Jim," Sergei said.

What both *my moms want?* Jimmy thought, but he didn't say it.

James Winslow was impressed that the Soviet wrestlers kept gauze pads and plaster and hypodermic needles in their locker at the Turnhalle Leopold. "They're Russians, Jim," Leo told him privately. "Even Russians who aren't med students can get hypodermic needles on the black market."

Before his roommates had left for the holidays, Jimmy had told them that Zander and Sergei were going to take him to a nightclub in Favoriten; he'd mentioned the belly dancer, the Egyptian, who was probably not an Egyptian.

"The poor belly dancer!" Claude cried, in empathy for underdogs.

"Maybe the belly dancer could carry your baby, Jimmy," Jolanda said. "Your family would only have to pay her more than she makes as

269

a belly dancer, which probably isn't much." Jolanda and Claude knew the Winslow family could afford to pay someone to have Jimmy's baby, but Honor was fearful of the unknown legal factors.

"No, no, *no*—not the poor belly dancer," Claude moaned. Claude still believed that Jolanda's ex-girlfriend Mieke was the best mom for Jimmy's ticket out of Vietnam. Claude remained convinced that Jolanda should hold Mieke's head and talk to her throughout the knocking-up process.

But Claude and Jolanda were in Paris and Amsterdam now for Christmas, leaving Jimmy and Hard Rain in Vienna. Keeping the dog hidden in the sleeping hours fell to Jimmy, who experimented with taking her to wrestling practice. The wrestlers loved the dog, but Hard Rain didn't like how the mat felt under her paws, and the thud of bodies on the mat frightened her. The dog hid in the locker room area, cowering in a crapper stall. When Hard Rain crept upstairs to the salon, Helene and the hairdressers were delighted. The various sprays and hair products made the dog sneeze, but Hard Rain was happy among the hairdressers and their female clientele.

Zander and Sergei invited Leo Spiegel to join them when they took Jimmy and Sol and Simon to Die Ägypterin in Favoriten. Kleiner Spiegel expressed his doubts about the Israelis going there. Once, in Favoriten, Little Mirror had run into a couple of Turkish wrestlers he knew from a long-ago tournament. "Kleiner Jude," one of the wrestlers had called him. ("Little Jew," the Turk had said.) Then Little Mirror locked up with the Turkish wrestler and threw him.

"Ich habe geworfen," Leo said. ("I threw," Leo told the freestyle wrestlers.)

Little Mirror politely declined to go to Die Ägypterin.

The night the Soviets took Jimmy and the Israelis to Favoriten, they stopped on their way at the Kaffeehaus Nachtmusik, where they left Hard Rain. If Jimmy was still at Die Ägypterin past Dagmar's closing time, Hard Rain would go home with Walter—the good dishwasher, as everyone now thought of the kindly, one-eared man.

James Winslow was distracted in the way someone writing a novel is. For a young man who hadn't seen a belly dancer, his mind was focused on his fictional characters and their story. He had just finished a long conversation on the phone with his grandfather, who'd assured him it was okay for a novel to be loosely autobiographical. "The more *loosely,* the better," Thomas Winslow had said. Jimmy was further distracted by what his grandfather told him about the orphanage at St. Cloud's. Jimmy was surprised his grandparents even knew that Honor Winslow wanted Chantal Beaudette to have Jimmy's baby. It was better to adopt a baby from the orphanage at St. Cloud's, Thomas had said. Both Thomas and Constance Winslow were disappointed when Honor rejected Thomas's idea. After all, their fourth daughter had grown up in a family with wonderful orphans; yet Honor adamantly wanted to know more about the birth mother of Jimmy's child than one can ever know about orphans' parents. In the long talk with his grandfather, there'd been no mention of Honor's backup plan—clearly unknown to the senior Winslows. Jimmy didn't talk about the bullet in his patella or cutting off the index finger on his writing hand—the repercussions of his failing to knock up someone.

While James Winslow was thus preoccupied on the way to Favoriten, the Soviet med students discussed how menstruation might affect a belly dancer. The Israeli wrestlers were more worried about anti-Semitism. Sergei thought most belly dancers were at their best in their thirties or early forties. "After they've had children, they have more of a belly," Zander said.

"In the first three days of her period, a belly dancer's abdominal movements could cause her some excessive bleeding," Sergei speculated.

"No hip drops or hip shimmies, or do them gently," Zander suggested.

"No pelvic locks or reverse undulations—they'll hurt," Sergei said.

Sol asked the Soviets about the nightclub's clientele. Were they mostly Turkish men, or were the Turks only a small percentage of the patrons? Simon wanted to know if the belly dancer mingled with the audience after her dance. The Russians had noticed only the Turks with cauliflower ears; the wrestlers represented a small percent of the clientele. The belly dancer, they said, was very discreet about her mingling. She touched no one. There was no anfassen allowed—no touching or feeling. The belly dancer discreetly moved among the tables of men, just making conversation; some men pushed their chairs away from the tables, hoping the belly dancer would sit in their laps. Zander said the belly dancer chose to sit in only one man's lap. Sergei said there was no anfassen during the lap-sitting—nothing overtly sexual.

James Winslow was typically withdrawn and introspective, even when the conversation concerned a belly dancer's moving hips—her pelvic thrusts and erotic undulations. The Russians had reserved a table near the stage at Die Ägypterin. The wrestlers would have a close-up view of the belly dancer.

"It's a lesbian's fantasy or a nightmare that I'm living with two guys in their twenties who've never had sex," Jolanda had told Claude and Jimmy—this was before she went home for Christmas, hoping to make up with Mieke.

This was odd for Jimmy to remember while he was waiting with his teammates for the belly dancer. And if Jimmy actually had sex with Mieke—imagining that Mieke gave birth to Jimmy's child—wouldn't their child want to have some sort of relationship with her? This was what Jimmy was thinking at Die Ägypterin. He also remembered his conversation with Fräulein Eissler—when he'd asked her to ask Esther, his birth mother, if he could write to her. Not meet her, or speak to her, but *just write* to her. Jimmy started to tell Annelies about the pact between Honor Winslow and Esther, but Annelies stopped him. "I know who gave birth to you, Jimmy," she'd told him. Did James Winslow want to write Esther *because* he was becoming a writer, or was it only natural or inevitable that he would seek to have some contact with his birth mom? These were Jimmy's thoughts when the house lights dimmed; the shapes of the men at their tables were unmistakable, even in semidarkness. On the spotlighted stage, the motionless belly dancer appeared to be looking straight at Jimmy, who guessed she was in her mid-thirties—about Esther's age when she'd given birth.

"There's something wrong with you if you don't get a hard-on," Zander, Jimmy's workout partner, whispered in his ear when the music started and the belly dancer began to move her hips. Her undulations, especially the way she could move her whole pelvis, gave Jimmy a hard-on. Yet he wouldn't have called the dancing pornographic—erotic, yes, but he hadn't realized how much a belly dancer had to learn. It was an art form, Jimmy was thinking—as the belly dancer's hip-shimmying kept pace with the music, rising to a crescendo. Now the men stood and applauded. The dance was done; the belly dancer bowed to her audience and left the stage.

"The way she was moving, she's not having her period tonight," Sergei said. The Soviets explained how the belly dancer would soon mingle with the patrons, beginning at the tables farthest from the stage and making her way forward. That way, she could once again bow to her audience from onstage—bidding them farewell from there. Like many of the men, the wrestlers pushed their chairs back from their table—in preparation for the lap-sitting. Jimmy was relieved that his hard-on had subsided. If he had an erection, he would have kept his lap under the table. Truly, all James Winslow was thinking was that it would be fun for him to bring Jolanda and Claude to Die Ägypterin to see the belly dancer.

With the house lights up bright, Simon and Sol were straining to overhear the conversation of the men at the nearby tables, but with everyone talking—and there was still some music playing—it was hard to hear what language (or languages) the men were speaking. James

Winslow wouldn't have known the difference between Turkish, Kurdish, and Arabic—not that he'd distinctly heard what anyone was speaking. "If the dancer speaks to us, we should speak in English to her," Zander suddenly said.

"That would be better than speaking German, with our respective 'foreign' accents," Sergei told his teammates. At this moment, even Jimmy was thinking that the Soviets sounded cagey; they sounded more like KGB operatives than med students.

Simon had noticed some women in the audience, but not many. "There are even a few women who look your age, Jim," Simon told him.

"Most of the women don't look Turkish," Sol was whispering when the belly dancer finally made her reappearance. In her dancing costume, she'd never looked like a stripteaser. There were long frills on her unrevealing brassiere; she'd shown no cleavage. She'd worn a long skirt with a slash and only rarely flashed a bare thigh. Black stockings had covered her knees. And now she'd changed her clothes to mingle. She was dressed like a businesswoman.

It would be necessary, later, for the Israelis and the Soviets to explain to Jimmy that Turkish women were not required to wear hijabs or headscarves in public. The belly dancer wore no hijab or headscarf—just a long-sleeved, loose-fitting blouse with trousers and a jacket (like a man's suit jacket). The severe way the woman dressed made her look somewhat masculine. Moving among the tables, the dancer was as comfortable speaking with the women as she seemed with the men.

When she approached the wrestlers' table, she ignored Sergei but smiled at Zander. "We'll speak English, if you can, because our friend is an American," Zander told her.

"I speak English," the belly dancer said, smiling at Sol.

"He's the American," Sol said, pointing at Jimmy.

The belly dancer didn't hesitate to sit in Jimmy's lap. The way she put her hands on Jimmy's shoulders, it was unclear if she intended to hug him or she meant to prevent him from hugging her. There was polite applause, then silence. "If you know what you want to be, tell me," the dancer said.

"I'm writing my first novel, or I'm trying to. I'm not really a writer yet, but I want to be one," Jimmy told her.

The belly dancer pulled him close to her, whispering in his ear. "Don't tell anyone, but I'm not an Egyptian and I'll never be one," she whispered.

When she'd pushed him away from her, Jimmy realized the crowd was waiting for him to say something. "Don't worry—I won't tell anyone," Jimmy promised the belly dancer. Everyone laughed; the older woman kissed him on his forehead. Then the belly dancer was back onstage, bowing again. When she was once more backstage, and everyone was leaving, the Soviets confided to Jimmy and the Israeli wrestlers that the evening always ended this way. When the dancer sat in someone's lap, she always whispered in his ear. "And the guy always says he won't tell anyone!" Sergei declared.

"What did she whisper, Jim?" Zander asked his workout partner.

"She asked me not to tell anyone," Jimmy answered seriously.

"Come on, Jim—tell us what she whispered!" Simon told him.

"The whispering is part of her *act*, Jim—you can tell us," Sol said. But James Winslow wouldn't even tell his teammates what the belly dancer whispered. Jimmy was sincere about writing his first novel, or trying to; he was sincere about not being a writer yet, but wanting to be one. The dancer had sounded sincere to him. James Winslow would not betray her confidence, even if what she'd whispered was only part of her act.

"A secret is still a secret," Jimmy insisted to his teammates.

It wasn't so late that the Kaffeehaus Nachtmusik had closed. The teammates had a few more beers before last call. The wrestlers teased Jimmy about his fidelity to the belly dancer's secret. "If a guy can keep a secret, a woman feels safe sleeping with him," Dagmar told the wrestlers. Over the Christmas holiday, Jimmy and Walter took turns bringing Hard Rain home with them, and Jimmy just kept writing and wrestling.

There was a Christmas card from Claude, who asked if he could write Chantal. Jimmy had called Chantal and asked her if she wanted to hear from Claude. Irmgard had explained to Jimmy how he could reverse the charges; he could call Chantal collect. "It's called person-to-person collect, Jimmy," Irmgard told him. Chantal wanted Jimmy to give Claude her address. Claude had seen the photo of Chantal, who Siegfried and the Frau still thought was Jimmy's mother. Chantal told Jimmy to ask Claude to send her a photo.

Jimmy had a long letter from Jolanda, too. Mieke was still interested in "trying it" with a guy, but both Mieke and Jolanda had some questions about the pregnancy part. "If Mieke has your baby, Jimmy, we want to be the baby's mother (or mothers) some of the time," Jolanda had written.

"Tell Mieke that the baby will want to know you, too," Jimmy wrote to Jolanda. "I know this because I want to know both my moms," he added.

In a toy store, James Winslow bought a small German shepherd of indeterminate sex for Siegfried. The painted dog was bigger than Siegfried's plaster soldiers and made of metal; it was a match in size and weight to the garlic press. With any luck, it might replace the garlic press, Jimmy was hoping. The small Christmas tree in the living room of the Schwindgasse apartment was also made of metal. There were only a few presents under the tree, where Jimmy put his Christmas present for Siegfried.

On Christmas Day, Jimmy was still in bed when Siegfried came into his room carrying the metal German shepherd instead of the garlic press. The boy climbed into the bed and gave Jimmy a hug. Then Siegfried ran into the hall, leaving the bedroom door open. Irmgard came in and gave Jimmy a hug, too; her face was wet with tears, and she couldn't speak.

NOT AN EGYPTIAN

Later, that same Christmas Day, Jimmy called home. Grandma Connie answered the phone and accepted his collect call. Jimmy talked to Grandpa Tommy and his mom. Everyone said how much they missed him. Honor Winslow didn't speak of knocking up anyone. During the call, Jimmy watched Siegfried mutilate and destroy his plaster soldiers with the metal German shepherd—a sturdier weapon than the garlic press.

In the week between Christmas and New Year's, both the Kaffee-haus Nachtmusik and Helene's hairdressing salon were closed, but Leo kept the Turnhalle Leopold open for the wrestlers. Sol and Simon took Hard Rain with them for some overnights, and Leo did, too. Zander and Sergei said there were no dogs allowed where they lived; the med students made it sound like they lived in a dormitory. "I doubt those two live together, or in a dormitory," Little Mirror said. "Russians just do what they do, Jim."

To Zander and Sergei's credit, the Soviet wrestlers were the ones who warned Jimmy he was being followed. "The same three thugs who were following the Dutch girl—she's the one they're interested in," Zander said.

"But now there's a woman with them," Sergei told Jimmy.

"Does the woman have tattoos?" Jimmy asked them.

"It's winter, Jim—she's wearing outdoor clothes—but she's definitely the dishwasher who tried it with the Dutch girl," Zander told him.

"Who else could it be—who else has it in for the Dutch girl?" Sergei asked Jimmy.

"If you go anywhere at night, take your teammates, Jim," Sol said.

"Take *all* your teammates with you at night," Simon told him.

"Me, too, Jim—I've never thrown a dishwasher!" Kleiner Spiegel said.

"Listen to Leo, Jimmy—the wrestlers are on your side," Annelies told him. She also informed Jimmy that he could expect to hear from Esther. "I don't want you to be *hurt*, Jimmy, but I don't see Esther as the

277

mothering type—nor do I think she'll be much of a pen pal," Annelies said. "What's more, you'll always be writing her or hearing from her in care of someone else. Esther has no permanent residence—she's a woman of no fixed address."

"Ich weiß," Jimmy said; he'd overheard his grandfather's complaints about Esther's itinerant nature. Jimmy wondered if *he* had an itinerant nature.

On New Year's Eve day, after wrestling practice, the Greco guys had showered and left the Turnhalle Leopold—except for Leo, who was always the last to leave. Little Mirror had showered and dressed; he was wearing his socks as he paced up and down the mat with a wet cloth, looking for spots of sweat or spit or blood to wipe clean. Jimmy sat on the mat in his socks. He was ready to go and was just waiting for his teammates. Sol and Simon were getting dressed in the locker room; Zander and Sergei were still in the showers. No one was screaming or yelling obscenities in the showers, because Helene and her hairdressers were on holiday; for once, they hadn't used up all the hot water. There was an ongoing negotiation between Helene and Leo concerning the need for a hot-water heater, either a new one or an auxiliary one—and who was going to pay what for it. At this moment, in the unusual absence of screaming and obscenities, Annelies came downstairs and into the wrestling room. She took off her boots before she stepped barefoot on the mat, painted toenails and all; she sat down, artfully facing away from the showers.

"It must be nice to have no hairdressers and lots of hot water, Leo," Annelies said.

"I'm in a hot-water war with Helene," Little Mirror told her.

Sol and Simon had heard her voice, and they could see Annelies from the locker room, where they were only half-dressed; they made no effort to conceal themselves. "It's just the Eissler," Sergei said to Zander; both of them went on showering.

"And you're *just* the Soviets, just *Russians*—your dicks are no big deal to me!" Annelies called to them. Everyone laughed, Sergei and Zander the loudest. Leo paced around Annelies, looking closely at her toenails. "Don't even think about painting your toenails, Leo," Annelies told him.

"I'm thinking about lifting you—not throwing you, just lifting you," Kleiner Spiegel said.

"I'll tell you when I want you to lift me, Leo," Annelies told him.

When Jimmy's fellow wrestlers were dressed, they just sat on the mat; it was as if they were waiting for instructions from Fräulein Eissler. Little Mirror just kept pacing—not lifting, not throwing. "You *wrestlers*," Annelies began. "You have no social lives—well, none to speak of—do you?" she asked them. Jimmy's teammates hung their heads; Jimmy knew he had no social life. "It's New Year's Eve and you have no plans, do you?" Annelies asked them. They could hear Hard Rain whining; the dog was alone in the locker room, but she wouldn't venture out onto the wrestling mat.

"Hard Rain has no social life and no New Year's Eve plans, either," Kleiner Spiegel said, for no discernible reason. He was still pacing.

"I know somewhere to go on New Year's Eve, and we can bring the dog," Annelies told them. It was a Hungarian place, with roasted paprika chicken and goulash with paprika. The teammates could hear one another over the zither player. Afterward, Sol and Simon escorted Annelies home, Leo took Hard Rain with him, and Sergei and Zander walked Jimmy to the Schwindgasse.

"No one's following the Eissler—she can get safely home herself," Zander had complained to Sergei.

"The Israelis worship the Eissler—they can't leave her," Sergei said.

"I worship her, too—I'm in love with her!" Jimmy told the Russians.

"We know, Jim," Zander told his workout partner.

"Even the Eissler knows you're in love with her," Sergei said.

When Claude came back to Vienna in early January, he told Jimmy and Jolanda he was in love with Chantal Beaudette. "Her written French is as good as mine, but I haven't heard her speak!" Claude lamented. His mother had asked him if Chantal had a French-Canadian accent; this was when Claude asked his mother to take some photos of him to send to Chantal. "I don't care if Chantal quacks like a duck!" Claude cried. He'd not sent Chantal his mom's photos, after all; in them, he looked like an angry, pouting child. Jolanda now photographed Claude in various poses in their adjacent bedrooms.

"I'm not taking any penis pictures, Claude—you'll have to ask Jimmy if you want to send Chantal any penis pictures," Jolanda said.

"Poor Chantal—no penis pictures!" Claude had cried.

Jolanda had returned to Vienna with photos of Mieke. Claude and Jimmy thought Mieke was more of a girly girl than Jolanda, who was tomboyish.

"You mean Mieke is more femme, and I'm more butch," Jolanda said. "You mean Mieke is prettier than me—she's more submissive than I am, too," Jolanda told them. "And Mieke is more sensitive than me— meaning her feelings are more easily hurt than mine," Jolanda went on; she was more emotional than usual, Claude and Jimmy thought. "I don't want Mieke coming to Vienna if those thugs are still following me—not now, not when Hildegund is hanging out with them," Jolanda told Jimmy and Claude.

James Winslow knew that Annelies and Jolanda must be talking. "Let the Eissler and Little Mirror make a plan for the followers, Jim," Sergei said. Zander nodded his assent to this.

"Mieke doesn't have to come to Vienna at all. We don't have to do this—not if you two have any misgivings about it," Jimmy said to Jolanda.

"We want to do this, Jimmy—for you and for us," Jolanda told him. "We think sharing a child would be fun for us—if you were the full-time parent, and we were parents only part-time," Jolanda said. She took photos of Jimmy for Mieke, who wanted to see what he looked like.

"No penis pictures for Mieke—she's too sensitive for penis pictures!" Claude wailed. Jolanda agreed that Mieke was too sensitive to see penises.

Simon and Sol had also confided to Jimmy about Jolanda's followers. "What's the plan?" James Winslow asked the Israeli wrestlers.

"Hildegund is one of those straight women who feel guilty for trying it with a woman. Some straight women and straight men who've tried it with the same sex are the worst homophobes, Jim," Sol said.

"But what do Annelies and Leo have to do with it?" Jimmy asked.

"In the end, the Russians will take care of Hildegund and her thugs—the Russians will do what they do. Annelies and Leo are setting up everything," Simon told Jimmy.

Setting up *what?* James Winslow wondered, but it was easier to let Jolanda photograph him in a variety of settings—while he went along with everything the wrestlers wanted. In the beginning, this meant that Jimmy and Claude took Jolanda no farther than their local café on the corner. If the roommates ventured as far as the Augustinerkeller or the Café Hawelka, the wrestlers met them there; they were taking no chances.

Through the first week of February, the ambiance at the Kaffeehaus Nachtmusik was enhanced by the alpine skiing at the 1964 Winter Olympics. Because of the mild weather, snow had to be trucked into Innsbruck and packed down by the Austrian army. "If you were Austrian, your mom might be more relaxed about your being a soldier," Claude told Jimmy.

"Jesus F. Christ, Claude," was all Jolanda could say.

The skiing in Innsbruck got off to a bad start. During a training run for the men's downhill, an Australian skier lost control and hit a tree; he died of a head injury. The Austrian men fared better, a gold in the downhill, a gold in the slalom, a silver and a bronze in the giant slalom. Dagmar was whooping it up for the Austrian women, who swept the downhill.

Claude was happy for France. The Goitschel sisters each won medals in the women's slalom and giant slalom, and two Frenchmen won medals in the men's alpine events. Jolanda was disgruntled that the Dutch skaters didn't do better; a Soviet woman speed skater won four medals. However, a Dutch figure skater won the women's singles, and a speed skater from the Netherlands took silver in the men's 1,500 meters. Jolanda was unimpressed, or perhaps she was just bored with her nightly confinement in the Kaffeehaus Nachtmusik.

Jolanda also bitched about Jimmy's wrestling teammates—now her constant companions and bodyguards. "It's too much testosterone for me to be around," Jolanda told Jimmy and Claude.

"It's better than being raped or beaten to death!" Claude cried.

"You're such a comfort to me, Claude," Jolanda said.

Jimmy knew Jolanda was inclined to chafe at too much supervision.

"Little Mirror is creepy—he's always looking at me, and the troll only comes up to my *waist*," Jolanda had complained.

"Kleiner Spiegel isn't *that* short—he's not a troll," Claude argued.

The way Leo looked at Jolanda, Jimmy couldn't tell if Little Mirror desired Jolanda or he wanted to throw her. Either way, Leo couldn't resist lifting Jolanda—his hands tightly locked under her butt. "Not throwing, just lifting!" Kleiner Spiegel assured her—his head like a cannonball below her breasts. Knowing Jolanda, Jimmy imagined she might rather be thrown.

The way the Soviet and Israeli wrestlers looked at Jolanda, Jimmy knew they desired her—more than other women, because the wrestlers understood she was a woman's woman and off-limits. When the roommates met Jimmy's teammates at the Café Hawelka, the wrestlers gathered around Jolanda at an oval table. Jolanda didn't speak; she scowled, breathing hard. Claude talked compulsively about being in love with a woman he hadn't met. Chantal had saved him from the Parisian heiresses his mother wanted him to have children with. Jolanda just scowled more and breathed harder.

To escape Claude's conversation, the Soviet med students told Jolanda about the male and female cadavers they shared with other med students.

"I don't want to know how you *share* the female cadaver," Jolanda said.

"The way you're breathing, you sound like you're going to throw up—you should go outside and get some fresh air!" Claude told Jolanda.

"If I go outside, I could be raped or beaten to death," Jolanda reminded Claude. Leo got out of his chair and was pacing around the table; he lightly touched Sol first, on one shoulder.

"No one will hurt you when we're close to you," Sol said to Jolanda. Little Mirror was bouncing on the balls of his feet; he patted Simon's head.

"We *lure* the dishwasher and her thugs," Simon told Jolanda. Leo had moved on to Zander, pulling the Soviet's ear.

"If Jim was on crutches, like he was injured, and you were alone with just Jim and Claude—well, you get the idea, don't you?" Zander asked Jolanda. Kleiner Spiegel put both his hands on Sergei's shoulders.

"But we'll know where you are—we'll get there in time," Sergei said. Sergei was sitting next to Jolanda, who sat with the palms of her hands pressed flat on the table, as if she alone kept the table from drifting away.

"What's wrong with the table? Is the table *levitating*?" Claude cried.

"There are so many hard-ons under the table, Claude. I was worried the table was rising," Jolanda told him. Claude looked under the table.

"I'm on crutches—just *pretending* to be injured, right?" Jimmy asked his teammates, all of them nodding. Little Mirror's hands were on Claude's shoulders. Claude had spotted no evidence of hard-ons under the table, which wasn't rising.

"You look like you can run, Claude. Are you a good runner?" Leo asked him.

"It's the only thing I'm good at—just running!" Claude lamented.

"Where will we be when Hildegund and her thugs attack us?" Jolanda asked. She was looking at Leo, the setup man. Jolanda flinched when Kleiner Spiegel held her wrists, the way wrestlers do.

"Between the Augustinerkeller and the Hawelka, but closer to the Hawelka—because the Dorotheergasse is a darker street," Leo told her.

"The Eissler says a darker street is less conspicuous," Sergei said.

"The Eissler means the Augustinerstraße would be more conspicuous than the Dorotheergasse," Zander explained to Jolanda.

"Annelies says Hildegund and her thugs have been hanging out around the Turnhalle and the Café Meisel," Sol said.

"This means they know when Jim is with us—when you and Claude are alone," Simon told Jolanda. Leo was too agitated to sit down.

"It won't matter what they know when we eliminate them!" Little Mirror cried. He was still bouncing on the balls of his feet when Jolanda pushed back her chair and stood up from the table. The way Kleiner Spiegel danced in circles, Jolanda waited until his back was turned to her. Then she bent her knees and lifted him; with her long arms locked around his waist, she bent over him and kissed his neck. The suplay-meister was a Greco guy; he'd expected to be thrown, not kissed. When Jolanda gently put him down, Kleiner Spiegel was speechless; he stood as still as a statue.

"Thank you, Leo—I love you!" Jolanda said. Jimmy and his teammates could see this meant almost as much to Little Mirror as her kissing him.

"I love you, too, Leo!" Claude cried, bursting into a flood of tears. It was not unnoticed by Jimmy how Jolanda kept hugging Claude until Claude could stop crying. "I want this to be *over*!" Claude kept saying, but Jimmy's teammates knew the details of the setup required rehearsal; like wrestling, the setup needed more practice.

"We'll be ready after Easter," was all Annelies would say.

Easter was early that year, the last weekend in March. Ash Wednesday was in the middle of February—in a Catholic country, noticeable by the gray smudges on the foreheads of one's fellow passengers on the Straßenbahn. The roommates saw the ashy smear on Siegfried's forehead after the Frau brought him home from Mass; the little soldier looked like he'd been singed by gunpowder. While the Frau was busy burning sausages at the stove, the five-year-old beckoned Jimmy (with his toy shepherd) to where the boy sat at the kitchen table. Whispering slowly, as if he were confiding to Claude, Siegfried said he'd been praying for a dog—a female German shepherd.

Jolanda and Claude had made plans for the long Easter weekend. They wanted to take Hard Rain to the mountains to let her play in the snow. In Zell am See, they'd found a Gasthof that welcomed dogs. This was in the Kitzbühel Alps, accessible by train from Vienna. Jimmy, of course, intended to stay in the city. "It'll be a good time to write," he'd told Fräulein Eissler.

"You and your writing, Jimmy. You're a Pferd mit Scheuklappen," Annelies said. (A "horse with blinders.")

According to Dagmar, her mother's dog with balls showed no sign of dying soon—nor did her mother. Dagmar had stopped flirting with Jimmy, who assumed her interest had been feigned or fleeting, but Jolanda said the widow manager's hopes were dashed on the night she got a look at Fräulein Eissler. "Dagmar knows she can't compete with a hottie like Annelies," Jolanda told Jimmy.

Claude shed more light on Jolanda's observation. The night Anneliese picked up Jimmy at the Kaffeehaus to go see the prostitutes, Dagmar had asked Claude and Jolanda who the pretty woman was. "Oh, Annelies is Jimmy's German tutor—he's gaga about her," Jolanda told the widow manager. "If they're not already fucking, they soon will be."

When Claude gave Jolanda away, Jimmy asked her why she would say such a thing to Dagmar. "I didn't like how she was flirting with you, Jimmy. I don't think she was sincere enough about it," Jolanda said. At times, Jimmy's junior year abroad would be lonely and confounding, but he made two friends who'd be his friends for life. Claude and

Jolanda made Jimmy's foreignness bearable. It would help him to see himself as a horse with blinders—a good analogy for a working novelist, Jimmy realized. As things would turn out, Claude and Jolanda wouldn't get to go to Zell am See for the long Easter weekend. (Not with all the practicing.)

March in Vienna didn't feel like spring. "No thunderstorms today," Claude kept saying every day, for the first week of March. For a while, Dagmar didn't play "A Hard Rain's A-Gonna Fall" at the café. Jolanda and Dagmar said they needed a break from the Bob Dylan song. Jimmy and Claude missed hearing it. Who knew what Hard Rain thought about it?

When the Soviet med students brought the wooden crutches to the Turnhalle Leopold, they made sure Helene and the hairdressers saw them. "Who are the crutches for?" Helene had asked them.

"Injuries happen—the crutches are just in case," Sergei said.

"Knee injuries are inevitable," Zander told Helene.

"Animals!" a hairdresser, washing a lady's hair, called out to the Russian wrestlers, who knew the hair-washing used up the hot water.

The choreography with the crutches required rehearsing. It was easy for Jimmy to learn how to use the crutches like someone with a knee injury. The passing off of one crutch to Claude on a dead run took more time. Like Hard Rain, Claude didn't like the feel of the wrestling mat—either in socks or barefoot. As for swinging one crutch like a baseball bat, Claude had never swung a baseball bat; he had to practice the grip. Annelies wanted Jolanda to practice getting her bicycle pump out of the holster when the holster was down around her ankles. "If one of the thugs pulls your jeans down, the holster won't be where you're used to it," Fräulein Eissler told her. Unlike Claude and Hard Rain, Jolanda liked the feel of the wrestling mat. In front of the wrestlers, she was brave about lying on her back on the mat—with her six-gun holster *and* her jeans down around her ankles.

Jolanda accepted this as part of the rehearsals; the wrestlers would see her flopping around on her back in her panties. But Jolanda drew the line about the wrestlers seeing her when she was sitting on a toilet in one of the crapper stalls with no doors. "No looking *and* no listening!" she called from the wide-open locker room.

When Jimmy and Fräulein Eissler went together to the Turnhalle Leopold, they got dark looks from Helene and her hairdressers. Annelies didn't resemble Jimmy's usual workout partners—not that Claude and Jolanda looked like wrestlers. When it was *finally* time to act out Jimmy's knee injury, Helene and her hairdressers had grown used to Annelies—they'd even stopped giving the hairy eyeball to Claude and Jolanda.

Helene and her hairdressers were used to the way the wrestlers screamed when they were taking cold showers. There was never any hot water at the end of the day, not after the hairdressers had been washing hair since the morning. But the way Leo had coached Jimmy to scream was a higher pitch of agony than Helene and her hairdressers had heard before. There was also the sound the ice machine made in the locker room when the wrestlers used it—the ice scattering on the bathroom tiles, where Hard Rain chomped on the fallen cubes and Jimmy just kept screaming.

While Sergei and Zander packed the ice around Jimmy's knee, they also wrapped his knee with an elastic bandage. Jimmy just screamed louder. Between breaths, he heard Helene at the top of the stairs, yelling down to the wrestlers. Helene sounded hysterical. Jimmy heard her say "Polizei" and "Krankenwagen," the words for "police" and "ambulance." He didn't get another word Helene yelled, but Annelies translated for him. "She says, 'You animals must be killing someone!' She's calling the police and an ambulance if the screaming doesn't stop," Jimmy's Jewish German tutor told him. "Just tone down the screaming a little, Jimmy," Annelies whispered in his ear. And now another hairdresser replaced Helene at the top of the stairs; it was her turn to yell at the wrestlers. Little Mirror shouted up the stairs to the hairdresser.

Fräulein Eissler translated their exchange. "You could kill one another more quickly and quietly if you used knives!" the hairdresser had yelled to the wrestlers.

"A wrestler has been injured!" Kleiner Spiegel yelled back. "Your lack of empathy is apparent. You hairdressers deserve to be strangled with your own hair!" Leo had shouted.

"The wrestlers and the hairdressers sound like they're *married*," Annelies observed. She'd already told Jimmy she would never be married. She also let Jimmy know her feelings about childbirth. "If and when I want a kid, I'll adopt one. Lots of kids need to be adopted, Jimmy." Sergei and Simon, the bigger wrestlers, carried Jimmy upstairs. Sol and Zander, Jimmy's fellow lightweights, carried his crutches.

At the top of the stairs, Helene and her hairdressers were waiting; they wanted to see the injured wrestler who'd been screaming. "He looks like he's still alive," Helene said to Leo. She sounded disappointed. (Annelies had translated for Jimmy without comment.)

When Fräulein Eissler spoke in German to Helene and her hairdressers, she spoke slowly enough that even Jimmy could understand her. "You women should do something about your hair—you look truly terrible," Annelies told them. Leo added something that shocked Helene and the hairdressers. Jimmy saw they were shocked, but he didn't get what Little Mirror had said to them.

What mattered was that Claude and Jolanda were waiting with the taxi and the driver. Out on the sidewalk, provided they were watching the Turnhalle Leopold, Hildegund and her thugs would have seen how awkward Jimmy was with his crutches; he appeared to be in pain when he was helped into the front seat of the taxi. Jolanda and Claude crowded into the backseat with Annelies. The crutches across their laps made them more uncomfortable. In the taxi, Fräulein Eissler reluctantly told Jimmy what Kleiner Spiegel had said to Helene and the hairdressers.

"She's a champion woman wrestler," the suplay-meister had told Helene and the hairdressers, pointing to Annelies. "She can tear off your tits and twats—she'll hide them where you'll never find them!" Jimmy knew Fräulein Eissler wasn't a wrestler; he understood why she'd hesitated to translate such a vulgar thing. In his heart, Jimmy was just thinking that Leo was a truly loyal little guy.

"And you say the wrestlers and the hairdressers sound like they're *married,*" Jimmy reminded Annelies.

"Like they've been married *forever,* Jimmy," Fräulein Eissler said.

In Vienna, the Straßenbahn rails and the cobblestones could be tricky or slippery for someone on crutches, and there was an unforeseen complication with the crutches. Hard Rain liked to lick (or gnaw on) the rubber tips on the ends of the crutches. The dog's feelings were hurt if you told her to stop it.

When Jimmy started his alleged rehab routine at the Turnhalle Leopold, the wrestlers were glad to see him. Helene and her hairdressers gave Jimmy their grudging respect. The hairdressers were visibly relieved when Fräulein Eissler wasn't with him. Little Mirror swore they'd believed him; Helene and her hairdressers thought Jimmy's Jewish German tutor was a champion woman wrestler—one who was poised to tear off their tits and twats, and somehow hide them.

The Easter weekend came and went. The appearance of a routine had been established. Claude and Jolanda, and Jimmy on crutches, went to the Kaffeehaus Nachtmusik, or they met with Jimmy's wrestling teammates—either at the Augustinerkeller or the Café Hawelka. Then, one night, the roommates pretended to yield to Jolanda's last-minute whim; after all, she was a girl inclined to whims. They appeared to be on their way to meet the throw-meister and Jimmy's teammates at the Café Hawelka when Jolanda proposed a spontaneous change of plans—suited to her free spirit. "Let's stop first for a beer at the Augustinerkeller," Jolanda told her roommates.

"The Augustinerkeller isn't really on our way to the Hawelka—it's not exactly a straight line to the part of the Dorotheergasse where we're going," Claude pointed out.

"For fuck's sake, Claude—just one beer!" Jolanda said. "I need a beer before I get the waist-high once-over from the troll, and before the Russians tell me all about their studies of obstetrical and gynecological procedures."

Jimmy and Claude couldn't argue with that, and the Augustinerkeller was kind of on their way to the Café Hawelka. Jolanda had downed only half her beer when Claude, who was choking, got a glimpse of the dishwasher's thugs. Jolanda checked out the women's room, where Hildegund herself was hiding out.

"How's Jimmy's knee doing, cunt?" the ink addict had asked Jolanda. "That's what he gets for wrestling," Hildegund added.

When Jolanda came out of the women's room, Claude and Jimmy were ready to leave; it was time to join forces with the Red Army wrestlers and the Israelis at the Hawelka, but they were some distance away from the Dorotheergasse. Jimmy (on his crutches) was supposed to have trouble keeping up with Claude and Jolanda. The roommates knew the dishwasher and her thugs would catch up to them, but not until they got to the relative darkness of the Dorotheergasse, where an attack would be less conspicuous.

The roommates didn't start running until they heard Hildegund and her thugs coming up behind them. Jimmy tossed one crutch to Claude when they were running. Jolanda and Jimmy let Claude get ahead of them before they stopped running. Jolanda and Jimmy stood back-to-back as Hildegund and her three thugs surrounded them. "Hit Hildegund first. The thugs won't be expecting that," Annelies had directed Jimmy. He held his crutch like a baseball bat, at the tip end; it was no Louisville Slugger, but it was wooden, and Jimmy hit Hildegund with the heavy end. As Kleiner Spiegel directed him to do, Jimmy then knee-capped her. Annelies had prepared Jimmy for the thug who thought he knew which of Jimmy's knees was the bad one. The thug came in low, reaching for Jimmy's knee. Jimmy sprawled, the way wrestlers do; he got behind the guy and put him in an arm bar. Jimmy didn't need the crutch to separate his assailant's shoulder.

The two thugs attacking Jolanda had her pinned on the pavement; one of them held her down while the other one unzipped her jeans and yanked them all the way down to her ankles. Jimmy saw that her holster was also at her ankles, but Jolanda had practiced how to reach for it. She quickly took hold of the bicycle pump; she was beating the face and ribs of the thug trying to mount her. Her panties were near her knees, but the guy trying to mount her was getting the worst of it.

"Fuck her, you idiots!" Hildegund was crying. Jimmy was surprised he understood her. Even carrying a crutch, Claude ran so fast to the Hawelka, he'd already run back—ahead of all the wrestlers. Claude started swinging the crutch the crazy way he'd rehearsed it. He hammered on the thug who was holding Jolanda down. Jolanda was already beating to death the thug who'd tried to mount her.

Claude had broken the nose and half-blinded the thug who'd been holding down Jolanda. The thug who'd tried to mount Jolanda was bloodied and sobbing. Hildegund, who'd been kneecapped, was struggling to stand; the thug with the separated shoulder had managed to get to his feet. The first of the wrestlers to arrive was too low to the ground for Jimmy to see, but Jimmy recognized the fierce grip of the throw-meister's locked hands. It was a belly-to-back suplay—a lights-out throw, a headfirst landing.

Hildegund was now standing. She and Jimmy were holding his crutch between them; it would be a short-lived standoff. Little Mirror locked his hands at Hildegund's hips. She must have known whose hands they were. "Kleiner Jude!" she said. (It seemed fitting that her last words were "Little Jew!") Jimmy let go of his end of the crutch.

"Goodbye," he told the tattooed dishwasher. The suplay-meister had Hildegund locked up; Jimmy knew the crutch would be no help to her. It was as well executed a throw as Jimmy ever saw. The dishwasher didn't land on a wrestling mat—the ink addict landed on the back of her neck and head on the Dorotheergasse.

Jimmy didn't feel sorry for Jolanda's two attackers. They deserved the way Jolanda was working one of them over with her bicycle pump, while Claude kept whacking the other one with the crutch. What the Red Army wrestlers did to them seemed a little unnecessary. Sergei bear-hugged the thug who'd tried to mount Jolanda; Sergei drove him flat to his back on the pavement. When Jimmy saw how the thug held his chest, as if he were afraid to breathe, Jimmy asked Sergei (who was, after all, a med student) if he thought the guy had rib damage.

"Could be ribs, Jim—could be a cracked sternum," Sergei said.

"*Now* you Russians show up—you could have come *sooner!*" Jolanda berated them. She was finally able to pull up her jeans. As for the poor fucker Claude was beating, the thug who'd been holding down Jolanda, he was somehow still standing when Zander dropped under him and hit him with an outside single-leg takedown, blowing out the thug's knee. At least Jolanda's two attackers were still conscious, Jimmy was thinking.

"We'll take care of this mess," Sergei was saying, indicating the carnage on the sidewalk. "You can go inside—we'll wait for the police. You can go inside, too," Sergei said to Leo.

"I'm sorry we were slow to arrive at the scene of the crime," Zander told Jolanda. "We were busy calling the police."

"It matters which police you call," Sergei said.

"What does 'which police' mean?" Claude was asking, as the roommates walked along with Leo to the Café Hawelka.

"Let the Soviets do what they do, Claude," Kleiner Spiegel said.

Jimmy knew Leo's two big throws had relaxed him. Little Mirror seemed almost normal by the time the roommates got to the Hawelka. Claude wanted to know which of the thugs was Hildegund's husband, but Jolanda had no idea. "Jesus Mary Joseph, Claude—we weren't formally introduced!" she told him.

Jimmy was carrying the crutch he'd used as a weapon, but Claude had left his crutch at the scene of the attack. "Jimmy doesn't need it, and it was bloody with someone else's blood!" Claude cried.

"Look at me, Claude—*I'm* bloody with someone else's blood! I'm glad you didn't leave *me* behind!" Jolanda told him.

That's when the man in a suit and tie came into the Café Hawelka. He brought Claude's bloody crutch to the roommates' table. "Aren't you the American? Isn't this your crutch?" he politely asked—in English, with a Russian accent. The man in the suit might have been a plainclothes cop—except for his accent and the kind of suit it was. It was true, as Leo said, the Russians could get anything on the black market. But, as Jolanda would say, men's suits weren't what the Soviets did well. Jimmy just thanked the guy for returning the crutch. If he'd been an actual policeman, the roommates knew, the man in the bad suit would have asked them some questions.

Claude was curious; he followed the unlikely plainclothes cop outside. When he came back to the roommates' table in the Hawelka, he was agitated. No bodies were lying on the pavement; the dishwasher and her thugs had just disappeared. Claude walked to the Graben. No cops in uniform, only men wearing ties and bad suits; they all spoke Russian.

"Not virgin births, Claude—they *are* Russians!" Jolanda told him. "Don't you get it? There are no policemen, *only* Russians."

Little Mirror was humming to himself, as happy as Jimmy had ever seen him. "Let the Soviets do what they do," Leo sang like a song.

"But what happened to Hildegund and her thugs?" Claude asked the little throw-meister.

"For fuck's sake, Claude—let it go!" Jolanda told him.

When the former Red Army wrestlers finished with their business, they joined the roommates and Kleiner Spiegel at their table. After the mess they'd cleaned up—after Sergei's sternum-cracking bear hug, after Zander's single-leg takedown—the Soviets might have celebrated a little, but all they ordered was their usual beer.

"You guys don't ever lighten up, do you?" Jolanda asked them.

"They're Russians—they can't help it. They just do what they do," the throw-meister reminded Jolanda. Jimmy could tell that Sergei and Zander wanted to change the subject.

"You're the real hero, Claude," Sergei said. "You have no idea what you're doing, but when Jolanda was in trouble, you just started swinging."

"That's you, Claude—you're a hero with no idea what you're doing," Zander said.

"Not much training—just balls, Claude," Sergei told him.

"You're all balls, Claude—a true hero!" Zander said.

"All balls!" Little Mirror shouted, toasting Claude with his beer.

"You're my hero, Claude—you always will be," Jolanda told him. "I would do anything for you—you know I would, don't you?" It was hard to tell if Claude was overwhelmed by everyone's high esteem of his heroism, or if Jolanda's offer to do *anything* for him was worrisome.

"For Christ's sake, Claude—not *that* kind of anything," Jolanda said, to put him at ease.

There were hugs all around when the roommates and the wrestlers said, "Auf Wiederschauen," though Claude and Jolanda were anxious about hugging Leo. Everyone should be anxious when hugging Greco-Roman guys, and Little Mirror was a big hugger. He couldn't hug you without lifting you—a little. "Please don't lock your hands, okay?" Jolanda asked Kleiner Spiegel, before he hugged her. Of course the throw-meister's hands were locked when he lifted her, just a little. Greco-Roman guys can't help it—lifting you with locked hands is what they do.

On the roommates' way home, Claude pointed out to Jolanda that Leo's head came up to her boobs—not to her waist, as Jolanda once said.

"Please don't remind me, Claude. I can feel exactly where the troll's head was," Jolanda told him.

"You're the crutch-meister, Claude—you're the real hero!" Jimmy told the brave Frenchman.

"You're *my* hero, Claude—forever and ever," Jolanda told him, hugging him to her. Jimmy couldn't help noticing that Claude's head didn't come up much higher than Jolanda's boobs, and that Jolanda's hands were locked when she lifted him.

Jimmy was walking fine without his crutches, which he'd given to one of the waiters at the Café Hawelka. The rubber tip at the end of Claude's crutch had been lost. Without the rubber tip, the crutch was a hazard. But the waiter's son was in a school play. The director was asking parents of the cast if they could donate crutches as stage props. Jimmy was happy to give the waiter his bloody crutches. The roommates were passing the Staatsoper before they realized what an early night they were having. Looking at his watch, Claude said, "When you're in a fight, it feels like an eternity, but all that violence actually took no time at all!"

"Some violence can take an eternity, Claude—some violence is fucking eternal," Jolanda told him.

They'd been thinking they'd have to hurry to pick up Hard Rain before closing time at the Kaffeehaus Nachtmusik, but the night was young. They had lots of time. Jolanda said she wanted to take a bath. As she told Jimmy and Claude, she'd been lying on the filthy pavement in her panties, and her assailant had bled on her. It was a good time to take a bath, Claude conjectured, in his nerdy way. "Irmgard will be out—it's too early for after-hours bath. Frau Holzinger and Siegfried will have gone to bed," he commented.

When they got back to the Schwindgasse apartment, Frau Holzinger was wide awake and fretting; it was past her bedtime, but she was excited, making her harder to understand than usual. Even in close quarters, in the hall by the roommates' bedrooms, the Frau was almost incomprehensible.

"Your *mother* was here!" the widow Holzinger exclaimed, taking hold of Jimmy's hands. "She's so pretty, so beautiful!"

"My *mother*?" Jimmy asked. The door to the bathroom was open, and there was no one in the bathtub.

"She wouldn't stay, but she's coming back," Frau Holzinger said. "I asked her to stay—I said she could wait for you here—but we couldn't understand each other. I told her you might be at the café on the corner, but I don't know if she understood me."

"Are you sure she was Jimmy's *mother*?" Jolanda asked the Frau. "You heard the *Mutter* word, did you?"

"Ja, Yimmys Mutter!" the Frau declared.

"Wait, wait, *wait*!" Claude cried, jumping up and down. "Your *mom* doesn't want you to make *her* pregnant, does she?"

"Jesus Mary Joseph, Claude!" Jolanda said. "I'm going to take a bath. You two can sort this out," she told Jimmy and Claude.

Frau Holzinger had all the while been babbling incoherently. "So pretty, so beautiful," Jimmy heard her repeat, "und mütterlich," the Frau added ("and motherly"). "Of course your mother is welcome to stay here," the Frau told Jimmy. "There's nothing like Mutterliebe!" the widow Holzinger declared—at the moment Jolanda reappeared in a bathrobe, carrying a towel and swearing to herself.

"There's nothing like *what*?" Jolanda asked Claude and Jimmy.

"There's nothing like *motherly love*," Claude translated.

"Don't make me vomit, Claude. I'm going to take a bath before I throw up," Jolanda said, but she was still in the hall, not in the bathroom, when Frau Holzinger spoke again—this time, more slowly and comprehensibly. Who knew how Frau Holzinger could rhapsodize on the holy subject of *motherliness*?

"Mütterlichkeit!" the Frau cried, in ecstasy. "Your mother is so pretty, and so *young*!" she exclaimed. With the *young* word, the roommates realized Frau Holzinger's misunderstanding. She'd seen a photo of Chantal; she still thought Chantal was Jimmy's mother. If she'd recognized the *mother* word, Chantal had probably told her she was a *friend* of Jimmy's mother.

"It's not just you, Claude—we're *all* idiots," Jolanda said. "It's *Chantal,* isn't it?" she asked Jimmy.

22.

In the Future

Of course it was Chantal who'd said she was a friend of Jimmy's mother. *Yimmys Mutter* was the way the Frau said it. A *J* in German is pronounced like a *Y*.

In German, Claude couldn't keep straight the two words that mean "accident"—*Unfall* and *Zufall*. A Zufall can be good or happy—it just happens by chance, unexpectedly.

"Oh boy, oh *boy*—is this an Unfall or a Zufall?" Claude asked.

"It doesn't matter what you call it, Claude. "It's Chantal. *You're* the one who should take a bath," Jolanda told him.

"Do you see, Yimmy?" the Frau asked; she pointed into his bedroom. Chantal's big backpack was on the floor, at the foot of his bed. "Your mother left her things—she's coming back," the Frau said. "She's looking for you at the café on the corner, if she understood me."

"We'll take turns in the bathtub later, Claude. We'll go to the Nachtmusik *now*," Jolanda said. She stomped back to her bedroom, taking off her bathrobe before she got there. Claude went into Jimmy's bedroom, where he struggled to lift Chantal's backpack.

"Maybe your mom is *in* the backpack!" Claude was saying to Jimmy, when Frau Holzinger hailed them from the far end of the hall.

"Gute Nacht!" the Frau called to Jimmy and Claude. They saw she was turning out lights in the living room. The Frau left one light on, maybe for the woman she thought was Jimmy's mother. It was unclear if Irmgard had gone out; she might still have been dressing to go out.

It was a moment of clarity for James Winslow. When he and his roommates were walking together to the Kaffeehaus Nachtmusik, he assured Claude and Jolanda that his mother and Chantal weren't crazy. True, Jimmy's mom had gone to extremes to have him—not what most women who wanted a child would have done. Yet it suddenly made sense to Jimmy why his mother would go to extremes to keep him out of a war. And Chantal loved and admired Jimmy's mom; Chantal would do what Honor Winslow wanted, but only up to a point.

"Chantal is here for *you*, Claude. You get it, don't you?" Jolanda asked.

"I just hope she *likes* me!" Claude cried, closing his eyes, praying while he was walking. There were some ancient stone hitching posts along the curbside of the Schwindgasse—not that anyone was still tethering horses on the sidewalk. Perhaps the thigh-high pillars of stone were expensive to remove. Jolanda sharply cautioned Claude to open his eyes.

"Watch where you're going, Claude! It wouldn't be a good night to neuter yourself on a fucking hitching post!" Jolanda warned him.

Their experience earlier in the evening gave Jimmy a new perspective on going to extremes. What Hildegund and her thugs tried to do to them was extreme. How the Red Army wrestlers retaliated was extreme. Jimmy's mother and Chantal were different, but they weren't dangerous. As for knocking up someone, Jimmy had grown fond of Mieke from her photo. Now that Hildegund and her thugs were gone—now that Jolanda was safe—Jimmy trusted that Mieke would be coming to Vienna. It was the first night in James Winslow's life when he felt like a grown-up, walking into the Kaffeehaus Nachtmusik and seeing Chantal sitting with Dagmar and Fräulein Eissler. A stranger would have thought this trio of attractive women were fast friends. Hard Rain's big head looked bigger than usual in Chantal's small lap. "The Ride of the

Valkyries" from Wagner's *Die Walküre* heralded the roommates' arrival. (Don't think for a minute that Dagmar, Chantal, or Annelies resembled those maidens of Odin, the guides to Valhalla.)

"Chantal looks just like her picture!" Claude was whispering.

"Keep your pecker in your pants, Claude," Jolanda told him.

"Why is Fräulein Eissler with them?" Claude asked Jimmy and Jolanda. Jimmy understood that Annelies had always known when Chantal was coming.

"Annelies doesn't just know what's happening, Claude—I think she arranges almost everything," Jolanda said. Jimmy was sure Annelies knew what had happened on the Dorotheergasse, near the Café Hawelka. Hard Rain was happy to see her roommates. Chantal and Jimmy were glad to see each other, too. But Fräulein Eissler gave the lion's share of her scrutiny to Jolanda. Annelies was certainly relieved to see that Jolanda looked okay, but she had noticed the blood in Jolanda's hair.

"Dear girl, is that their blood or your blood?" Annelies asked.

"Not mine," Jolanda answered. Annelies gave her a hug.

Naturally, Claude asked Annelies if she had any idea what ultimately happened to Hildegund and her thugs.

"Keine Ahnung," Fräulein Eissler automatically said. ("Not the slightest idea.") "There's snowmelt in the Danube every spring—a lot of water in the river this time of year," she added. There were no crocodile tears for the tattooed dishwasher and her thugs, who were headed down the Danube—the second-longest river in Europe. They were bound for Bratislava—as the river flows, sixty kilometers away.

Dagmar had already moved on. She'd put "A Hard Rain's A-Gonna Fall" back on the café's playlist. Everyone knew Bob Dylan wasn't to blame for the departed dishwasher's bad behavior.

"Hard Rain is a great name for a dog—for *this* dog," Chantal said, as she held Hard Rain's head in her lap, but Chantal was looking at Jimmy, who was looking at her. "Your mom misses you, Jimmy, but

I guess you'll have to make do with me," Chantal said. Now she was looking at Claude.

"Wait, wait, *wait!*" Claude started to say, but Jolanda stopped him.

"For Christ's sake, Claude, speak *French!*" Jolanda said.

Jimmy and Jolanda had never heard Claude speak French. Naturally, the roommates didn't understand what Claude was saying, but Claude sounded confident and composed. In French, Claude was impassioned but controlled; he sounded like another person. The patrons of the Nachtmusik were stunned, Dagmar among them. They'd heard the French boy's accent, in English and German, but they'd not heard his French before. Hard Rain had perked up her ears. This was a different Claude, even to a dog.

Of course, Claude overdid it. He didn't pause to let Chantal speak. Claude might have gone on talking until closing time if Jolanda hadn't purposely interrupted him; she kicked him under the table.

"We take turns sleeping with Hard Rain. We also take turns sleeping with each other—not in the way you might think," Jolanda told Chantal.

Chantal smiled at Jolanda and her roommates. "I guess you'll have to make do with me, too—not in the way you might think," Chantal said. She said something in French to Claude; whatever she said, it made him moan. Then Chantal turned her attention to Fräulein Eissler. "We've been talking about Siegfried's dog, about saving Siegfried," Chantal said. "We like your part-time-moms idea, Jolanda," Chantal told her. "Now that there's a plan to save Jimmy from the war in Vietnam, we'll move on to saving Siegfried." Jimmy knew that moving on was what Annelies did best. Unwitting draft dodger that Jimmy was, he trusted Jolanda and Mieke to save him from the war in Vietnam. He was aware that saving Siegfried was Fräulein Eissler's next salvation project. What Claude had in mind was saving Hard Rain, but Claude had started something more; he had set a story in motion. Claude made Siegfried want a female German shepherd. This was a writing lesson James Winslow would learn.

"You're the writer, Jimmy, or you want to be," Fräulein Eissler said. "Tell us how Hard Rain and Siegfried save each other. You're the story-teller. Tell us how we bring them together."

At the time, beginner writer that he was, Jimmy only knew he was being asked to finish a story Claude had started—or Annelies had started it, by urging the roommates to somehow save Siegfried. Either way, Jimmy knew he was starting his story by finishing theirs. For Jimmy, the writing lesson entailed beginning a story with an ending—namely, he had to figure out how Hard Rain could become Siegfried's dog.

Walter, the one-eared dishwasher, saved him. By suddenly showing up at the table, the former child soldier and POW bought Jimmy a little more storytelling time. Everyone saw that Walter was worried about something. Dagmar's new dishwasher didn't beat around the bush. A Gewitter was coming. Walter had seen or heard a weather forecast. A thunderstorm was expected in the wee hours of the morning. Walter reiterated his concerns; he didn't want Hard Rain to be "embarrassed." In the event of thunder and lightning, Walter wanted her to have "a place to go."

"I'll leave the bathroom door open for her, even if I'm taking a bath," Claude told the kind-hearted dishwasher.

"I'll let Hard Rain shit in the bathtub when I'm in it," Jolanda said.

"I'll let Hard Rain into the bathroom, even if Irmgard is in the bath-tub!" Claude cried. (His newfound heroism knew no bounds.)

Fräulein Eissler had been translating the one-eared dishwasher's words for Chantal, including Walter's repeated expression of empathy for Hard Rain. ("If only the poor girl could tell us her thoughts.") From the safe haven of Chantal's lap, Hard Rain stared lovingly at her protectors.

"This dog can't be a bathtub shitter—not *this* dog," Chantal said. "I've heard of only one dog who shit in a tub during thunderstorms," she went on. "I just assumed it was a New Hampshire thing," she said.

"Of course it was!" Claude cried, but Jolanda looked as disconcerted as Jimmy. They'd not heard about an actual bathtub shitter before. If there was another dog who did it, Hard Rain could be a bathtub shitter, too. Thunder and lightning were coming. This could complicate the plot to bring Hard Rain and Siegfried together, but Jimmy was grateful to Walter for warning them, and for buying him more storytelling time.

To anyone who listens to music, it's discordant to go from Wagner to the Beatles. At the Nachtmusik, the playlist went from "The Ride of the Valkyries" to "I Saw Her Standing There"—it was quite inharmonious. More dissonance followed with "The Blue Danube Waltz." From the Beatles to Johann Strauss II was a stretch, and tonight wasn't the night for the roommates and their friends to dwell on the Danube, where the tattooed dishwasher and her thugs were going downstream— they were no longer waltzing. No maidens of Odin were guiding them to Valhalla. Hildegund and her thugs were headed to the Black Sea— they weren't having a "Blue Danube" kind of night. That night, at the Kaffeehaus Nachtmusik, the approaching thunderstorm helped Jimmy to focus. It was the night when storytelling became James Winslow's business.

Frau Holzinger had simply misheard Chantal. It wouldn't be hard to explain to her that Chantal was a friend of Jimmy's mother. But Jimmy decided to make it his mom's idea to give Siegfried a dog, the very dog he wanted. The way the story would go, Jimmy had told his mother that he lived with a five-year-old. Jimmy's mom had asked him if there was anything Siegfried wanted. Naturally, Chantal hadn't brought a female German shepherd from the United States. This was where Fräulein Eissler would enter the story. She had arranged for the perfect female German shepherd—spayed, regularly shampooed, and with all her shots. Furthermore, the Holzinger family could share Hard Rain with the café on the corner of Argentinierstraße. The widow manager was a dog person and the one-eared dishwasher had built Hard Rain her own doghouse. And, by the way, the shepherd was welcome to sleep with the student boarders—until such a time as the Frau, Irmgard, and

Siegfried made other sleeping arrangements for the dog. How could the Holzingers refuse a Geschenk from Jimmy's Mutter? Surely the Frau and Irmgard would accept a gift for Siegfried. If Fräulein Eissler had a hand in it, wouldn't it be too obvious if the Holzingers turned the dog down? Jimmy had learned a little in Vienna, after all. (Some anti-Semites don't like to be too obvious about their anti-Semitism.)

Jolanda liked Jimmy's story. Claude had been taking notes. Dagmar was disconsolate; she regretted that her mother's dog with balls was still alive, but Dagmar promised she would share Hard Rain for as long as the Holzingers wanted to.

"What's the title for this novel, Jimmy?" Annelies asked him.

"*A Boy's First Dog*!" Claude cried, bursting into tears. Jolanda kicked him under the table.

"*Eine Hündin für Siegfried,*" Jolanda suggested. But Fräulein Eissler thought *A Female Dog for Siegfried* sounded strange in English.

"I'm still thinking of a title," Jimmy told them. But for now he had a plan, and he was sticking to it. Hard Rain had no discernible reaction to Jimmy's story, but what if she didn't want to become Siegfried's dog? Jimmy was worrying. He hoped Hard Rain was a dog who liked children. Not all dogs do. It occurred to Jimmy that he couldn't write the future, but he had an ending-driven plot. It was a start.

There was back-to-back Bob on the playlist as the roommates were leaving the café with Chantal and Annelies—kisses all around. "Don't Think Twice, It's All Right" was playing.

"You be a good girl," Dagmar said to Hard Rain.

Jimmy took it as a good omen that the next Dylan on the playlist was "A Hard Rain's A-Gonna Fall," but Claude had a couple of convulsions when he heard it. Claude never knew an omen that wasn't evil. Presentiments of doom caused him violent and involuntary muscle contractions, which Jimmy and Jolanda found hard to ignore.

Bob Dylan sang something about a newborn baby surrounded by wolves, which clearly didn't comfort Claude.

"Get a grip, Claude," Jolanda said.

Bob Dylan just kept singing. It was something about young children handling guns. Claude's convulsions had subsided, but he was quietly moaning. Outside the café, the nighttime sky was overcast, the air humid and still. The roommates knew how oppressive and unmoving the air always was before a thunderstorm.

Claude was scanning the glowering sky, looking for lightning, when he walked into one of the stone hitching posts. Everyone waited for him while he got back on his feet and resumed normal breathing.

"*You're* the one who's going to shit your brains out in the bathtub, Claude," Jolanda told him. Chantal, who took hold of Claude's hand, gave him a reassuring squeeze.

"I'll tell you a title—just call it *A Gift from Yimmy,*" Annelies said. "Siegfried will remember *you,* Jimmy. Siegfried never met your mother." She kissed everyone good night before she went her own way.

Hard Rain, bless her heart, took a dump; everyone had to wait for this. Then Jimmy and Chantal waited on the sidewalk with the dog, while Claude and Jolanda made sure the coast was clear in the Holzinger apartment. It was the time of night when Irmgard was working in the Krugerstraße hotel, and the Frau and Siegfried were sleeping. Those two could be expected to sleep through the night.

"What did you say to Claude in French?" Jimmy asked Chantal.

"I said he would hear my French when we were alone together. 'I'll always speak French when we're alone,' I told him," Chantal said.

Claude took the first bath, insisting that Hard Rain be there—in the bathroom, while he was in the tub. "That was tragic," Claude said, after his bath. He didn't think Hard Rain knew anything about bathtubs. The whole time Claude was having his bath, Hard Rain had kept her distance from the tub. "If you ask me, the poor girl is wary of baths—or of people in bathtubs!" Claude cried.

Jolanda took the next bath. "Hard Rain seems bored with bathtubs," she said. The dog fell asleep on the bathmat while Jolanda was having her bath and slept through Jolanda drying herself and wrapping herself in a towel. "I'm not used to being ignored when I'm naked," Jolanda said.

Claude had shipped his encyclopedia set in a steamer trunk from France. No, not the entire set, which wouldn't have fit in the steamer trunk. Claude had ventured a guess as to which letters of the alphabet to leave out. He was always complaining that he'd left the wrong encyclopedias at home, but not this time. The encyclopedia for all things beginning with the letter D was in the steamer trunk. After Claude and Jolanda took their baths, it was Chantal's turn in the bathroom with Hard Rain. Claude translated his French encyclopedia for Jolanda and Jimmy. Claude imparted his obsession with the course of the Danube to his tired roommates. Budapest was some three hundred kilometers downstream from Vienna, Claude explained. Belgrade was some five hundred kilometers downriver from Budapest, he carried on.

"You should've read this to Hard Rain in the bathroom," Jolanda told Claude. "You would've given Hard Rain such a boring bathroom experience, the poor girl would never shit her brains out in a bathtub— she would shit her brains out anywhere but a bathtub!" Jolanda said. By the time Jimmy took a bath, Hard Rain refused to go in the bathroom.

Chantal and Jolanda had been towel-drying their hair in Jimmy's bedroom, but they were ready for bed now. Jolanda had put her pajamas on; she'd opened the window by Jimmy's writing desk, where she said she was listening for thunder, but Jimmy knew the open window was for her cigarette smoke. "I can't imagine listening to Claude getting laid without having a last cigarette," she whispered to Jimmy.

"If Siegfried were my five-year-old, and anyone gave him a German shepherd without telling me first, I think I'd be pretty pissed off about it," Chantal said to the roommates.

As Jimmy told Chantal, he would almost certainly see Irmgard first. "Irmgard takes a bath as soon as she's home from work," Jimmy explained. He'd pointed out that his bedroom was across the hall from the bathroom.

"I hope Irmgard won't be *in* the tub when the thunderstorm starts," Jolanda said.

This had occurred to the roommates. They agreed Hard Rain should start out sleeping with Claude and Chantal, and Jolanda would sleep with Jimmy in his bedroom. This way, Jimmy and Jolanda could tell Irmgard about the gift from Jimmy's mother. Later, Irmgard could meet Hard Rain and be introduced to Chantal—not necessarily in that order.

Was it going to be a night of comedy or a night of conscience? Jimmy turned off the light in the hall. Irmgard would turn it on when she came home. Jimmy's bedroom lights were off, but there was more light than usual in his room. Jolanda had left the window open, and she'd not closed the curtains. She wanted to be sure they could hear the thunder and see the lightning. If Jolanda slept at all, her tossing and turning kept Jimmy awake. Jimmy thought he heard Jolanda tapping her fingernails on the wooden frame of the bed—as if she were waiting, impatiently, for the thunderstorm.

"You hear the rain, don't you?" Jolanda asked Jimmy. They listened to the patter of rain on the balcony window; it sounded a little like fingernails tapping on wood, James Winslow was thinking. They started talking about anything and everything, in no particular order.

"Sometimes I wish I was romantically involved with Fräulein Eissler," Jimmy admitted to Jolanda.

"I can identify with that, but I'm being faithful to Mieke now," Jolanda said. The rain was pelting down; there was no mistaking it for fingernails. Because Jimmy and Jolanda were talking, they didn't hear Irmgard come home. The flashes of lightning were coming closer. When Irmgard turned on the light in the hall, Jimmy saw her unmistakable shape in the frosted-glass panel on his bedroom door. He and Jolanda watched Irmgard undress and wrap herself in a towel.

"I can hear two of you, Jimmy," Irmgard said. "Is she old enough?" Irmgard asked.

"She's old enough! I'm with Jolanda!" Jimmy called.

"I want to see her," Irmgard told him, opening his bedroom door.

Like most tall people, Jolanda had a way of making herself look taller when she wanted to. In her tent-size bath towel, Irmgard filled Jimmy's bedroom doorway. "Yes, Jolanda is of age, but Claude must be sleeping with someone—I heard their voices, too," Irmgard said.

"Claude is sleeping with a friend of my mom's. Her name is Chantal—she's older than Claude. Chantal has a Geschenk for Siegfried—a gift from my mother," Jimmy told Irmgard. He didn't know how much more he could have blurted out, in three deep breaths, and Chantal was already in the hall.

"I'm Chantal," she said, offering to shake Irmgard's hand. From the way that went, Jimmy would have guessed that Irmgard didn't have a lot of experience shaking hands. "It's a very *active* gift to transport from the U.S.—I needed Fräulein Eissler's help to arrange it here," Chantal told Irmgard.

"Annelies is good at arranging things," Jolanda ventured to say.

"Fräulein Eissler is an *arranger*, all right," was all Irmgard said.

Claude must have been holding back Hard Rain. There was a clap of thunder—no more distant rumbles, Jimmy was thinking. He got out of bed; he didn't want to be in the bed when Claude let Hard Rain go. Jolanda had gotten out of bed, too. She and Jimmy thought Hard Rain wouldn't jump on an empty bed, but who knew what Hard Rain would do?

"I'm not crazy about baths in thunderstorms," Irmgard said, edging her way into the hall. "If it's all the same to you, I'll try to get in and out of the bathtub before the storm," she told Jimmy and Jolanda.

Claude took the next resounding thunderclap as his cue. "Wait, *wait*!" Claude cried from his room. "No one has been killed by lightning in a bathtub—not when a dog was watching," Claude said.

"Not when *Siegfried's* dog is watching—*this* dog watches over you," Chantal said to Irmgard.

"I'm sorry, but I told my mom that Siegfried wanted a female German shepherd. I should have known what this might prompt my mom to do," Jimmy told Irmgard.

"Your mother got Siegfried a *dog*?" Irmgard asked. She was standing on the threshold to the bathroom.

"You can always give her back if you don't want Siegfried to have a dog," Jolanda said, shrugging.

"Her name is Hard Rain!" Claude cried. This caused a commotion in Claude's bedroom, where Hard Rain had heard her name.

"For Christ's sake, Claude—let her out!" Jolanda cried. "Her name, Hard Rain, is from the Bob Dylan song," Jolanda explained to Irmgard.

"Hard Rain," Irmgard said, interrupting Jolanda. Irmgard then started singing it—the where-have-you-been bit, and the blue-eyed-son business.

Irmgard was kneeling in the open doorway to the bathroom. It's not easy to kneel in a bath towel, but Irmgard managed to do it. She must have known that dogs prefer meeting you when you're down at their level.

There was a new person in the hall, and Hard Rain couldn't wait to sniff her. The new person's clothes were in a pile on the floor in the hall. When Hard Rain sniffed the clothes, she sneezed, banging her big nose on the floor. The new person's face was close enough to lick, so Hard Rain licked her. "Oh, where have you been, my darling young one?" Irmgard was singing. When Irmgard took Hard Rain into the bathroom, even after she closed the door, Chantal and the roommates could still hear her singing.

The Gewitter was a serious one, but no one was worried now. There are five verses to "A Hard Rain's A-Gonna Fall," and the chorus is repeated five times. It's a long song to sing in a bathtub, but Irmgard kept singing it. Chantal and Claude and Jolanda and Jimmy cuddled together on his bed, listening to her sing. The roommates knew Irmgard would be singing a different song if Hard Rain were shitting her brains out in the bathtub. If you can sing to a dog, you will make a friend.

It was the spring of Jimmy's junior year abroad, 1964. The roommates didn't have many more nights in Vienna together. Later, when they passed through the Holzinger living room, they saw who was watching movies with Irmgard—on the same sofa. In the semidarkness—in the flickering light from the TV screen, in the constant staccato of dubbed German—the roommates knew it wasn't Irmgard who thumped her tail on the sofa.

That first night, following her bath, Irmgard didn't linger with them. She was almost shy when she thanked Chantal and the roommates. In the morning, when Jolanda and Jimmy woke up, Siegfried was staring at them. He'd been told there was a Geschenk for him—from Yimmys Mutter! It was a weekend morning; Siegfried was still in his pajamas. Jimmy made the boy get in bed with Jolanda. Then Jimmy went to wake up Claude and Chantal, and to bring Siegfried his gift. Jimmy knew Hard Rain would be happy to jump into bed with a little person and a tall one.

"That went well," Jolanda told Jimmy later, "but Siegfried peed in his pajamas." Hard Rain had been as excited by Siegfried as he'd been by her. (Hard Rain had also peed in Jimmy's bed, but just a little.)

When they weren't fucking, Claude and Chantal spoke French all night. Jolanda was smoking up a storm at Jimmy's balcony window.

When Jolanda wasn't smoking, she slept with Jimmy and Hard Rain in Jimmy's bedroom. When Jolanda was smoking, she focused better on when Mieke was coming to Vienna. Thinking about Mieke made it hard for Jimmy to study for his philosophy exam at the Institute for European Studies. The exam was mostly on Ludwig Josef Johann Wittgenstein. That spring, the IES students were driving themselves crazy by repeating Proposition 7 of Wittgenstein's *Tractatus*. "Wovon man nicht sprechen kann, darüber muss man schweigen," Jimmy kept saying to himself. ("What we cannot speak of, we must leave to silence.") Just hearing this made Jolanda smoke more. Just thinking about when Mieke was coming made Jimmy and Jolanda crazy.

When Chantal went home to New Hampshire, Claude went crazy for a few days. Claude and Chantal were a love story; Chantal was moving to Paris soon, and Claude was insanely happy. Claude was just missing Chantal like crazy. This made Jolanda smoke more, too. An insanely happy Claude *or* a crazy Claude gave Jolanda fits.

"Jesus Mary Joseph, Claude—Hard Rain should sleep with *you*," Jolanda told him. "Hard Rain won't let you hump your pillow."

Even with Jolanda's smoking, it seemed right that Jolanda and Jimmy slept together—just the two of them—now that Mieke was coming.

Now that Hard Rain was Siegfried's dog, the five-year-old's sudden affection for the roommates changed how Jimmy and Jolanda felt about the boy. He'd stopped mutilating his toy soldiers. Hard Rain might choke on the soldiers' body parts, Irmgard had told him. When Siegfried hugged them, Jimmy and Jolanda could imagine how their shared child might hug them. Claude was so besotted with Chantal, he was oblivious to Siegfried's hugs. When Jimmy and Jolanda looked at Siegfried, the blond, blue-eyed boy didn't look like he belonged to the dark-haired, dark-eyed Irmgard. Who would Jimmy and Mieke's child look like? Jolanda was wondering. Jolanda was no less obsessed with what she called Mieke's "fertility window," and everything to do with Mieke's ovulation. In Jolanda's estimation, Mieke had a "fairly regular" or a "fairly reliable" cycle. The *ovulation* and *cycle* words caused Claude to have muscle spasms.

"For fuck's sake, Claude, you're getting married—you should know that women have some sense of when they're ovulating," Jolanda told him. "You get symptoms like premenstrual syndrome—like cramps or bloating or breast tenderness—but you know it's way too early to get your period," Jolanda went on, while Claude kept convulsing. What Wittgenstein wrote could apply to ovulation and women's periods, Jimmy thought to himself.

It might have been funny if Jimmy actually said, *What we cannot speak of, we must leave to silence,* but Jimmy knew better than to say it. Ovulation and women's periods were scary to Claude, and Jolanda was taking seriously everything to do with Mieke's "fertility window," as she kept calling it. Mieke had counted the days since the start of her last period. Fourteen days later, when she was expecting her period in a couple of weeks, Mieke would be in Vienna. "You and Mieke will do it for three days, Jimmy. These will be days twelve, thirteen, and fourteen of Mieke's cycle." Even the math gave Claude muscle contractions.

Jimmy's German tutor was a distraction to him when he was studying for his philosophy exam; she was more of a hindrance than a help. Fräulein Eissler said she disapproved of Wittgenstein's wealthy family; they claimed to be Roman Catholics, but they were of assimilated Jewish ancestry. "I only half like Wittgenstein, Jimmy," Annelies said; she was sitting on his bed, unbuttoning her short-sleeved cardigan. "Don't get the wrong idea—I'm just showing you my tattoo," she told him. Below her collarbones and above both breasts was the first line of Proposition 1 from Wittgenstein's *Tractatus,* "Die Welt ist alles"—no comma after the *alles* word. The rest of Proposition 1 wasn't tattooed. "Just 'The world is all' or 'The world is everything'—the rest of it is Wittgenstein screwing around with rhymes, Jimmy," Annelies said, buttoning up her sweater.

Fräulein Eissler didn't like the end line to Proposition 1—in German, "was der Fall ist," which means "that is the case." James Winslow decided he only half liked Wittgenstein, too, but he never forgot his brief glimpse of Annelies's tattoo and the tops of her breasts in the cups of her bra.

Jolanda told Jimmy that she hated the haircuts he'd been getting. "Your Friseur or your Barbier is furchtbar, Jimmy," Jolanda said. (His "hairdresser" or "barber" was "terrible.") He'd been going to a barbershop somewhere on the Argentinierstraße, but Jolanda took him to see Helene and her hairdressers, above the Turnhalle Leopold. It was in the morning. The wrestling room below them was strangely silent—no thudding on the mat, no screaming from the wrestlers in the ice-cold showers. While the women fussed over him, Helene kept patting Jimmy's knee—the one she thought had been injured. "He has an important *date* coming up," Jolanda told the hairdressers. "Jimmy's a *virgin*, you know," she also told them.

"I'm glad your *thing* is all better!" Helene said, patting his knee again. There were gales of laughter from Jolanda and the hairdressers, who went on and on about Jimmy's important date—not to mention his being a virgin.

Claude was almost as excited to meet Mieke as Jimmy was. "Keep your pecker in your pants, Claude. It's Jimmy's turn to lose his virginity—you've had your turn," Jolanda told him.

With his loss of virginity pending, it might not have been the best time for Jimmy to write to Esther, but he'd heard from her—as Annelies said he would. "Dear Honor's Child," Esther's letter to Jimmy began, making herself clear from the start. "You may write to me, but I'm not your mother—she's the one who raised you and did all the work. All I did was get pregnant and give birth to you." It was a typewritten letter. She'd not signed it; she'd just typed her full name, Esther Nacht. Her return address was in Tel Aviv. As Fräulein Eissler had forewarned Jimmy, it was in care of someone else.

"Dear Esther Nacht," Jimmy began his first letter to his birth mother. "There is a foreignness inside me, not only when I'm in Vienna. There is more make-believe than reality inside me, and I'm wondering where this comes from. I'm becoming a fiction writer (more make-believe) and I'm just wondering if you ever wanted to be a writer—if the foreignness inside me is also inside you." He'd typed his letter, but he wanted to sign it in longhand. *Love, Jimmy*, he almost wrote, but he typed "James Winslow" instead.

At wrestling practice, Sol and Simon teased Jimmy about his haircut—his "hairdo," Leo called it. Helene and her hairdressers had been talking.

Even the Greco-Roman guys knew all about Jimmy's important date. Jimmy was grateful to the hairdressers, who'd not told the wrestlers he was a virgin. If they'd known, the wrestlers would have been merciless to him about that.

"Where are Zander and Sergei?" Jimmy asked Leo and the Israelis. Even the Greco guys looked uncomfortable, and what would they care if two freestyle wrestlers skipped practice? Sol and Simon just looked at Leo.

"They're Soviets, Jim—Soviets are always moving on," Sol said.

"But they're med students—how do med students move on?" Jimmy asked; he was looking at Little Mirror, who was dancing all around. "Are they now *interns*, or something—did they just become *doctors*?" Jimmy asked.

"The Russians do what they do, Jim—they just go where they go," Kleiner Spiegel said. The former Red Army wrestlers had moved on. Now Sol was Jimmy's only workout partner, and Simon didn't have one. No live wrestling for Simon, who just drilled moves with one of the Greco guys. One day, Jimmy understood, Sol and Simon would move on. The Israelis had other work to do. Like the Russians, Jimmy knew, the Israelis also did what they did—they just went where they went, too.

James Winslow remembered how Esther made him read Arthur Schnitzler's *The Road into the Open*. While Jimmy was waiting for Mieke to come to Vienna, he reread the passages he'd marked in Schnitzler's novel. Among Georg von Wergenthin's friends, the death of Georg's stillborn child with Anna Rosner arouses no pity for the child who never lived, and Else Ehrenberg feels no pity for Georg. "She had no idea of how the death of the child had shocked him," Jimmy read. "How could she have had an idea, either? What did she know of the hour when the garden had lost its color for him and the heavens their light, because his own beautiful child lay dead within the house?" This was the moment when James Winslow realized that Esther had always known he was destined to be a father. Esther knew that Honor Winslow would want her child to have of a child of his own.

Yet when Jimmy asked Fräulein Eissler what she thought of Esther's intentions—of why she'd made him read *The Road into the Open*—Jimmy's German tutor reminded him that he knew how to write Esther. "That's something you should ask Esther, Jimmy," Annelies said. "We're studying for your German exam—today we're reviewing strong and irregular verbs. That's my job, remember?" There were more than two hundred strong and irregular verbs in German, and Jimmy knew he would be asked to recite the present tense, the past tense, and the past participle of the verbs on the test. Knowing Jimmy wanted to be a writer, Fräulein Eissler began with an easy verb for him. "I write, I wrote, I have written," Annelies said softly.

"Ich schreibe, ich schrieb, ich habe geschrieben," Jimmy said loudly.

"I think, I thought, I have thought," Annelies said more softly.

"Ich denke, ich dachte, ich habe gedacht," Jimmy recited, robustly. Irmgard, passing by in the hall, didn't hear Fräulein Eissler—only Jimmy.

"I sleep, I slept, I have slept," Annelies whispered sleepily.

"Ich schlafe, ich schlief, ich habe geschlafen!" Jimmy said, shouting.

"You sound like you need to get laid, Jimmy," Irmgard said from the hall. Then Irmgard heard Fräulein Eissler laughing.

"I speak, I spoke, I have spoken!" Annelies cried out.

"Ich spreche, ich sprach, ich habe gesprochen!" Jimmy called out to Irmgard, who shouted back to them from the kitchen.

"Ich trinke, ich trank, ich habe getrunken!" Irmgard yelled.

"I drink, I drank, I have drunk," Annelies softly translated for him.

"Ich weiß, ich wusste, ich habe gewusst," Jimmy quietly told his German tutor. ("I know, I knew, I have known.") It was their last tutorial together, an anticlimactic one—just verbs.

"I'll come say goodbye before I go, Jimmy," Annelies told him.

"Where are you going?" Jimmy asked her; he'd followed her out on the Schwindgasse sidewalk.

"I've got other business, Jimmy. I'm in the Jewish business—I just go where my Jewish business takes me," Fräulein Eissler said.

"You made *me* your business. You were more than my German tutor—you looked after me!" Jimmy told her.

"Esther made you her business—*she* looks after you, Jimmy. Looking after Esther is my business," Annelies said. She'd made plans with Irmgard, Fräulein Eissler wanted him to know. Annelies assured him that she and Irmgard were going to do things differently with Siegfried.

They were standing on the corner of Argentinierstraße. "I love you!" Jimmy told her; he thought his heart was breaking.

"Oh, don't be silly, Jimmy—just have fun with Mieke and Jolanda," Fräulein Eissler said. "I'll come say goodbye before I go," she repeated. Then she walked away from him, in the direction of the Karlskirche, where the eighteen-year-old Hedwig Kiesler, who later became Hedy Lamarr, married a thirty-three-year-old Austrian armaments dealer. Where he stood crying, Jimmy could hear the song from the Nachtmusik.

Bob Dylan's "Girl from the North Country" was winding down when Jimmy found Claude and Jolanda at their usual table in the Kaffeehaus. The roommates knew Fräulein Eissler had stayed later than usual. Jolanda and Claude could see Jimmy was crying.

"No tears tonight, lover boy. Guess who's in town tomorrow?" Jolanda asked him. Claude stood up and hugged him, but Jimmy kept crying. "You should try to think of something positive, Jimmy. Mieke's boobs are bigger than mine," Jolanda told him. She knew how to uplift the spirits of a twenty-three-year-old virgin.

Later, back in the Holzinger apartment, Claude confided to Jimmy when Jolanda was in the bathroom. "You're short and Jolanda is tall," Claude began, as if this weren't obvious. "Mieke is as tall as Jolanda, but don't worry, Jimmy—when you're lying down, it doesn't matter." Now that Claude had had sex, he was speaking as an expert.

It was early in the evening of the following day when Jimmy came back to the Holzinger apartment after wrestling practice. Siegfried was playing in the hall with Hard Rain. "Mädchen im Schlafzimmer," was all Siegfried said. ("Girl in bedroom.") He meant Mieke.

That night at the Nachtmusik, as the three roommates and Mieke sat around their table, Jolanda suggested that Mieke might feel more relaxed if she got to know Jimmy better before they did it. "Since it's your first night in Vienna, maybe you and Jimmy should sleep together but just *talk* to each other—or something," Jolanda said to Mieke.

"Okey doke," Mieke said. Her English was more American than Jolanda's. Mieke's German was okey doke, too, Jimmy noticed.

"Should Mieke and I sleep in my bedroom, and you sleep with Claude and Hard Rain?" Jimmy asked Jolanda.

"You and I and Mieke will sleep in your bedroom, Jimmy," Jolanda said.

"Okey doke," Mieke said, but she was looking at Jimmy.

"Okey doke," Jimmy repeated, looking at Mieke.

"I've never been on a date as awkward as this one!" Claude cried.

"Jesus and family, Claude—it's not your date!" Jolanda told him.

It was no less awkward when Jolanda and Mieke and Jimmy were in bed together—Mieke in the middle. Jolanda had opened the curtains at the balcony window, so that Jimmy and Mieke could see each other in the streetlight. Jolanda turned away from them, facing the bedroom door. "Touch each other, talk to each other—you know, just *figure out* each other, like I'm not here," Jolanda told them.

"But you *are* here," Mieke reminded her. Jolanda had instructed Mieke and Jimmy to wear only their underpants, so Mieke's breasts were bare.

"I don't want to see Jimmy's penis, Mieke, but *you* should see it," Jolanda said.

"I don't want to see your penis, Jimmy, but can I touch it?" Mieke asked him.

"Okey doke," Jimmy said. When Mieke held his penis, he got a boner.

"Oh!" Mieke said; she'd felt him get bigger.

"Well, what did you *think* would happen to a penis if you held it?" Jolanda asked her girlfriend. Jimmy tentatively touched Mieke's breasts.

"Is *this* okay?" he asked Mieke.

"Yes, it's *fine*," Mieke told him.

"Is *what* okay? What's *fine*?" Jolanda asked them. Mieke said something in Dutch; she sounded angry. "Well, then—you should just *do it*, Mieke!" Jolanda told her. "Look out the window, Jimmy—don't watch us," Jolanda said. Jimmy turned his back to them, staring into the light from one of the streetlamps on the Schwindgasse. He could hear Jolanda and Mieke; maybe they were kissing. He heard the moment when Mieke's breathing changed. "Take off your underpants, Jimmy—now," Jolanda told him.

Of course it wasn't what Claude had imagined. Jolanda didn't hold Mieke's head and talk to her. Jolanda turned her back to them; she lay curled on the far side of the bed. Maybe her eyes were closed or she stared at the frosted panel of glass on Jimmy's bedroom door. Mieke's eyes were open when Jimmy kissed her, and she kissed him back. When she guided him inside her, she was wetter than Jimmy expected. It was more wonderful than anything Jimmy ever imagined; he never wanted it to stop, but then it was so suddenly over. He lay still on top of her; they stared into each other's eyes. "Holy shit—that was fast! Is everything all right?" Jolanda asked them.

"That was superfast but better than all right," Mieke told her, smiling at Jimmy. Later, Jolanda took her T-shirt off, but she kept her panties on. She and Mieke lay cuddled together. Mieke's back was turned to Jimmy. He lay staring at the streetlight; he drifted asleep, he woke up. When Jimmy was awake, he heard Jolanda and Mieke whispering in Dutch. "She's telling me what happens when the prostitute comes home from work—how she takes a bath and everything," Mieke explained to Jimmy, who fell back to sleep.

When Irmgard came home and undressed in the hall, and after

she'd covered herself in a bath towel, she heard the two girls whispering in Dutch. "How many girls are with you tonight, Jimmy?" she asked, opening his door.

Mieke must have wanted to get as far away from the behemoth in a bath towel as possible. She didn't want to be in the middle, between Jimmy and Jolanda. Mieke scrambled over Jimmy; now she was on the window side of the bed, with Jimmy in the middle. "She looks old enough," Irmgard said, meaning Mieke.

"Ein Dreiecksverhältnis," Jolanda told Irmgard.

"A love triangle," Mieke whispered in Jimmy's ear, translating for him.

"Das ist mir Wurst," Irmgard told Jolanda, closing the bedroom door.

"She said, 'That is *sausage* to me'—what the Christ does *that* mean?" Mieke asked Jolanda.

"It means, 'I couldn't care less'—it's a Viennese thing," Jolanda said.

"Irmgard only cares if you're old enough," Jimmy explained to Mieke. They could hear the bath running, but Irmgard wasn't singing to herself. Hard Rain was sleeping with Claude. "Please say the word for *love triangle* again—it sounds ridiculous," Jimmy said to Jolanda.

"Don't even think about a love triangle, Jimmy," Jolanda told him.

"Dreiecksverhältnis," Mieke whispered in Jimmy's ear, reawakening his penis. He was lying naked between two girls with bare breasts, and Jolanda was the only one with her underpants on.

"I heard you, Mieke—no more whispering," Jolanda said. "No playing with Jimmy's penis, you two," Jolanda told them.

"I like being in the middle," Jimmy said.

"I like being in the middle more," Mieke told him.

"Give your reproductive parts a rest, you two," Jolanda told them.

In the morning, Siegfried seemed disappointed to find Jimmy and Jolanda in bed with the new girl—not with Hard Rain. Jolanda just made Siegfried repeat Mieke's name. Soon Siegfried liked saying it. Mieke was an easy name for a German-speaking boy to say, and the five-year-old stayed with them awhile. Then Jolanda told Siegfried to go wake up Claude. Hard Rain would be happy to see Siegfried, and Jolanda had to pee—as did Mieke and Jimmy. Mieke also had a bath. "I didn't want Siegfried to see two girls with bare boobs—not to mention your penis, Jimmy," Jolanda said. Jimmy just knew he had two more nights to make Mieke pregnant.

"How'd everything go?" Claude couldn't wait to ask the three of them, after the chaos of Hard Rain's reunion with Siegfried had subsided. Jolanda once more explained to Claude that Mieke would be back in Amsterdam before she even knew if she'd missed her period. Jolanda said it would be a few weeks after that before Mieke could go for a pregnancy test. In the 1960s, the only way to test for pregnancy was to make a doctor's appointment, give a urine sample, and wait two weeks for the results. "I know, I know—I just meant how it went with the *doing it*!" Claude cried.

"It went fine—I really liked it," Jimmy said to Claude.

"It went superfast, but it was better than all right," Mieke answered.

"Jesus F. Christ, Claude," was all Jolanda could say.

"I don't like the stuff that keeps coming out of me," Mieke told them, matter-of-factly. "I even had a bath, but the stuff just keeps coming out," she said to Jimmy, who didn't know what to say. "Isn't the stuff supposed to stay *inside me*?" Mieke asked Jolanda. Claude, of course, looked appalled.

"Aren't you glad you asked, Claude?" was all Jolanda could say.

Claude had read that the woman's urine was injected into a rabbit. If the rabbit ovulated, pregnancy had occurred. Sometimes the rabbit died. Even Claude had better sense than to ask Jolanda and Mieke about this; he asked Jimmy, who knew nothing about the rabbits. "Maybe that was a long time ago, Claude. I don't believe rabbits will ovulate or die if Mieke is pregnant," Jimmy answered.

The next two nights, with Mieke in the middle, Jimmy tried to make the doing-it last longer. Mieke said lasting longer was better than superfast.

"The longer you do it has no influence on Jimmy's sperm count," Jolanda informed the lovers. After Jimmy ejaculated, Jolanda didn't want him to dillydally over withdrawing his penis. "Why are you just *lying there* on top of her, Jimmy?" Jolanda asked him. As soon as they did it, Jolanda made her girlfriend lie on her back and hug her knees to her chest. "Then maybe Jimmy's stuff will stay inside you longer," Jolanda said.

"Okey doke," was all Mieke said. The third and last night they did it, when the doing-it was over, the three of them were just lying on their backs. Mieke was still in the middle when she spoke to them. "You both should know I *never* want to do this again, but I *will* do it again if I'm not pregnant," Mieke said. "Thank you both for letting me *try it*," she added. As usual, Jimmy didn't know what to say. He'd been hoping to himself that Mieke *wasn't* pregnant—because, naturally, he wanted to keep doing it—but now he felt awful at the thought of Mieke having to do it again when she didn't want to. "I don't mean it was unbearable, Jimmy—I'd just rather not do it again if I don't have to," Mieke told him. By how quickly she moved her hand away, Jimmy knew she'd not meant to touch his penis.

"I hope you don't have to do it again, Mieke," Jimmy consoled her.

"If you're not pregnant, Mieke, I'll do it with Jimmy," Jolanda said.

"No! You might end up *liking it!*" Mieke told Jolanda. This made Mieke and Jolanda laugh. Jimmy laughed, too. Even Jimmy knew enough to know that Jolanda was in no danger of *liking it*—not to mention the funky smell. On their third morning together, Siegfried sniffed and wrinkled his nose. The five-year-old thought it was a Hard Rain kind of smell, but it was a semen smell—or so Jolanda said, after she sent Siegfried to wake up Claude and Hard Rain. "I think it's semen *and me*—it's both of us together!" Mieke declared. "It's why I can't wait to take a bath—it's the stuff running out of me!"

"*Semen and Me*—it's a good title," Jolanda told Jimmy and Mieke.

"It's a first-person novel by a woman," Mieke said. This was how

Jimmy and Mieke learned they were both trying to be fiction writers; like Jimmy, Mieke was writing her first novel. Jolanda didn't want them to know.

"Just don't fall in love, you two. It would kill me to lose both of you," Jolanda told them.

"Losing either of you would kill me—or losing Claude!" Jimmy cried. Hard Rain, racing in the hall, ran into Jimmy's bedroom. Siegfried was crying; Hard Rain had knocked him down when they were racing. Claude had heard the *losing Claude* exclamation all the way from the kitchen.

"What about *losing* me—why would you ever *lose* me?" Claude was wailing. "Hard Rain didn't *mean to* knock you down," the three lovers heard Claude say; he was trying to comfort Siegfried.

"I'm taking a bath—the semen-and-me smell is getting to me," Mieke whispered to Jimmy and Jolanda. The smell was getting to Hard Rain, too; the poor dog was sneezing her brains out.

"All of you remain calm!" Jolanda screamed, just for the hell of it. Jimmy thought it was the happiest day of his life—he just hoped this wasn't the end of it. The rest of it, the legal rigmarole, reminded Jimmy of Dickens; he thought his grandfather would get a kick out of it. While Claude and Jolanda stayed in Vienna, Jimmy and Mieke took the train from the Wien Westbahnhof to Amsterdam. They left at seven in the morning; they wouldn't get to Amsterdam before eight or nine that night. They must have changed trains three or four times; Jimmy wouldn't remember. The whole time, Mieke and Jimmy just talked about the novels they'd read—the ones that had made them want to write novels.

In the morning, the couple went to the civil registry office in the town hall—"het Stadhuis," Mieke called it—to get their marriage license. Mieke explained that the announcement of their intended marriage would be made public for six weeks, to be sure there were no formal objections to it. "I'm not a bigamist, Jimmy. Are you?" Mieke asked him. In six weeks, Jimmy would be back with Mieke in Amsterdam, in the same registry office—in the presence of four witnesses, two for each of them. It would be a simple civil ceremony. The witnesses could be family or friends; if needed, the witnesses could be civil servants of the town hall, or random people off the streets.

Claude and Chantal promised they'd come from Paris to be Jimmy's witnesses; Mieke's mother and Jolanda would be Mieke's witnesses. Mieke's mother was "in on it," Mieke had told Jimmy. Jolanda's mother and father were "not yet informed," as Mieke put it. If Jimmy had intended to live in Amsterdam, he would have needed a residence permit in order to get married. But since Jimmy intended to live in the United States, this requirement didn't apply to him. The legal minutiae of everyday life were not on Jimmy's mind on the long train ride back to Vienna. He was more concerned for Mieke, all alone in Amsterdam, where she would wait to see if she missed her period—and only if Mieke missed her period could she go for a pregnancy test a few weeks later. Jimmy knew it would be an anxious six weeks for Mieke. And meanwhile, back in Vienna, there weren't that many weekends remaining before Jimmy and his roommates parted.

At Fräulein Eissler's prompting, the three roommates made plans to do something with Siegfried and Hard Rain on one of their last weekends. First they took Siegfried to their café on the corner of Argentinierstraße, so the boy could meet Dagmar and Hard Rain's "other family." Then the roommates went with Hard Rain and Siegfried to the Stadtpark. They didn't know the rules for dogs, but they had Hard Rain on the short leash in her Seeing Eye harness, and they walked close to the perimeter of the park. Some filmmakers were shooting a scene in a movie. The roommates and Siegfried stopped to watch. Naturally, Siegfried was confused. Why would they shoot the same scene again and again? Siegfried kept asking.

A young man has a telescope on a tripod. He wants his girlfriend to look in the telescope, but she is upset by what she sees. She slaps him; she leaves him alone with the telescope. The young man is more interested in what he sees in the telescope than he is in his girlfriend. That's the scene.

It would have been better if Claude had never tried to explain the purpose of a telescope to Siegfried, but Jolanda and Jimmy didn't pay close attention to what Claude said to the five-year-old. The filmmakers were finished shooting. They had a lot of equipment, which Hard Rain had been sniffing. Maybe Siegfried was the only kid around—not that Jimmy would remember. One of the filmmakers asked if Siegfried would like to look through the telescope. To everyone's surprise, Siegfried wanted no part of the telescope. Jolanda and Jimmy wondered what Claude had said to make a magnifying optical instrument sound so terrifying. Jolanda and Jimmy looked through it. There was a park bench at a distant corner of the Stadtpark, across the Stubenring from the Wollzeile. The face of a young woman sitting on the park bench was as close as one's reflection in a bathroom mirror.

"Nicht die Zukunft!" Siegfried said. ("Not the future!" the boy begged—he was afraid of seeing the future.)

"Jesus Mary and the cuckold, Claude!" Jolanda screamed. "What did you *say* to him?"

In German, it was a small mistake for Claude, but it made a big difference to Siegfried. Claude had said the *Zukunft* word when he meant *Entfernung*. A telescope lets you see "in the distance"—a telescope "brings the distance closer," Claude meant to say, but he'd said the *future*, not the *distance*. A telescope lets you see "in the future"—a telescope "brings the future closer," Claude had told Siegfried, frightening him.

"Nicht die Zukunft!" the five-year-old had cried. ("Not the future!")

(Siegfried didn't want to see his dog die, the boy told Jimmy later.)

In the Stadtpark, Jolanda had tried to calm Siegfried down. "Die Entfernung, nicht die Zukunft," Jolanda kept telling the five-year-old, but Siegfried would not go near the telescope, where the future might loom.

Claude felt awful for his mistake; he himself would always be afraid of the future. The night after that misadventure in the Stadtpark, Jimmy persuaded Irmgard and Frau Holzinger to let Siegfried sleep in his bed with Hard Rain. Jimmy slept in Jolanda's bed with Jolanda, and Claude left their bedroom door open. Siegfried slept peacefully through the night; he had no telescope nightmares. "Everyone wants to sleep with this dog," was the way Irmgard put it. It meant a lot to Jimmy that Irmgard had thanked Fräulein Eissler for her part in the gift of Hard Rain.

Those last few weeks, Jimmy and his roommates slept with their bedroom doors open; this allowed Hard Rain to come and go. When Irmgard came home from work and had her bath, she always sang to the dog in the bathroom. The widow Holzinger remained convinced that Hard Rain was the ghost of the German shepherd she'd once known; yet the Frau was no less kind to the dog because of it. It was Jimmy's final impression that the distinction between Jimmy's mother and Jimmy's mother's *friend* remained murky to Frau Holzinger, who persisted in speaking of Chantal with a reverence reserved for mothers.

The academic year finished differently at the University of Vienna than it did at the Institute for European Studies. Claude and Jolanda had been done a week before Jimmy. They'd gone home, to Paris and Amsterdam, leaving Jimmy alone in the Schwindgasse apartment. Jimmy was glad that Jolanda and Mieke would be together, waiting for the results of Mieke's pregnancy test. (It was good news for all concerned that Mieke had missed her period.)

Jimmy went one afternoon to the Turnhalle Leopold, but Sol and Simon didn't show up at wrestling practice. Jimmy just drilled moves with Leo, who told him the Israelis were packing for a long trip.

"A trip *where*?" Jimmy asked Little Mirror, who seemed sad.

"They're Israelis, Jim—they go where they have Israeli business," Kleiner Spiegel said, giving Jimmy a hug and a lift, but not throwing him.

"Where are they going, Leo?" Jimmy asked again. The little throw-meister shrugged—as if it didn't matter where anyone went these days.

"I heard it was Argentina, Jim—maybe they're going to Argentina," was all Leo said about it, giving Jimmy another hug and lift.

Jimmy was sleeping in his bed with Hard Rain, with his bedroom door open, when Irmgard came home from work. She sang "Girl from the North Country" to Hard Rain in the bathroom; there was no question Irmgard knew the music the dog liked best. After her bath, Irmgard came into Jimmy's bedroom to talk to him. Hard Rain got in bed with Jimmy, but Irmgard sat almost primly at the foot of his bed.

"I owe you," she began; Irmgard was strictly businesslike about it. She had paid Berta to have sex with Jimmy. Everything was arranged; all Jimmy had to do was find Berta, and Berta would take care of the rest. "Don't worry—I got you a student discount," Irmgard told him. She had an accurate but cruel way of imitating what the scar from the mayonnaise jar had done to Berta's lip. "Annelies isn't the only one who can arrange things," Irmgard said, smiling. She was being nice to him, Jimmy knew—as nice as Irmgard knew how.

It was Jimmy's last week in Vienna. He had a paper to write on the Victorian novel. It was hard for him to think about the Brontë sisters and Dickens and Hardy and Eliot and Kipling when he was thinking about the future. Claude had scared the shit out of Siegfried with a telescope that sees in the future—worse, Jimmy's tutorials with Fräu-lein Eissler had come to an end. Where would Annelies go? Jimmy wondered. It was that time of night when the Frau and Siegfried were asleep, in their quarters. Irmgard had gone out, or she was dressing to go out. Hard Rain and Jimmy were on their own for a while. Jimmy was trying to decide if he should study in his bedroom or go to the café on the corner. When the first pebbles pinged against his bedroom window, Hard Rain got the jitters. Jimmy went to the balcony window and saw Annelies on the sidewalk. The window was open, and he could hear her clearly. "I'm not your tutor tonight, Jimmy—I've just come to say goodbye," Fräulein Eissler said. But wouldn't she *always* be his tutor? Jimmy imagined.

No, she wasn't coming inside tonight, and she didn't want Jimmy to join her on the sidewalk, Annelies told him. She had to pack for a long trip. She was going to Argentina. "Simon and Sol don't speak Spanish, Jimmy, and I'm good at languages," she added. (As Sergei once said, the Eissler was working for Wiesenthal, or for the Mossad.)

"I hope you get to be what you want to be, Jimmy—a writer, if that's what you choose," Annelies said. "You don't get to choose everything, but being a writer is your choice," she told him.

"What *don't* I get to choose?" Jimmy asked her. (He should have known where she was going with the choice business.)

"You don't get to choose to be Jewish, Jimmy—you just *are* Jewish," Fräulein Eissler told him. "No matter what your two moms say, your father and your birth mother are Jewish. You're a *Jew*, Jimmy," Annelies said. "In your case, you don't have to do anything differently—you can be any kind of Jew you want to be, but you *are* Jewish." She thereupon turned and walked away from him in the direction of the Argentinier-straße. Fräulein Eissler knew how to move on.

"I'm still learning from you! I didn't get to choose to *lose* you!" Jimmy called out the window, but Fräulein Eissler was walking to Argentina.

It was only a fifteen-minute walk from the Schwindgasse to those side streets off the Kärntner Straße. Jimmy wouldn't remember if he found Berta on Johannesgasse or Annagasse, but she took him to the whore hotel on Krugerstraße. True to what Annelies told him, Berta explained that prostitutes didn't kiss their customers. In Jimmy's case, however, Irmgard had arranged for Berta to kiss him. Irmgard must have known that the slight disfigurement of Berta's upper lip got to him. That was Jimmy's last night in Vienna—his bittersweet goodbye to the city on the Danube.

Jimmy was in his bedroom—packing for Amsterdam, with Hard Rain sniffing through his things—when Irmgard came home to take her nightly bath. If Irmgard knew he'd seen Berta, she didn't mention it. She stretched out on Jimmy's bed, still in her working clothes, but she wasn't coming on to him. Irmgard wanted Hard Rain to jump on the bed with her, which Hard Rain did. The dog was a miracle, not only for Siegfried. Jimmy told Irmgard that he was still upset about what happened to Siegfried in the Stadtpark—the five-year-old's fear of a telescope that brings the future closer, as Claude had told the boy. "I hope Siegfried is over the fright," Jimmy said.

"I don't think *you're* over it," Irmgard said.

Jimmy told Irmgard that he was happy to hear she'd made plans with Annelies—for the two of them to do things differently with Siegfried. Jimmy went so far as to say that Annelies was a good person for Siegfried to know.

"If Siegfried is lucky, Annelies will adopt him," Irmgard said. She was taking off her clothes in the hall, as if Jimmy weren't there—as if he weren't watching, or he didn't care. In Vienna, Jimmy couldn't tell the difference between what was truly undisguised and what was merely cynical.

Hard Rain's tail was wagging as she followed Irmgard into the bathroom, where Irmgard paused and faced Jimmy in the open doorway; because Irmgard was naked, Jimmy looked down, then he turned away.

"There *is* a telescope that sees into the future, Jimmy—it's called the passage of time. Just wait and see," she said, closing the door.

Jimmy said his goodbyes to the Frau and Siegfried and Hard Rain in the morning. Jimmy knew Irmgard would be sleeping in. When people asked the five-year-old about his German shepherd, Siegfried told them, "Hard Rain ist ein Weibchen"—meaning "Hard Rain is a female." The boy had asked Jolanda how to say this in English.

Jolanda liked to fool around. "Hard Rain is a woman," Jolanda had taught Siegfried to say. Siegfried understood that this sounded funny in English. The boy liked to say it; he always got a laugh out of it.

This was how Jimmy and Siegfried said their goodbyes—telling each other, "Hard Rain is a woman." All Frau Holzinger kept telling Jimmy was to pay her respects to his sainted mother.

Jimmy had so many bags to take to the train station, he needed a taxi. From the Schwindgasse sidewalk, waiting for his ride, Jimmy could see Siegfried and Hard Rain in the window of his former bedroom. Hard Rain had perked up her ears when Jimmy called her name. Siegfried silently mouthed the words. Jimmy could read the boy's lips. The five-year-old just repeated, "Hard Rain is a woman," until Jimmy's taxi came.

23.

The Last Faculty Meeting

A t twenty-three, James Winslow was a daydreaming boy. All fiction writers are daydreamers. What Jimmy knew of the passage of time came from those nineteenth-century novels he loved. As Irmgard had told him, the passage of time was the only way to see in the future. As he learned from the novel he was writing, a novelist's job was imagining the future. Jimmy knew he would be writing a death scene for the character based on his grandfather.

James Winslow didn't remember or care how many times he changed trains from Vienna's Westbahnhof to Amsterdam Centraal. Fourteen hours on a train amounted to uninterrupted writing and reading to a young writer. For the first time, he was reading Tolstoy's *Anna Karenina*—the novel that had made Mieke want to be a novelist, she'd told him. Long ago, his grandfather had recommended the book to him. Novels in translation were neglected by English teachers, Thomas Winslow once told him. Jimmy had written to his grandfather, but Thomas wasn't writing back—not the way he used to. "All families with children who have children are complicated in their own way," Jimmy had begun his letter to Thomas. "Guess what I'm reading, Grandpa?" he asked him, but there'd been no reply.

Didn't Jimmy's grandfather get the joke? There'd been jokes in the Winslow family about the opening sentence of *Anna Karenina* long before Jimmy started reading the novel. How those Winslow sisters made fun of that opening sentence! "All happy families are alike; each unhappy family is unhappy in its own way," Tolstoy begins the novel, but how those Winslow daughters had disagreed.

"*We're* a happy family, but we're not like *any* other family!" Faith said.

"We Winslow girls aren't even like one another!" Hope maintained.

"Yeah—each of us is happy in her own way!" Honor cried.

"What makes *you* happy, Honor, wouldn't work for *anybody*!" was how Prudence put it, making everyone laugh—Thomas and Constance included. Jimmy remembered that well. He recently wrote to his mom about it. He'd told her how Grandpa Tommy wasn't writing letters like he used to, but Honor Winslow hadn't written back. Naturally, mailing letters internationally was slow; even airmail took forever. Jimmy gave Irmgard his forwarding address and gave her money for postage. He made sure Irmgard knew the names of his grandfather, his mother, and now Esther. On the train to Amsterdam, he put an unopened letter from Esther in a safe place—her eagerly anticipated letter was Jimmy's bookmark in *Anna Karenina*.

"Dear James Winslow," Esther's answer to Jimmy's first letter began. "Blame me for the make-believe inside you. I never wanted to be a writer, but I didn't get to grow up Jewish. I was too busy making up my life to be a writer. Your grandfather was the only father I knew. My mother didn't live long enough to be a mother. I didn't want to be someone my mother didn't get to be. I'm just trying to be the best Jew I can be. You bet your ass there's a foreignness inside me! I'm told you managed to learn a little German," she went on. "Ich wünsche Dir alles Gute," she ended her letter. ("I wish you all the best.") This time, she signed her first name—just Esther. Her return address was a new one, now in Jerusalem—as before, in care of someone else. For now, Jimmy thought, Esther's letter was a suitable bookmark for *Anna Karenina*, which was almost certainly a novel of betrayal, faith, family, marriage, and desire—or so Jimmy imagined. He'd read only the first part, when

Vronsky gets his first look at Anna, and Anna sees the railway worker killed when he accidentally falls in front of a train. The accident did not bode well for Anna's future, James Winslow was thinking; Anna should be wary of trains, he thought. Jimmy wished Irmgard would be wary of dogs with balls when she and Siegfried were walking with Hard Rain, but Irmgard had been dismissive of the dogs-with-balls business.

"No one likes dogs with balls, Jimmy, but castrated males hate dogs with balls more than Hard Rain does," Irmgard had said. "Hard Rain knows what to do when horny males try to hump her. No one likes being humped by a beagle with balls—I know the feeling." He couldn't wait to tell Claude and Jolanda how Irmgard felt about males in general.

"Dear Esther," Jimmy wrote on the train. "I confirm that there's mostly make-believe and foreignness inside me, too. I know you correspond with Grandpa Tommy. I'm worried about him. I correspond with him, too, but he doesn't write me back the way he used to. I wonder, have you noticed a decline in the way he writes to you?" This time, when he signed his name, he wrote, "Love, Jimmy."

In one of the notebooks where he wrote his novel, James Winslow did the math on Grandpa Tommy and Grandma Connie. They were the same age, born in 1880—an easy number for Jimmy to remember because he'd been born in 1941, when his grandparents were sixty-one. And there wasn't anyone in the Winslow family who hadn't heard the story that Prudence was ten when Constance Winslow was "starting to show." At the time, Hope was twelve and Faith fourteen.

In 1919, when Honor Winslow was born, Thomas and Constance were thirty-nine—in those days, Jimmy knew, this was old to be having a child. In the fall of 1963, when Jimmy went to Vienna, his grandparents were eighty-three. Those two were long-distance walkers; they were still slim and fit and walked everywhere. They were as alert as they'd always been; they showed no signs of needing The Meadow, the town's much-maligned retirement home—also dubbed The Last Faculty Meeting by the academy's retired teachers and staff who were residents there. This name somewhat consoled those who were still teaching at Pennacook Academy—their wives, less so. In 1964, when James Winslow would come home from his year abroad, Jimmy's grandparents would be eighty-four.

"Dear Aunt Faith," Jimmy wrote to the eldest of his aunts. He knew those Winslow girls weren't reticent to speak, and Faith usually spoke first; she didn't mince words. He explained why he was worried about Grandpa Tommy. He'd written to his mom, and to Esther, he told Faith. "When I left for Vienna, I saw no hint of The Meadow on the horizon," he wrote to her. Jimmy had two letters to mail in Amsterdam, and no idea how long he might be there. He made no mention of his efforts to knock up Mieke in his letters to Esther or Faith. He didn't want to jinx Mieke's being pregnant. Jimmy just hoped, for Mieke's sake, there would be no more knocking up to do.

When he arrived in Amsterdam Centraal, Amsterdam's central station, he saw Jolanda from afar. She was waving her arms, and she was taller than anyone around her. "Hey, Sperm Man, way to go—you knocked up my girlfriend!" Jolanda yelled. The way people looked at him, Jimmy knew that many Netherlanders understood English. In the taxi to his hotel on the Oudezijds Voorburgwal—one of the high-walled canals that ran through the red-light district—Jolanda explained that the walls were ramparts to control flooding. The red-light district was called de Wallen, for the ramparts. There were no ramparts to control her parents, she explained. "My dad is a pussy-whipped lawyer, my mom is the pussy-whipper," Jolanda told him.

After he checked in and left his bags at the hotel, Jolanda took him for a walk in de Wallen. The prostitutes who were not with customers were visible in their windows or doorways. They didn't like it when women looked at them, Jolanda had observed, but she knew how to look at the prostitutes discreetly. Jolanda whispered her favorites to Jimmy, but a few of them were with customers. Jimmy didn't dare say who two of his favorites were, but he often liked the ones Jolanda liked. "It's okay to *look*, Jimmy, but don't go back and *visit with* one of them. You're here to get *married*, remember!" Jolanda told him. "Mieke is already acting like a bride who's expecting—she won't even have sex with me until after the ceremony, when you get your marriage certificate. Two unvisited vaginas till then. Now *there's* a title, Jimmy! *Two Unvisited Vaginas!*" Jolanda cried. The way the prostitutes in their doorways looked at her, Jimmy guessed they understood English. Jolanda regretted how she drew the women's attention; she'd meant no disrespect to them. Jimmy tried to imagine *Two Unvisited Vaginas* as a marriage novel. He realized only later what Jolanda was worried about, when she'd walked back to his hotel with him. Her parents were meeting Jimmy for breakfast, when Jolanda would be back in Amsterdam Centraal; she was meeting Claude and Chantal's train from Paris.

Knowing Jolanda, it was hard for Jimmy to imagine Mr. and Mrs. Lammers as the epitome of uptightness Jolanda described, but Jeroen and Els Lammers were still processing that their daughter was in a long-lasting lesbian relationship. Then, suddenly, Jolanda and Mieke were having a baby—a child they would somehow share with a man who wasn't interested in an actual marriage. Yes, Jimmy and Mieke's civil ceremony would constitute a legitimate marriage—in the sense that the child would be born of parents lawfully married to each other—but Mr. Lammers foresaw, in his lawyerly way, a sea of possible legal wrangles ahead. And Mrs. Lammers, in her pussy-whipping way, could not countenance a married couple who didn't intend to live together. "At breakfast, Jimmy, you have my permission to throw up—just don't go out and console yourself with one of those poor women in a window or a doorway," Jolanda told him. Jimmy didn't tell her how he'd consorted with Berta in Vienna—consoling himself, no doubt, for how much he missed sleeping with Mieke and Jolanda.

Both Jeroen and Els Lammers were as tall as Jolanda. Before they were seated at breakfast, Jimmy felt apprehensive about how short he was. "If the child is only your height, a girl would likely be happier than a boy," Jeroen Lammers told Jimmy.

"Girls are also happier when they're taller, Jeroen," the pussy-whipper told her husband, not looking at Jimmy, who had no doubt he would have been happier as a girl—as either a tall girl or a short one. Given the critical opprobrium emanating from the Lammers, Jimmy's newfound confidence surprised him. It was a storyteller's confidence; it came from writing. Jimmy told them his two-moms story. It was a long story, and he told all of it; he barely ate any breakfast. His two moms were the heroes of Jimmy's story.

"Yet I wish I *knew* my birth mother. I wish I could spend time with her," he told the Lammers. "My child should spend time with Mieke and Jolanda—he or she should really get to know them," Jimmy said.

"Your mother—the one who wanted you, the one who raised you—works as an obstetric nurse," Mrs. Lammers kept reiterating. "I suppose she'll want to be on hand when the child is born." Jimmy assured her that his mom would want to be there for the birth; his having a child had been his mother's idea, Jimmy reminded Mrs. Lammers. "I already like your mother—both of them," the pussy-whipper told him. No one threw up at breakfast, not even Mr. Lammers. Jolanda twice sneaked a peek at them in the café, but she wouldn't interrupt them—not while Jimmy was talking. Jolanda had already taken Claude and Chantal on a tour of de Wallen.

Fortunately for Jimmy, Jeroen Lammers reserved his lawyerly scrutiny for the foreseeable shortcomings of Dutch law. The child would be a dual citizen of the Netherlands and the U.S.; Dutch citizenship didn't expire, regardless of how long the child lived abroad. "You just need to renew the child's passport," Mr. Lammers said. He was more critical of the divorce plan. It was Jolanda's idea that Jimmy and Mieke would get divorced when the child was three or four. Divorce was permitted only in the case of a jail sentence of four years or more, or in the case of abuse, neglect, or adultery. "It's simplest for the husband to admit to adultery," Jeroen Lammers told Jimmy. "Hopefully, this compulsory lie will one day no longer be required," the lawyer said. (It seemed likely to Jimmy that he wouldn't have to lie about the adultery—not if he and Mieke were married for three or four years.)

As for Jolanda's relationship with Mieke, lesbian couples could make "cohabitation contracts," but these arrangements were not "legally recognized," Mr. Lammers told Jimmy. There was no mention of civil unions or same-sex marriage in their conversation. If Jimmy remarried, and a child or children came of this subsequent marriage, it could affect the future custody of Jimmy and Mieke's child—or so Jeroen Lammers speculated, in his lawyerly way.

"Friendships last longer than many marriages. Friends stay friends—it's the lovers who split up," Jimmy said to Jolanda's father, who remained skeptical of his daughter's unusual relationships.

By the time Jimmy was reunited with Claude and Chantal, Claude had recovered from the red-light district, where Jolanda said he'd burst into tears. Claude thought the prostitutes on display needed to be rescued from their sexual enslavement. Jolanda didn't dispute that some of the women in the windows and doorways probably were in need of being rescued, and Claude's emotional response to them only made Chantal love him more. Jolanda said she needed a break from the lovey-dovey cooing in French that was nonstop between Claude and Chantal—and from their wedding plans, which were open to dispute. Claude favored a New Hampshire wedding, to avoid his mother's extravagant aspirations; Chantal dreaded exposing Claude and his mother to the overbreeding Beaudettes, who didn't speak French, who just changed diapers. Chantal hoped that not many Beaudettes would venture to Paris for her wedding; Claude hoped to escape his mother's manipulations in New Hampshire. Jimmy just wanted Jolanda's help to mail his letters to Israel and New Hampshire.

"You'll be back in New Hampshire before this letter," Jolanda said.

That night, Mieke's mother took them all to dinner at a restaurant—

maybe on the Rokin, near Dam Square. Or maybe it was a restaurant on Dam Square, near the Rokin—Jimmy wouldn't remember. Both Mieke and Jolanda had forewarned him about Mieke's mother, Bente. "She flirts with young men—she'll definitely flirt with you, Jimmy," Mieke told him.

"If Bente gets out of hand, just say the *penis* word, Jimmy—it's the same word in Dutch, German, and English," Jolanda reminded him. She'd already told him the story of Mieke's father; he'd abandoned Bente before Mieke was born. Mieke had grown up without a father— it had been just her and Bente.

The flirting was fine with Jimmy. Bente just stared soulfully at him—her hand on his thigh, under the table. "Thank you, Jimmy," she whispered, as if his knocking up Mieke had been an ordeal.

"*Moeder*! Both hands on the table," Mieke said. (The *mother* word in Dutch sounded like "mooder.")

Jimmy liked Bente. She said the baby should be born in Amsterdam, where Mieke would have all the doctors and nurses she needed. "*I'm* the one who'll need a nurse, Jimmy. I hope your mother will come and be *my* nurse," Bente told him. Jimmy thought his mom might like coming to Amsterdam. Honor Winslow knew how to be a nurse to babies, and to mothers.

Early the next morning, Chantal went to the Anne Frank House alone. When she returned to the hotel, she went to bed for the rest of the day. That was why Claude asked Jimmy to go with him when he went; he knew better than to go alone to the old canal house on the Prinsengracht. Jimmy cried there as much as Claude did. They cried for Anne as a kid, and for Anne as a Jew, but Jimmy cried for her as a *writer,* too.

After seeing the enslaved women in their windows and doorways in the red-light district, and given his experience in the Anne Frank House, Claude was emotionally on edge at Jimmy and Mieke's civil ceremony. Following their vows, Claude saw that the married couple were given something, but he didn't see exactly what it was. He asked Jolanda, but she was crying. "It's a *trouwboekje*!" she blurted out, still sobbing.

"Not a *trouwboekje*! Poor Jimmy and Mieke!" Claude cried.

"It's just a *booklet*, Claude. Their marriage certificate is in the booklet," Jolanda told him. It was that kind of wedding. Both Jimmy and Jolanda kissed the bride, and Bente kissed Jimmy a little too hard. Jimmy thought he bit his tongue, but Mieke was sure her mother had bitten him. "Don't forget the *penis* word if you need it, Jimmy," Jolanda reminded him.

Under the circumstances, it was not the kind of wedding night a groom might choose to remember, but James Winslow was as happy as he'd ever been. He would never forget that night, or how many times he imagined he would be coming back to Amsterdam in the future. The child was the one who mattered the most, and the three of them were in sync about the baby. The name for a boy would be Jimmy's choice; a girl's name was up to Mieke and Jolanda. Jimmy chose *Leo*. (He'd not told Little Mirror; he knew Kleiner Spiegel would be disappointed if Jimmy had a girl.) Mieke and Jolanda said a girl should be named Vienna. "Because *Vienna* is a pretty name for a girl, and because it's where we *did it*!" Jolanda shouted.

Jolanda's father begged to differ, in his lawyerly way. "Technically, Jolanda, only Jimmy and Mieke *did it*," Mr. Lammers said, but Mieke and Jimmy just shook their heads; they knew Jolanda was part of the doing it.

"All three of us *did it*, Daddy—this child took all three of us," Jolanda told her father, with Mieke and Jimmy now nodding their heads. There was no doubt about it—this child would have one dad and two moms, Jimmy was thinking. Claude and Chantal had stopped arguing about where to get married; they went on murmuring in French, and kissing. "It won't matter where you *do it*, Claude—I'm going to raise a ruckus," Jolanda had told him.

Perhaps because he was expecting a child, something had changed in James Winslow. On the plane back to America, he made a major revision in the novel based on his beloved grandfather. The saintly English teacher is not a confirmed bachelor; he isn't an asexual like Honor Winslow, Jimmy's mom. Teacher Tom, the eponymous Dickens Man, is a family man. He wants his students who are lonely and depressed to be as happy as his own children. The homophobic faculty wives and students don't think this English teacher is a nonpracticing homosexual. James Winslow understood where this revision came from; he knew he was already thinking protectively, like a father. And with this thought, Jimmy felt more empathy for his mom; her overprotectiveness of him was more understandable. The Dickens Man still seeks out and saves those lost boys; Teacher Tom finds the Dickens novel that will lift their spirits. Jimmy realized he was making the main character of *The Dickens Man* more normal—to make him safer—and this thought led Jimmy to a darker place. He remembered a story Grandpa Tommy told him—a story Dr. Larch had confided to the Winslows. When Larch told the rabbi in Portland that Esther didn't believe in God, the rabbi declined to judge Esther's beliefs. The rabbi said Esther deserved to know how much her mother was afraid for her. "Fear is love," the rabbi had said.

As James Winslow now understood, even parents who aren't normal want their children to be. *Aren't normal children safer?* he thought. This led Jimmy to fear for his own child. Given the landmark loss of Jimmy's virginity, and how out of it he was at the time, Jimmy doubted his own child would be normal—not to mention Mieke's contribution, and Jolanda's. And with this thought, Jimmy also realized that the more you fear for a child, the more you must love it. Jimmy never doubted that Mieke and Jolanda would feel the same way. If their child was a gay boy, they would be more afraid for him, they would love him more. It would be the same with a lesbian girl; the more fear they felt for her, the more they would love her.

All this on the plane back to America, where being a father would save James Winslow from a misbegotten war. By the time he landed in New York, and before he boarded his connecting flight to Boston, Jimmy knew there must be something wrong with his grandfather. There was a fear-is-love thing going on; those Winslow daughters were protecting him from what had happened to Grandpa Tommy, or so Jimmy thought. He just knew someone would meet his plane in Boston. Faith and Hope liked to drive, and Hope had a station wagon. His mom and Prudence might be at work. Nurses and doctors were always working, Jimmy thought.

At the baggage carousel in Boston, Faith saw him before he saw her. As usual, she spoke first. "Hope has the station wagon—we knew you'd have a lot of stuff," she told him. "Plenty of room for you and Prudence in the backseat, Jimmy," Faith said. He hadn't expected three of them.

"Prudence isn't working?" Jimmy asked his aunt.

"You need to hear it from the doctor, Jimmy. Hope and I can interpret for you, when Prudence goes overboard with the medical jargon," Faith said.

At some point, Thomas Winslow began to have "spells"; he tried to keep these episodes to himself, not wanting to worry Constance. Initially, the spells abated in an hour or two. He suddenly developed an acute shortness of breath, weakness, and lightheadedness; he felt a rapid, irregular pounding of his heart. There were moments, Prudence told Jimmy, when Grandpa Tommy looked alarmed; once or twice, someone in the family noticed that he seemed unsteady when he made his way to a seat. But he seemed fine when he was sitting down. These episodes ended as abruptly as they'd started, leaving Thomas completely recovered.

"Are you all right, Tommy?" the Winslow daughters had all heard Connie ask when he made a hasty exit—often into the bathroom.

"No more locking the bathroom door, you two," Prudence told them.

"At their age, people die in bathrooms while the rest of the family is trying to break down the door, Jimmy," Faith informed him. Jimmy knew Grandpa Tommy always thought of Dickens. In 1870, Charles Dickens had died of a paralytic stroke; at death, his eyes were closed but a tear was observed on his right cheek. Dickens was fifty-eight.

Hope interjected something while she was driving. Connie had known enough to be worried about Tommy, because he kept saying how unjust it was that he should live so long—while someone as important and productive as Dickens had died when he was so young. "Daddy must have known he had heart palpitations, like Dickens," Hope told Jimmy.

"Daddy had developed paroxysmal atrial fibrillation, Jimmy—the attacks became more frequent and lasted longer," Prudence continued. In the rearview mirror, Jimmy saw Faith close her eyes and grimace at the medical babble, but Prudence was determined for Jimmy to see the situation they'd kept from him. In atrial fibrillation, the small chambers of the heart no longer pump blood into the large chambers; the small chambers just "fibrillate" (they "quiver," as Prudence put it). The blood still gets into the larger chambers, but the "electrical signals" are disrupted. Because the heart is pumping so quickly, there's no time for any significant amount of blood to fill the chambers, and almost no blood is being pumped out. This was what caused Thomas Winslow's lightheadedness, his fatigue, and the shortness of breath—his rapid, uncoordinated heartbeat.

"Cut to the killer, Prudence," Faith interrupted. "Jimmy has jet lag, and he's been trying to knock up a Dutch girl. He doesn't need to know how the heart is *supposed to* work," Faith told her younger sister.

Prudence doggedly persisted. If the small chambers are no longer "pumping purposefully," she said, the blood in the chambers stagnates. The stagnant blood forms clots. "When an episode ends, and the small chambers start to pump again, the clots fly out—sending a massive number of emboli to the brain, causing a stroke. Brain tissue dies, Jimmy—that's what it means to have a stroke," Prudence said. There was no interrupting her—medical details were a doctor's business.

Thomas Winslow had been in the bathroom—he was probably feeling poorly, in the middle of an episode. Then the episode passed; he felt better, only to be hit with what Prudence called "a shower of emboli." His left middle cerebral artery was occluded, killing off Broca's area—the "speech region of the brain," as Prudence put it. Thomas collapsed. Constance must have heard him fall; she rushed into the bathroom.

"Mommy tripped over him. The left side of Daddy's face was already paralyzed—the left side of his mouth was askew and drooling," Prudence continued. "Daddy can't speak, Jimmy, and he has paralysis on the right side of his body. But he can hear—he understands everything. When Mommy fell, she hit her head on the bathtub—she was unconscious—but she also fractured her hip," Prudence said.

Faith and Hope had stopped interrupting. Thomas's atrial fibrillation might have been manageable, but the stroke damage was permanent. He was conscious but unable to speak; he couldn't use the right side of his body. He was fed through a tube because he couldn't swallow. Thomas Winslow was bedridden and incontinent—unimaginably, he was unable to communicate, except with his left hand. Connie was in worse shape. Her hip would normally need surgery, but given her age and the head injury, the surgery was risky; the Winslow daughters decided to let her slip away. She'd also sustained what Prudence called a "brain bleed," which wouldn't kill her immediately but kept her comatose. Constance was being fed through a tube, too. "Mommy could last up to a month," Prudence told Jimmy. Thomas was torturously aware of his own and his dear wife's situation—they were now in the intensive-care part of The Meadow.

"They were hospitalized for two weeks, Jimmy—before they were transferred to The Meadow," Faith said. She now felt free to interrupt. There were no more medical details, Jimmy guessed.

"Daddy could die at any time, in the next few years or imminently, but Mommy will almost certainly predecease him, Jimmy," Hope said.

"I just got your letter, Jimmy—not that there was time to answer it," Faith told him. "We've been taking turns, answering your letters to Daddy—not that we managed to fool you."

"It was mostly your mom who answered your letters to Daddy, Jimmy," Hope had told him.

"It was *all* of us, correcting one another—that's why we fucked it up! There was no way *all* of us could sound like Daddy!" Prudence exclaimed.

"Remain calm—we'll take Jimmy to The Meadow tomorrow. Now I just want to know how it's going with knocking up the Dutch girl," Faith said.

"It's the first thing your mom will ask you, Jimmy. Is the Dutch girl knocked up, or isn't she?" Hope asked him.

"If she isn't, you should still be doing it, Jimmy," Prudence said.

"Mieke is pregnant. She and her girlfriend—my roommate Jolanda—are behaving like they're *both* expecting," Jimmy told them.

"Those girls sound *wonderful*!" Hope cried.

"Sure as shit, those girls sound like *us*!" Prudence put in.

"That's what Hope means, Prudence. Those girls will fit in fine, Jimmy," Faith told him. It seemed fitting he was a backseat passenger—he was just along for the ride, Jimmy was thinking.

James Winslow would be a single parent, but his child would have no lack of mothers. "I'm actually looking forward to being a father," he said from the backseat. Given all the help he would have, Jimmy knew he had no excuse not to be a good father.

"Your mom knows you've been writing to Esther, Jimmy," Hope said.

"Esther and Honor are always writing each other," Prudence told him.

"There's a recent letter to you from Esther—as recent as your letter to me from Amsterdam," Faith said.

There was no keeping anything from those Winslow girls, or from Esther, Jimmy was thinking. He knew there would be no keeping anything from Mieke or Jolanda. This was a good idea for someone who wanted to be a writer and a father. There were hugs and kisses from his mom when Jimmy came home to the Winslow household. Honor was so happy to hear Mieke was pregnant, she was slow to give him Esther's letter.

"It's a thin one," was all Honor said, when she handed it over.

"Notwithstanding what Annelies told you, it's too late for you to be Jewish—you didn't grow up afraid, Jimmy," Esther had written him.

"Aren't *all* of Esther's letters thin ones?" Faith asked Honor.

"In my experience, if I ask Esther questions, her answers are short," Honor said, looking at Jimmy.

"On the subject of *Jewishness,* or what's going on in Israel, Esther keeps it *very* short!" Hope cried.

"Esther is protecting us from her Jewish business—that's who she is," Honor said.

"Esther isn't just *your* nanny, Honor—she's a nanny to *all* of us!" Prudence put in.

"In this case, I didn't ask Esther a question—it was something my German tutor said," Jimmy told them, handing Esther's letter to his mom. Naturally, all those Winslow girls read Esther's letter; it didn't take long.

"Annelies was Jimmy's *Jewish* German tutor," Honor explained.

"Annelies is the one named for Anne Frank," Prudence put in.

"Did you like her, Jimmy?" Hope asked him.

"I had a crush on her, but Annelies discouraged that," he said.

"Very professional—good for Annelies!" Prudence shouted. Honor changed the subject to what mattered most at the moment: moving ahead.

"Do you have photos of Mieke to show us, Jimmy?" his mom asked. As he remembered, Jolanda was the one who'd taken most of

345

the photos—yet she also had managed to be prominent in many of the photographs. It seemed disloyal to Jolanda to say Mieke was the pretty one, so Jimmy didn't say it; he just showed the photos to his mother and his aunts.

"Is Mieke the pretty one?" Faith was the first to ask him.

"Yes, that's Mieke," Jimmy said, pointing to her in one of the photos.

"The tall one was your roommate, right?" Hope had asked him.

"Yes, that's Jolanda," Jimmy said, pointing to the tall Jolanda.

"Jolanda is pretty is her own way," Prudence said.

"Yes, she is," was all Jimmy could say.

"Mieke is going to have a good-looking kid," his mom said. The way those Winslow girls hovered over Mieke's photos, assuring themselves of the good looks of Jimmy's child, served as an ill omen to the writer James Winslow would become; he hoped this hovering over the imagined beauty of Mieke's baby didn't constitute the writing on the wall. Good looks did not ensure a child's well-being. Jimmy's sudden fear for his child's safety served as a harbinger of the father he would become—his fear was not only a portent of his literary imagination.

"You're going to like Mieke and Jolanda—they're a lot of fun," Jimmy said. This did not appear to go over well with his mom and his aunts. Maybe the urgency in their desire for him to knock up someone did not take into consideration that the knocking up itself could be fun. Once more, Honor changed the subject.

"You better prepare yourself to see your grandparents, Jimmy," his mom said. "Mommy is completely unresponsive, but Daddy is sadder. He knows what's happening, he understands it all, but he can't *speak*—and you know how that man could *talk*."

Yes, Grandpa Tommy certainly could talk—especially about Dickens, Jimmy was remembering. "And Dickens overpunctuates!" Thomas Winslow had exclaimed. Jimmy even remembered his granddaddy saying that Dickens's punctuation was "a form of stage direction." The man could talk.

"*Fuck* Dickens's punctuation, Daddy!" Honor had shouted to her father. (Jimmy remembered this, too.)

"I'll read to Grandpa from the novel I'm writing—*The Dickens Man*," he told them. This went over about as well as his describing how fun Mieke and Jolanda were.

"Is it a novel about your grandfather, Jimmy?" Faith asked first.

"The main character is a teacher loosely based on Granddaddy—he teaches Dickens, but he uses Dickens in a lifesaving way," Jimmy said.

There wasn't a Winslow who didn't know that Thomas never intended to "burden" his grandson with the outdated desire to be a novelist like Charles Dickens. "A dinosaur of an ambition," was what Thomas Winslow called it. Thomas regretted how he'd inspired his beloved grandson to become a nineteenth-century novelist; he'd only hoped to enlighten the struggling boy as a reader.

"*How* 'loosely based,' Jimmy?" Faith was first to ask.

"*How* does Dickens save lives?" Prudence (the doctor) wanted to know.

"I don't recall Daddy as a magnet for suicidal students!" Hope cried.

"Daddy had some depressed students. Maybe Dickens helped them," Jimmy's mom said to her sisters.

"I think 'loosely based' means not exactly," Jimmy said. As a first-time fiction writer, he was learning he would be criticized for writing about real people—whether he did it exactly or inexactly. "Granddaddy will let me know if I got Dickens right. It won't matter to him if he is or he isn't like the Dickens Man," Jimmy told them.

Or so Jimmy *hoped*, his mom and his aunts imagined. To their thinking, he was being presumptuous—he was taking a liberty with sacred family property merely to title a novel *The Dickens Man*.

"We'll take you to The Meadow tomorrow, Jimmy." Faith told him.

"I'll drive—I could drive there blindfolded," Hope said.

"I can't take two days off in a row," Dr. Prudence informed them.

"I'm working," was all Jimmy's mom said, not looking at him.

"We'll tell you everything," Hope assured Honor and Prudence.

Jimmy had pictured Grandpa Tommy as his only audience. As fiction writers learn, your whole family reads you, looking for themselves. They're angry if they find themselves, disappointed if they don't. *Whose aunts are these?* Jimmy's aunts would wonder when they read Jimmy's novel. *Whose mother is this?* Honor Winslow asked herself when she read it. Neither James Winslow's classmates nor his wrestling teammates saw themselves among the lonely, depressed, and suicidal students Teacher Tom saves in *The Dickens Man.* These students in need of rescuing were figments of Jimmy's imagination. Those lost boys, Jimmy knew, were potential versions of his most insecure self. If Arnaud or Chantal Beaudette hadn't been there, what might have happened to Jimmy?

More germane to Jimmy's survival at the academy, what if Coach Ted or Jonah Feldstein or Grandpa Tommy hadn't been there? How lonely and depressed might Jimmy have been if he'd never read Charles Dickens? In *David Copperfield*—remembering his life as a reader in his attic room, in the Chatham of his childhood—Dickens wrote, "I have been Tom Jones (a child's Tom Jones, a harmless creature)." James Winslow didn't doubt Grandpa Tommy would understand. Jimmy imagined he might have been hopeless had he not read *Great Expectations.*

The Chatham of Dickens's childhood is reborn in *Great Expectations*—in the churchyard graves he could see from his attic room, in the black convict hulk, "like a wicked Noah's ark." Dickens saw it offshore on the boating trips he took on the Medway to the Thames, when he saw his first convicts. Thomas Winslow would recognize the model Jimmy used to illustrate the landscape of Pennacook— its two rivers, its two communities, the stark differences between the academy and the town. The academy was the ruling class of Pennacook. James Winslow, the writer, would scorn the townspeople of Pennacook—as they had scorned the Winslow family. The landscape of *Great Expectations* owes much to Chatham's landscape—the foggy marshes, the river mist, even the nearby house where Miss Havisham lives. On walks from Gravesend to Rochester, Dickens and his father paused in Kent and viewed the mansion atop the two-mile slope called Gad's Hill. His father said if Charles was hardworking, he might get to live there one day. Given his family's circumstances, his father's money problems, this must have been hard for young Charles to believe. Yet Dickens did get to live there—for the last dozen or so years of his life. He wrote *Great Expectations* there; he died there. Truthful exaggeration was real to Dickens.

As Jimmy's grandfather had told him, "For readers who find Dickens's imagination farfetched, they should look at his life." Impoverishment forced the family to move away from the Chatham of Dickens's childhood.

"I thought life sloppier than I had expected to find it," Dickens wrote.

Self-pity had no place in his novels. "His weapons were those of caricature and burlesque," his biographer Edgar Johnson writes, "of melodrama and unrestrained sentiment."

In reading the opening pages of *The Dickens Man* to Grandpa Tommy, Jimmy emphasized that Teacher Tom's classroom was an emotional battlefield; low comedy and pathos were at play. A student's roommate had committed suicide; he'd hanged himself in the dormitory shower room after leaving a note on his pillow. "I'm in the shower," he wrote his roommate.

The parents of one of Teacher Tom's students were divorcing. They were sleeping with the same woman—she'd been the student's favorite teacher when he was in elementary school. During one school vacation, he'd accepted a job as her house sitter when she was gallivanting with a girlfriend around the Caribbean. He'd masturbated with his head in her underwear. The Dickens Man read aloud to the troubled boy—imitating Mr. Sleary's lisp in his plea for the circus artists in *Hard Times*. "Don't be croth with uth poor vagabondth. People must be amuthed. They can't be alwayth a learning, nor yet can they be alwayth a working, they ain't made for it. You *mutht* have uth, Thquire. Do the withe thing and the kind thing, too, and make the betht of uth; not the wortht!"

In the room at The Meadow that Thomas and Constance Winslow shared, there were standing curtains on casters. The comatose Connie lay facing her husband, where he could see her—except when the nurse's aide, Alma, rolled the standing curtains closed. This was done for Connie's privacy, when Alma needed to attend to cleaning her. Although Connie was comatose, the nurse's aide also rolled the curtains closed when she attended to cleaning Tommy. "After urination and defecation, they need privacy," Alma told Jimmy.

Alma was a tireless supporter of privacy and personal hygiene. With the peeing and pooping going on, there were interruptions to the narrative momentum of Jimmy's heartfelt reading of *The Dickens Man*—not to mention the behind-the-curtains exhalations, gasps, and rigorous holding of breath by Aunt Faith and Aunt Hope, whose criticism was expressed by breathing. Once or twice, Hope had laughed; her girlish giggles prompted a thumbs-up from Grandpa Tommy's left thumb. Dickens's readers, Jimmy understood, were encouraged to love or hate his characters—as Dickens did.

"Look at Orlick—you're *supposed* to hate him," Teacher Tom tells his students. In *Great Expectations,* Orlick is as dangerous as a mistreated dog. Dickens has little sympathy for the social circumstances underlying Orlick's villainy. Orlick is a bad one, plain and simple—he means to kill. "Look at Joe—you *have to* love him," Tom tells the boys. Joe is proud, honest, hardworking, uncomplaining, and manifesting endless goodwill despite the clamorous lack of appreciation surrounding him. Joe is a good one, plain and simple—he means no one any harm. "Dickens believed in good and evil. He believed there were truly good people and truly bad ones, like *you* do. You boys are incapable of indifference," Teacher Tom tells his students. "You love or hate, like Dickens does. I know you do."

Yet, in *Great Expectations,* Dickens shows more fear of Jaggers than loathing for him—as if Jaggers is too dangerous to despise. "When I was a teenager, I thought Jaggers was always washing his hands and digging with his penknife under his fingernails because of how morally reprehensible (how morally *dirty*) his clients were," Teacher Tom tells his students. "It was a case of a lawyer trying to rid his body of the contamination contracted by his proximity to *the criminal element.* I think now that this is only partially why Jaggers can never be clean. I am far more certain that the filth Jaggers accumulates in his work is dirt from *the law itself*—it is his own profession's *crud* that clings to him!" Tom tells the boys.

Jimmy read on and on. It was hard not to address his reading to his grandfather's left hand, instead of to the dying man's disfigured face. Jimmy continued with the "permanent contamination of Jaggers," how the lawyer's home is as businesslike as his office—how the presence of his housekeeper, Molly, "casts the aura of a prison over Jaggers's dinner table." Molly is a murderess, spared the gallows *not* because she was innocent but because Jaggers got her off. It would break Jimmy's heart to get another thumbs-up from his devoted grandpa's left hand.

In *Great Expectations,* Magwitch was Jimmy's hero—the convict who risks his life to see how his creation has turned out. It's just like Dickens that Magwitch will be spared the answer. The convict's creation hasn't turned out very well. "It's Magwitch who enlivens the novel's dramatic beginning—an escaped convict, he frightens a small boy into providing food for his stomach and a file for his leg-iron," Teacher Tom tells his students. As Jimmy read to his bedridden grandfather, when Magwitch returns to London a hunted man, he also enlivens the novel's dramatic ending. Magwitch as effectively destroys Pip's expectations as he has created them. "You think *you* have troubles," Tom tells the most troubled, near-suicidal boys. "Be glad you're not Pip, who discovers his benefactor has all along been Abel Magwitch—the escaped convict. And don't feel *too* sorry for Pip—you should feel *sorrier* for Magwitch!"

Teacher Tom tells his students. "Don't tell me you're *homesick*," the Dickens Man tells the homesick boys. "Look at Magwitch. He provides us with the missing link in the story of Miss Havisham's jilting. Magwitch is our means for knowing who Estella is, and where she comes from, but don't tell me Magwitch is just a *plot device*!" As Jimmy read to the dying man, Pip can never rid himself—or Estella, by association—of Magwitch's prison "taint."

That was as far as Jimmy got in his first reading of *The Dickens Man* to his grandfather. Grandpa Tommy had emitted a gassy, liquid sound. There then emanated an overpowering odor from the dying man's diaper. The standing curtains on casters were rolled aside, as if the sound and the odor summoned Alma. There were tears on the cheeks of the nurse's aide, and Jimmy could see that his aunts were crying; they'd all been listening to *The Dickens Man*. Not many writers have such a gratifying audience response to their first novels. As for his devoted Grandpa Tommy, there was another thumbs-up from the man's left hand—another heartbreaker. Tears were streaming down Thomas Winslow's cheeks. Despite his half-frozen face, Jimmy's grandfather was crying uncontrollably from both eyes.

"Don't worry, Jimmy," Alma told him. "Post-stroke patients are emotionally labile—they'll frequently cry over the smallest trigger. Their emotions are fast to appear, with little or no filtering." This didn't fully explain to the young author why the nurse's aide and his aunts were all sobbing. Jimmy hoped that *The Dickens Man* amounted to more than *the smallest trigger* for Grandpa Tommy. And Alma's vocabulary confused Jimmy; he didn't know the word *labile*, meaning emotionally unstable or liable to change. Jimmy thought *labile* was related to *labia*.

Poor Alma. She thought Jimmy looked suddenly stricken, not realizing he was trying to imagine his unfortunate grandfather as emotionally vaginal, as if post-stroke patients were somehow vulnerable to resembling the inner or outer folds of the vulva. "What do post-stroke patients have to do with *vaginas,* or with just the *labia,* maybe?" Jimmy asked the nurse's aide. The question was sufficient to stop Jimmy's aunts from sobbing. Faith and Hope were aghast; they were now the stricken-looking ones. Jimmy's grandfather was the only one who realized this was a language problem, having nothing to do with strokes or vaginas. The fast thumbs-down from Grandpa Tommy's left hand seized everyone's attention. As Faith and Hope would later tell Jimmy in the car when they were driving away from The Meadow, if their dear daddy could have laughed, he surely would have.

"Don't you know what *labile* means, Jimmy?" Faith was first to ask in Thomas and Constance's room. Alma seemed to be experimenting with the stricken look and Hope had burst out laughing. The Winslow sisters and Jimmy did their best to assure Alma that the *labile-labia* confusion was just one of those language or vocabulary misunderstandings.

"Blame it on Latin!" Hope had cried. She said *labile, labia, vulva,* and *vagina* all came from the Latin. This got a thumbs-up from you-know-who.

Back in the Winslow household, Prudence and Honor were anxious to hear how Jimmy's reading from *The Dickens Man* had been received. "It was all thumbs-up until Jimmy told a vagina joke to Alma," Faith said first.

"Poor Alma!" Prudence exclaimed, while Hope howled with laughter.

"No vagina jokes to nurse's aides, Jimmy," his mom intoned to him. After the labia business was explained to death, Faith and Hope told Honor and Prudence how the opening pages of *The Dickens Man* made them cry—even Alma. "It's not like Alma to cry!" Honor declared. "I want you to read *The Dickens Man* to me, Jimmy," she told him.

"I'll read the novel myself—I hate being read to," Prudence stated.

The ending of his novel was all-important to the writer James Winslow would become. When you tell a story to a dying man, you better know where you're going—you better know how your story ends. The dying man knows *his* ending. Jimmy had imagined the end of *The*

Dickens Man, but he'd not written it. He imagined the ending more exactly when he was reading to his grandfather. He could see the students Teacher Tom had saved—they came to a place like The Meadow to pay their respects to the dying Dickens Man.

"I have a medical question for Prudence, not about Granddaddy, but my fictional character is also dying—at the end of the novel," Jimmy began.

There ensued a Winslow-sister hullabaloo about dying in real life—as opposed to portrayals of death in novels. Jimmy's medical question for the doctor in the house was passed over in the emotion of the moment.

"Your fictional character shouldn't die in the same way as Daddy," Faith said matter-of-factly to Jimmy.

"And don't read your character's death scene to Daddy, no matter how your Dickens Man dies," his mother told him.

"Daddy is hanging on your every word, Jimmy—slow the story down, put off the dying, don't ever get to the ending," Hope advised him.

"I'm a long way from writing the ending. I've written less than half the story," Jimmy admitted to them.

"You should be writing ahead, except when you're reading to Daddy," Faith said.

"First you read as much as you've written to me, all at once—then you write your ass off, Jimmy!" his mom ordered him.

"Daddy is nobody's fool, Jimmy. When you slow the story down, he'll know you're stalling because you haven't written the rest," Hope had said.

"What's your *medical* question, Jimmy?" Prudence asserted herself.

"Might someone like Grandpa Tommy be able to *write*?" Jimmy asked.

Jimmy knew his grandfather could move the fingers of his left hand, and the post-stroke patient understood everything. That he couldn't speak didn't preclude his ability to write with his left hand, or did it? If paper on a clipboard were positioned in a way that Grandpa Tommy could reach it, might he be able to write his thoughts? A character *like* his grandfather—provided the stroke hadn't robbed him of his ability to form sentences in his mind—might be able to hold a pen and write. Yes?

Faith, not Prudence, was the first to answer Jimmy's medical question. "Daddy is right-handed, Jimmy—he was proud of his handwriting. Daddy wouldn't want us to see his left-handed writing," Faith said.

"A fictional character could be left-handed, Faith," Hope pointed out.

"Daddy doesn't want to articulate his thoughts in writing, Jimmy. In his condition, a thumbs-up or down is all he wants to say," his mom said.

"Speaking *as a doctor,*" Prudence interrupted, "your fictional character can conceivably use his left hand to write; his cognition could be intact, and he can articulate his thoughts in writing. If his cognition far exceeds his ability to communicate, he could be frustrated over his inability to make his thoughts known. He can grunt and flail his hand, he can pantomime holding a pen—he can be a whole lot angrier than Daddy is, Jimmy," Prudence said.

This was all Jimmy needed to know; he would write his ending. In his future novels, Jimmy knew, there would be more loved ones dying. Prudence, his doctor aunt, would be his first reader. The dying details mattered in an ending. The Dickens Man was discouraged to see that not all his students had been saved. The grown men in need of rescue were too old to be saved by Dickens; their formative years were behind them. Teacher Tom understood that Dickens's best characters were redeemable. It hurt him to realize that students were more redeemable than adults. He wrote, with his left hand, what his stroke didn't let him say. Teacher Tom hoped to *scare* his former students who still needed saving; it was too late to inspire them. Jimmy believed Grandpa Tommy would approve of the passage the Dickens Man reads to the pathetic adults among his former students—from *Great Expectations,* when Pip imagines a night cold enough to kill a man lying out on the marshes: "I looked at the stars, and considered how awful it would be for a man to turn his face up to them as he froze to death, and see no help or pity in all the glittering multitude." Jimmy remembered how his grandfather had admired this passage.

Real life, Jimmy and his grandfather knew, wasn't plotted like a novel. When Constance Winslow died, unresponsive as she was, her dear Tommy was the first to notice; he interrupted Jimmy's reading by pointing with the index finger of his left hand to the space between the curtains. Alma came as soon as Jimmy called her name; the tears on his Grandpa Tommy's cheeks indicated to Jimmy that Grandma Connie was gone. If Thomas Winslow could have spoken, Jimmy knew what the crying man would say. Jimmy said it for him. "Right you are, Connie!" Jimmy cried. It was the exuberance of the thumbs-up from his grandfather that let Jimmy know the man who loved him and Dickens was ready to pack it in.

The everything-he'd-written reading to his mother—"all at once," as she'd directed—was attended by Faith and Hope. The three sisters' tears were interspersed with their laughter—a gratifying response to a first novel. What remained of his reading at The Meadow would be short-lived. After Constance Winslow's passing, her bed was removed, but Alma was still listening behind the curtains. Jimmy didn't want *The Dickens Man* to be a burden to his grandfather, who just wanted to die. Upon finishing a short reading, Jimmy waited for Alma to slip away—to dry her tears unseen. When he bent over Grandpa Tommy, their foreheads almost touched.

"I'll stop now, Grandpa," Jimmy whispered, hoping Alma was out of hearing. "I just wanted you to know I can do this thing—I can be a writer," Jimmy said. The strength in his grandfather's left hand surprised him. The dying man seized his grandson's neck in a wrestler's collar tie, holding him cheek to cheek. This was how Alma would find them—as if they were frozen in time, or they wanted to be.

After that—as Alma would say she'd seen before—Thomas Winslow refused feedings and resisted all care. With his strong left hand, he would pull out his tubes. Jimmy's grandpa, the good teacher who had inspired *The Dickens Man,* died within days of his dear Connie.

24.

The Passage of Time

The townspeople of Pennacook knew that Alma, the nurse's aide, had shepherded many endings at The Meadow. Alma tended to downplay the Winslows' back-to-back deaths. She was a woman who said she'd seen everything before; yet Alma's high esteem for Thomas and Constance Winslow's love story had a humbling effect on the townsfolk. The ladies of the town were conspicuously silent. Did those ladies wonder if their husbands would have pulled out their tubes to die within days of their wives? Was it due to their regard for Alma, who had a history of experience with the dying, that the townspeople of Pennacook exhibited more respect for Thomas and Constance Winslow in death than they'd shown for them when those two were alive? Bouquets of flowers came to the Front Street house.

It was Alma who became a catalyst for a rare rift among the Winslow daughters—or if *rift* is too strong a word, at least a difference of opinion. Alma herself was the opposite of a troublemaker. The Winslow sisters loved her and had the utmost respect for her. Constance had first met Alma at the library. An unmarried Mexican American around Faith's or Hope's age, Alma Vásquez had already been a reader as a young woman.

"I loved reading novels, but my nursing studies came first. I also had to learn English and emigrate from Mexico," Alma told Constance when they met. "Now I want to read novels again—this time in English." Constance guessed that Alma was in her late twenties or early thirties. The library had a book club—all women, older than Alma. The book club wouldn't work out for Alma. She was too well-spoken and a better reader than the ladies of the town, and there were almost no Mexicans in New Hampshire. Alma's brown skin and coal-black hair set her apart; she was statuesque with chiseled features and a jutting bosom, and she was single. Alma preferred to talk about the novels she read with Constance. But no one had ever read a novel aloud to Alma, not until she heard Jimmy Winslow read from *The Dickens Man.*

Given Alma's devotion to their beloved departed parents, the Winslow sisters were welcoming to Alma when she first dropped by the Front Street house to ask Jimmy how *The Dickens Man* was coming along. What Alma really wanted was for Jimmy to read to her, but she was shy if his mom and one or more of his aunts were around. When the doorbell rang in the Front Street house, the Winslow sisters raced one another to the door. The third time Alma dropped by, she got up the nerve to say what she wanted.

It helped that Honor Winslow was alone when she answered the door. Alma and Honor had their nursing in common. "Jimmy is probably writing in his room, but I'll go get him for you," Honor said.

"I want him to read to me, if that isn't strange," Alma blurted out. She explained to Jimmy's mom that she'd loved listening to him read from *The Dickens Man.* "Now I associate the novel with his voice. I want to *hear* it, not read it," Alma said.

"It isn't strange. I like listening to Jimmy read, too," Honor told her. Jimmy's mom found him writing in his room. Jimmy said reading to Alma was strange. "It *isn't* strange. It would only be strange if you read to her in your pajamas, Jimmy," his mother said. He often wrote in his pajamas, but he put on jeans and a T-shirt to read to Alma.

Jimmy read to her in what was called the reading room of the Front Street house. Thomas and Constance used to sit there when they were reading their respective books—usually not talking to each other. The TV was in what was called the living room—or the family room, after Faith and Hope had children. That day, when Faith and Hope dropped by, they could overhear Jimmy reading aloud. "Who is Jimmy reading to?" Faith asked Honor.

"Or is Jimmy writing out loud in the reading room?" Hope asked. When Honor explained about Alma, Faith and Hope were shocked.

"Alma must be my age—she's almost *sixty*!" Faith exclaimed.

"Even if Alma is only *my* age, she's still too old for Jimmy!" Hope said. She was fifty-seven.

"Jimmy is just *reading* to Alma. They're not having sex," Honor explained. She was laughing, which outraged her older sisters more. "It wouldn't be the worst thing if they were having sex—or if they do have sex one day," Honor whispered. Faith and Hope just stared. "I mean that Jimmy's not really married—he's going to have sex with *someone*, one day. If he does it with a woman Alma's age, she won't get pregnant, will she? It would be the best thing for this family if Jimmy doesn't knock up someone else!" Honor declared.

That was when Prudence got home; she and Honor still lived in the Front Street house. Faith and Hope told Prudence that Jimmy and Alma were "starting something" in the reading room, where "there was more than reading going on."

"Alma is too old to get pregnant, isn't she?" Honor asked Prudence, who was Alma's doctor and knew exactly how old she was. Prudence was also discreet.

"Alma is older than I am," Prudence told Honor. "Alma is younger than you two," she told Faith and Hope. Alma was fifty-six, they now knew. "It's highly unlikely that Alma will get pregnant, and if she did, she and I would know what to do," Prudence said to her sisters, while Jimmy read on.

That day, when Jimmy was reading to Alma from *The Dickens Man*, it never occurred to them to have sex with each other. They learned that Jimmy's mom wished they *would* have sex only when Honor took Alma aside and asked her to prevent the budding author from knocking up a younger woman. Faith and Hope cornered Jimmy when he was writing in his room. They told him that his having sex with Alma was "an inevitable perversion"—what his reading to her would surely "lead to." But his aunts had a more major message to get across—one that wasn't about Alma.

"You must have noticed, Jimmy—there's an *opaqueness* to your mom when it comes to sexual matters," Faith said first.

"It's okay that she's asexual, it's totally fine, but your mom is sexually opaque in other ways, Jimmy. It feels like there's a *hole* in her—like there's something *not there,* sexually speaking," Hope said.

"We don't mind if Honor isn't *normal,* Jimmy—Prudence doesn't have an entirely normal sex life," Faith started to say, but Hope interrupted her.

"Prudence *had* a boyfriend who wanted to marry her, Faith," Hope jumped in, "but Prudence went to med school instead. Okay, so Prudence has a thing for arm's-length relationships—at least she *has* relationships, Jimmy," Hope said.

"I'm sick of hearing how your mom and Esther were 'kindred spirits,' Jimmy. Big deal! Esther did *everything* for your mom. It's as if your mom didn't get to *be* a teenager or a young adult," Faith told him.

"It's fine that your mom wanted you to knock up any girl you could—okay, so she's a somewhat overprotective mother," Hope said. "But you're a young adult now, and you're going to be a father—you can't let someone who's never had sex manage your sex life, Jimmy," Hope told him.

Jimmy was, as he often was, speechless. When it came to his sex life, he worried that no one would ever be as exciting as Jolanda and Mieke—specifically, the way those two had *managed* Jimmy's first sexual experience. And although Jimmy didn't like the way Faith and Hope talked about his mother, he felt there was a vagueness Honor shared with Esther. His mom and Esther lived in the background, like peripheral characters in a novel.

Alma Vásquez said it would be "better" if Jimmy read to her in his room. They were in his bedroom when Alma told him what she meant by *better*. "Your mom thinks we should have sex, Jimmy, but I have more in common with your mom than she knows," Alma began. She'd left Mexico, where she didn't want to become a nun, nor did she ever want to have sex—not to mention (worst of all) be married with children. "Sound familiar?" she asked Jimmy. Alma thought it would be easier—in the sense of "more acceptable"—to live alone as a Mexican American woman in a small New England town.

"Faith and Hope think it's an 'inevitable perversion' if we have sex, and my mother *wants* us to have sex," Jimmy repeated to Alma, like a poem he'd learned by rote in childhood.

"If you keep reading to me in your bedroom, Jimmy, we can pretend we're having sex," Alma told him. "We'll make your mom happy, and your aunts will have the satisfaction that comes with being right," Alma said.

In a Winslow-sister talkathon, where Jimmy was present but didn't say a word, Faith and Hope were fearful that the townspeople of Pennacook would hear of the shameful relationship. They were concerned that Alma's reputation would be compromised, but Prudence disagreed. "Maybe if the town knew Alma had a younger boyfriend, some older men in the town—mostly married men—would stop making improper advances." Faith and Hope were shocked to hear of such repugnant behavior, but Honor wasn't. As a single mom, she was familiar with wayward advances from some older, married men in Pennacook.

Jimmy couldn't wait to tell Alma, who decided he should occasionally read to her in her rooming house, which was adjacent to the textile mill in town. The millworkers would notice Jimmy's visits and tell their wives, or the landlady of the rooming house would surely say something to the ladies of the town.

"This will *enhance,* not compromise, my reputation, Jimmy—the older men who pester me will be embarrassed to know I'm seeing a *younger* man. They'll be ashamed to compete with you and they'll leave me alone," Alma said.

For the writing of *The Dickens Man,* James Winslow had a real listener. Like his hero, Charles Dickens, Alma Vásquez taught Jimmy that the reader mattered. And Alma was a fictional girlfriend in another important way. "When you have sex with a young woman—and you will, Jimmy—you don't have to hide her from me. I won't kill you for cheating on me. I'll be happy to advise you about the precautions you can take not to knock her up. There *are* some useful precautions, you know, Jimmy," Alma told him.

"I know," Jimmy said, as he'd been used to saying in Vienna.

That summer of '64 was a productive one for James Winslow. "Don't stop!" Alma would cry out from his bedroom when he stopped reading.

"Louder," Jimmy got used to whispering, and Alma upped the volume on her *Don't stop!* act. Jimmy enjoyed writing to Jolanda and Mieke about his older girlfriend. Those two would meet Alma that August, when Claude and Chantal were married in Pennacook, and Claude's French family stayed in the Front Street house—though there might have been more room for them with the Beaudettes. Many of the Beaudette children were grown up now, with children (and houses) of their own.

With Claude's family in the Front Street house, Prudence and Honor shared a room, and Jimmy slept in the same bed with Mieke and Jolanda. He was very happy. "No fooling around, you two," Jolanda told them. It was just like Jolanda to sleep in the middle, to keep Jimmy and Mieke separated. There was a lot of looking at (and touching of) Mieke's baby bump. Mieke wished it was bigger. Because Jimmy had a hard-on, he was glad he wasn't sleeping in the middle; he lay awake worrying that Jolanda would notice his erection. One morning, when they were awake but lying in bed together, Jimmy confided to Mieke and Jolanda; he said having sex with them was certain to be the pinnacle of his sexual experience.

Jolanda snorted like a horse and Mieke cried, prompting Jolanda to say pregnant women had surging hormones. Claude's mother was a major disappointment to Jolanda; she wasn't as bad as Claude had made her out to be. The Winslow sisters had prepared themselves for being with a snooty Frenchwoman by putting on airs to one another, which Jimmy found annoying. Chantal had urged the Beaudettes to be on their best behavior. Meaning what, exactly? Were the Beaudettes not supposed to display their overbreeding tendencies *publicly*? (The Beaudettes' withholding of their overbreeding tendencies must have disappointed Claude's French family.)

Jolanda saved the ruckus she'd promised to make at Claude's wedding for the reception. In her toast, Jolanda said nonstop sex with Chantal was the only thing preventing Claude from panic attacks. As Claude's former roommate, Jolanda wanted everyone to know that living with Claude and Chantal having nonstop sex was better than living with panicky Claude on his own. "You call that a *ruckus*—that was just the truth," Claude whispered to Jolanda later, kissing her ear. Jolanda and Jimmy were very happy for Claude; they'd never seen him so relaxed. Chantal, on the other hand, was a wreck. The sheer number of Beaudettes at the wedding, and at the party afterward, was overwhelming to her, but Chantal was the only one who noticed the Beaudettes outnumbered all the other guests.

The Winslow sisters were unanimous in their opinion: the Beaudettes were always well-behaved. As Constance once said, "The reproductive habits of the Beaudettes are their own business—surely not the domain of the townspeople of Pennacook." As for those two tall Dutch girls with their arms draped around Jimmy Winslow's shoulders—or the very tall one and the pretty one, who were both taller than Jimmy—the ladies of the town weren't mistaken to imagine the Dutch girls were a new kind of two-moms idea, a twosome of motherhood in the making.

And of course Arnaud Beaudette came home to see Chantal get married. He was grateful to Jimmy for introducing his unmarriageable aunt to Claude. Arnaud had pitied Chantal, seeing her as someone destined for spinsterhood. Arnaud noticeably (if silently) disapproved of Jimmy's draft deferment in gestation, not to mention his marriage to Mieke. Jimmy was disappointed that his former best friend was such a straight arrow. Perhaps, unbeknown to Jimmy, Arnaud had always had an uptight moral barometer. The officer in training clearly looked down on Jimmy's relationship with Jolanda and Mieke, what he saw as a marriage in name only.

Jolanda sensed Arnaud's holier-than-thou opinion of her room-mate's sex life, *and* of Jimmy's future family life. That August wedding weekend, whenever Arnaud was around, she addressed Jimmy as "Sperm Man." Jimmy was heartened by her solidarity. Arnaud was no less uptight about Jimmy's much older girlfriend, Alma Vásquez. It was heartening to Jimmy that Chantal, who was only a little older than Claude, stood in solidarity with Alma. When Chantal saw Jimmy and Alma together, she made a point of praising older girlfriends and younger boyfriends. It turned out that Alma and Chantal already knew and liked each other. As a nurse's aide, Alma had lent a helping hand at the birth of more Beaudettes than she could count—likely *not* at Chantal's birth, not that either of them would remember.

Jolanda tried not to feel left out when Mieke and Jimmy talked about their writing—even when they were in bed, with Jolanda lying between them. Both Mieke and Jimmy were aware they were writing nineteenth-century novels—Mieke's was more like Tolstoy than Dickens.

"The passage of time is like a major character," Jimmy ventured to say.

"The passage of time *is* a major character!" Mieke exclaimed.

"In real life, the two of you are totally oblivious of the passage of time," Jolanda told them. This was true. As the years passed, the beginnings, the middles, and the ends of Jimmy's and Mieke's novels marked where those writers stood in time. The years when their novels were published would be Jimmy's and Mieke's milestones. When their child was born, Jolanda observed, the age of the blessed child was the only indication of *real time* the two writers noticed.

Vienna Winslow was born in Amsterdam in March 1965. Jolanda always said she would be a girl. Jimmy and his mom were there, staying in the hotel on the Oudezijds Voorburgwal—the canal running through the red-light district. Before the birth, Jolanda took Honor on a walk in de Wallen, showing her the prostitutes in their doors and windows. At the hospital, Honor sat beside Bente, Mieke's mother—the two of them holding hands. Jolanda sat beside Jimmy, holding his hand. When the nurse emerged from the delivery room, the Dutch word for *girl* ("meisje") was unintelligible to Honor and Jimmy, but Jolanda yelled, "It's a *Vienna!*"

Jolanda's parents—the pussy-whipped lawyer, Jeroen, and his wife, Els, the pussy-whipper—took Jimmy and Honor to dinner at their favorite restaurant in Dam Square. Honor's postpartum nursing talk was better received by Bente than the Lammers, whose dinners were disturbed by any mention of Mieke's "bleeding" or "swelling"—also her "nipples."

Jolanda took Honor to the Anne Frank House, where they both cried, and Honor told Jolanda something that she'd never said to Jimmy. Not the part about "the driving force behind the creation of Israel." (He'd heard this before, how "anti-Semitism could compel countries to persecute their Jewish population—anywhere, and at any period of time.") But Honor also said, "Some Palestinians are raised on hatred of the Jews—they believe in martyrdom, in death as the path to glorious paradise." This seemed harsh to Jimmy; it sounded more like Esther than his mother, he told Jolanda.

Jolanda just shrugged. She said there were Palestinian refugees in the Netherlands. She'd heard them say there should be no Israel—there should be only Palestinians in Palestine. With Mieke still recovering in the hospital, Jolanda was more interested in keeping Bente's hand off

Jimmy's thigh, or at least making sure that Bente wasn't touching Jimmy's penis. Mieke wasn't with them at dinner; she wasn't there to say the *moeder* word when Bente was groping Jimmy under the table. But this time Bente didn't bite Jimmy's tongue when she kissed him, and Jimmy didn't need to say the *penis* word to summon Jolanda to restrain Bente. When Mieke and Vienna were home from the hospital, and Mieke was breastfeeding the baby, Jimmy and his mom flew back to Boston.

On the plane, as if to test her son's propensity for speechlessness, Honor said: "I know Bente is attractive, and she's younger than Alma—she's still too old to get pregnant." Jimmy just waited. "Bente is the *kind of* woman you should sleep with, but you shouldn't actually sleep with her—not with the mom of your birth child's mother, Jimmy," Honor said. *For fuck's sake!* as Jolanda would say, and Jimmy was thinking, but he didn't say it.

That spring semester of '65, before he graduated from the University of New Hampshire, Jimmy was sleeping with a girl in his creative writing class. Before they had started sleeping together, he had told Maud he was married to a Dutch girl—a lesbian who had a girlfriend in Amsterdam. Maud said this sounded like fiction. She'd read an excerpt from *The Dickens Man* in their writing class; she thought Mieke and Jolanda, and now the newborn baby, were just characters in Jimmy's novel. He had to show Maud photos of Mieke and Jolanda and Vienna to convince her of what Jimmy and his grandfather understood: "Real life isn't plotted like a novel," he told Maud. Then (somehow) Maud heard about Alma. Maud didn't believe Jimmy when he said he wasn't really sleeping with Alma. Maud's graduation present to Jimmy was a dose of the clap, with the usual symptoms. The gonorrhea made him cry out loud when he was peeing. Naturally, Alma overhead him.

"It sounds like an issue for Dr. Prudence—it sounds like Maud has been sleeping around, Jimmy," Alma told him, when she heard him yelp when he was pissing. Alma was no less the supporter of personal hygiene and privacy than she'd always been. Jimmy just knew it was true—real life isn't plotted like a novel.

"Mind over matter, Jimmy. What don't you get about condoms?" Prudence asked him.

In those days, only Stanford and Iowa offered a master's degree in creative writing, but James Winslow wasn't moving away from Pennacook, where Vienna now lived and had those four Winslow women serving as mother substitutes. Jimmy pursued a master's degree in Victorian literature at the University of New Hampshire, where the English Department faculty already knew he was devoted to *Great Expectations* and *David Copperfield* as models of the bildungsroman. One of the fiction writers in the UNH English Department introduced Jimmy to his literary agent. An editor who was a big deal at Random House bought *The Dickens Man* when the novel was half-done, and Jimmy was still studying for his master's. By then, even Honor Winslow knew Jimmy wasn't really sleeping with Alma, who was so familiar with Jimmy's reading voice that he didn't need to read aloud to her anymore. Alma preferred reading to herself.

Jonah Feldstein had just published a first collection of short stories with a university press. There were only a few reviews, and no sales to speak of, but the reviews were good ones. This led Jonah to a full-time job at a university in the South, where he was teaching English and creative writing—Jonah also had a full-time girlfriend. Jonah's sister Sarah wrote Jimmy about the girlfriend: "There's been no mention of marriage or children—not nearly as original as your situation, Jimmy." Thus began their correspondence; if he couldn't sleep with Sarah Feldstein, there was no reason he couldn't write her.

By then, Mieke Koster published her first novel in the Netherlands—her maiden name sounded better in Dutch than her married one, Winslow. The title was taken from the first sentence of George Eliot's *Middlemarch*—the epigraph to Mieke's novel: "Miss Brooke had that kind of beauty which seems to be thrown into relief by poor dress."

Thrown into Relief would be the title in English—like *Middlemarch*, Mieke's novel was about the nature of marriage and the status of women. Also like *Middlemarch*, Mieke's novel would be published to a mixed reception, but there were a lot of reviews. Jimmy's editor at Random House would publish *Thrown into Relief* in English, and Mieke Koster had a U.K. publisher in addition to her European translations.

Vienna Winslow would be four in 1969, when her father's first novel, *The Dickens Man*, was published—like *Middlemarch* and *Thrown into Relief*, to an abundance of mixed reviews. It was no coincidence that Mieke's Dutch publisher was among the first to issue James Winslow's many European translations. For a literary novel about a teacher who saves his troubled students with Dickens, *The Dickens Man* was an unusual bestseller in a lot of languages. Jimmy made close friendships among his foreign publishers—not only with the one in the Netherlands, but with his other Western European and his Scandinavian publishers as well. The epigraph to *The Dickens Man* was a line James Winslow loved from the fourteenth chapter of *Great Expectations*. "It is a most miserable thing to feel ashamed of home." The most troubled students, the ones in need of rescuing, were the ones who were ashamed of where they came from; maybe this resonated with readers who needed saving, too.

Claude, in his nerdy way, noticed a French review of Mieke's *Thrown into Relief* and one of Jimmy's *The Dickens Man*—two different reviews, by different reviewers—that complimented both novels for the same quality. The French word both reviewers used was "intertextualité." According to Claude, *intertextuality* was a new word in English—meaning "the interrelationship between a text and other texts, creating a new text."

"Leave it to Claude to make something that was perfectly clear completely incomprehensible," Jolanda said.

When *The Dickens Man* was published, Jimmy was teaching English and coaching wrestling at Pennacook Academy. He was also a full-time father with a houseful of mother substitutes. With the international success of his first novel, he would become self-supporting as a writer—he could write full-time now. Mieke Koster was also an international success and a self-supporting novelist. Naturally, the fact that the two of them were married to each other—in a somewhat unusual way—would be written about. They had a real marriage, but Mieke had a lesbian partner—her relationship with Jolanda was her only actual relationship—and Jimmy was free to have a girlfriend (or as many girlfriends as he wanted). Vienna Winslow was a shared child; the way it worked was that Vienna had two moms and one dad. "Vienna has a bunch of moms—if you count my mother, and my three aunts, too," Jimmy always said.

Although she was a fiction reader, Chantal Beaudette—now Madame Guilbert—was slow to read *The Dickens Man*. It wasn't only that she waited to read the French translation. Second Lieutenant Arnaud Beaudette—Company A, 502nd Infantry, 101st Airborne Division—had been killed in action.

Chantal's nephew had died amid a rocket attack and small-arms fire, searching for the body of a missing soldier in Vietnam, in February 1968. James Winslow understood why Chantal took her time reading his novel. Compared to Arnaud, in Chantal's mind, Jimmy was a draft dodger.

Esther's letter to Honor about Matzpen ("Compass" in Hebrew)—a revolutionary socialist organization, founded by former members of the Israeli Communist Party—was in step with Esther's thinking, but the ideological splits within the group pissed her off. There was a Trotskyist split and a Maoist split, not to mention a Matzpen Tel Aviv and a Matzpen Jerusalem; the latter group had adopted the name Matzpen Marxist. "Intellectualizing fuckheads!" Esther said, sounding very characteristic of Esther to the Winslow sisters.

Matzpen had issued a declaration—a sweeping generalization that rubbed Esther the wrong way. Matzpen asserted: "It is both the right and duty of every conquered and subjugated people to resist and to struggle for its freedom."

"Not if these same people seek to eliminate the Jews," Esther said.

In 1973, James Winslow would publish a historical novel. *The Doctor's Rules* is set in a fictional orphanage based on St. Cloud's, where the fictional doctor is based on Dr. Larch, who gives women what they want—they can either get an abortion or leave behind an orphan. Jimmy's third novel would also be historical. Set in Vienna in 1963–64, it parallels Jimmy's junior year abroad, but the characters based on Jolanda and Claude are both women. *Roommates in Vienna* (1977) is a roman à clef—a male American student is sharing two rooms and one bathroom with a Dutch lesbian couple. The Dutch girls want a child of their own; their roommate makes the baby. "An alternative family saga," a reviewer described the story. Frau Holzinger has another name—as does Irmgard, who isn't a prostitute. The American boy who's based on Jimmy has a prostitution problem—he can't stop visiting them. The Dutch girlfriends won't let him make a baby until he gives up the prostitutes. In *Roommates in Vienna,* the Jewish German tutor is not called Fräulein Eissler, and she isn't working for the Israelis. Her single agenda is to cure the anti-Semitic landlady and her family of their anti-Semitism—thereby saving the character based on Siegfried, who is a five-year-old girl. Jimmy's third novel is dedicated to his daughter, Vienna.

As Fräulein Eissler had told him, James Winslow was a Pferd mit Scheuklappen—a "horse with blinders." He was always imagining; he was always writing. He seemed more engaged with the characters he created than with what was happening or being said around him. An exception was how closely Jimmy paid attention to Vienna, and the friendship Jimmy maintained with Jolanda and Miele was no less constant. Their travel between New Hampshire and the Netherlands became routine. Jimmy and Mieke didn't want to get divorced; they liked being married. In 1971, when Jimmy and Mieke could have filed for divorce in Amsterdam—without Jimmy admitting to adultery—

Vienna Winslow was a six-year-old. She was old enough to have friends whose parents were divorcing, or already divorced. Vienna was a happy little girl; she wouldn't have wanted her parents to get a divorce. Jolanda's parents and Mieke's mother didn't want their happy grandchild to go through a divorce. As Jolanda's lawyer father, Jeroen Lammers, said: "The only reason for Mieke and Jimmy to get divorced is if Jimmy wants to remarry."

James Winslow liked to say he was happily married to a Dutch girl. After a pause, he liked saying (even more) that they shared a child together. "My Dutch wife has a lesbian partner—they're a happy couple," he added, after a longer pause. This kept his more serious-minded girlfriends at bay. Why would Jimmy be in a hurry to get divorced? He didn't want to remarry. The girlfriends would come and go; they were transitory. Being married to Mieke, and being a full-time father, kept the girlfriends at arm's length. Being a writer was what made James Winslow a Pferd mit Scheuklappen. And a horse with blinders is just a German way to describe a workaholic, as a writer like Jimmy is more commonly called in North America.

Vienna Winslow's Dutch passport could be renewed at the Dutch consulate general in New York, but Jimmy, Mieke, and Jolanda always did it in Amsterdam. This took them back to the office at the town hall where Jimmy and Mieke had been married. That's where they were in 1971, when the American Academy of Pediatrics found "no valid medical indications for routine infant circumcision."

Was there a correspondingly weird symmetry to Esther's not allowing Jimmy to be Jewish? As a father, Jimmy could appreciate how Esther had protected him. Jimmy wouldn't want Vienna to be Jewish.

James Winslow's fourth book, his second Vienna novel, would be published in English in the fall of 1981. *Not an Egyptian* is another roman à clef. In Jimmy's first Vienna novel, *Roommates in Vienna*, there's no wrestling (not even any wrestlers). There's no Turnhalle for wrestlers on Währinger Straße. The focus is on the three roommates and their local Kaffeehaus, not called the Nachtmusik, where the Dagmar character is named Maria, and Hard Rain is the only dog—there are no dogs with balls.

James Winslow had saved the wrestlers for *Not an Egyptian,* based on Jimmy's first time back in Vienna since he'd been a student—in 1978, when he was promoting the German translation of *Roommates in Vienna.* He went to Leopold Spiegel's gym on Währinger Straße, but the gym was gone.

"Keine Turnhalle mehr—Gott sei Dank!" Helene told Jimmy, when he went to her hairdressing salon. ("No more gym—thank God!") "Kleiner Spiegel ist weg," she said. ("Little Mirror is gone.") It was fourteen, almost fifteen years ago that, as Helene put it, Leo had followed "his people" to Israel—to a wrestling club in Haifa. Given Jimmy's "awful injury," Helene said she was happy to see he wasn't limping.

With the help of a publicist from his German publisher, Jimmy tried to locate the belly-dancing club in the Favoriten district. It turned out the club wasn't called Die Ägypterin—that was just the name of the belly dancer. No one could remember the name of the club. Jimmy inquired about the belly dancer herself, but no one knew what had become of her. In a Turkish coffeehouse in Favoriten, Jimmy's German publicist spoke to some older Turkish men, only one of whom remembered seeing Die Ägypterin. His ears didn't look like wrestlers' ears, but the older man agreed with Jimmy: "The belly dancer was not an Egyptian," he confirmed.

In *Not an Egyptian,* Jimmy's roommate in Vienna is a fellow IES student—a Jewish wrestler from New York. The Institute for European Studies is wise to put them together. The novel is a flashback to the days when the two IES students see more of their wrestling teammates in a gym on Währinger Straße than they see of their fellow Americans. Jimmy's fictional roommate is a conflation of Jonah Feldstein and Claude, but his future is modeled on what happens to Arnaud Beaudette. The roommate is a Feldstein—a Noah, not a Jonah. The gym is Turnhalle

Daniel, but Daniel is still a Spiegel. The suplay master is a Danny, not a Leo, but he's still called Little Mirror. James Winslow didn't change the names of the Soviet or the Israeli wrestlers; their names might not have been real in the first place, he decided.

In *Not an Egyptian*, the Noah character has Claude's panicky but lovable qualities. A virgin, Noah is seduced by a dangerous dishwasher at a Bierhalle the wrestling teammates go to after practice. (Jimmy decided not to change Hildegund's unsuitably old-fashioned name. It served her right.)

Not an Egyptian is the first James Winslow novel where the character based on Jimmy becomes a writer. He's back in Vienna, on a book tour for a German translation, when he discovers that Turnhalle Daniel no longer exists and that Danny has joined his people in Israel. Unlike Jimmy, his fictional character is contacted by the belly dancer after he makes inquiries about her in the Favoriten district. She remembers that he wanted to be a writer, from when they whispered in each other's ears; she's happy for him that he got to be what he wanted to be. As for her, she's too old to be a belly dancer anymore, but she tells him she's still not an Egyptian.

The underlying story is what happens to Noah, the character based on Jonah Feldstein and Claude—and a little bit on Arnaud Beaudette. (Noah is killed in action in Vietnam in 1968.) In *Not an Egyptian,* the belly dancer also remembers what Noah wanted to be—they'd whispered in each other's ears, and Noah had told her he was going to be a soldier. "He had no doubt about it," the belly dancer says.

Yes, the belly dancer notices that the former wrestler, now a writer, has a limp. There's a flashback to his intentional knee injury in Turnhalle Daniel; all his teammates are in on it. He tells Noah that his mom is hoping for an injury worthy of a draft deferment; Noah tells the Soviets and the Israelis. Danny, the little suplay master, is in on the intended injury, too.

James Winslow would publish four novels in a span of twelve years, from 1969 until 1981. Those Winslow sisters were not surprised that Jimmy's first novel, *The Dickens Man,* got the best reviews; his homage to Dickens found favor with the critics. The later novels, in their different ways, were political. "Your social conscience isn't everyone's social conscience, you know," Jimmy's mom told him about *The Doctor's Rules*—his "abortion novel," she called it.

"What you see as one of society's injustices, Jimmy, is not shared by homophobic dickheads," Faith was first to say about *Roommates in Vienna*—his novel about the lesbian couple modeled on Mieke and Jolanda.

Hope clearly admired the Jewish German tutor who cures the family of their anti-Semitism in that novel. "Annelies was definitely working for Esther, Jimmy," she said.

As for the doomed roommate in *Not an Egyptian*—the Jewish boy who becomes a soldier and will die in Vietnam—Prudence would prepare Jimmy for a few of his unfavorable reviews. "Sure as shit, Jimmy, between the gung-ho Vietnam vets and the anti-Semites, you'll make some enemies."

Nor did it surprise the Winslow sisters that Jimmy's two favorite European publishers were Jewish. His Swedish and French publishers knew Jimmy was an ally—to women's rights (including abortion rights), to lesbian rights (including the rights of other sexual minorities), and to the rights of Jews. Because of these European Jews, James Winslow had an Israeli publisher from the beginning. Jimmy had confided to his Swedish and French publishers about his birth mother, and how she had protected (even prevented) him from being Jewish. Maybe Jimmy was hoping one of these European Jews would tell him he should be a Jew.

"Just be an ally to us Jews and call it a day, Jimmy," Matthias said—he was Jimmy's Swedish publisher, a German-born Jew.

"Keep being a good writer, Jimmy—that's enough of a burden," Gabrielle told him. She was Jimmy's French publisher; she'd somehow evaded the Vichy Nazi puppets in a Catholic convent school for girls.

"Be a good father, Jimmy—that's your foremost job," Matthias said.

Back in 1971, Esther had voiced solidarity with Jimmy's Swedish and French publishers. They, like her, were left-wing, nonobservant Jews. That summer, there was rioting in Jerusalem because the Egged bus service was operating on a Saturday. "The ultra-religious are protesting Sabbath desecration," Esther wrote to Honor. There were more than two hundred Orthodox demonstrators, led by a rabbi. The police used water cannons to disperse the religious zealots. Esther loved the water cannons. Even in the early 1970s, those two European Jews who published Jimmy said the prospect of a more religious society in Israel was on the horizon, the right wing on the rise. They were worried about it—as was Esther, Jimmy could only guess.

Later on, when his Swedish and French publishers talked about taking him to Jerusalem, Jimmy thought of Annelies more than he thought of Esther. Why wouldn't he? When he'd been back in Vienna on the translation trip, Jimmy had gone to the Schwindgasse, but—like Little Mirror—Frau Holzinger's family was gone. Jimmy could only imagine that Fräulein Eissler might have adopted Siegfried, as Irmgard had hoped. Why wouldn't Jimmy imagine that Annelies could have taken Siegfried to Israel to save him?

And hadn't Irmgard been right about the passage of time? It really is a telescope that sees into the future. Vienna Winslow was growing up. She wasn't a little girl anymore. In the summer of 1978, Vienna was thirteen. The Winslow sisters were saying it was time for Vienna to think about a bra. Jimmy wanted nothing to do with his daughter's bras. Vienna had her own ideas. "I can get better bras in Amsterdam than in Pennacook, Dad," she whispered to her father. When it came to bras, even Jimmy knew that Mieke and Jolanda wore more up-to-date bras than the Winslow sisters did.

Esther was already writing Honor Winslow about the first settlement established by HaMa'arakh ("The Alignment" in Hebrew)—an Israeli alliance of social democratic parties—when James Winslow was still a student looking after a two-year-old. The settlement was the reincarnation of Kfar Etzion—not that Jimmy knew, or would remember. He was busy with fatherhood and writing.

In the decade between 1967 and 1977—when, according to Esther, "the right wing took over"—almost thirty settlements were established. They were located where there was a sparse population of Palestinians, "not justifiable for security reasons," Esther wrote—in her opinion, "a huge mistake." She said the settlements were "against international law"—citing the Fourth Geneva Convention, concerning the protection of "Civilian Persons in Time of War." Esther wrote that she had "a sometime boyfriend who was a peace activist"—he refused to go into the army. The Winslow sisters were buzzing about Esther as an uncharacteristic and unlikely peace activist.

In the 1977 elections, Herut—now as a part of the Likud, the right wing Esther had in mind—reached power. Menachem Begin became Israel's prime minister. According to Esther, the Begin government started to establish settlements close to the Palestinian population. She said the settlements hindered a peaceful resolution to the Israeli-Palestinian conflict. But Jimmy wasn't paying attention to what was happening in Israel.

In the fall of 1979, Vienna Winslow was almost the age Esther had been when she came from St. Cloud's. Vienna was a first-year student at the academy; her fancy bras, from Amsterdam, were the envy of the other girls. Pennacook Academy had become a coeducational school in 1973. The academy faculty knew that Vienna was the great-granddaughter of *The Dickens Man*—the daughter of the novel's author, and a better student than her father.

In the fall of 1980, when she was fifteen and a half, Vienna started learning to drive—at first with her father, then with one of her aunts. She was also enrolled in a driver education program. Vienna would take her driving test the summer of 1981, when she was sixteen—a tall, pretty girl (taller than her author father).

Prompted by his European Jewish publishers. Jimmy would go to Israel in April 1981, at the invitation of what was then called the Jerusalem International Book Fair. Matthias and Gabrielle had longstanding ties to Israel and knew Jerusalem well. They'd invited Jimmy to stay with them at the American Colony Hotel. They told him that international journalists and diplomats, as well as U.N. officers, liked staying there.

Jimmy hoped he would see Esther in Jerusalem. In writing to Esther, Honor had given her all the details of Jimmy's itinerary. But Esther, as always, was elusive and vague. She didn't commit herself to seeing Jimmy. "At her age, Jimmy—she'll be seventy-six when you're there—Esther has most likely retired," his mom told him.

"Retired *from what*? It's as unclear as always!" Faith said first.

"Once upon a time, Esther *must have* worked for the Mossad," Hope reminded Jimmy, who often looked like he'd forgotten everything.

"Moreover, Jimmy, Esther *must have* had a high rank in the IDF—*before* she went to work for the Mossad," Prudence told him.

What Esther said on the phone to Honor Winslow, who'd asked her what she was *doing*, was that she no longer *did* anything. "I'm just advising, or occasionally information-gathering," was the vague way Esther put it.

There was something the Winslow sisters weren't telling him, Jimmy was thinking. "Has Esther stopped sending photos of herself, or have you stopped showing me her pictures?" he asked his mom. He knew how those sisters waited for one of them to go first. Faith was the one who told him there'd been no photos of Esther since she lost her arm. Hope said Jimmy should know about the arm before he saw Esther in Jerusalem—provided Esther chose to see him. Prudence chided Honor for not telling Jimmy about Esther's missing arm. It had happened three years ago.

"You're the doctor, Prudence—you know more about missing arms than I do. *You* tell Jimmy how Esther lost her entire arm!" Honor cried.

"There were no medical or surgical details," Prudence told Jimmy.

"There were no details of any kind, Jimmy," his mother told him.

Faith had answered the phone when the young IDF soldier called, a boy who asked for Honor. "This is about Esther—she's going to be all right," the soldier said. Faith told Honor there was a soldier on the phone.

"Something's happened to Esther?" Hope asked Faith, who said the soldier sounded too young to be shaving; he wouldn't tell Honor his name.

"No sensitive information, no unnecessary details," the young soldier said. He kept repeating that Esther was *going to be* all right. This call came after the coastal road massacre in 1978. Palestinian militants had crossed into Israel from Lebanon and hijacked a bus on the Coastal Highway near Tel Aviv, killing thirty-eight Israeli civilians, a third of them children. (The bus had exploded, bursting into flames.) The PLO claimed responsibility for the attack, which had been planned by Fatah. The purpose for the attack was to disrupt Israeli-Egyptian peace negotiations. Three days later, Israel invaded southern Lebanon, attacking PLO bases nearest the border. "When our command car came under heavy fire and Esther was wounded, we were not on a military mission—we were only information-gathering," the young soldier told Honor, who'd seen pictures Esther sent of the M325—a light truck, fitted with machine guns, a patrol vehicle and weapons carrier.

"What kind of *heavy fire*—machine guns, grenades?" Honor had asked.

"Submachine guns, definitely—maybe two grenades," the soldier said.

Esther had not been so badly wounded that she couldn't give orders. Her commands to the soldiers escorting her in the M325 were crystal clear.

"Leave me, or leave my arm," Esther commanded them. The young soldier told Honor that this had become a mantra among IDF recruits. The story of how Esther lost her arm in Lebanon got around.

"But how *did* she lose her arm in Lebanon?" Honor Winslow asked.

"No sensitive information, no unnecessary details," the soldier said.

Esther had earlier expressed her leftist allegiance to Israeli prime ministers of the Labor Party, opposing Menachem Begin, and she was dismayed when he was made leader of the Likud coalition in 1973. The Winslow sisters remembered how angry Esther was when Menachem Begin became prime minister of Israel in 1977, ending years of left-wing leadership. Esther had criticized Begin's uncompromising position on Israel's retaining the West Bank and the Gaza Strip—which were occupied by Israel during the 1967 Arab-Israeli War. Esther had even complained how Begin dressed. (He'd been a soldier, but he wore formal-looking suits and ties.)

Yet when Honor called Esther to tell her Jimmy knew about the arm, the Winslow sisters were surprised by the photo Esther sent of herself—a news photograph, torn from an Israeli newspaper. The one-armed Esther was saying something to Begin and the prime minister was listening. In contrast to how formally Begin was dressed, Esther wore dark slacks, like men's trousers, and ankle-high boots—no laces. Her white polo shirt was untucked and unbuttoned. The stump of her right arm protruded only an inch or two below the short-sleeved cuff of her shirt.

When Vienna Winslow, Jimmy's sixteen-year-old, saw this photo, Vienna sounded more like Jolanda than Mieke. "Maybe Esther is saying, 'Leave me, or leave my arm,' to Prime Minister Begin," Vienna said.

25.

Honor's Child

At sixteen, Vienna Winslow was of an age to wonder if the Latin motto of Pennacook Academy possibly applied to her and the whole Winslow family. Finis Origine Pendet, The End Depends Upon the Beginning, accurately presaged what Vienna knew of the circumstances of Esther's birth. Esther's childhood and her early adolescence foreshadowed Esther's ending up in Israel, or so Vienna Winslow had told her dad—smart girl.

There was no second-guessing Esther Nacht, Jimmy knew, but he didn't contradict his darling daughter. "Where Esther came from certainly led to where she ended up," was the way Jimmy put it. This reminded him of the origins of his daughter's name.

When Vienna was older, Jolanda stopped calling Jimmy "Sperm Man," or she only occasionally whispered it in his ear. As for Jolanda's tempting title, *Two Unvisited Vaginas,* it wasn't meant for Vienna to hear.

"Or for fucking mainstream publishing in the eighties," Mieke said.

Real life wasn't plotted like a novel, Jimmy and his grandfather knew. Yet, with or without the lisp, what Mr. Sleary says in Dickens's *Hard Times* emerged as a guiding principle in James Winslow's and Mieke Koster's writing. "Do the *withe* thing and the kind thing, too, and make the *betht* of *uth;* not the *wortht*!" (It was Mieke who chose to *accent* Sleary's lisp.)

Having a child of his own, and loving her, gave James Winslow some illuminating insights into his own childhood and early adolescence. He'd grown up with the story that his grandmother had chosen his aunts' names; he was aware that *Faith, Hope,* and *Prudence* were *virtue* names. He'd known from the start that his mom had an *expectation* name, and that his grandfather had named her. "*Honor* is a name like *Chastity*—an expectation isn't necessarily a virtue," was the way Constance put it. To the townspeople of Pennacook, especially the ladies of the town, *Honor* nonetheless sounded like a hard name to live up to. In retrospect, Jimmy thought, the *expectation* part of his mother's name wasn't something she had struggled to live up to. It was her expectations for *others* that could be a burden—not least what she'd expected of Esther, and of Jimmy.

Constance Winslow had heard her husband say (more times than she could count) that religion was the bane of civilization. Those Winslow sisters grew up saying this to one another—later, to Jimmy. The Winslow girls and Jimmy were liberal Democrats. In the 1980s, President Ronald Reagan and the Christian Right, a.k.a. the Moral Majority, were in favor of school prayer and opposed to abortion— evidence that religion was the bane of civilization. In 1981, what would become the AIDS epidemic was detected when doctors noticed Kaposi's sarcoma and pneumocystis carinii pneumonia in homosexual men. This was early in the Reagan presidency. In his anti-abortion zeal, Reagan devoted his time to lamenting the plight of the unborn—more than he cared about the death of gay men, or the women who'd died in those days when abortion was illegal and unsafe.

It was no coincidence that Jimmy's European Jewish publishers were nonobservant Jews; they had their own reasons for believing that religion was the bane of civilization. It was a sore point with them that Haredi men were exempted from mandatory military service. This began with the birth of the State of Israel, the 1948 War of Independence. "A deal was made with the Haredim, if their full-time occupation was Torah study," Matthias said.

"The Haredim were permitted to study their religion in yeshiva instead of serving in the miliary—torato umanuto, 'his Torah is his occupation,' as they put it," Gabrielle told Jimmy.

Matthias complained about high birthrates in the Haredi community—the "*ultra*-Orthodox Jews," he called them. "They don't believe in interfaith marriages, they have a dozen children—hence their population grows exponentially," Matthias said. What he called "the Torah world" had nearly disappeared during the Holocaust. Matthias said that Orthodox Judaism was growing now—in no danger of disappearing. In 1977, under Begin's Likud government, the Knesset had removed the cap on the number of exemptions under torato umanuto.

Among the Haredim, the Orthodox Jews, Jimmy had trouble sorting out the non-Zionists from the anti-Zionists.

"The non-Zionists don't object to the State of Israel—they just don't take it that seriously, or pay much attention to it," Gabrielle told Jimmy.

"Whereas the anti-Zionists oppose the existence of any Jewish State—that is, before the coming of the Messiah," Matthias said, rolling his eyes.

"Now *there's* a title, you two—*Before the Coming of the Fucking Messiah*," Jolanda exhorted Mieke and Jimmy.

Jimmy had a feeling he would hear more from Jolanda before he left for Israel. While he was away, Jolanda and Mieke would be coming to New Hampshire. They could stay in Jimmy's room; Mieke would write there during the day. The two Dutch women could spend more time with Vienna. Jimmy also knew the Winslow sisters were looking forward to having Mieke and Jolanda to themselves while he was in Jerusalem. "The house will be full of girls!" Vienna Winslow had happily cried.

"Nowadays, I'm the only boy who's ever here," Jimmy reminded them. He was forty. Vienna had not brought a boy home from school—not yet.

When Jimmy was packing for Jerusalem, his mom was more talkative than usual about Esther. Jimmy's aunts were drawn into the conversation, which was more about Esther's hiddenness than it was about anything new. Naturally, Vienna was interested in hearing more about Esther, too.

Jimmy's mother began with a story about a rabbi—she'd talked to a rabbi about the biblical Esther, the queen who hides her Jewish identity. "God does not appear in the Esther of the Christian Old Testament or in the Esther of the Hebrew Bible—even God is hidden, Jimmy," Honor said.

"The queen our Esther is named for—I know who you mean," Jimmy assured his mom. (As if any Winslow didn't know *that*.)

"In the holiday of Purim, when the Jews read the Scroll of Esther, they wear masks to hide their faces—more hiding, Jimmy," Faith told him. She didn't say if she'd talked to the same rabbi, or to a different one.

"Passover is the next big Jewish holiday after Purim. A symbolic piece of matzoh is hidden at the start of the Seder meal—you can't finish the Seder until the matzoh is revealed. Passover is like a bridge from hiddenness to revelation, Jimmy," Hope had added. (Jimmy *knew*, heaven knows!)

"It's forty-nine days until Shavuot—the Jewish holiday that celebrates the revelation of the Torah on Mt. Sinai, Jimmy," Prudence said.

"Sure as shit, *our* Esther isn't a rabbi girl—the Torah isn't *her* occupation!" Vienna cried, sounding more like Prudence than Prudence.

"Our Esther *is* Queen Esther—she's *that* Esther, Vienna," Honor said. "But just remember, Jimmy—a Nacht will always be a Nacht."

James Winslow knew the *Nacht* warning was nothing a rabbi imparted to his mother. He should have known those Winslow sisters weren't done with warning him. "Remember our Esther's Charlotte Brontë business, Jimmy," Faith was the first to say.

"Our Esther will show you her *Jane Eyre* tattoo," Hope told him.

"Don't forget our Esther's no-bra business, Jimmy," Prudence said.

"Don't gross me out—a seventy-six-year-old woman with no bra won't show her birth child *all* of that tattoo!" Vienna Winslow declared.

"You don't know Esther, Vienna," Honor said, unbuttoning the top two buttons of her shirt—using only her left hand, the way the one-armed Esther would have to do it. When Honor unbuttoned a third button, you could see her collarbones and the topmost part of her bra. "The *I care for myself* and *The more solitary* are above Esther's breasts—let's hope that's all she shows you, Jimmy," his mom said. He knew the Charlotte Brontë quotation, for heaven's sake. Jimmy just hoped he would see Esther, tattoo or no tattoo; he didn't know if she would choose to see him.

"If you see Esther, Jimmy, I'll bet her shirt's untucked," Faith said. The last two lines of the *Jane Eyre* tattoo were below Esther's belly button, Jimmy knew—both *the more I will* and the *respect myself.* Faith, Hope, and Prudence bet Esther would show him her belly—not the top of her breasts.

"Esther will show you *something*, Jimmy—if you see her," Honor said. What would stay with Jimmy, all the way to Jerusalem, was the business about *a Nacht will always be a Nacht.*

But why was a trip—to somewhere he'd never been—making him so *nostalgic*? James Winslow would wonder. Was this part of his being a fiction writer? Of course, he'd *imagined* going to Jerusalem before—too many times. Even the travel arrangements made Jimmy nostalgic. He'd considered a connecting flight from Vienna to Tel Aviv. It might be fun to spend a night or two in Vienna—or so Jimmy thought, before he mentioned this idea to Mieke and Jolanda.

"Jesus and the gang—don't you remember, Jimmy?" Jolanda asked him on the phone. "In Wien kann man keinen Spaß haben," she told him. ("In Vienna, you can't have fun.") Jimmy vaguely remembered the Viennese expression; it was something Irmgard would say, sarcastically. Knowing Jolanda, she just might have meant he couldn't have fun in Vienna without her and Mieke.

As it turned out, his connecting flight to Tel Aviv was from Frankfurt. A layover in Germany wasn't nostalgic. In April 1981, when Jimmy went to Jerusalem, he was marginally aware of the trouble in Lebanon. He knew the Lebanese Civil War was ongoing. He'd heard there were PLO bases and Syrian forces in Lebanon. "A war with Lebanon is coming," Matthias said.

"The Golan Heights will forever be a problem" Gabrielle had added.

In early April Jimmy rode in the car with Matthias from Tel Aviv to Jerusalem. Jimmy was embarrassed that he didn't know where the Golan was in relation to Lebanon and Syria. This set Matthias off on the subject of what Prime Minister Begin might do about the Syrian forces in Lebanon. Jimmy couldn't contribute to this conversation in any meaningful way. He just lamely commented that the book fair started on April 7.

What James Winslow wanted to say was that he didn't know who he was. He might be Honor's child, but he didn't feel like a Winslow. If he wasn't Jewish, who was he? He couldn't even imagine how it felt to be a Jew. When he arrived at the American Colony Hotel, Jimmy said nothing about not knowing who he was to Matthias and Gabrielle. Those two Jews knew James Winslow well, but they knew his writing best.

The American Colony was like a European hotel. It had a Swedish sauna, which Jimmy went to in the late afternoon. There were two swimming pools. The bougainvillea was climbing the walls all around There is no spring to speak of in New Hampshire, but spring comes early to Jerusalem. Jimmy was late joining his European publishers for dinner. He didn't know if they were in the main dining room of the hotel or on the patio with the fountain. Jimmy knew they must have started with some wine, because Gabrielle's laughter led him to them. She had a lighthearted laugh when she'd had a glass or two of wine.

It wasn't the first time his European Jewish publishers were laughing about Jimmy's Israeli publisher. He'd not met Yehuda; now Jimmy learned he wouldn't meet him. Yehuda was famous for his remoteness; he kept his distance from his authors who weren't Israelis. He had been known to delegate an editorial assistant to deal with his *foreign* authors.

Matthias had assured Jimmy it was a good house with a good list of authors. Even so, at the Frankfurt Book Fair, Matthias had heard the house was facing a buyout from a bigger, better publishing house. Gabrielle told Jimmy that Yehuda had a standoffish relationship with the Jerusalem book fair. "Yehuda believes the book fair should bear the burden of hosting their international writers. Maybe Yehuda thinks God forbids Israeli publishers from hosting their *foreign* authors," Gabrielle said, in her serene way.

No one had met Anat, the editorial assistant. "I'm sure she's good. Yehuda delegates *everything* to his editorial assistants—he picks good ones," Matthias said. A German-born Jew, Matthias was more interested in James Winslow's Hebrew translator—a very good one. Yaakov Himmelman had translated *Roommates in Vienna,* and now he was translating *Not an Egyptian.* There was a lot of German in those two Vienna novels, and Yaakov knew German.

Matthias thought Jimmy should know that Yaakov was an Austrian-born Jew who'd been a prisoner at the Mauthausen concentration camp in Upper Austria. At first the prisoners were all men—Germans and Austrians—and then, during the second half of the war, Mauthausen had women prisoners, too. Mauthausen was a forced-labor camp; the gas chamber wasn't used until 1942. The prisoners at Mauthausen were forced to work in the granite quarries, Matthias told Jimmy, and the Hebrew translator had once carried stones on what were called the "stairs of death." Often men collapsed under the weight of these heavy stones, crushing the prisoners who followed them up from the quarry. The U.S. Army had liberated Mauthausen in 1945, when Yaakov Himmelman was thirty-two. His American liberators were the reason he had wanted to learn English.

Gabrielle had calmly done the math. Yaakov Himmelman would be sixty-eight now. "But back to Anat, James—she's the one overseeing Himmelman's translation of *Not an Egyptian,*" Gabrielle said. She'd talked to Anat on the phone; the assistant's English was better than Yehuda's.

Gabrielle found much to admire in Anat's "outspokenness"—about the army and Israeli society. Anat had recently finished her military service; she had "miserable memories" of that time, Gabrielle told them.

"It is not uncommon to have 'miserable memories' of that time in one's life," Matthias said, in his dour way.

Gabrielle was more measured than Matthias; yet she could also be more exact. Gabrielle told them that Anat had served as a journalist in the army; she'd participated in basic training, in guarding missions, in kitchen duties. Anat told Gabrielle that she'd had "an excellent position with much freedom"; yet Anat had described the environment in the army, and in Israeli society, as "sexist, militarist, and brutal." Gabrielle saved for last what Anat had said about "today's secular society"—how it was "slipping away." All this made Jimmy happy to meet Anat; to a forty-year-old, Anat sounded young and rebellious.

Where Jimmy walked with Anat, from the American Colony Hotel to the Old City, he liked best the chaotic food places on The Prophets Street—nearest to the Damascus Gate, where they entered the Old City Wall into the Muslim Quarter. The rest of the twenty-minute walk was easy but unmemorable. The American Colony itself was more memorable. In the late nineteenth century, an American Christian family had founded it. They were joined by Swedes from the U.S. and Sweden. The hotel had the reputation of being politically neutral; Jews and Arabs could comfortably meet there. Jimmy would remember the patios—the one with the gazebo, and the better one with the fountain. The ceramic-topped tables were Armenian. Although James Winslow was just a beer drinker, he would remember the wine cellar with the see-through iron doors—off the main dining room with its white tablecloths.

One of the round tables for four was perfect for Jimmy and his two favorite European publishers. Every morning those European Jews and Jimmy hoped that Anat would join them for breakfast. She never did; she either skipped breakfast or had already eaten when she showed up to take Jimmy to his Hebrew translator in the Jewish Quarter of the Old City.

In Anat's opinion, the American Colony was "more cool"—even "more super cool"—than the King David Hotel. It was definitely "more international," Anat had said. She often joined Jimmy and his European Jewish publishers in the evenings in the cellar bar of the American Colony, which was very popular at night. It was downstairs from the main dining room and the patio with the fountain. The curved arc of the bar's low ceiling reminded you that you were in a cellar. There were cozy, connected nooks with comfy furniture.

Jimmy loved his morning walks with Anat through the Damascus Gate into the Muslim Quarter. Anat explained that they could have gone more directly past the Church of the Holy Sepulchre in the Christian Quarter, on their way to the Jewish Quarter of the Old City. They could stay on Khan Ez-Zeit—rather than staying on El Wad, the road from the Damascus Gate to the Via Dolorosa. But Anat wanted Jimmy to see the Christian pilgrims following the Way of Sorrows, where Christ carried the cross to be crucified. Besides, Khan Ez-Zeit was the main market street of the Old City. Jimmy could tell Anat was impatient to pass by the more aggressive sellers in their bazaars; the aggressive ones resembled hawkers.

It was also clear to Anat that Jimmy was a fellow nonbeliever; they both enjoyed seeing the zealousness of the Christian tourists, kneeling (even weeping) at the Fifth Station of the Cross on the Via Dolorosa. There were more cats in evidence on the main market street, Khan Ez-Zeit—as if the cats were disturbed by the praying (sometimes wailing) Christian pilgrims. It took no time to pass from the Muslim to the Christian Quarter, by either route. They always ended up where the worshipful Christians were going—where Christ ended up, at the Church of the Holy Sepulchre. Even in the morning, there was a line of Christians waiting their turn to kneel (or pray, or wail) at Christ's tomb. Jimmy admitted to Anat that he was curious to see the tomb.

"Maybe one afternoon, when we're walking back," Anat said. Yet after the first three days of wending their labyrinthine way through the Old City—the Muslim Quarter, to the Christian Quarter, to the Jewish Quarter, and back again—even Jimmy knew there were usually *more* Christian tourists in line in the afternoons.

Walking with Anat from the Church of the Holy Sepulchre, they sometimes took Muristan Road, entering the Jewish Quarter on David Street, where they turned left—then a right, on Jewish Quarter Street. Less frequently, Anat would take him past the Church of the Holy Sepulchre to Christian Quarter Road, where (once again) they turned left on David Street to Jewish Quarter Street—a longer walk past the bazaars on David Street. Maybe these were the mornings when Anat had more to say—or she was more outspoken than usual. Jimmy was just trying to learn what was what.

On Jewish Quarter Street, Anat took her time. She felt more at home there; she made more eye contact with the people passing by. There was a left turn on Lokhamei Ha-Rova Be Tashakh—"Street of the Fighters for the Quarter in 1948," Anat had translated for him. This brought them to what Anat called "the ruin square." This was the ruin of the Hurva Synagogue. "It was destroyed by the Jordanians in 1948," Anat had told him. (Sometimes she said "razed" or "bombed" instead of "destroyed.") For reasons Anat didn't explain to Jimmy, the synagogue had been left in ruins—even after the reunification of Jerusalem following the Six-Day War.

There was a narrow, almost hidden apartment building, where Yaakov Himmelman had a second-floor walk-up at the junction of two small streets off the ruin square. HaUgav—"The Harp," Anat told Jimmy. Bonei HaHoma—"Builders of the Wall," Anat had said. From Yaakov's apartment, Anat explained, they were nearest to the Zion Gate in the Old City Wall, but Jimmy understood they would return to the American Colony the way they'd come—through the Jewish Quarter, to the Christian Quarter, and the Muslim Quarter, to the Damascus

Gate in the Old City Wall. The Jerusalem Jimmy saw seemed like such a peaceful place.

Jimmy admired his Hebrew translator's diligent attention to detail; he also loved listening to the man's Viennese accent, in German and in English. Yaakov never laughed; yet he demonstrated an affection for those parts of *Not an Egyptian* that were funny. Jimmy also grew fond of Yaakov's Palestinian housekeeper, Naur, and her five-year-old son, Omar. Nour always wore a hijab. She kept herself busy, cleaning Yaakov's apartment or preparing food. Jimmy assumed that his Hebrew translator had taught his housekeeper and her son some English. After all, translating from English was Yaakov's work. Yet, even as Nour got used to Jimmy working with Yaakov at the kitchen table, there was no conversation between Nour and Jimmy. Only a few words of English were exchanged between Jimmy and Omar. The five-year-old liked to bring Jimmy an object—a spoon, a ballpoint pen, the case for Yaakov's glasses. Jimmy said the name for the object in English. Omar was very excited to repeat the word.

The kitchen table, where Jimmy and Yaakov worked on the translation of *Not an Egyptian,* was very long. There was no dining room in the apartment; this was Yaakov's only table. When Nour and Omar were in the kitchen, it was Jimmy's impression that they were listening to his conversation with Yaakov—Nour certainly was. When Jimmy and Yaakov were working, Nour and Omar were always there.

Yaakov Himmelman's devotion to translating *Not an Egyptian* endeared him to Jimmy, but Yaakov wouldn't be drawn into extraneous conversation, particularly not of a political kind. James Winslow wondered if Yaakov's silence was characteristic of concentration camp survivors, but Jimmy felt it would be incorrect of him to ask his European Jewish publishers or Anat. Yet because Jimmy trusted Yaakov's sensibilities, Jimmy kept asking Yaakov what he thought of something Jimmy had been told. Matthias and Gabrielle were always saying something to Jimmy of a political nature, and Anat was very outspoken. There were also things Jimmy's interviewers asked him or said to him. Jimmy was constantly seeking Yaakov's opinion—to no avail. This was the Yaakov who knew and understood Jimmy's *writing* so well. It was frustrating that this same Yaakov would not respond to Jimmy's inquiries of a more contemporary kind.

Nour certainly overheard all these political questions. Yet when Yaakov and Nour spoke to each other, it was in Arabic. Yaakov had explained to Jimmy that he couldn't be a good translator of Jimmy's English into Hebrew without knowing Arabic, too. The dialogue between Jimmy's characters was often profane—or vulgar, or sexually explicit. There were no Hebrew words for what Yaakov called "these unmentionable things." In a Hebrew translation, the words for such things were Arabic, Yaakov told Jimmy. That Yaakov must have taught Nour and Omar some words in English was most imaginable to Jimmy, but he had no grounds for thinking Nour could understand English—much less that she could speak it.

From the translation trips he'd taken as an author, James Winslow had learned to write down what people said in a small notebook. In Israel, he'd written down those things Matthias and Gabrielle had said—and what Anat told him. When he repeated them to Yaakov Himmelman, he read them verbatim from his small notebook. This was an excessively fastidious thing to do, but Jimmy was a *writer,* after all—he wanted to be *literal* in what he quoted to his esteemed Hebrew translator.

"When people talk about the Israelis *displacing* the Palestinians, they make it sound as if this was *always* and *only* the land of the Palestinian people," Gabrielle had said to him. "As if the Land of Israel never previously existed, as if the Jews hadn't been murdered here, and exiled from here—for *centuries* before there was a Mandatory Palestine," Gabrielle had added.

"When people speak this way, they're taking a very short view of the *long* history of the Jews in the Land of Israel—long before the twentieth century," Matthias had pointed out. He was the one who'd escaped with his family from Germany to Sweden. Of Jimmy's two European Jewish publishers, Matthias was the one who insisted on the importance of peace and reconciliation with the Palestinian people; what he called "the ominous consequences of the settlements" weighed on him. Yet Jimmy had heard even Matthias say, "If the Palestinians insist on killing us—on *eliminating* us—we will have to kill more of them than they kill of us, or they will kill us all."

"We Jews just went back where we *came from,*" Gabrielle repeated.

"The Jewish Diaspora began in the eighth and six centuries B.C.—and if you've read Exodus, you might remember Moses leading the Israelites from slavery in Egypt long before then," Matthias said, as if reciting in school. (He was a student when he'd fled to Sweden from Germany.)

"A basic premise of anti-Zionism is false," Anat told Jimmy; she didn't beat around the bush. "Those Sephardic and Ashkenazi Jews—those Jews from the Middle East, and from Europe—were going *home*. Once upon a time, the Land of Israel was their homeland. Now it's ours," Anat had said.

Matthias reminded them of the intractable pain to both sides caused by the eternal conflict. "Reconciliation with the Palestinian people is the only path to peace," Matthias said. With Matthias, there was always a long pause. Then he said: "We share this little land with the Palestinians, but if we don't maintain some measure of control over them, they will kill us all."

This was the refrain Jimmy kept hearing. "If we don't . . . they will . . ."

Was this Israel's constant echo? James Winslow wondered. He knew his European Jewish publishers were leftists. He was aware they'd criticized Begin's right-wing Likud government for accelerating the settlements in the West Bank. The Likud government had declared "the right of the Jewish people to Eretz Yisrael." Did this mean the entire historic Land of Israel was the inalienable heritage of the Jewish people?

As Jimmy's leftist publishers explained to him, there might already be such a Jewish presence in the West Bank and the Gaza Strip that Palestinian self-determination could be more difficult to achieve. "A two-state solution to the Israeli-Palestinian conflict could slip away," Gabrielle had said in her measured way.

Jimmy was confused. He grew up with great empathy for the Zionists who'd led the persecuted Jews from Europe (and elsewhere) back to the Land of Israel. Now the Jews called Zionists were linked to the settlements—to the Israeli-occupied territories. This sounded a little like racial segregation to Jimmy, who was reminded of the civil rights struggle in the United States. His European Jewish publishers and Anat dismissed this analogy. Yet Anat didn't hold herself back about the "settler vigilantism in Hebron," and what she called "illegal activities" perpetrated by settlers against local Palestinians in the West Bank—not to mention the "overly harsh suppression" of any Palestinian pushback. This still sounded a little like a segregation issue to Jimmy, but what did a New Hampshire boy know about politics in Israel?

Then there was the interview Jimmy did with an Israeli journalist at the King David Hotel. "Why would James Winslow ever come to Israel?" the reporter challenged him. *You're not even Jewish,* the guy seemed to be saying, or so Jimmy imagined; he was having second thoughts about why he'd come.

"Well, the book fair *invited* me," Jimmy began. He said he was working with his Hebrew translator on *Not an Egyptian,* which would soon be published there. Jimmy ventured to say that he'd always been a supporter of Israel and the Jewish people. This last bit seemed to provoke or irritate the Israeli journalist more.

It was easy for the "fuckhead," as Anat called the reporter, to find a subject that exposed James Winslow's ignorance of Israel.

The guy asked Jimmy for his thoughts concerning the disputed origins and various usages of the phrase "from the water to the water," or "from the river to the sea." Jimmy had no idea what the guy was fishing for. It sounded like a setup—even to Jimmy, who was just a New Hampshire boy.

"Please ask me about my *writing*—if you've read any of my novels," James Winslow said. "I was invited to the book fair because of my *writing*."

Anat called the editor of the Israeli newspaper to complain. "In the first place," Anat told Jimmy, "I'd said no interviewers who haven't read your novels—at least one of them. This fuckhead *never* reads novels. What this fuckhead asked you was predicated on making you look bad. There's no way you can talk about 'from the water to the water,' or 'from the river to the sea,' without offending *someone*," Anat said to Jimmy.

"It's toxic—no matter who says it, or how you say it," Gabrielle said. "It can seem anti-Semitic *or* anti-Palestinian," she told Jimmy.

"From the Jordan River to the Mediterranean Sea means the entirety of what was called Mandatory Palestine, if you're Palestinian—or the whole of the Land of Israel, if you're Israeli," Matthias said, pausing.

In 1977, Matthias told them, the election manifesto of the right-wing Likud party had declared: "Between the sea and the Jordan there will only be Israeli sovereignty." The Israeli journalist was definitely a troublemaker.

"I get it," was all James Winslow could say.

"You may *hear* it, just don't *say* it. 'From the river to the sea' can mean they will drive us *into* the sea—meaning they will *annihilate* us," Anat said.

In contrast to the American Colony, according to Anat, the King David Hotel was associated with "the establishment." She meant that the King David was a symbol of "Israeliness"—it was constructed "under the British Mandate." His only experience with the King David was the Reading Room, off the lobby. Jimmy never understood why some of his interviews took place there. An imposing Oriental rug was under the huge center table, often festooned with flowers. The painted ceiling was adorned with the Star of David. On the beige-colored walls were four menorah candelabras. The seven-branched candles of the temple menorahs shed little light on the ominously dark room. Squat, upholstered chairs surrounded small, marble-topped tables. There were long curtains draping the windows. It could have been night or day outside; you'd never know. The dim lighting might make it a challenge to *read* in the Reading Room, or so Jimmy had imagined. The room's somber colors and the dim light made Jimmy's interviews at the King David feel like interrogations.

Thinking of interrogations, Jimmy was wondering about the soldiers. Young men and boys, young women and girls—their uniforms and their weapons were noticeable. Jimmy had questions about the soldiers, but he was sensitive to Anat's "miserable memories" of her time in the IDF. A few times, when Anat was busy with her other publishing responsibilities, a couple of young soldiers took Jimmy through the Old City to his Hebrew translator, or the soldiers walked with him back to the Damascus Gate—from which he knew his way to the American Colony. Jimmy had asked two women soldiers about their duties in the IDF; they sounded disappointed when they said women were mostly restricted to administrative jobs.

Anat was angry she'd been replaced by soldiers—they weren't her idea. Her boss, Yehudah, whom no one liked, had told Anat that the "one-armed one" had requested the soldiers. As Anat understood, despite Esther's opposition to Begin's expansion of Jewish settlements in the occupied territories, she had the prime minister's ear.

"But there's no need for a *writer* to be escorted by soldiers in the Old City!" Anat exclaimed to Jimmy. He'd noticed the soldiers who appeared to be on guard duty at the International Convention Center, where the book fair was. Some of the soldiers attending the book fair events were without their rifles; Jimmy wondered if the unarmed soldiers weren't on duty, but he didn't want to provoke Anat by asking her about the soldiers. Anat knew that Esther Nacht was Jimmy's birth mother—both the former nanny and a close friend of Honor Winslow.

This was only a scandal to the terrible townspeople of Pennacook. To everyone else, especially to James Winslow's publishers, it was a good story.

The International Convention Center was connected by a long, outdoor corridor to a tall Hilton Hotel. From midafternoon—through the late afternoon and into early evening—there was a wind blowing through the palm trees at the main entrance to the convention center. In the main hall—Ussishkin Hall, where Jimmy had his onstage interview—he noted the horseshoe-shaped balcony above and surrounding the stage, and the utilitarian sturdiness of the seats. "Typical modern architecture of the fifties—simple, humble, but above all *ugly*," Anat had said.

Anat spoke of the fifties as if they'd happened centuries ago and were accordingly outdated. A floor below the hall was the agents' center and the exhibition areas, where the various publishers had their stalls of books. After Jimmy's main event at the book fair—this being his onstage interview—Jimmy's book signing was in his Israeli publisher's exhibition space. To have an autographing session in the midst of his publisher's stalls of books contributed a kind of chaos—reminiscent to Jimmy of the traffic around Jerusalem's central bus station, across from the convention center. The *ugly* modern architecture of the fifties was certainly not Anat's only criticism of the convention center, where she declared the crimson carpeting "simply awful."

Anat didn't accompany Jimmy to all his events at the book fair. She'd skipped a panel discussion Jimmy had with other authors, his onstage interview in Ussishkin Hall, and the book signing afterward. From the convention center, there was always someone returning to the American Colony Hotel—or there were two of Esther's soldiers. James Winslow's onstage interview drew a big audience, and there was a long line of readers at his book signing. Many people brought their own copies of books to be signed—some in English or in European languages.

The bookseller was happy, but she was impatient to keep the line moving forward; a bossy, domineering woman, she stopped conversations of any duration in the signing line. The unfamiliar Hebrew names were hard for Jimmy to spell, and some of the more complicated inscriptions readers asked for required clarification. A young salesman for the Israeli publisher offered pencils and paper to the readers in the signing line. "*Spell* your name—*write out* any inscriptions!" the bossy bookseller kept shouting in English and Hebrew.

Jimmy didn't notice the blond, blue-eyed soldier until he was next in line at the book signing. The book the young soldier held out for Jimmy to sign was an English-language edition of *Roommates in Vienna*.

"Eissler, Siegfried Eissler—you know how to spell it," the young soldier told Jimmy. "And you know what the inscription should be," Siegfried said. He had a deep, resonant voice. Siegfried was about the age Jimmy had been when they first met, garlic press and all. When Jimmy stood up from the signing table to hug him, the writer was aware that he was eye-level to the breast pockets of the tall soldier's uniform.

"Hard Rain is a woman!" they shouted to each other, which is what Jimmy wrote in Siegfried's copy of *Roommates in Vienna*. Jimmy was "James" to everyone in the writing world, but he wrote "Jimmy" when he signed Siegfried's book. James Winslow knew he was still a *Yimmy* to Siegfried.

Fräulein Eissler had adopted Siegfried before his mother died—when Irmgard was in her forties. (*Of what* Irmgard died, Siegfried wouldn't say.) Because of Annelies, Siegfried was Jewish now; he lived full-time in Israel. Siegfried said he wouldn't go back to Austria again; Israel was his home. Hard Rain was gone, and Siegfried didn't mention his grandmother. Jimmy just assumed Frau Holzinger had passed away.

"And how is Annelies?" Jimmy asked Siegfried. His fellow soldiers were standing close to him, the way young friends do. It surprised Jimmy when Siegfried leaned over him and whispered in his ear, as if Siegfried had something to say that he didn't want his comrades-in-arms to hear.

"Annelies told me, Yimmy—I knew Esther Nacht gave birth to you, before everyone knew. The one-armed one is *inside you,* Yimmy!" Siegfried whispered. Why was Esther such a damn secret? James Winslow wondered. Now Jimmy was whispering to Siegfried, too.

"I don't know if I'll see her when I'm here, or if she *wants* to see me," Jimmy whispered. "I don't even know how she lost her arm in Lebanon!" he said to Siegfried, his voice rising.

"No one knows how she lost her arm—no one asks," Siegfried said, not whispering now. There was something of the soldier's rigidity of training in his voice. "The story I tell myself, Yimmy, is that the angels asked Esther if they could have her arm, and Esther gave it to them."

"Seriously, dear Siegfried—is this what you believe?" Jimmy asked the good soldier.

"I don't believe in God, just in angels—your Esther is our angel, dear Yimmy," Siegfried said.

One of the soldiers standing closest to Siegfried was a young, pretty woman—as tall as Siegfried. "Your Esther is *Israel's* angel, Mr. Winslow," she said.

James Winslow knew that it must have been Annelies, the good tutor, who'd made Siegfried a reader. Jimmy tried to say that, from his perspective, there was something more mythical than actual about Esther. Like a literary character, didn't the one-armed one seem more symbolic than real? Jimmy asked Siegfried.

"If you *see* her, Yimmy, her missing arm will be real—not symbolic," Siegfried said.

"I'm also hoping I see Annelies—if she's in Jerusalem," Jimmy said. He knew Siegfried had tried to steer him away from the Annelies subject.

Fräulein Eissler had maintained her IDF connections. In 1967, she'd served as an interpreter in the Six-Day War, and Siegfried said she was in the Sinai in 1973, during the Yom Kippur War—when Siegfried would have been eight and fourteen respectively. "She was good at languages, as I know you know," Siegfried said, with sudden awkwardness.

That was when Jimmy knew she was gone. "She was so glad you got to be what you wanted to be," the tall soldier told Jimmy, with no hint of his birth mother's cynicism.

There was not much of a signing line left, but the bossy bookseller was agitated with Jimmy and Siegfried—their conversation was holding things up. Siegfried's comrades-in-arms were among those in the line.

"What happened to Annelies?" Jimmy asked her adopted son. The same tall woman soldier—the prettiest one—squeezed Siegfried's hand.

It had happened in Hebron, in the West Bank, where Annelies was working as a mediator—what people who are good at languages do. "It was a roadside bomb, a car bomb," Siegfried said. Some Palestinian children had been curious about the abandoned car. Fräulein Eissler must have believed the kids were too close to the car; she'd made them move away. Yet there'd been something about the car that drew Annelies to take a closer look.

James Winslow told Siegfried where he was staying and gave him a number he could reach him at. They talked about having dinner—or just breakfast, if dinner didn't work out. Jimmy didn't doubt that Siegfried Eissler was a young man with lots of options. *Don't be afraid of the telescope—only the passage of time sees into the future!* Jimmy almost said to him. But the soldier resembled Annelies, the singular woman who'd saved him; like Annelies, the tall and handsome soldier knew how to move on.

As suddenly as Siegfried had shown up, the blue-eyed one and his comrades-in-arms disappeared. James Winslow had calculated that the young soldier must have been twenty-two or twenty-three. *He won't call me—we won't have dinner, or even breakfast,* Jimmy knew, as certainly as he knew Fräulein Eissler was gone.

Naturally, Jimmy told his Hebrew translator, Yaakov Himmelman, all about encountering Siegfried—the Austrian boy who'd been the inspiration for *Roommates in Vienna*. "Die Vergangenheit ist nicht Siegfrieds Freundin," Yaakov told Jimmy. ("The past is not Siegfried's friend," Yaakov had said.)

Jimmy knew that Yaakov had been a prisoner at Mauthausen concentration camp and had been forced to transport stones on the "stairs of death." Jimmy understood that the past wasn't Yaakov's friend, either.

One time, when Jimmy and Yaakov were working on the translation of *Not an Egyptian,* Yaakov took a bathroom break—as he often did when Jimmy sought his opinion of the current situation in Israel. Yaakov was still in the bathroom when Omar brought Jimmy the rock.

The five-year-old needed both hands to carry such a heavy stone. "*Stone,*" Jimmy said, and Omar studiously repeated the word *stone*. Not a souvenir from Mauthausen, James Winslow had hoped. "Maybe Omar should put this back where he found it," Jimmy said to Nour, handing her the stone. She seemed to understand him, or perhaps Nour just knew—as cleaning women do—where everything belonged.

After his encounter with Siegfried, now a full-grown man, it was hard for Jimmy to get used to being a "James" again, but he was always that to everyone who knew him as a writer, including Nour and Omar. Just to be sure, Omar liked to point at Jimmy—as if Jimmy were an unnamed object Omar had found. "*James,*" Jimmy told Omar, who laughed when he repeated the funny-sounding name.

"*Yames,*" Omar usually said first, before he said the name correctly.

Then there was the day Jimmy repeated to Yaakov something that Anat had told him. He'd been frustrated by the *them* and *us* designations his European Jewish publishers gave to the Palestinians and the Israelis. Anat was frustrated with the Europeans for another reason. The Israeli policy was not to call them Palestinians, Anat told him—thereby not acknowledging that Palestinians had national identity.

Jimmy admitted to Anat that he was uncomfortable with the way the Israelis *restrained* the Palestinians. He'd asked Anat if this restraint didn't amount to *suppression* or *repression* of the Palestinians.

"You can call it 'suppression' or 'repression' if you want to, James," Anat had told him. "But if we don't restrain them, they will drive us into the sea—they will *annihilate* us," Anat said.

This was what Jimmy repeated to Yaakov Himmelman. Yaakov took another bathroom break, his response to Anat's "If we don't . . . they will . . ." Jimmy just sat at the long table in the kitchen, where Nour and Omar were watching him. Nour looked like she wanted to say something, or so Jimmy thought, but there were no words between them. There was nothing in Omar's hands—no object for Jimmy to name, no name for Omar to repeat.

It was one of those days when a couple of soldiers were supposed to fill in for Anat, who was busy, but no soldiers showed up. Yaakov explained it to Nour in Arabic. "It's not difficult for Nour and Omar to take you through the Old City to the Damascus Gate—to where you know your way back to the American Colony," Yaakov told Jimmy. Walking with Nour and Omar delighted Jimmy. They were the only Palestinians he knew, and they were wonderful. Omar held Jimmy's hand, not his mother's.

It was Omar, not Jimmy, who noticed there were no Christians in line outside the Church of the Holy Sepulchre—waiting their turn to kneel (or pray, or wail) at Christ's tomb. Omar had dropped Jimmy's hand; the boy was tugging on his mother's hand now, beseeching her to do something. "Omar wants to see where Jesus died. Jesus is dead in there," Nour said to Jimmy.

"I know—I want to see Christ's tomb, too," Jimmy told her. They went into the cool darkness of the church together. The darkness made Omar hold Jimmy's hand again. The towering height of the dome of the church made them look up at the skylight above them. The sobbing Christian surprised them; he was already crying when he came inside the church, and he didn't hesitate to enter Christ's cavelike tomb. Omar had questions for his mother about the sobbing Christian. The candle-light in the darkened tomb did not make the weeping Christian visible. They all heard him cry out, more loudly, just before he emerged from the tomb—his face streaked with tears, his smile radiant.

"Jesus *touched* me—I felt him *touch* me!" the lunatic Christian cried.

Nour needed to reassure Omar more; the five-year-old didn't want to enter the tomb. The sobbing Christian had left the Church of the Holy Sepulchre, still claiming he'd been touched by Jesus.

When Jimmy cautiously entered the tomb, Nour and Omar didn't follow. It may only have been in Jimmy's imagination that the candle-light flickered at the same moment the cat brushed against his leg. The cat's plaintive yowl made Omar and his mother laugh. The cat and Jimmy came out of Christ's tomb together. It was a warm afternoon in the Old City; one of a hundred cats was seeking and had found some-where cool and dark.

"Not Jesus," Jimmy said to Omar, who perfectly repeated it. Omar didn't say *Yesus* the first time; the boy had gone straight to the *Jesus*.

"Not Jesus," Nour had also repeated—the three of them laughing.

When they got to the Damascus Gate, where Jimmy knew the rest of the way, he had to restrain himself from hugging Nour. Anat had warned him not to be too familiar. "Her hijab means you should re-spect her, you shouldn't even look at her closely—her hijab means she is modest in the presence of a man who isn't her husband or a blood relation," Anat said. The way her hijab haloed Nour's head gave her a saintly or a holy presence, or so Jimmy thought. They had an awkward goodbye at the Damascus Gate.

"And we *will*," Nour said quietly.

"And you will *what*?" Jimmy asked her.

"We will drive them into the sea—we *will*," Nour told him.

"We *will*," Omar repeated, beaming at Jimmy.

"We will *annihilate* them," Nour said, hitting all four syllables.

This was what Esther had been protecting him from, James Winslow realized—this eternal conflict, this everlasting hatred. When Nour turned away from Jimmy, she wasn't smiling. Omar was still beaming when he called out, getting the *James* right the first time. The five-year-old pointed at Jimmy—the way Omar had pointed at the stone Yaakov might have carried with him from those stairs of death at Mauthausen.

After what she said at the Damascus Gate, Nour wouldn't speak to Jimmy. She stayed out of the kitchen when Yaakov and Jimmy were at work on the translation. For the most part, Omar stayed close to his mom. When Omar ventured into the kitchen alone, it was usually when Yaakov went to the bathroom and Omar had an object for Jimmy to name. James Winslow would remember one such object, a framed, black-and-white photo of Yaakov in his early twenties—before Mauthausen. The older couple must have been Yaakov's parents; the two girls were Yaakov's younger sisters. Jimmy knew their stories; they died in other concentration camps, not Mauthausen. The children died at Dachau, the parents at Auschwitz—or the other way around. It pained Anat that Jimmy couldn't keep straight who died where.

"*Family,*" Jimmy said, and Omar repeated the *family* word. Nour must have heard the word, because she quickly came to take the family photo and put it back—perhaps on the night table at Yaakov's bedside, where a photo of such tragic magnitude belonged. (Or so James Winslow believed; he was just guessing where Yaakov kept that family photo.)

There was one last book signing, in a chain bookstore on Jaffa Street, a Steimatzky's—or this was what Jimmy thought Anat had said. Anat wasn't with him. The one-armed one had arranged for a couple of soldiers to see he got safely back to the American Colony. The bookstore had his backlist titles, in Hebrew and English—even *The Dickens Man* was there—although James Winslow was mostly signing copies of *Roommates in Vienna.* The aisles between the bookshelves were as labyrinthine as the snakelike signing line. Jimmy knew this was his last chance to see Esther, if she chose to show up.

Wasn't Esther's hiddenness of biblical proportions? Wouldn't Esther keep moving to the end of the signing line? Didn't it suit the one-armed one to be incognito—to be the last in line? Jimmy was resigned to not seeing her, but he still hoped he would—if only to thank her for looking after him and his mom. If only to *hug her,* James Winslow was thinking—provided someone as elusive as Esther would allow herself to be hugged.

Although she was seventy-six, Jimmy had expected Esther to be as invincible as her story. As always, Jimmy noticed the soldiers. Were soldiers inclined to take up the end of a line? Jimmy wondered. It struck him there was no one left in the line who *wasn't* a young soldier. Who knew soldiers were big readers? James Winslow was thinking. Jimmy imagined Esther would still be tall and thin, but her hair was white, Jimmy knew, remembering how her white hair stood out in the photo of her with Prime Minister Begin.

Jimmy saw soldiers who were tall and thin—some of the young women included. Up close, Esther's white hair indeed stood out, but Jimmy didn't see her until she was the next in line. The one-armed one was accompanied by two *very tall* girl soldiers.

"These two will take you to the American Colony," Jimmy's birth mom said. One of the young women was clinging to Esther's remaining left arm. The other tall soldier kept her distance from Esther's missing right arm. When he saw the stump, Jimmy instantly felt a sharp pain in his right arm. He'd been bent over the signing table, autographing a book for one of the young male soldiers, when Esther was suddenly the next in line—she just stood there when the pain made Jimmy drop his signing pen.

The tall girl soldier who'd been hanging on to Esther spoke to Jimmy first. "It happened to me when I saw it—the pain goes away," she told him. The other young woman, who stood apart from Esther's stump, spoke next.

"I feel the pain every time I see it—the pain just subsides," she said.

"Just don't think the pain you feel is *genetic*, Jimmy," Esther told him, laughing at herself—thus inviting the young soldiers to laugh along with her. Even Jimmy laughed a little, although the pain in his right arm was no joke.

Esther was wearing faded blue jeans with an untucked red polo shirt. Jimmy saw the long fingers of her left hand lift the bottom hem of her shirt. Even at her age, the one-armed one had a flat stomach. The last two lines of the *Jane Eyre* quotation were above the waistband of her blue jeans, below her belly button—both *the more I will* and the *respect myself.*

"I'll bet you've read Charlotte Brontë, haven't you?" Esther asked him.

Jimmy knew Esther's story better than he could remember Jane's. When he stood up from the signing table to give Esther a hug, she hugged him so hard (with one arm) that he thought he broke his nose against her breastbone. Jimmy knew firsthand that there would never be a bra for Esther. "It's like Annelies said—you just *are* Jewish. You're a *Jew*, Jimmy," Esther whispered in his ear. "You feel the pain because you're Jewish."

Later, when he was signing books for a whole gang of girl soldiers, the one-armed one stood behind him—her left hand on his right shoulder. Jimmy was relieved she'd not shown him the rest of the *Jane Eyre* quotation.

When Esther leaned over him, to whisper in his ear, he could feel her strong left hand—her long fingers digging into his right arm, which was still hurting. "You know how long I waited to catch up on being Jewish," she whispered. "Please wait to be a Jew until your two moms are dead, Jimmy. But what about your daughter?" Esther asked him. "If somebody loves you—if there's anyone you love—just be a Winslow, Jimmy," Esther told him. "Remember how the townspeople of Pennacook hate your family, Jimmy—just for being Winslows! Isn't their hatred enough? Don't you relish their hatred?" the one-armed one asked him. His signing hand was throbbing.

When the last soldier's book was signed, there were some boy soldiers standing there. Jimmy realized the young men weren't just hanging around because of the young women. No less than the girls, the boy soldiers were enthralled by Esther. All Jimmy could think of was the three-year-old girl who'd been left at the orphanage—her mother murdered by anti-Semites. Here is Queen Esther with her devotees, Jimmy was thinking, when Esther whispered once more in his ear. "Just be a Winslow, Jimmy," she repeated.

That was when the photojournalist, a young man who'd all the while been taking photos, asked Jimmy to tell him Esther's name. The young man spoke English with a German accent. He was an Israeli correspondent, a German photojournalist; he was covering the Jerusalem book fair for a German newspaper, as he explained to Jimmy and to Esther.

"You don't need to know my name, young man," Esther told him. Then the one-armed one repeated herself in German.

"But the resemblance between you and your son is so striking. If my newspaper wants to use one of my shots of the two of you, I'll need to know your name—it won't suffice for me to say you're the author's mother," the young photojournalist said, speaking both to Esther and to Jimmy.

From the uncertain way James Winslow and Esther Nacht stared at each other—as if they'd just now noticed the resemblance between them—the photojournalist imagined he'd made an embarrassing mistake. "Es tut mir leid," the young German said to Esther. ("I'm sorry," he'd said.) "I shouldn't have presumed you were James Winslow's *mother*," the young photographer said. James Winslow was, as he often was, speechless. Had he told the story so many times that he was tired of telling it, or was Jimmy just relishing the hatred of the townspeople of Pennacook?

"Young man," Esther said, taking the photojournalist's right wrist in her unshakeable grip, "James Winslow's mother is a dear friend of mine." Then she released the young German. "This precious boy is Honor's child," Esther said, no less fiercely seizing the wrist of Jimmy's writing hand, like she'd never let him go. They watched the photographer gather up his gear—he took no more pictures of Jimmy with his birth mom. Jimmy couldn't feel his fingers; he believed the blood had stopped circulating to his right hand.

At last, James Winslow knew who he was. Forbidden to be a soldier, he'd not been born to die in a misbegotten war. Jimmy knew he was Honor's child—a daydreaming, woebegone boy with a brave Jewish girl inside him. His right wrist would be bruised by how tightly Esther took hold of him, before she let him go. This was when the New Hampshire boy knew he had the heart of the Winslows' last orphan. The Jewish one was the best one. James Winslow would forever be an ally of Queen Esther.

Acknowledgments

Robbert Ammerlaan

Hannah Brown

Rabbi Michael Cohen

Ornit Cohen-Barak

Dean Cooke

Amy Edelman

Julia Fermentto-Tzaisler

Ari Folman

Anne Freyer

Per Gedin

Khalida Hassan

Kati Hertzsch

Eva Irving

Janet Irving

Gili Izikovich

Jonathan Karp

Diana Kogan

Ada Paldor

Marty Schwartz

Jackie Seow

Alix Shaw

About the Author

JOHN IRVING was born in Exeter, New Hampshire, in 1942. His first novel, *Setting Free the Bears*, was published in 1968, when he was twenty-six. He competed as a wrestler for twenty years and coached wrestling until he was forty-seven. He is a member of the National Wrestling Hall of Fame in Stillwater, Oklahoma.

In 1980, Mr. Irving won a National Book Award for his novel *The World According to Garp*. In 2000, he won the Oscar for Best Adapted Screenplay for *The Cider House Rules*. In 2013, he won a Lambda Literary Award for his novel *In One Person*. Internationally renowned, his novels have been translated into almost forty languages. His all-time bestselling novel, in every language, is *A Prayer for Owen Meany*.

A dual citizen of the United States and Canada, John Irving lives in Toronto. *Queen Esther* is his sixteenth novel.

Discussion Questions

1. "Not enough was known about where those orphans *came from*. With orphans, too much is missing; there's always something you don't know" (page 7). Discuss the importance of familial belonging in *Queen Esther*. What does it mean to "come from" somewhere? How does the novel challenge or uphold your understanding of having a "home"?

2. From the Book of Esther, after which Esther Nacht is named, to Charles Dickens's *Great Expectations*, to Jimmy Winslow's *The Dickens Man*, stories play a major role in *Queen Esther*. Discuss the role of stories and storytelling in the novel. What does it mean to "have a story"? How is the importance of storytelling to Jimmy similar to or different from its importance to Esther? Why do you think Jimmy is attracted to being a storyteller?

3. The threat of Hard Rain's "alleged overreaction to thunderstorms" (page 227) hangs over Jimmy's stay in Vienna. What role does Hard Rain play in *Queen Esther*, and how might we interpret her fear of thunderstorms? Is it significant that, when a thunderstorm does come, Hard Rain *doesn't* "overreact" in the way Jimmy, Claude, and Jolanda have been anticipating?

4. "Hard Rain is a woman" is a phrase repeated several times in *Queen Esther*. It's one of the first things Jolanda teaches Siegfried to say in

English, and it's what Jimmy writes in Siegfried's copy of *Roommates in Vienna* when they meet in Jerusalem. What is the significance of this refrain in the novel?

5. Although Jimmy is a heterosexual man, he is surrounded by sexual minorities: Honor is asexual, Jolanda is a lesbian, and Mieke is a lesbian who wants "to *try it* with a guy" (page 197). Discuss the portrayal of sex and sexuality in *Queen Esther*. What role does sex play in Jimmy's life? In what way does the novel either challenge or uphold traditional notions of sex and sexuality?

6. *Queen Esther* starts with a history of the Winslow family in America: "Beginning in Puritan times, more Winslows kept coming" (page 1). Why do you think the novel begins this way? What role does family history play in *Queen Esther*? How, if at all, does personal history intersect with national history?

7. In Chapter 8, we learn that Esther wants the following quote from *Jane Eyre* tattooed on her chest: "I care for myself. The more solitary, the more friendless, the more unsustained I am, the more I will respect myself" (page 71). Why do you think Esther is so drawn to this quote? What do you think Jimmy would make of it? If Jimmy were to get a tattoo, what words or image do you think he might choose?

8. "In *Great Expectations*," says Thomas Winslow to Jimmy, ". . . you will love the characters you're supposed to love, and you'll hate the ones you're supposed to hate" (page 138). How does Tommy's reading of *Great Expectations* play out in *Queen Esther*? Do you think we're "supposed to love" some people, and "supposed to hate" others? How does the novel reaffirm or complicate this conception of love and hate? Support your ideas with reference to the text.

9. Esther is left at the orphanage at St. Cloud's by two female "anti-Semites" (page 65); Jimmy is raised with two mothers and no father; Vienna, Jimmy's daughter, is raised with a father and two mothers; and Siegfried is adopted by Annelies when the anti-Semitic Irmgard dies. These are just a few examples of how motherhood is portrayed and reconfigured in *Queen Esther*. Discuss the novel's portrayal of mothers and motherhood. What do you think of the idea that "giving birth to a child and being a mother [are] two separate choices" (page 154)? Support your ideas with reference to the text.

10. "'There *is* a telescope that sees into the future, Jimmy—it's called the passage of time. Just wait and see,' [Irmgard] said, closing the door" (page 329). Discuss the significance of this quote, and of the passage of time more broadly, in *Queen Esther*. What does it mean to see into the future by means of the passage of time? From the very first Winslow on board the *Mayflower* in 1620, to Jimmy Winslow in Jerusalem in 1981, the novel covers a long span of time. How is the passage of time portrayed in the novel?